SUZANNE F...

...Winner of the *Ro...* Writer" Award

...The #1 National Be...ing ...thor who "has firmly established herself as one of the brightest lights in the romance genre."*

*Romantic Times

Also by Suzanne Forster . . .

The sensual, suspenseful national
bestseller

SHAMELESS

Forced into marriage with Luc Warneke, the man she most fears, Jessie Flood fights desperately to protect herself, her child—and her heart . . .

"So strongly written the passion will envelop you as these two transform before your eyes. I loved every breathtaking word."
—*Rendezvous*

"Sizzling!"—*Romantic Times*

"A stylist who translates sexual tension into sizzle and burn with bold, dangerous heroes you want to lie for, die for, and cry for."
—*Los Angeles Daily News*

"SHAMELESS is shamelessly wonderful . . . Passionate and emotional . . . and beautifully written. Suzanne Forster is a truly gifted storyteller—and a wonderful gift to readers!"
—Bestselling author Katherine Stone

Berkley Books by Suzanne Forster

SHAMELESS
COME MIDNIGHT

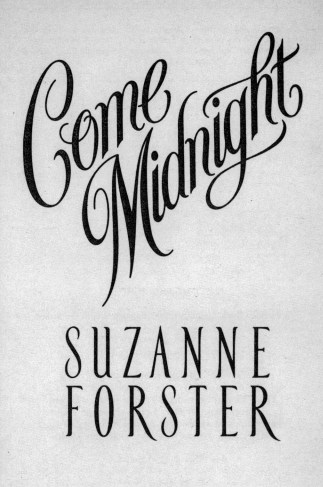

Come Midnight

SUZANNE FORSTER

BERKLEY BOOKS, NEW YORK

COME MIDNIGHT

A Berkley Book / published by arrangement with the author

PRINTING HISTORY
Berkley edition / February 1995

All rights reserved.
Copyright © 1995 by Suzanne Forster.
This book may not be reproduced in whole or in part,
by mimeograph or any other means, without permission.
For information address: The Berkley Publishing Group,
200 Madison Avenue, New York, New York 10016.

ISBN: 0-425-14565-4

BERKLEY®
Berkley Books are published by The Berkley Publishing Group,
200 Madison Avenue, New York, New York 10016.
BERKLEY and the "B" logo
are trademarks belonging to Berkley Publishing Corporation.

PRINTED IN THE UNITED STATES OF AMERICA

10 9 8 7 6 5 4 3 2 1

CHAPTER
·· ONE ··

SHE WAS BEING stalked. A shadow darted across the wall of the crumbling parking garage and the sound of stealthy footsteps warned Leigh Rappaport that someone was following her. She dug in her shoulder bag for her car keys, but the zippered compartment where she usually kept the large brass ring was empty.

The *ching* of a metal blade brought her to a halt.

She whirled in panic and saw him materialize from the gloom of a nearby parking stall, sinuously tall and menacing. His mirrored sunglasses bounced light and his red bandanna wrapped jet-black hair that curled at his neck like Medusa's snakes. As he sauntered across the pitted concrete toward her, his animal arrogance announced who he was—a self-proclaimed god of the barrio underworld, armed to the teeth with evil intent.

He was going to rape her.

That was Leigh's first thought. Her only thought. If she'd seen him sooner, she might have been able to make a run for her car. But she'd left it on an upper tier of the parking structure, and now she was caught in a maze of cement walls that seemed to have no exits.

Leigh's thoughts raced crazily as her assailant hesitated some twenty feet away. He wasn't giving her a chance to escape, she realized. He knew there was nowhere to run. More likely he got some twisted satisfaction in prolonging her fear. He wore savagely slashed jeans, and the red bandanna might have represented gang colors, but his clothing wasn't buttoned up and baggy in the style of L.A. gangs. The sleeves of his chambray work shirt were rolled up above his elbows, and the shirt was hanging open, revealing a sweat-stained white tank top, amber skin, and whorls of gleaming muscle. A silver bracelet coiled around his wrist like a snake. Gang member or not, he was clearly dangerous.

And Leigh was clearly in the wrong neighborhood. She must have taken a wrong turn on Salerno Street. She'd pulled into the garage thinking to ask someone for directions, but she should never have left the protection of her car in this godforsaken place. She'd agreed to evaluate the defendant in a recent homicide case. She'd been told the man was free on a million-dollar bond, but if she'd known her appointment would take her into a Los Angeles slum, she never would have risked making the trip alone. Someone from the prosecutor's office was supposed to have escorted her, but had failed to show up.

Her assailant swept the mirrored glasses up onto his head and started toward her. His eyes flashed over her body, carbon hot, a flicker of recognition in their depths. Leigh's hands flew up defensively. She inched back. He was too big to fight off, and there was no chance she could outrun him.

Scream, she told herself. The impulse set her nerves on fire. But she never had the chance. He was on her before she could draw a breath. Engulfing her with terrifying speed, he clamped a hand over her mouth and forced her up against the cement wall behind her. His other hand claimed her throat in a rough caress.

"Look like you're enjoying this," he whispered harshly. "Or you're dead, *chica.*"

The caustic sting of fear filled Leigh's throat. She tried to push him away, but he shouldered her back, slamming her up against the wall with a force that knocked the fight out of her. Cold concrete bit through her clothing, bruising her shoulders and buttocks. Hot hands branded her skin and snuffed off her breathing.

A high-pitched sound rang in her ears. The room spun dizzily, and she went limp, dragging at his clothing blindly. And then, just as unexpectedly as he'd captured her, he released her. She gulped in air, but before she could speak, before she could even think about speaking, he jerked her to her feet and swung her around so that she could see the two gang-bangers who were stalking her.

"The bitch is mine," he warned the men, his voice low and savage. He buried his hand in Leigh's blond pageboy, gathering up a fistful of hair as he pulled her up against him.

The men hesitated, hovering like jackals. Each one had a crude gang insignia tattooed on his face. If they couldn't make the kill, maybe they'd watch—and share the spoils?

Leigh's hoarse protest was cut off as her captor scooped her into the sheltering wedge of his shoulder, burying her face in the material of his chambray shirt. "Touch me," he breathed against her hair.

Leigh reacted instinctively, touching his forearm.

"Not there. Touch me like a woman who wants it." He nudged her with his leg and Leigh shuddered, dropping her hand, sliding it along the stony muscles of his thigh.

"There are worse things," he whispered. "Like being dead."

The jackals inched forward eagerly.

Leigh's captor whipped a stilettolike blade from a leather sheath secured to the waistband of his jeans. The flash of deadly silver lit up the gloom, riveting the eye and the heart. The air smelled of fear and sweat. "This isn't show-and-tell, you bastards," he snarled at the men. "Get the hell out of here. *Vete de aquí.*"

One of the men spit like a snake. But they both slunk back in a sullen retreat, scowling at Leigh as they disappeared behind the same block wall that prevented her from moving. She heard the hydraulic hiss of a stairway exit door and realized how close she'd been to making her escape. If she'd kept going instead of turning, she might be in her car now and heading for home.

Leigh gasped as she was abruptly released. She was shaking so violently, she nearly slid down the wall in a heap. "Thank you," she whispered, looking up at the man who had come to her aid. The words died in her throat. His eyes were black with loathing—beautiful, burning eyes. His face was all flaring shadows and sensual bones. Up close he was one of the most compelling men she'd ever seen in her life.

"*Pertida, chica,*" he said softly. "Get lost."

He was telling her to go? After risking his life for her? Leigh swayed, unsteady on her feet. It felt as if there was something she must do, something she had to say. But what? And what was she expecting? That he would be the kind of man she could reach out to in gratitude? A hero, if she even understood what that meant? She must have been naively hoping for some sign of compassion. But whatever she expected, it wasn't this—the seething silence, the fires of hell in his eyes.

Confused, still stiff with fear, she stumbled away from him and began to run toward the exit door she'd heard moments before. The musty stairwell looked empty when she got there, and without checking any further, she darted up a flight of stairs, heading for the level she'd parked on. Her lungs were burning and her thighs ached with every lunge, but she didn't stop until she was locked inside her shiny white Acura.

The red snake sauce was too hot, the tiny, trendy Santa Monica restaurant was too crowded, and the overhead air conditioner was blowing damp rivulets down Leigh's collar. Worse, the waiter had done a vanishing act just when Leigh needed some ice water. She knew her mouth must be smoking as she reached for her fiancé's dripping glass of Corona beer to put out the fire.

One icy-cold quaff brought relief—and a grin from Dawson Reed.

"Told you so," he teased, indicating the nondescript blob that was a stuffed white flour tortilla, oozing with guacamole, on his own appetizer plate. "You should have ordered the duck quesadilla."

"I should have ordered a beer," Leigh countered, taking another sip of his. The slippery glass nearly got away from her as he reached for it, and she impulsively pretended she wasn't going to give it back. "Oh, sorry!" she cried as beer splashed onto his worsted wool slacks.

So much for whimsy, Leigh thought.

Dawson swore softly and grabbed for a napkin to blot the stain. Watching him, Leigh wondered why she always felt so left-handed around her fiancé. Even discomfited as he was now, he had a certain smoothness of manner that she envied, one of those fortunate human beings born to easy grace. He also had a body made for designer clothes, and his round, tortoiseshell glasses were the perfect counterpoint to a chiseled, square-jawed face that might otherwise have been too handsome. Luckily she found bright, well-dressed men very sexy. And Dawson was certainly that.

"Have you considered my proposition?" he asked, dipping his napkin in his water glass and continuing to attack the offending spot.

"I didn't know you'd made one," Leigh said quite truthfully.

He glanced up. "The Montera murder trial."

"Oh, that." Leigh had already explained that she didn't want to be involved in such a spectacular case. The defendant was a photographer, and Dawson seemed to think her background in art therapy and the diagnostic technique she'd helped to develop on a research grant at Stanford would make her the perfect expert witness for the prosecution. She didn't agree, but Dawson wasn't L.A. County's district attorney for nothing. To him, no wasn't an answer, it was an incentive.

"Who else around here has your practical experience, Leigh?" he argued, abandoning his cleaning project. He was clearly in pursuit and loving it. "You're a licensed psychologist with a specialty in art therapy. You've worked with a wide range of clients, including convicted felons. You've developed a method of testing that reveals latent aggression. I'll never find anyone else with your track record."

"I can give you a half-dozen names without even consulting my American Psychological Association Directory," she assured him.

The maître d', an older man with a stone-gray ponytail and lots of Indian jewelry, chose that moment to seat another couple next to Leigh and Dawson, at that table which wasn't even elbow room away. Leigh wanted to thank the man for the distraction, but Dawson wasn't so easily put off. He simply lowered his voice and continued arguing his case.

"Are any of them young women under thirty, whose scholarship has turned the psychometrics community on its ear? Are any of them writing a definitive book on psychological testing? Besides, I want my expert to be a woman, Leigh. Montera dusted a woman."

"He's accused of killing his girlfriend," Leigh reminded him. "And lest you forget, *I* was nearly dusted yesterday when I tried to keep my appointment with him. Apparently your assistant didn't realize Nick Montera's studio is in the middle of the barrio."

"*One* of his studios. He has another in Coldwater Canyon. It was our mistake," Dawson admitted gallantly, refraining from reminding Leigh that she made the trip without an escort. "I'll arrange to have Montera come to your office in the future."

Leigh stood firm. "I'm not taking this on, Dawson. I have no experience as an expert witness, and the very fact of our engagement could diminish my credibility on the stand." In fact, Leigh wasn't quite as inexperienced as she claimed. Her mentor, Carl Johnson, the man with whom she developed the Johnson-Rappaport Art-Insight Survey, had used their test in expert testimony many times, and Leigh had a reasonably good understanding of the process through him.

"You're the originator of a state-of-the-art diagnostic technique. That's credibility enough for anyone. Come on, Leigh." He tantalized her with the half-full bottle of beer. "I'll even give you the rest of my Corona."

Leigh glanced over at the couple who had just been seated, a busty brunette in her fifties whose fashion tastes seemed to have been influenced by too many Jane Russell movies, and a sun-bronzed younger man with enough muscle layering his neck to bulletproof Dawson's entire upper torso. Though neither looked Leigh's way, they were clearly intrigued by the little drama going on next door.

"Dawson, you're not listening to me," Leigh said under her breath, as emphatically as she could manage at that volume. "I've told you very clearly that I don't want to take this case. I used the N-word, Dawson. No. You have to respect my no's."

Dawson plunked down the beer bottle, laughing softly. When he'd recovered sufficiently, he tapped the end of Leigh's nose with a wet finger. "I do respect it, Leigh. It's one of the cutest noses I've ever seen. . . . Okay, okay, if you don't want to testify, that's that. I'll round up somebody else, one of the flunky headshrinkers the office has been using for years."

Leigh smiled, pleased but wary. She adored Dawson, but she'd recently come to realize that he had a great deal in common with her mother. They were both controlling personalities who worked their wiles with such easy finesse, you hardly knew you were being "managed." But they rarely gave up until they had what they wanted. She and her mother had reached an uneasy truce some years ago, and she didn't want to fight the battle for her autonomy all over again. So if she was a little surprised that her fiancé had capitulated so easily, she was also relieved. Perhaps, it meant that she wasn't about to marry her mother.

The maître d' made another appearance, hovering at the next table to take the new couple's order. Leigh was tempted to advise them against the frijoles with red snake sauce. She needn't have worried.

"Duck quesadilla for two," the sun-bronzed one said. "Hold the guacamole."

"I've never known *anyone* like him. The sex was supernatural!"

Frowning, Leigh glanced up from the journal article she was reading while riding her vintage stationary bicycle. The television was playing and a stunning redhead was being interviewed on the five o'clock news. Leigh had been trying desperately to concentrate on the article. It was crucial research for her book, a study on fantasy aggression in adolescent males, but it couldn't compete with supernatural sex. Apparently the redhead was rhapsodizing about a former boyfriend.

Curious, Leigh swept damp hair off her forehead and strained to hear over the whir and click of bicycle wheels.

"Of course, I don't believe he killed anyone," the woman insisted. "He's a wicked man in many ways—all the best ways, if you want my opinion, which I guess you do or you wouldn't be interviewing me. But he's not a murderer. I'd bet my own life on that."

Leigh slowed her pumping legs and swiped at her dripping brow. She could feel a stillness growing inside her, the calming quiet that overtook her when her imagination was awakened. She'd devoted so much of her career to developing a projective test that placed science over subjectivity that she'd all but forsaken her trust in her own intuitive responses. But something had triggered them just now. This woman was the cause.

"Were you ever afraid of him?" the male reporter asked, holding the microphone to the woman's glossy peach-frappé lips.

"Oh, always!" Her blue eyes sparkled with laughter.

"Why? What did he do?"

"What *didn't* he do? The man is gifted. If I hadn't escaped him, I would have expired of ecstasy." She winked as if to say it was all a joke, and the golden bangles on her wrist clinked madly as she tucked a black bra strap into the confines of her pastel sweater.

"Seriously, though," she continued, "he had the most incredible effect on me. There were times when I felt as if he were hypnotizing me or something—taking over my will, you know? Isn't that silly? I loved him madly, but I had to leave him. I was losing control of my life. . . ."

The Exercycle's front wheel spun madly, but Leigh was no longer pedaling. The papers in her hand dropped to the floor as Nick Montera's image flashed on the screen. The carbon-hot gaze and sensual bone structure were unmistakable. He was the same man who'd come to her rescue in the parking garage.

Touch me like a woman who wants it.

Leigh could still remember the shock of excitement she felt when she'd stroked his thigh. She'd been in fear of her life, but the sexual charge, though disorienting, had been unmistakable. She didn't know how else to describe it. So *that,* she thought, watching the dark image fade from the screen, is Nick Montera.

CHAPTER
··TWO··

ALEC SATTERFIELD WAS widely known as the vampire bat of California's criminal litigators. It was rumored that he gauged a witness's fears by the rush and squeak of blood through the distended veins on his temple. And it was a cherished belief among his partners at Gluck and Satterfield, the prestigious Century City law firm, that he went for his opponents' throats with a melancholy smile and beautifully bared fangs. His pale skin, elegant sable hair, and penchant for black turtlenecks undoubtedly contributed as much to his macabre image as the trail of figuratively bloodless bodies he left behind him. Beyond that, he was reputed to drink nothing but deep-frozen Russian vodka, thawed to the consistency of slush. And Bloody Marys, of course.

Satterfield had made his name defending prominent white-collar criminals—junk-bond dealers, international financiers, and veteran politicians, many of whom had worked to deliberately defraud the public. But he was also known to take on the odd high-profile murder case.

At the moment he was thoroughly fascinated with his latest client . . . the man who'd refused to take a chair when he entered Satterfield's penthouse office just moments ago, and who was now fashionably, if rather negligently, slouched against the Italian green marble mantel of the fireplace, his hands loosely tucked in the pockets of his crumpled silk slacks.

Nick Montera was one of the coolest, most lethal characters Alec Satterfield had ever come across in his twenty years of lawyering. Alec prided himself on being able to assess the psychopathology of his clients quickly and accurately, but Montera was a fascinating enigma. According to his file, he'd grown up in a drug-infested barrio, lost his mother at ten to gang violence, and done hard time on a murder rap at seventeen.

And yet somehow, despite all that, Montera had outrun his past, become an "art" photographer and rocketed to prominence on the West Coast. A scholarship program in grade school had provided the photography classes, and the press had given his career a jump start by dubbing him as something of a sexual sorcerer, though not because of his love life, which no one seemed to know much about until recently. The reputation the media had been referring to sprang from his hauntingly intimate portraits of women, and the way his subjects seemed willing, if not eager, to abandon themselves to the magnetic force of his camera. The notoriety his work brought had quickly won him a cult following.

Alec smiled secretly. Women. They loved the unholy bastard. Montera's mother had been Anglo, possibly of French extraction, but the dark sensuality in Nick's features was the legacy of Latin bloodlines on his father's side. He had the moody good looks of a matinee idol, but even with his rapier cheekbones and rich onyx hair, he could never have made a living off his looks. His eyes were too disturbing. They were arctic blue and impenetrable. As was Nick Montera.

Fire-and-ice metaphors were woefully inadequate ways to describe the man, Alec had concluded. Montera was a glacier with the internal flashpoint of TNT. It was a deadly combination . . . and perhaps the *perfect* combination for committing the crime of which he was accused, the premeditated murder of one of his former models. The killer had even gone so far as to arrange the lovely model's body in a pose that was identical to the way Montera had once photographed her.

Needless to say, Alec had found the case irresistible.

Alec rose from his chair, strolled around to the front of his desk, and sat on the edge. "You're in deep guano, shall we say, Mr. Montera," he said, folding his arms thoughtfully.

Montera glanced up from his casual observation of the woven Navaho carpet beneath his feet. "That's why I hired *you*, Mr. Satterfield. To dig me out. Rent a shovel, if you must."

"A bulldozer might be more helpful. You have no alibi."

"And they have no witnesses," Montera pointed out. "No one saw me kill her, did they?"

"As a matter of fact . . . someone did."

"I beg your pardon?"

I'll bet you do. Alec was pleased. At least now he had Montera's attention. His client had not yet parted company with the fireplace mantel, but those acetylene-torch eyes of his were suddenly, scorchingly, focused. Wait until he hears the rest of it, Alec thought. He might even take his hands out of his pockets.

"Apparently you're as interested to learn about this as I was, Mr. Montera. A next-door neighbor who was sitting on his front porch claims he saw you enter the dead woman's apartment around six P.M. on the night of the murder. Forgive my curiosity . . ." Alec lowered his voice for effect. "But why the *fuck* didn't you tell me you were at Jennifer Taryn's apartment that night?"

Montera's faint smile didn't thaw his icy gaze in the slightest. "That's pretty obvious, isn't it? I didn't want you—or anyone else—to know."

Alec Satterfield was having trouble hanging on to his legendary sangfroid. He was used to respect, if not outright reverence, from his clients. They were drowning, and he was their lifeline. It was a simple, fear-based relationship, the sort he greatly preferred, but Montera didn't seem to understand the dynamics.

The death penalty had been reinstated in California, which meant his client's life was at stake, and yet Alec couldn't get a rise out of the guy. By now Montera should have been swearing he didn't do it and imploring Alec to believe him. Alec knew the photographer could lighten up and turn on the charm when he wanted to. He'd seen the man with women, seen the effect he had on them. It was nothing obvious at all, just a subtle focusing in of those uncanny blue eyes, and the speech centers of the female brain seemed to disengage.

"Do I have to give you the standard lecture about trusting your lawyer, Mr. Montera?" Alec asked. Frustration sharpened the edges of his normally modulated tones. "The one where I inform you that you have to tell me everything, that I can't represent you unless you tell me *everything*?"

"Trust *you*, Mr. Satterfield?" Montera drew his hand from his pocket, a wad of paper money entwined in his fingers. "*This* is what I trust." He held up a hundred dollar bill. "I've been through the criminal courts before, and I'm intimately familiar with justice. She's a very expensive whore, but luckily, I can afford her this time around."

With a snap of his thumb and forefinger, Montera flicked the bill at Alec. "I think we both know what that makes you, Satterfield."

The money landed on the expanse of gleaming hardwood floor between them.

Alec felt warmth creep up the back of his neck. Anger? He couldn't remember the last time he had gotten really hot with a client. That just didn't happen these days. His sort of people generally had impeccable manners. "You're a smart-ass," he hissed under his breath. "A goddamn smart-ass. I should call the guards and have you thrown out of here."

Montera shrugged his agreement. "That would be my move. But it won't be yours. This case is a big deal, even for you. And it's exactly the sort of dirt you love to dig in, manicured nails and all. The media's going to swarm this trial. The blitz has already started, and unlike me, you'd like nothing better than to be caught in the blinding glare of flashbulbs. You're an exhibitionist, counselor. You want the exposure. And the glory."

Alec brushed some lint from the sleeve of his Armani suit and realigned the cuff with a precise tug of his fingers. "You're mistaken, Mr. Montera. *Sadly* mistaken. I've had more than my share of glory. My career does not need a booster shot of notoriety, thank you."

God, this was absurd. A farce! Alec Satterfield's outfit might be immaculate, but his heart was flipping like the vertical hold on a broken television set. Worse, he felt almost prissy in his refusal, like an adolescent girl playing hard to get.

"You're excited, aren't you, Satterfield?" Montera pressed his advantage. "I can hear it in your voice. This case excites you, doesn't it? And that's why you won't throw me out of here. You can't. Because nothing else has made you feel this way in a very long time."

Alec sighed quickly, almost bitterly. It was true. Championing crooked politicians just didn't do it for him anymore. Perhaps it never had. Every once in a while he needed to grab hold and shake things up, to dance on the edge of the cliff and flirt with a plunge into oblivion. That's why he wasn't going to send Nick Montera packing. But God, he should.

"What about the bruise on Jennifer Taryn's throat?" he snapped. "The coroner's office says it was made by the imprint of a ring—a snake's-head ring. The mark is so distinct, they've even got an outline of the damn thing's tongue."

Alec found himself staring at the snake bracelet Montera wore. It was a chillingly beautiful piece. A silver serpent coiled wantonly around the man's powerful wrist, its tail entwined around its sleek, gleaming head. "Where is your ring, Montera? The one that matches your bracelet? The police report says you claimed it was stolen."

"It *was* stolen."

"Yes, but when? How? I need more information, details. I can't mount a defense on quicksand."

"I haven't got details. It turned up missing the same week Jennifer was killed. I don't know the exact date, but I always leave my things—watch, jewelry, spare change—on the dresser at night. When I woke up the next morning, the ring was gone."

"It was stolen before the attack on her? Or after?"

"Before . . . maybe two days before."

Alec had read the police report. Montera told the arresting officers he'd taken a hot shower that night, had a couple of glasses of wine, and fallen asleep on the couch. He hadn't seen anything, heard anyone.

"Nothing else was missing?" Alec asked, beginning to sort through the possibilities. "Just the ring? Is there any chance you were set up? It's a damn flimsy defense, but it may be the only one we've got at the moment. Do you have any enemies?"

Montera rubbed his jaw, then lifted his hand. "Who doesn't? An insanely jealous husband, maybe? My photographs get pretty intimate. I've had problems with some of my models' husbands—even with their boyfriends."

"You're screwing them? Married models?"

"I said the *photographs* got intimate."

"So you're *not* screwing them?" Alec made a small sound of derision. "No one's going to buy that. Not with your reputation."

"You're talking about my *reputation*," Montera said. "You're not talking about me."

Alec twisted the gold signet ring on his little finger, leaving it slightly askew. His client didn't seem to be playing games at the moment, but he was clearly a genius at manipulating people, especially women. If his manipulations hadn't been working on Jennifer, maybe he'd resorted to an extreme solution. It was also possible he'd only wanted to frighten her and things had gotten out of hand.

"You still haven't told me what happened that night," Alec said, looking up. "You claimed you hadn't seen Jennifer in weeks, but the neighbor saw you entering her place, and the police found your prints all over her apartment. Fresh prints."

Montera stepped over the money that was still lying on the floor and walked to the window that looked out over Century City. The bright afternoon sun formed a silver aura around his head and shoulders, casting his face in deep shadow as he turned back. Alec wasn't a photographer himself, yet he couldn't help but think what an incredible portrait the scene would have made.

"She called and asked me to come over," Montera admitted. "She'd been drinking when I got there. We argued, and I left."

"Argued about what?"

"Our relationship."

"I thought you said there *was* no relationship."

"There wasn't. She wanted one."

"Oh, Christ! You know how they'll construe this, don't you? A lovers' quarrel that turned violent. Only they'll twist it around. They'll make it look like she rejected you. They'll try to establish that you killed her and left your 'mark' on her."

"It didn't happen that way—"

"How did it happen? The lab reports verify that the skin under her fingernails was yours. The hair on her clothing was yours. There was evidence of a fight—"

"She tried to stop me when I left. She was drunk."

"Jesus! This stinks, Montera. It stinks on ice. You have no alibi. You were spotted at the scene of the crime. You 'argued' with a woman who was found strangled to death. And the corpse had your mark on her throat—a snake's head."

Alec hesitated, giving Montera plenty of time to digest the bad news. This was his client's official cue to swear he hadn't done it. Alec had brought some of America's mightiest to their knees—distinguished senators accused of taking bribes, wealthy financiers accused of making them. Now it was Nick Montera's turn. *Get down on your knees, lover boy. Swear you didn't off the silly bitch!*

But lover boy didn't take the bait. He didn't blink so much as one long, black eyelash.

It would have brought Alec immeasurable satisfaction to see his client humbled, but he had to admit to a twinge of admiration when Montera didn't bow to the pressure. Alec's heart had begun to pound again, insistently this time, almost violently. He'd been denied the satisfaction of making another man grovel, and yet he was secretly pleased. Impassioned denials had never persuaded him of anything except a client's desperation. Matters of guilt or innocence were the least of his concerns when he took on a case. Younger lawyers dreamed of breaking new ground, establishing legal precedents. They wanted to be heroes. Alec had long ago given up heroics. He wanted to play creator—God or the devil, it didn't matter which—as long as he had the power to work miracles.

He slid off the edge of the desk and walked around to his chair, gracefully suggesting that their consultation was over. "I trust you have no objections to a woman on the team," he said, glancing at his desk calendar to check on his next appointment. "It will help offset the illusion of a war between the sexes."

Montera moved out of the glare with a silence that was somehow aggressive. "I don't care if a Martian defends me, as long as I walk. However, I am paying a fortune for *your* services."

"I'll be there when the need presents itself," Alec said, waving away his client's concerns. "In the meantime we'll want as many women as possible on the jury, of course. The more the better, as long as they're not ball-busting feminists."

"If we're lucky, maybe NOW will picket the trial."

Alec flared. "How do I make you understand that this is a catastrophe, my friend? You could be a candidate for the death penalty. And speaking of luck, do you have any idea how fortunate you are to be walking around loose? There is *no provision for bail* on a Murder One charge with special circumstances. If I hadn't convinced the judge to make an exception in your case, you'd be in the slammer now. So, Mr. Montera, if you really want to help, there are three things you can do. Stay out of trouble, wear a blue suit in court. And for God's sake, cut your hair."

Montera raked back the darkness that had fallen onto his forehead. "Don't mess with my mind, Satterfield," he warned softly. "The judge made an exception because of my work with kids in the barrio. What's more, only one person in four charged with murder in this country gets convicted, and those who do jail time are out in less than twelve months on average."

Alec pressed his fingers to his desktop and leaned forward. "How the hell do you know that?"

"I've made it my business to know."

"Then maybe you should represent yourself."

"If I could, I would. In the meantime, instead of trying to convince me that I'm going to fry, why don't you start earning your money. We've got a four-to-one shot working. With those odds, almost any pimp lawyer could save my sorry ass—even you."

Alec watched in startled silence as his client swung around to leave. Montera walked to the door and cranked it open, then hesitated. "Oh, and by the way," he said, turning back. "In case you're wondering. I didn't do it."

Jesus, Alec thought as the door crashed shut. He'd just been screwed without being kissed. And Montera hadn't been gentle.

CHAPTER
·· THREE ··

THE LOS ANGELES Art Council's Marina West Guild was holding its annual Winter Carnival, a gala charity auction that had become the signal event of the season, and on this temperate January evening, the Ritz Carlton's grand ballroom was filled to capacity with the cream of Southland society.

Leigh Rappaport had been pressed into service for several years running by her mother, whose enormous powers of persuasion were legend. Kate Rappaport was artist, hostess, and coordinator of the spectacular affair, and tonight, moving among the black-tie crowd, beguiling her guests with her quick wit and charming eccentricities, Kate was undeniably the woman of the evening as well.

There were many more beautiful women in the room, including Leigh herself, but none who commanded attention the way Kate did. Her presence turned heads and stirred whispers of admiration, and if some of the women's comments were edged with envy and focused pointedly on "how well Kate was aging at fifty-three," the men's resonated with frankly erotic interest, irrespective of age, hers or theirs.

Leigh admitted to being one of those admiring, yet ambivalent women. Standing with the cool crystal of her champagne flute pressed to the hot flush of her cheeks, she watched her mother's flawless performance and wondered how the magnificent Kate could ever have produced a child so opposite to her in temperament. She adored her mother, as almost everyone who knew her came to eventually, but Leigh had long ago learned not to hope for attention when Kate was in the room. It was a losing proposition.

Tonight, Leigh's long golden hair was woven into a rather severe coil at the nape of her neck, her makeup was spare, and her ankle-length Ann Taylor black crepe was accented with a paisley tunic and high-heel boots in black suede with eyelet laces. It was a striking outfit, taken alone, but demure next to Kate's violet de la Renta.

Not that anyone would have called Leigh shy, exactly. Reserved, perhaps. Contemplative. If she was intense in her way, the energy was contained and inward. Leigh was a "deep pool of moonlit water, much more inaccessible and mysterious than her radiant mother," or so a magazine society column had once claimed. Kate had taken exception. "Do they really think I'm not mysterious?" she'd wondered aloud after reading the piece at the breakfast table. "How very odd."

Now Leigh watched with some amusement as her mother came upon Dawson Reed holding court with a group of young lawyers. Kate affectionately straightened his tuxedo tie and then summarily dismissed him to fetch her some cranberry juice and Perrier, the strongest thing she ever drank. Leigh could almost see the veins pop in Dawson's temples as he made his excuses to his protégés and went off to do Kate's bidding. No one in the civilized world would dare to treat Dawson Reed like a gofer but her mother.

It was one of the reasons Leigh loved Kate.

It was also high on the list of reasons why she loved Dawson. He couldn't stand her mother. He and Kate were far too much alike to be compatible. At least they couldn't gang up on Leigh to be more social. They both considered her too reclusive and a bit of a grind where her work was concerned.

"Kate's in top form tonight," Dawson grumbled moments later as he joined Leigh at the back of the ballroom, where she was quietly watching the crowd take their seats in anticipation of the auction. Leigh had always been more an observer of life than a participant. Her professional life especially had contributed to distancing her, until a few days ago . . . when a man she'd never seen before had pressed her up against a wall, manhandled her outrageously, and told her to act as if she liked it.

Leigh smiled impishly and held up her brimming flute of champagne. "What would you do if I tweaked your tie and sent you off to get me fresh champagne?"

Dawson colored, realizing he'd been compromised. "I'd turn you over my knee, wench."

Leigh blushed, too, something she did well. "In that case, I'd better do it, hadn't I?"

"Quick! Somebody buy this nude beauty!" the celebrity auctioneer called out from the podium. "Or I'm going to hang her on the men's locker-room wall of my tennis club!"

The auction had started and the master of ceremonies, a stand-up comedian and local TV weatherman, was attempting to tantalize the crowd with a reclining nude of Rubensesque proportions.

"She'd go great next to my Bud Lite poster, don't you think?" he called out.

Within moments the crowd was groaning and hooting at the comedian's irreverence in the face of fine art. But the bidding was spirited, much to Leigh's relief. Both her mother and Dawson were active on the Arts Council Board, and Kate had been heavily involved in planning the fund-raiser, which was more than a mere excuse for a gala this year. The council's funds had been heavily cut, and their grants program to schools in underprivileged areas was in danger of being discontinued.

Most of the donations came from successful local artists, but a few prominent collectors, including Dawson, had donated valuable pieces from their personal collections, which made the bidding hotly competitive. The comedian's ribald humor kept the atmosphere festive, and even when the amounts occasionally rocketed into the six-figure range, everyone shouted out their bids and complained vigorously when they didn't win. There were no hand signals or discreet raisings of silver Tiffany pens at this pricey garage sale.

"Well, well—what have we got here?" The emcee held up a photograph in sepia tones of a man and woman in a startlingly erotic situation. The subjects were both fully clothed, but it was the nature of their encounter that made the picture so arresting. The man's hand was encircling the woman's throat in a slow, almost unbearably sensual caress, and his thigh was insinuated between her parted legs.

"It's a Nick Montera photograph," he told them, lifting the large-framed piece high over his head. "Wait until you catch the title. What am I bid for *Come Midnight*?"

Leigh turned to her mother and Dawson in surprise. She could hardly find her voice to speak. "How did one of Nick Montera's photographs get in the auction?"

"It must be the emcee's idea of a joke," Dawson said.

"Not at all," Kate countered. "The artist has contributed heavily to our grants program this year. Montera volunteered to teach photography to schoolchildren in the barrio, and he donated some photographs to our planning committee over a month ago. So I thought, well, since he's such a cause célèbre these days—"

"Cause célèbre? Mother, he's accused of murdering one of his own models. Of *strangling* her." The man in the photograph looked like Montera himself, Leigh realized, chilled at the thought.

"Oh . . . really?" Kate scrutinized the photograph the auctioneer was holding up. "Oh, dear."

"Come on, folks!" the emcee urged. "We're asking for a minimum bid of five thousand, but this photograph is worth ten times that. By tomorrow, it could be worth more."

"Fifty-five hundred," someone called out.

"Six!" another shouted.

The bidding began in earnest then, the price quickly climbing higher. A kind of frenzy broke out among the bidders as they maneuvered for a closer look at the photograph. But Leigh was aware of something else, an undercurrent of shock and disbelief spreading through the crowd. Some of them were horrified by what was going on, and she sensed that trouble was about to erupt.

Kate seemed to understand this, too, as she was already heading for the podium. "I'm sorry," she cried out. "There's been a mistake!"

The emcee reluctantly surrendered the mike as Kate swept up onto the stage. "I'm very sorry," she explained, her silvery voice vibrant with regret. "But the Montera photograph was put up for sale by mistake. It's quite beautiful, and I'm sure it must be very valuable, but it's not the policy of the guild to profit from others' misfortunes, so if you'll be patient for a moment, we'll move on to the next item. . . ."

As her mother and the auctioneer tried to regroup, Leigh became aware of the whispering among the guests. "If that photograph is submitted as evidence," a man near her muttered, "Montera's going to fry."

"Murder One," another agreed.

"The jury won't even have to deliberate," a third predicted.

The auctioneer had placed the photograph with its face to the wall, but the images had burned themselves into Leigh's mind. It was as if she'd seen the photograph before in a more primitive form—a dream or subliminal flash from the depths of some subconscious ocean. She'd been plagued with unbidden erotic thoughts since a frightening incident in her childhood— an encounter with one of her mother's young male protégés that had left her confused about her desirability and wary of her own sexual impulses. But this was different, more like a long-suppressed dark fantasy searching for expression.

"Maybe it's just as well that you're not evaluating Montera," Dawson said, taking her hand in his protectively. "He's too sick and twisted for me." He encircled his forefinger around hers as he'd done many times in the three years they'd been together. It was more than a gesture of affection. It had become a symbol of their solidarity. Their bond.

But instead of reassuring Leigh, the sight of their linked fingers brought on a wave of near panic. She wanted to jerk her hand away for some reason, but she couldn't bring herself to do it. "I've changed my mind, Dawson," she said in a soft rush of resolve.

"Changed your mind? About what?"

"About Nick Montera. I want to do the interview. I'm going to take the case."

Leigh wasn't ready for Nick Montera. She'd had her assistant set up an appointment with him for this morning, and he was due in a few moments, but she hadn't yet received the files she'd requested from the DA's office. She didn't plan to rely heavily on police reports to make her evaluation, but she wasn't comfortable proceeding without even a look at his background information. Her plan was to interview him extensively and administer a battery of tests, including the Johnson-Rappaport Art-Insight Survey, the projective test she'd developed with Dr. Carl Johnson, her mentor at Stanford.

She didn't want to be blindsided again, not by the courts or by Montera. To that end she intended to do her "doctor" thing to the hilt. If necessary, she would armor herself with every interview technique and diagnostic device known to psychotherapy. In her dealings with clients, the goal was to achieve a relationship of trust and intimacy, to overcome distance, but Montera wasn't seeking out her advice and counsel. The state of California was. They were asking her to document their case, if they had one.

She glanced at her watch, annoyed at herself for not making better use of the free time Montera's late arrival had created. Undoubtedly it was the way she'd met him that had her on edge. He'd intervened at great risk to himself in what could have been a brutal assault. He might even have saved her life. She ought to have been feeling grateful instead of vulnerable and defensive. Overcompensation, she imagined. She was trying too hard to recover from the first round of a power game that he'd won, hands down. Take a deep breath, Leigh, she thought. Relax, as you so often tell your clients.

Across her tenth-floor office, showcased on a credenza that fronted a window overlooking the Santa Monica coastline, sat a huge terrarium where two small box tortoises made their home. In her graduate-school days, when Leigh was doing art therapy with children, the clinic where she'd interned had used the tortoises as a way to coax the children into interactive play. Leigh had become so attached to the creatures' slow, blinking sweetness that she'd convinced her supervisor to let her have the pair when the clinic had been closed down for lack of funds.

Now she rose from her desk and walked to the terrarium. Sig, named for the father of penis envy, was dozing in a ray of sunshine from the window. Frau Emmy, named for one of Freud's most famous patients, was lolling in the wading pool. Leigh stroked her finger along Emmy's hard, ridged shell and found herself envying the turtle's built-in armor. But for all her seeming protection, Emmy had a fatal vulnerability. She had only this one game plan. The shell she relied on to protect her soft underbelly was a primitive and inflexible strategy. If she came across a smart predator, one who knew how to upend her, she was utterly helpless to defend herself.

That was often what the hardest armor was protecting, Leigh had realized in her practice—the soft, fragile heart of the beast. Almost everyone was vulnerable, if you found the way to upend them. Sig blinked up at her with his huge, sad eyes, but when Leigh reached out to stroke his head, it immediately disappeared. Smart cookie, she thought.

The intercom gave out several staccato bursts, which meant Nancy Mahoney, Leigh's assistant, was either feeling uneasy or impatient. "Mr. Montera is here," Nancy announced in her typically husky, grabbing-for-the-next-breath fashion.

Uneasy, Leigh decided. She returned to her desk and hit the intercom button. "Did the files from the DA's office ever arrive?"

"Not yet. Shall I put in another call?"

"Yes, would you please? And send Mr. Montera in."

Leigh sighed and glanced at her watch. She would have to make do without the files. Clearly the DA's office had fouled up again. She was going to have to speak to Dawson about that.

Leigh rarely sat behind her desk when dealing with clients, but she was going to today. In fact, she wanted to be sitting and busy at something when Montera entered . . . perhaps even too busy to notice that he was there.

A latch bolt slid out of place and clicked.

She busied herself as the door opened, perusing a study that had employed her own test, the Johnson-Rappaport, to measure the aggressive behavior of juvenile offenders. The findings lent support to one of Leigh's earlier theories concerning the inverse relationship between fantasy aggression and behavioral aggression. It seemed the juveniles who actively fantasized about aggression were less likely to act upon such impulses. "Interesting," she murmured.

Leigh waited for the latch to slide back in place, telling her the door had closed, but the sound never came. A pencil lay near her fingertips. She picked it up and made a couple of notations on a yellow legal pad, then tapped her chin with the eraser end, all very nonchalant and thoughtful.

The silence surprised her. Why hadn't he said something? It was possible he'd recognized her as the woman he'd rescued, and his surprise was causing him to hesitate. It was also possible he simply intended to wait her out, knowing that the one who spoke first conceded an enormous amount of power. A man with his apparent instinct for seduction would be aware of that sort of thing, perhaps intuitively.

What kind of game are you playing, Mr. Montera?

She continued to make notations, her pencil pressed hard to the paper. The low rumble of traffic from the street below was punctuated by the occasional horn and the sudden screech of car brakes.

Leigh started as a shadow flitted across her desk, crossing her arm for an instant. In the split second before she took action, several frightening possibilities flashed through her mind. Had something come at the window? Clouds? A plane?

"Oh!" She sprang from the chair so quickly she sent it flying backward. "What are you doing?"

He was there—*right there*—on the opposite side of her desk.

His dark, expressive brows slanted warily as he studied her, whether from suspicion or confusion, she couldn't tell. Her heart was racing so fast, she could hardly think, but she realized something as she took in his silent presence. This was not the terrifying barrio outlaw of their first encounter. He carried no visible weapons this time, wore no gang colors. Viewed as a whole, he was tall and stunningly attractive, but with eyes that could burn holes through reinforced steel. No wonder women dropped like gnats. No wonder.

His oversize trench coat would have touched the floor on a man with less height. It was slate gray and duster length, flowing almost to the hem of his blue jeans. The black V-neck he wore beneath the coat had a deep groove that revealed prominent collarbones and body hair as soot dark as some unlit corner of his heart. The matching wealth of hair on his head was gathered into a lush ponytail at his nape.

"Nick Montera?" It was the most unnecessary question Leigh had ever asked.

"Is there a problem?" he wanted to know. "Your assistant said you were ready."

"No problem, I just . . . didn't hear you enter. Please"—she waved to one of the fanback chairs that faced her desk—"have a seat."

He nodded, but remained where he was. Leigh touched her fingers to her desk, realizing that the game hadn't played itself out yet. He wasn't going to sit until she did. Was that it? He was waiting for her to go first, very much like a predator waits patiently for its victim to bolt. You run. I'll chase.

She would not make that mistake, she resolved. Ever.

His focus intensified, shimmering until it pierced, and with each second that Leigh waited, the air in the room seemed to thicken until it became an effort to breathe it in. This man could stare you to your knees, she realized.

"So it's Dr. Rappaport?" He broke the trance casually, glancing around her office, hesitating as he read the brass nameplate on her desk. "And we have met before, haven't we?"

You know damn well we have, Montera. "As I recall, you told me to get lost."

Something flickered in his expression and was gone, the shadow of a smile, perhaps, or the briefest flaring of sexual awareness, as if he were thinking about the intimacy he'd forced on her in order to ward off her attackers.

"You didn't take my advice, did you?"

He was referring to today's meeting, Leigh realized, not their earlier encounter. But before she could come up with an answer, he'd already pulled up a chair and made himself comfortable.

"Thanks." His mouth shaped itself into an ironic curve. "I think I will sit down. How about you?" He settled back, despite the fact that his six-foot frame made the spindly chair look like stick furniture, and took in her rather stark taupe suit jacket with its notched lapel as if he could hear the clatter her heart was making beneath the breast pocket.

With a quick snap of her wrist, Leigh drew up her chair, sat, and opened the file Nancy had prepared. Technically, she'd won. So why did she feel as if she'd blown a game of Simon Says?

"Generally, I have my assistant handle the intake information," she explained, her voice sharpening. "In this case, I thought it more appropriate that I interview you myself."

"Works for me," he said. "Personal service . . . with a smile?"

Leigh was not smiling. "Your birth date, Mr. Montera?"

The rapid-fire questions Leigh posed confirmed that Nick Montera was thirty-seven, a California native, and that he'd never been married or even engaged. Leigh didn't find this too surprising, since Dawson had already told her Montera was raised in an East Los Angeles barrio and that he'd done time in prison as a young man. Still, she would have expected at least one serious relationship somewhere along the line.

"Sex?" she asked without thinking.

He let the question linger, hanging in the air between them until Leigh looked up. "Right here . . . ?" he wanted to know.

She could feel a damp spot forming in the curve of her upper lip. "I think we can safely say that you're male." She made a bold check in the *M* box.

"You're good at this." Amusement lent his voice an attractive huskiness as he glanced at her licenses, diplomas, and the commendations on the wall adjacent to her desk. "Must have taken years of training."

"Years," she acknowledged softly. "And I'm very good at this."

They were both testing wary smiles by then, and Leigh realized he'd disarmed her rather handily in just a matter of moments. He'd turned a tense situation around so deftly that she'd barely noticed him doing it. Thawed of their ice crystals, his eyes were the color of a sparkling arctic summer, a blue so sharp and pure, it flashed out and physically struck you with its beauty.

With great reluctance Leigh realized something that both surprised and disturbed her. She rather liked this enemy of the people, this "dangerous" outlaw who could crack jokes and smile. It was engagingly sexy, his smile. She wanted to see it again. And feel the warmth of his eyes. She was drawn to him at this moment, very drawn. It wasn't a conscious decision. It was an intuitive flash, but that didn't make it any less inappropriate for a woman in her situation.

She consulted her legal pad, aware of a lightness that made her grip the pencil more tightly. Her hand felt as if it wanted to float away like a balloon. So did her stomach. Was this the effect Montera had on women? To make them want desperately to know him better? His charm had a quality of intermittent reinforcement to it, she realized. Keep them waiting, keep them dangling, give them just enough to make them want more. It was one of the most powerful inducements known to the behavioral sciences. She smiled. Ask any white rat.

"I understand you had some trouble when you were younger," she said. "You did some time in Chino. Would you like to tell me about it?"

A shadow touched him, but Leigh wasn't sure what she'd seen. Pain? Regret?

"Not much to tell," he said. "I was seventeen, but they tried me as an adult and gave me five years. I served three."

"How did the man die?" She knew some of the details, but she wanted to hear the story in his own words. If he was lying to her—or to himself—correctly reading his body language would be crucial.

"Quickly. Painfully, I hope."

Leigh felt a chill run down her arms. He had wanted the man dead. That much was true, at least.

"It was self-defense," he explained. "But unfortunately, the jury didn't agree. The guy who attacked me sustained a half-dozen stab wounds, a few too many, apparently."

"But he did attack you?"

"He jumped me with a knife," Montera said evenly. "It pissed me off."

Leigh was careful not to register shock or any other emotion. Clients were always watching for cues from their therapist, signals that told them whether or not it was safe to reveal their darkest secrets to a stranger. Some of them tested the therapist, much like children did their parents, trying to see how much the doctor would accept before censuring them. In Montera's case, she knew that kind of testing could prove dangerous.

"You were very young," she went on. "Just seventeen. What did it feel like . . . killing a man?"

"It felt necessary. It was him or me."

Leigh had thought she might unearth some remorse, perhaps even discover what the shadow that had touched him earlier had been about, but she'd been too optimistic. He was staring at her with what looked to be casual interest, but his eyes were pale and hard.

"You don't get it, do you, doctor?" he said. "You think it boils down to a rational choice? To kill or not to kill? That's absurd. There are no choices in the barrio. There's only the quick and the dead."

Now he was making excuses, Leigh decided. "Everyone has choices."

A darkness moved through him, galvanizing him. "What choice would you have had if I hadn't shown up the other day?" Her silence brought him forward. "Answer me, doctor. What would you have done if I hadn't been there?"

Leigh set her pencil down in a very deliberate manner. Her spine was locked, and the uncomfortable lightness she'd felt before was invading her limbs again. She overrode it this time and knew a minor victory.

"I would have talked my way out of it," she said.

"*Talked* your way out of it?" Cold, derisive laughter erupted. "Just the way you did with me? There wouldn't have been time to talk. Those *cholos* would have been on you like animals."

"Just the way you were?" Leigh didn't realize for a moment that she'd spoken. The question had flashed into her mind like an accusation. "Mr. Montera," she said quickly, "I'm not unappreciative of what you did, but I have worked with violent clients before. And I do know how to defuse a situation. I would have been fine."

"In an office or a hospital, maybe. But not in the barrio. Not a chance, *chica*."

Even if his certainty hadn't provoked her, that last insolent word would have. "I worked in prisons with convicted felons," she insisted hotly.

"Surrounded by burly guards? Why the hell won't you admit the danger you were in?"

"I never said I wasn't in danger!" Leigh was startled by the low force in his voice. He was angry, but there was something tautly controlled in him, she realized. Exquisitely controlled, like a spring mechanism designed to measure force. "I'm aware that I might have been hurt—"

"You might have been raped, doctor. Or killed."

Leigh's chair wheels creaked beneath her. It sounded oddly like a cry for help. Her heart was tight, and it took a concerted effort to breathe. But there was a part of her that was still the psychologist—still the clinician—and she found it curious that a man accused of killing one woman would show so much concern over another woman's safety. Of course, *accused* was the operative term, as she kept reminding others.

"I tried to thank you that day," she told him. "You wouldn't let me."

"I didn't want thanks—" He broke off, a violent word on his lips.

"You wanted *what*?" she asked.

"Nothing. Forget it."

But Leigh was nearly paralyzed by the sudden rage that had arced through his gaze. It had only flared for an instant, but the message was as riveting as the day he rescued her. He might as well have said, *I wanted you, bitch.* She'd witnessed the same mix of hunger and black passion that day in the parking garage. She'd felt it burning through him into her. He'd glared at her as if he already knew her, as if he desired and despised her at the same time. But why? Why had he looked at her that way?

One of her diplomas was lopsided. That startling fact seized her attention as she glanced up at the wall that displayed her career and academic achievements. It was nothing—a crooked diploma—but for some reason, straightening it felt imperative. She rose abruptly from the chair and went to fix it.

For her, the wall symbolized almost everything she'd achieved that was of any consequence. It was only one aspect of her life, and she had probably invested too much importance in such things, but the plaques remained a source of great pride and pleasure. In some ways they had become markers of her worth, she realized, signifying who she was.

As she reached up to adjust the bronzed certificate, something made her hesitate and draw back. An instant later she heard a whir, a squeak, and a thud. "Ahhh!" Reeling backward, she stared at the gleaming knife blade that had hit the wall not a foot from the plaque.

She spun around, expecting to see Montera coming at her. "Are you *crazy*?" she cried. "What are you doing?"

He was still in the chair, settled back as if he'd never moved, his posture impassive, his expression indifferent. His gaze said what's the big deal, he threw knives every day, and this was nothing more than a momentary diversion, a little target practice. But if his attitude was blasé, his voice wasn't.

"You don't know the first thing about danger," he told her quietly. "Or about me."

Leigh forced herself to move. She started for her desk, only to halt in her tracks as he rose from the chair.

"No, please," she implored. "Stay where you are."

Freezing in place, she watched him come toward her, shuddering as he paused to have a look at her. His eyes brushed over her, then dismissed her as he walked to the spot where he'd stuck the knife in the wall. The blade made a rasping sound as he freed it and sheathed it in a leather case, boot-clipped to his jeans.

"Relax," he told her. "If I'd been aiming at you, I would have hit you. I was just making a point, so to speak."

Relax? Leigh felt as if she'd survived an earthquake, but just barely. She was trembling in every fiber of her being and was still unable to assimilate what had happened. She could hardly stand.

"How did that *feel,* doctor?" he asked her. "Did it feel like danger? Did you have any *choice* in the matter?"

She said nothing. Nothing. She had no idea what else might trigger him and she wasn't going to risk finding out. She didn't want another object lesson, thank you. She had to think how to get him out of her office, but in the meantime there was a more immediate problem. He'd moved behind her.

"I'm curious about something," he said. "Just curious, doctor. Did you get a look at those two gang-bangers in the garage that day?"

"What do you mean?"

"Did you see the gleam in their eyes? The lust?"

"No, I didn't see them," she lied. He was coming around the other side of her, circling her as if he were deciding what to do with her, just how and when and where he was going to make the blond *gringa* one of his trembling victims.

"They wanted you," he assured her, his voice slowing, thickening with Spanish inflections. "They wanted you bad. We *pachucos* have a thing about chicks like you, didn't you know that? You're every young barrio kid's wet dream—"

"Stop it, *please.*"

He exhaled laughter, flat and aching. "Oh, but it's true, doctor. You're the first thing that poor dumb *vato* thinks about when he wakes up in the morning. You're the last thing he thinks about at night. Fantasies of you eat him up alive, doctor. They make him thrash and sweat and abuse himself."

The duster coat flared as Montera stepped in front of her. He'd moved into the light from the window, and it threw his shadow against the far wall, creating a huge demonic silhouette. Leigh was praying he was done with her, but there was a predatory glint in his eye that told her he'd only begun to torment her, that he was feeding on her discomfort, that he'd waited a lifetime for this moment of reckoning.

"When he fantasizes, doctor—when that lonely street kid curls up in his poncho of many colors and dreams his pathetic barrio dreams—it's your pale skin he's yearning to touch. . . ."

Leigh didn't look at him as he went on, nor did she move. She tried to block out his voice, but she couldn't. Disdain fueled the low anger in his declarations, but even his contempt had a barbed, aching quality to it. Leigh's heart sank as she realized what must be going on. Up until this murder charge, Nick Montera could have had almost any woman he wanted. But it hadn't always been that way. He wasn't talking about *every* barrio kid, he was talking about himself, and a part of him hated what the Leigh Rappaports of the world represented. Sadly, another part of him wanted what she was, perhaps for the same reason he hated it . . . because he had grown up believing he couldn't have it.

"He fantasizes about firm, white breasts and pink-tipped nipples, doctor. He dreams about how they'd soften in his hands, sweeten on his lips. . . ."

Leigh tightened inwardly, painfully. She could feel his eyes all over her as he resumed his circling. His voice had a tactile quality to it, a velvet grip that made her aware of how tight her suit jacket was, how hot. She was moist between her thighs and in the rising heat of her armpits.

"You're the golden girl," he informed her, "the prize piece. You're everything he's ever wanted. But he can't have you, can he, doctor? *Can he?*"

The last question came at her like a whip, but she didn't dare look at him. She couldn't bear to see the loathing in his eyes.

"The barrio kid had the misfortune to be born in the wrong neighborhood, a ghetto. He doesn't exist in your world, except maybe as an object of pity. He's good enough for charity, a handout, but not good enough for—"

Leigh shook her head, unable to take any more. "Stop," she insisted, pleading with him. "Go back and sit down. We can talk about this—"

He moved in front of her again, his coat flaring darkly, his gaze as piercingly sharp as the knife blade.

"Talk about what, *chica*? About how the dreams hurt? How they make him want to hurt back?"

She shook her head. "I don't know who you're talking about, Mr. Montera, but it isn't me. It *isn't* me! I'm not that golden girl you're describing, and I don't deserve this abuse!"

He stared at her for a moment or two, his head lifted, his eyes measuring and wary, still lit with contempt. He didn't want to give her an inch, but perhaps she had surprised him a little, forced him to think of her in a new way. At last he stepped back, giving her room.

Leigh broke for her desk, barely able to control the trembling as she sank into her chair. Wheels squeaked across the acrylic platform, sending up that same helpless sound. Gathering herself together, she tensed protectively, elbows pressed to her sides. She would have to find a way to deal with this nightmare. There was no one to call for help now, no one to come to her rescue. Nick Montera would not save her. He was her assailant.

"Please sit down," she said finally, addressing him directly. It seemed the only way to proceed, to let him think she was going to continue the session. That would give her some time to decide what to do next.

He glanced over his shoulder at her, pulled away from whatever had drawn his interest outside the window. "No problema," he said, his tone sardonic. "We can play by the rules if that's the way you want it."

"There is only one rule in this office, Mr. Montera. No weapons. Don't ever bring that knife in here again. If carrying weapons isn't a violation of your bail, it should be, and I won't hesitate to report you."

The room fell silent as Leigh laced her hands on her desk. She was still vibrating, still shaking in every fiber, but she'd begun to think there might be some small hope for regaining control of the situation. If Nick Montera did as she asked, if he sat down and conducted himself appropriately, she would consider continuing the interview. If he didn't, she would summon the building's security guards and have him thrown out of the office. Dawson could damn well find himself another expert witness.

"Let's proceed then, shall we?" Leigh prompted.

Montera moved across the room toward her, stooping to pick up something on the way. Leigh watched him, wary but curious as he hesitated alongside her desk.

He gazed at her notes, then at her. "What kind of game are you playing?" he asked.

Leigh brought a hand to her throat protectively. "What do you mean?"

"It's there, on your notepad." He pointed toward the yellow pad where she'd been scribbling notes when he first arrived.

She glanced down in confusion and saw a question she didn't remember having written. *What kind of game are you playing, Montera?* She felt caught, exposed, and her reaction was instantaneous. She rose, coldly furious. "Are you going to sit down, Mr. Montera? Or am I going to call a halt to this session?"

"You dropped this." He held up her automatic pencil.

Leigh looked down at her desk in disbelief. How could she have dropped it? She'd set it precisely in the middle of her blotter. But it wasn't on her desk now. The goddamn pencil was in his hand.

"Apparently I did." Her fingers grazed his as she snatched it away. "Thank you."

"You're welcome," he said, his gaze fixed on the pencil. "Your hands are like ice, doctor. Why, I wonder?"

"You bastard," she whispered. "Stop trying to intimidate me!"

He smiled then, darkly, as if she'd finally said something he could relate to.

Leigh's only thought in coming to her feet had been to hang on to the small measure of authority she'd managed to assert.

But he was bigger than she was, so much bigger that her tough, get-out-of-my-face stance seemed to accentuate the difference in their sizes. She was beginning to feel a little ridiculous glaring at him, and the awkwardness only increased as she caught the shadings in his expression. He wasn't even the slightest bit daunted by an angry female psychotherapist. If anything, he seemed faintly amused.

"I was just going to sit down," he told her.

"Please do."

They made tentative eye contact, and Leigh's foot hit the chair leg. She was trying to back away, she realized. He was less than a foot away, and that was too close. Fear was still coursing through her, but it was charged with anger now, and the combination had created a taut, vibrating excitement that seemed to be short-circuiting her thought processes.

She was still in shock, it must be that.

Her senses had sharpened to the point that she was ultra-responsive, quivering like an antenna. She was even catching hints of the scent he gave off—the canvas of his duster coat, a piney masculine aftershave. And his eyes. She'd just realized what they reminded her of. They were that impossible shade of blue white that made one think of lightning during the first instant it struck.

"What's happening?" he asked, studying her. "You're perspiring."

Leigh's foot jerked again, but the chair leg had become an impassable barrier. It would have taken a weight lifter to budge it. She felt the metal digging into her ankle, the soft leather arm pressing into her thigh, nudging her insistently, but she couldn't move, either herself or the chair. The presence of her own office furniture seemed to have paralyzed her.

Something warm was purling down the inner length of her forearm. She didn't have the strength to look, but she knew it was him. He was touching her. *Yes.* He was touching the inside of her wrist with his fingers, stroking the sensitive area with a feather caress.

"Your pulse is wild," he told her, swaying closer, curious as he searched her features. A smile flickered, burning softly in his eyes. He gazed at her mouth, at the dampness on her lower lip, left there by a flick of her pink tongue.

"Feels good, doesn't it?" he asked.

Leigh had never been more aware. Of everything, anything. She could feel every inch of her own skin, every prickling hair on her arms, every tiny little goose bump. If sensation had been a sound, her body would have been singing with it. Good? she thought, her throat going dry and tight. Her heart going weak. Good? It felt wonderful.

CHAPTER
··FOUR··

"MR. MONTERA, I really think you should—" Leigh's voice thickened, becoming embarrassingly throaty.

"I think I should, too," he agreed.

Her fingertips stiffened against the desktop as Montera gazed down at her. There was no question that she ought to stop him from whatever it was he thought he should do, but she couldn't seem to manage it. She was too caught up in the moment to react, and at the same time she was wholly fascinated by what was happening, both as a psychologist and as a female. She didn't understand why she was responding so powerfully to his touch, especially after the stunt he'd pulled with the knife. How had he managed to reduce her to a mass of exposed nerve endings in just a matter of moments?

The analytical side of her personality wondered if this was the way he seduced his models—by frightening them half to death and then taking advantage of their weakened condition. Fear sometimes generalized to other kinds of arousal, including sexual. But Leigh's female side honestly didn't give a damn how he'd done it. She just didn't want him to stop. Her stomach was light as air, her breasts heavy with sensation. She could feel every silky inch of the cups of her lace bra. The sheer material was tight and confining against her flesh.

Lord, if she were this susceptible, one could only imagine how an eager, unsuspecting model might respond.

"Sit down, Mr. Montera," she said, infusing her voice with steely resolve. "And do it now."

A smile pulled at the corner of his mouth, and dark hair fell forward, drooping onto his forehead. "I thought there were no rules, Doctor, except against weapons."

His expression told her he intended to test her as she'd never been tested before. And his eyes, so strange and mercurial in their expression, were now flecked with diamond dust. He was a demon, she decided. One of Satan's own.

"Don't," she breathed as he shifted forward slightly.

She veered back, thinking he was going to try something crazy, like kissing her. But even before she'd regained her equilibrium, she realized he was only bending to sit on the edge of her desk.

"Whatever the doctor orders," he said. "You asked me to sit, I'm sitting."

"I meant in your chair."

"In that case . . ."

"What are you doing?" Leigh was incredulous as he leaned over and slipped a hand through the narrow space between her arm and her midriff. He was close enough to embrace her.

"Borrowing your pencil. Is there a rule against that?"

"Yes," she said, nearly out of breath by this time. "There is. I just made one." If her pulse was wild before, it was off the scale now. Her brain was fairly shouting at her to do something, but just as before, she made no move to stop him. Instead, she watched guardedly as he retrieved the pencil that lay near her hand, then picked up her notepad and sketched out a circle around the question she'd written. This could be a golden opportunity to observe him, she told herself.

She couldn't make out what he was drawing, but she was intrigued by his swift strokes. When he was finished, he tucked the pencil into the breast pocket of her suit jacket and dropped the notepad on her desk. Leigh glanced down at the sketch. He had drawn a snake coiled around the words: *What kind of game are you playing, Montera?* Her first impression was one of menace, and worse—of unmitigated evil—but she resisted the impulse to analyze what she saw. She would study the image later.

"The game is life, Doctor. And we're both playing it."

Leigh looked up at the sound of his voice, but not before realizing that the snake he'd drawn was an exact replica of the bracelet he wore on his wrist. She knew the details of the murder and that the dead woman had been found with a bruise in the shape of a snake's head on her neck. What she didn't understand was why Montera would want to openly associate himself with that symbol. He was still wearing the bracelet, but why? Was it defiance? Another way to flaunt society's rules? Or was Nick Montera part of some secret society that worshiped evil?

She had little doubt that he was capable of killing someone in the heat of passion. Most people were if the conditions were right. But was he cold-blooded enough to arrange his victim's body in exactly the way he'd photographed her? That was a chilling prospect.

By the time she sat down and faced him, Leigh was at war with herself. Common sense told her to end the session immediately and to consider taking herself off the case. He was a dangerous and unpredictable man, who seemed to harbor some deep-rooted hostility toward her, yet something kept her from acting on her own best advice. It was curiosity, she realized. He had aroused her deeply curious nature and more. He had galvanized her. She wanted to know about the golden girl who'd hurt him when he was a kid in the barrio. She wanted to know about the women he photographed, about the snake he wore. But more than any of that, she wanted to know if he was really a killer.

"There was a woman on the news the other night," she said, determined to resume the interview. "She spoke of having had a relationship with you. She said it went beyond the modeling."

He looked out her office window, his features seeming to harden against the bright light. In profile, his angular bone structure stood out in sharp relief, echoing the hawklike contours of his Spanish ancestors. Only the blue eyes, embedded in a fringe of dark lashes, softened him.

Leigh rarely thought of men in terms of beauty, but it was difficult not to with him. He was forbidding, but with a sinister grace about him that made one want to stare and try to discover what was so compelling.

"Paula Cooper has nothing to do with this case," he said.

"Perhaps not, but she spoke out in your defense. I'd like to know more about her—about you and her."

"I have nothing to say."

"Mr. Montera, do I need to remind you that I'm working with the district attorney's office, and that it might be in your best interests to cooperate?"

His laughter was quick, harsh. "Does it really matter what impression I make, Doctor? The DA wants a conviction, and you're being paid to help him get it. It's your job to make me look like a killer, right?"

"I'm being paid to evaluate you. And I intend to do it with professional dispassion. That's why I'll be analyzing your drawings and administering some psychological tests. They allow me to be objective . . . even when I personally find that difficult."

He grew quiet then, his trench coat hanging open, his right hand resting on his jeans-clad thigh. "No test is going to tell you who I am, Doctor. If you want to know me, you'll have to come where I am, enter my world. I dare you."

Fortunately she wasn't in a position to take him up on his challenge. "You're in my world now," she explained. "And that's the way it has to be. Neither one of us has the kind of freedom we might like in this situation, but there are reasons."

"Reasons of safety?" he asked. "Your safety?"

"I work here," she replied evasively. "My tools are here. Just as your tools are in your studio."

"What kind of tools tell you if a man's a premeditated killer? Is there one that pries open his heart and looks inside? Is there one that dissects his brain?"

Leigh had no response for that. She could find nothing within herself but a kind of sobering surprise. He had lifted his head as if waiting for her answer, and his gaze touched into hers expectantly, but she was empty-handed. There were no tests for looking into a man's heart. She sat back in her chair, aware that he had exposed perhaps the most profound drawback of her work, the abstract and impersonal nature of the tests she would give him. They would reduce him to numbers and percentages, and worse, if the results were misused, they would rubber-stamp a label on his forehead for all time.

He rose, brushed the creases from his jeans, and said without preamble, "If I'd killed a woman, why would I announce it to the world by arranging her body in exactly the way I'd once photographed her?"

Leigh was left to ponder that question long after Nick Montera had gone. There were no quick or obvious answers, and for some odd reason, she was rather glad. To her surprise she found herself preferring to think that he hadn't done it, though his aggressive behavior would certainly have encouraged her to believe otherwise. Eventually she did come upon one rationale that might have triggered the Machiavellian instincts of a sociopath. Nick Montera was a photographer, and the asking price of his work had skyrocketed since the murder charge was brought, with no signs of leveling off. The nature of the crime itself had drawn enormous attention to his work, and he was undoubtedly going to be a very rich man before the trial was over. A true sociopath wouldn't flinch at such a desperate publicity stunt, especially if he was totally convinced he could get away with it.

Why would I announce it to the world . . . ?

It was a good question.

"Okay, children, go forth and emote. Papa's next class is waiting with bated breath for their moment with the master."

A general clamor erupted in the Burbank acting workshop as twenty-plus students of all ages, creeds, and colors hustled to pack up their scripts and hurry off to auditions or dance classes or whatever else they had scheduled for the remainder of the morning. Their gravel-voiced, graying instructor, Gil Chambers, the legendary ex–Broadway actor, was the current guru of "Stick It," the latest in a seemingly endless series of acting techniques to hit Hollywood since the days of Stanislavsky's Method.

Paulie Cooper closed the script the class had been working from and tossed it into her unzipped tote bag, wincing as she realized she'd just crushed the Camembert and crackers she'd been planning to have for lunch.

"The eye is a slut, the ear is a virgin!" Gil called out to his departing devotees. "Keep those tape recorders running. Catch your mothers, brothers, and lovers in the act of being real and bring me back some gut-busting dialogue."

"The eye is a slut? What's that mean, Paula?"

Paulie turned to the hushed voice of her curvy brunette classmate and smiled. Jobeth Turner was a transplant from the heartland and, even after three years, a bit mystified by the Hollywood scene. Paula had always thought it was the secret of her friend's appeal. She could still be awed.

"It means we've seen everything, Jo," she said. "Seen it and probably done it."

"Oh . . . cool." Jobeth hoisted the strap of her huge canvas carryall over her shoulder as she rose, ready to follow the others filing out of the tiny storefront repertory theater.

Moments later the two women were strolling down the bustling sidewalk in the bright haze that passed for Southland sunshine. What neither noticed as they walked and talked was the nondescript, brown two-door sedan that crept alongside them and pulled into the first empty parking space.

"Isn't that illegal?" Jo asked Paulie out of the blue.

"What?"

"Taping people without their knowledge."

"Probably," Paulie admitted. "But I do it all the time. It's fun. Gives you a feeling of power, especially with guys." She laughed brightly. "Anything they say can be used against them."

"Oh!" Jo all but squealed as she got the picture. "Like those lying promises they make when they're horny?"

Paulie tapped her temple. "You're catching on."

"Time for coffee?" Jo wanted to know. "My voice coach canceled on me, so I've got a free hour before my workout." Jobeth was trying to lose her midwestern accent.

"Sorry!" Paulie sighed elaborately. "I'm meeting with the shampoo people about the yachting shoot." She tweaked the gold epaulets of her navy-blue cardigan, then pulled off her matching beret, letting her gleaming auburn hair fall in a cascade of brilliant highlights. "What do you think? Any good?"

"God, you're *lucky!*" Jo sang out enviously. "Fabulous hair and a shampoo commercial."

Paulie raked both hands through her rich, red tresses, lifting the heaviness away from her face. "I'm lucky? If I had your figure, I could be bald and get work."

Both women understood the value of physical attributes in a beauty-obsessed culture. Jobeth had great breasts and paid for her acting classes by being a body double in television and movie work. Paulie was a reasonably successful photographer's model. But both were also approaching thirty and feeling the pinch of the movie industry's lifelong indifference to women of age.

"Can I hitch a ride to my car?" Jo asked as they reached Paulie's dusty red Rabbit convertible. "I had to park a mile away."

"Good exercise," Paulie opined with a wink. "Help me put the top down."

Once they'd wrestled the heavy vinyl top into place, they threw their bags in the backseat and piled into the small car. With the sun in their eyes and the future on their minds, both were oblivious to the brown sedan as it crept into the traffic behind them and followed Paulie to the intersection, slipping into the left-turn lane just moments after she did.

"Hey, that's beautiful, *beautiful* . . . uncurl that gorgeous body and give me a grrrreat big stretch. Yeah, go with it. That's right . . . stretch it out for me, baby. Arms high, back arched, legs all the way to China. Oh, yeahhhh," Nick said, laughing richly, "that's it, hurt me, hurt me."

Nick rarely worked with color and he never did glamour photography, but he hadn't been able to resist today. Marilyn, an occasional model of his, was in one of her rare cooperative moods. A sleek and sensual female, she'd inspired a composition that was incredibly simple, yet employing a clarity of line and color that was as pure as anything he'd ever done.

He'd cut out a hill-like landscape from a sheet of plywood, lit it from behind, and arranged her in a languid pose in front of it so that her curves were aligned in sinuous counterpoint to the line of the hills. The tour de force was the rich glow of a tangerine-orange sunset, created from tungsten lighting on a painted backdrop.

The warm light sheened her limbs, creating deep pockets of shadow and feminine mystery. Nudity rarely inspired Nick. It lacked subtlety, but it was working today. Lying on her side, Marilyn had been a sphinx, the symbol of inscrutability. Now, stretched out on her back, she was a wanton creature, a lovely plaything.

Nick moved around her, enchanted by her long, slim beauty. He loved it when a subject resisted him at first, giving in only after he'd convinced her that she was extraordinary, a magnet to his creative vision. The rest came naturally. Murmuring, coaxing gently, he would ease past her guard and penetrate her defenses like a lover, bringing her into it, making her participate in her own seduction.

But it was the moment when she finally softened, surrendering to the experience, surrendering to his camera, that brought him the greatest satisfaction. Sometimes he wondered if that was what had attracted him to the field in the first place—the implicit power of the photographer over his subject, the subtle subjugation imposed by the camera.

Now Marilyn glanced up at him soundlessly, curiosity in her green cat eyes, and Nick realized he'd stopped taking pictures.

"Roll over," he told her, his voice dropping to a whisper. "Slowly, now, take it slow. Give me your back . . . come on, give me a peek of that beautiful backside. Good, good, *good* . . . a little more . . . just a little more. Keep it coming . . . keep it coming. That's it!"

He dropped to his knees to get a different angle, then rotated the lens to adjust the focus, snapping the pictures quickly, catching her before she could breathe, framing her while she was poised in exactly the way he wanted, with the small of her back arched and her rump practically in his face. "Jesus," he said, "hold that pose. I want you like that . . . just like *that*."

But Marilyn was getting restless. Nervousness rippled her graceful spine, and her eyes brightened with some fleeting distraction.

Nick quickly reset the camera's shutter speed, knowing he didn't have much time. "Stay with me, baby," he said, talking faster as she rolled over onto her stomach.

"Hold it," he pleaded softly. He had an idea for another shot, but it was too late. Marilyn was already sitting up and blinking into the distance. Her attention had been drawn elsewhere. She was clearly curious about a flash of light from the corner of the studio.

"Hold it!" Nick shouted.

But his subject had ceased to be interested in the frivolous concerns of men and their adult toys. She had spotted something: a furry, four-legged creature and she clearly intended to have it for dinner. If she could catch it.

In one uncoiling flash of strawberry-blond speed, Marilyn leaped from the set Nick had created just for her, sprinted across the studio like a small, fleet jungle cat, and pounced on the catnip mouse he'd picked up at the pet store, grabbing it by the head and shaking the red felt creature dramatically.

Nick laughed and set his camera down on the aluminum tripod. He'd done well to get her to cooperate for even a few minutes, knowing what a huntress she was. The cat had been there in his studio when he'd come home one day. He assumed she'd snuck in through an open skylight, and by the way she'd taken possession of his overflowing laundry hamper and made it her bedroom, it looked as if she'd come to stay.

He'd never seen a cat with blond hair before, but it was more the way she purred—quick, breathless, and sexy, as if she were slightly asthmatic—that had prompted him to call her Marilyn. He'd tried his damnedest to get rid of her. He'd checked around the neighborhood and put an ad in the paper, but no one had claimed her. So Nick Montera had become the proud owner of a blond bombshell with incipient asthma and a mean streak.

The catnip mouse spun across the glowing hardwood floor as Marilyn batted it with her paw. Nick swept it up and dangled it in the air, impressed by the cat's quivering excitement as she crouched to leap for it. Her ears flattened against her head, her eyes gleamed like gunmetal. Her tail twitched madly.

Something about her imminent attack made Nick think of the situation he was in. Marilyn was out for blood. Only they didn't call it murder in the cat kingdom. They called it survival of the fittest. The law of the jungle. But Nick's world—the human jungle—was run by the laws of a civilized and "polite" society, according to people like Dr. Leigh Rappaport. It wasn't kill or be killed. When they tried a man for murder and found him guilty, they either took his freedom or his life. They'd already taken Nick's freedom at seventeen.

There was only one thing left.

He felt a tug at his wrist and realized that Marilyn had snared the mouse. She'd pulled it from his fingers and now she was rolling across the floor, going at it tooth and nail.

Nick sprang up and grabbed for the camera. His fingers felt clumsy as he reset the focus, and somehow he triggered the strobe. The 35mm Canon began to flash wildly even before he had the cat framed in his sights. Marilyn hesitated in her glorious and uncivilized onslaught and gazed up at him, curious again. What's this guy doing? her expression asked. And why doesn't he find his own mouse?

Nick set the camera down. Even a half-assed photographer knew when the moment had passed. He was crouched near one of the tungsten lights he'd been using for his sunset composition. Marilyn's backdrop had only taken up one corner of the studio. The rest of the cavernous room was set up with an array of funhouse mirrors and prismlike reflecting surfaces for a future shoot he'd had to put on hold because of the murder charge.

This was the first time he'd held a camera in his hands since the night the police picked him up and took him in for questioning. Lately if he wasn't poring over law books to help prepare his case, he was fighting off the blinding headaches he'd suffered since childhood, thanks to a neighborhood gang who'd taken offense at his *gringo* eyes, cracked open his skull, and left him for dead. It had felt good losing himself today. No legalese. No mind-bending pain.

He heard a throaty meow and looked down.

Marilyn had stopped mauling the mouse by now and she was approaching him with great pride, half of the creature's body and all of its long red tail dangling from her jaws. She strolled up to him and dropped the mouse at his feet, a gift.

"Watch that stuff," Nick warned, deadpan. "It could get you a reputation as a killer."

CHAPTER
·· FIVE ··

WAS THERE ANY more Frango Mint ice cream in the freezer?
Leigh glanced up from her desk with that one urgent thought on her mind. She'd been studying the drawing that Nick Montera had sketched on her notepad, when a craving for the mouthwatering gourmet ice cream had struck her like a thunderbolt.

It was late, two in the morning by the watchman's clock on her home-office wall. She wasn't hungry, but her sudden craving was so imperative, it had to be a missive from her unconscious, trying to distract her from the sinister pull of Montera's sketch. Frango Mint was the one vice she had time for these days. She usually indulged to lift her spirits when she was feeling low, but she hardly needed reviving at the moment. A strange, insistent humming sensation had infused her. The feelings made her think of rain on a roof, pattering lightly at first, but gradually increasing to a soft frenzy.

She wasn't sure when the agitation had started, probably even before she'd dragged herself from the warmth of her bed, picked her way down the dark stairs, and voluntarily confined herself to this desk. She hadn't been able to sleep for the starkness of the images in her mind, so she'd decided to quit fighting the nervous energy and apply it instead.

Now she touched her finger to the drawing gingerly. The serpent seemed to be alive, as if it might come right off the page at her. There were tons of psychic energy trapped in that one symbol, she realized. Just as there were tons of psychic energy trapped in the man who'd drawn it. She had no doubt that Nick Montera was going to be one of the most intriguing subjects she'd ever analyzed.

She pressed her steepled fingers to her mouth, stifling a yawn. Her hands were like ice. Was that nerves, too? Or just another case of the chills she'd suffered as a child? She could remember them being so severe at times that she'd had to curl up in front of the floor heater in her room to get warm. Now her feet were icy, too, and though she'd long ago realized that it was probably nothing more interesting than poor circulation, she'd often wondered if she'd been responding to the lack of emotional warmth in her life, especially from her own mother.

In the more fantastical moments of her childhood, Leigh had imagined herself an alien, fearing that the hot red blood of humankind didn't run in her veins. She'd made the mistake of confessing her concern to her mother once. Kate's answer had been classic. "Oh, didn't I tell you? I got you from the lizard people. Be good or I'll give you back."

Leigh smiled ruefully and massaged her hands, pressing into the delicate bones and knuckles of her fingers and savoring the rising ache as her flesh fought against giving up its inner chill. She could laugh now, but she'd only been four at the time, too young to appreciate her mother's sense of humor.

She forced herself to get up from the desk and move around. The hardwood floor creaked softly as she crossed it with bare feet, her shadow flung out in front of her by the green banker's light on her desk. Her office had once been a bedroom until she'd added skylights and window seats and turned it into a solarium. The room's bright warmth during the day had prompted her to move in a desk and do her work here, too. But the cozy environment she loved so much in the daylight felt a little sinister now, at night. There was too much glass, too much exposure.

And darkness. Too much of that as well.

She folded her arms tightly over her breasts and tucked her hands into the warmth of her sides. She ought to have worn her heavy chenille robe, but she'd been in too much of a hurry and had run downstairs in her nightshirt.

Her shadow flared and disappeared in the black depths of the windowpanes as she paced the room, wondering what meaning the snake held for the man who'd drawn it. Her reference books said the reptile was a symbol as ancient and primordial as the creature itself, and its most powerful association was to the idea of evil. In the Garden of Eden the snake was the embodiment of Satan himself—and the instrument of Eve's seduction.

But in even more ancient religions, the serpent was a symbol of renewal. The snake shedding its skin or biting its own tail represented eternal return. It also implied the power of desire to ensnare the mind and body, not by force, but by willing surrender. "Imperialism of the soul" was how one reference had referred to romantic love, claiming that lovers were driven by their own desire to sacrifice themselves in order to prove their devotion.

A familiar scent came upon her as she halted, as if there were a window open, a breeze stirring up the room. The faint essence of mint rose in the air, bewildering her. Leigh turned, startled as she caught her reflection in the dark panes. With the light shining brightly behind her, she could see the outline of her body through her nightshirt. The glowing silhouette made her look like something holy and carnal at the same time—a naked angel protected by the gauzy light of her own purity. The radiance turned her sleek blond pageboy into a golden aura, and for the briefest moment she allowed herself to remember the incident from her adolescence. She could almost imagine someone standing on the other side of the dark panes, watching her.

Was this what he'd seen? she asked herself.

Her temples throbbed as she absorbed the erotic charge that seemed to glow from her own haunting image. Wisps of wintergreen triggered her senses, flooding her with more memories of that day. But she had been younger then, so very young. . . .

Finally Leigh forced the incident from her mind, but she couldn't erase the breathtaking sexuality that emanated from her reflection. It wouldn't go away. She wanted to believe it was an illusion, but people had told her she was desirable. Dawson had, many times, and yet she'd never felt desirable. As a teenager, she'd had the golden good looks of a prom queen, coupled with a crippling lack of confidence in her appeal. She'd always thought it was the legacy of an overpowering mother, but perhaps she'd been more profoundly affected than she realized by that young man, that strange day. . . .

She continued to stare at the windows, hypnotized by the contrast of darkness and light. Gradually her focus lengthened until she was looking past the glowing figure into the fathomless January night. Thoughts swirled in her mind like windblown leaves, a small cyclone that was starting to funnel itself into a pattern. Her mind always seemed to work this way when an idea was taking shape. Awareness springing from chaos. But in this case, it was more a hunch than a plan of action, and it had nothing to do with Leigh Rappaport and her desirability or lack thereof. It was about Nick Montera.

To her the snake bracelet had been overpoweringly sexual, but perhaps it had another meaning for him, a deeper meaning—

Her reflection dissolved in a stream of white fire as she turned. A high-tech message telephone sat on her desk. She started for it, knowing she couldn't wait until morning to set things in motion. If she didn't take care of this now, she wouldn't sleep. She rarely used the phone's speaker unit, but tonight she depressed the button automatically, then hit another button on a computerized panel that dialed the message machine at her office. After two rings, her assistant's recorded voice answered.

"Nancy—" Leigh's fingernails drummed a rapid tattoo on the telephone's plastic casing. "If you haven't already made me another appointment with Nick Montera, would you do that, please. I'd like to get him back in the office as quickly as possible. Thanks. See you tomorrow."

She hit the disconnect, then flipped her notepad on its face and went off in search of some Frango Mint ice cream.

A bomb was about to go off in the war room. Dawson Reed's strategy session had just come to a gear-grinding halt. Half of the six-member prosecution team were glowering at each other with homicidal intent across the conference table's water-scarred walnut surface. The other half were fidgeting nervously with their barrel cap pencils, clothing, or whatever else was handy, as if waiting for the detonation.

Even the room's heating system seemed set to blow. The intermittent hissing noises escaping through the wall vents could have been steam seeping from a bulging pressure cooker.

Dawson rose from the table and walked to the water cooler. He pulled one of the tiny paper cups from the receptacle, filled it up, and downed the tepid water in one gulp, then filled it again. He wasn't thirsty and he hated the flimsy little cups. He could hardly hold one in his hand without crumpling it, but he wanted to put some distance between himself and his embattled staff. To find another vantage point.

He wasn't unhappy about the internecine warfare. Quite the contrary. It gave him the chance to observe some of the newer members under fire and see firsthand how they handled conflict. He rarely assigned high-profile cases to rookies, but this case had some unique aspects that required him to be more flexible. To that end he'd been patiently observing their game of king of the mountain all morning, waiting to see who would muscle his way to the top. Or in this case, *her* way. The team didn't know it yet, but he'd already decided he wanted a woman to try the case. The question was, which woman.

He swished the water in his mouth, swallowing it with a grimace as he turned back to the deadlocked table. "The defense will probably request a change of venue at the preliminary hearing," he said, crushing the cup and lobbing it into an overflowing wastebasket. "They'll say Montera can't get a fair trial in L.A. The case is too visible. Anyone?" he asked, waiting to see who took the bait.

Maynard Keyes, an aggressive young attorney fresh out of Yale Law, jumped first. "They're right," he said. "Montera's become a national cult figure. The case is so damn visible he couldn't be guaranteed a fair trial anywhere, so he might as well stay here."

Dawson ignored the group's snickers. "What if the defense wants to deal? Are we open to a plea bargain on the charges?" He addressed the question to Carla Sanchez, a tall, handsome woman with a penchant for red blazers, who'd been with his office just over a year. She hadn't yet shown enough courtroom savvy to suit him, but he liked her self-assurance. Her legs weren't bad either.

"Why not?" she responded coolly. "Murder One requires malice *and* premeditation. Even if Jennifer Taryn pissed Montera off big time when she testified against him, that was twenty years ago. How do you prove someone held a grudge that long?"

There was some shuffling of papers and scraping of chair legs, a clear indication of dissension, but Maynard Keyes was the first to speak out.

"We don't have to prove it," he argued. "All we have to show is opportunity. Montera wasn't lying in wait for twenty years. She came back into his life, reopened the wounds, and presented him with the perfect opportunity to avenge himself."

A low hiss rattled the heating unit.

Carla crossed her long legs and settled back in her chair. "You're suggesting he had no shot at her before that? I don't buy it, Maynard. Besides, why jeopardize our case by reaching too high? Manslaughter or even second-degree murder would be a cakewalk, but what jury is going to send a thirty-seven-year-old second offender to his death?"

"He's already gone down for manslaughter!"

Maynard was getting perturbed and Dawson shared the sentiment. Sanchez was coming across as the voice of reason, so much so that her words could be construed as sympathetic to Montera's situation. Too bad, Dawson thought, imagining the scenario of a fiery young Latina, so incensed by this crime against all women that she wanted justice done, even if it meant prosecuting one of her own disadvantaged race, *even if it meant sending him to the gas chamber.*

She would have been perfect, but unfortunately she hadn't shown any such zeal. And this wasn't the first time Dawson had privately questioned her toughness. To his way of thinking, an effective litigator had to have a streak of ruthless ambition, not to further her career, but to win the case, which ultimately accomplished the same thing. She had to be hungry, but Dawson hadn't seen much evidence of that in Carla Sanchez.

He consoled himself with the fact that she would be a damn good prop at the prosecution table. Admittedly, this was tokenism at its worst, but he was willing to be accused of political incorrectness if that's what it took to win this case. And he needed to win. This was an election year, and a strong record was crucial if he wanted to avoid a contested primary. More importantly, winning the case would be insurance against a twenty-year-old skeleton in his closet, one that could easily come to light if Dawson weren't meticulously careful. He'd been involved in a peripheral way in Nick Montera's first trial, though even the old-timers in the office weren't aware of that fact. He intended to keep it that way.

"Maybe Carla is a fan of Mr. Montera's work?" one of the other women deputies suggested.

Laughter rippled through the small room.

Sanchez blushed. "Personally I find his work offensive. His subjects look like victims—Sleeping Beauties and Cinderellas—longing to be set free. And that one with the man's hands on the woman's throat, what's it called? *Come Midnight*? You can't tell if it's a kiss or some weird sexual thing, like autoasphyxiation. That piece alone should be enough to get him convicted."

Dawson's voice broke through her sermonette. "Convict him, Ms. Sanchez? Nick Montera was seen entering the victim's home the night she died, we have his fingerprints, we have skin and hair samples, and he has *no fucking alibi*. I don't want to convict his ass. I want it nailed to the cross. I want the death penalty and nothing less. Any questions?"

Carla Sanchez looked startled, then sucked in a breath and shook her head. No questions. None whatsoever.

Dawson curbed a smile. If she wasn't hungry, at least she was malleable. That was a start. By the time he was done with her, she'd be jumping for Montera's throat with a sharp knife.

"*Caramba!* What ees that weerd music you listening to? And why are you *naked*?"

Nick Montera glanced up from his reverie to see his housekeeper standing in the Moorish archway of his kitchen, staring at him in horror. She'd caught him daydreaming—leaning up against the tiled kitchen countertop in his briefs with a towel draped around his neck. He was hardly naked, but apparently Calvins were close enough to qualify for Maria Estela Inconsolata Torres.

Nick wasn't surprised. Estela, as she preferred to be called, was a Central American refugee who was overjoyed to have been living in the land of the free for the last several years. She didn't understand Nick's cynicism for one second, nor did she understand his preoccupation with the opposite sex. She was a devout believer in the faith of her fathers, the evil eye, and the importance of authentic chipotle chili peppers in her brick-red salsa. Not surprisingly, she disapproved of almost everything Nick Montera did, and had for years.

"Women, women, always the women," she'd complained about his photographs. "Why don't you take pictures of nature?"

"Women are nature," he'd explained. But she hadn't been mollified. They'd never discussed the murder charge against him, but it wouldn't have surprised him if she believed in her twice-consecrated heart that he'd done away with several of his former models with premeditated zeal. And yet she showed up week after week, faithful as the sunrise, to mop up after him. Her salsa was eye-popping, and she was a demon housekeeper. But he wouldn't want her sitting on his jury.

The kitchen and dining area of his studio were one open, sweeping space, decorated with an array of huge fan palms, bright red geraniums, Mexican pottery, and intricately carved Spanish chests. Moorish and Portuguese influences were evident in the woven cane furniture. Nick was a music lover, and in the adjoining living room, or *sala,* as Estela called it, an elaborate stereo system was thundering Dvorak's *New World Symphony* at a volume high enough to be a Memorex commercial. Nick had wanted to feel surrounded by the sound.

Estela clapped her hands over her ears, marched over to the wall unit, scanned the dials, buttons, and switches as if she were dealing with an instrument of the devil. *"La santissima madre de Dios,"* she muttered as she found the right dial and twisted it savagely. The music died and the studio went ominously silent, except for Estela's snort of satisfaction.

"What ees this beeg music?" she asked, darkly suspicious as she turned to Nick. "I think you like jazz."

"I do," he said. "I was in the mood for something different." It was true, except that when he'd turned on the stereo, he'd known exactly what he wanted to hear and gone in search of it. He even knew why.

Estela seemed baffled by his contemplative mood. "So . . . you like to stand around like that?" She swept a feather duster out of her equipment tray and propped her hands against her ample hips. "How do I clean with you stand around like that? You got your hairy butt hanging out!"

Nick glanced down for any evidence of the condition she was complaining about. He saw hairy calves and thighs, and there was a liberal dusting of the dark stuff on his abdomen and chest as well, but his butt wasn't hanging out, and even if it had been, there was damn little fuzz on it as far as he could remember.

Estela didn't return his slow grin.

"Okay, just for you, *señora bonita,*" he said. "Just for you, I'm going to remove my hairy butt from your presence."

"Bueno!" she huffed. *"Muy bueno.* Where you going?"

"I'm going to closet myself in the darkroom and sulk for a while, then maybe I'll develop some pictures."

She rolled her dark, expressive eyes. "Ay, pictures of women, I'll bet."

"You got that right." Nick was already halfway across the kitchen, but he whipped the towel off his shoulders and tossed it on one of the tall cane chairs at the breakfast bar. The least he could do was give Estela an unadulterated view of his back.

Her long-suffering moan made him smile. Inconsolata. They had named her well.

In the foyer of his studio he'd installed a small showroom with white walls, mahogany woodwork, and a domed glass ceiling. Beyond that stretched his work area—one cavernous room set up with the elaborate photography equipment that he used mostly for his advertising work, a couple of dressing rooms, a darkroom, an atrium with natural light, and a terraced garden for outdoor shots.

The formal showings of his work were held in galleries, but he'd realized it was good business to have an area in his studio where customers could see his work displayed. Not that anyone was lined up outside the door at the moment, but he had heard the galleries were selling out of his photographs since news of the murder rap broke. Nothing like a scandal to rev up interest. The only thing more advantageous than a scandal was death itself. That guaranteed instant fame.

Even for Jennifer . . .

He paused for a moment, studying the space where her picture had hung on the wall. The homicide detectives had confiscated it, but Nick didn't need the photograph to see the images in his mind. Beautiful Jennifer. Crazy, desperately unhappy Jennifer. Her serene face and lifeless body had been splashed all over the TV and on the front pages of major newspapers for days, weeks. She'd always said someday the world would stand up and take notice of her. They were standing now.

Nick wished he'd brought the towel. The studio was icy cold, but his neck was damp with sweat. Estela liked the heat off when she worked, and unless he had a modeling session scheduled, he tended to keep the place cold anyway. Gooseflesh felt like an indulgence when you'd grown up in a crumbling stucco shack in East L.A. with broken windows for air-conditioning. Fortunately he kept some cotton sweats in one of the studio dressing rooms for those days when he was able to sandwich a workout between photo sessions.

Sweat pants and a cropped black T-shirt hung on a hook behind the dressing-room door. *Si esta vibora te pica, no hay remedio en la botica.* Nick repeated the T-shirt's inscription as he pulled the soft cotton fabric over his head. It was a caution about playing with fire, but he strongly preferred the literal translation. "If this snake bites you, there's no remedy at the pharmacy."

He had rarely allowed himself to think about Jennifer since the media rampage. There was a line between passion and obsession, and she had crossed it repeatedly. If he regretted her death, it was mostly because she had brought it on herself. The modeling profession was rife with insecurity and narcissism, but Jennifer had been an extreme case. She'd been morbidly fascinated by the idea of suffering for love, perhaps even of dying for it. She sought out victim status, reveled in it. She was both saint and whore, perfect and fatally flawed, and in the end she had finally succeeded in making him despise her. God, yes, he regretted her death . . . but he wasn't going to the gas chamber for it.

The darkroom was as silent as a confessional.

Nick closed the door behind him and the inky blackness came aglow with crimson heat as he switched on the safelight. Moments later he was watching the face of his latest subject materialize in the developing solution. The woman taking shape before his eyes was very different from Jennifer. Her physical attributes were similar—both were slim of build and average in height—but their coloring was different. This woman's honey-blond hair was tied back in a ponytail, and delicate gold hoop earrings adorned her pierced earlobes. Though she was lovely, it was her pensive profile that drew the eye.

She carried with her the fragile air of emotional damage, and he found that irresistible in a woman. She was lonely, too. That much was obvious by the way she had abandoned her bicycle to gaze through the window of an oceanfront pet shop. A litter of kittens frolicked in the display window—but one wide-eyed little bundle of gray and white sat apart from the others, looking forlorn and frightened. The woman rested her forehead against the pane for a moment, totally sympathizing. The little misfit had opened her heart, Nick realized . . . and undoubtedly would one day break it.

He processed the next sheet, a shot of the woman riding away from the pet shop on her bike, without the kitten.

By the time he was done, he had a dozen shots hung up to dry. Normally he would have used a dryer for the prints, but he rather liked the old-fashioned home darkroom methods when he was processing for personal reasons. It reminded him of the magic he used to feel as a kid when he gazed at the moment of life he'd caught on film. Heartbeats, he'd called them then. Now his last shot showed the woman standing on a long pier, staring out at the horizon, a cone of melting ice cream in her hand. He'd caught one heartbeat. Hers.

When Nick left the darkroom a short time later and returned to the kitchen, the area was redolent with the sweet pungency of chilis and onions. A huge cast-iron kettle bubbled on the largest gas burner of the stove. Nick lifted the lid and inhaled with a sigh that bordered on the sexual. Estela had decided to favor him with some of her famous Salvadoran-style frijoles. Apparently his naked butt was looking a little too bony to suit her.

He glanced over his shoulder to make sure he wouldn't get caught, then dipped his finger in the hot, spicy mixture and popped it into his mouth. *Mother of God.* He was going to propose to the woman the minute she came back to the kitchen. The spicy stuff had his tongue aflame and his juices flowing. He could hear the nearby roar of an angry-sounding vacuum cleaner, but fortunately for Estela's Christian virtue, there was no sign of her. Apparently she'd gone off to liberate other areas of the studio from his grimy occupation.

The flashing red light on his phone machine told him some-one had called while he'd been in the darkroom. Either Estela hadn't heard it over the noise of the vacuum or she'd simply refused to answer it, as she often did. She had never approved of his "women."

A small throaty cry caught Nick's attention.

Marilyn leaped onto the countertop, rubbing herself up against him as he played back the messages on his machine. He indulged the undulating cat for a moment, petting her absently while the tape whirred backward. But she pressed against his hand hard, demanding his full attention.

The first message was from a nearly breathless female.

"Mr. Montera? This is Nancy from Dr. Rappaport's office. The doctor would like to see you again. Could you please call the office as soon as possible?"

Abandoning Marilyn to replay the phone message, Nick ignored the cat's soft yowl of displeasure. He'd been waiting for this call. He imagined most murder defendants would be reluctant to meet with an expert witness for the prosecution, particularly someone who had the ability to probe their psyches and strip bare their demons. However, he wanted all the time he could get with Dr. Leigh Rappaport. He wasn't concerned about her battery of tests and her fancy diagnostic techniques, because he knew that eventually he would persuade her of his innocence, no matter what those tests indicated. All he needed was the time and the opportunity. That was all he'd ever needed.

A sexy little growl gurgled in Marilyn's throat and she butted her head into the curve of his shoulder and then arched herself along his chest, finally turning so that her tail swished his face. Nick smiled and scooped the squirming cat into his arms, holding her gently but firmly while he worked his knuckles into the tiger-blond fur of her scruff.

"Wench," he murmured softly.

As she nuzzled into his caresses he stroked her velvet ears with his fingertips and flicked the underside of her chin with his thumbpad. The little whimper of pleasure she made was so languid it nearly melted him. Her throat vibrated against his fingertips with a tremulous beat that was as sensual as anything he'd ever experienced.

Marilyn was turned on, big time.

You're mine now, Nick thought, laughing softly. All mine.

He had always envied the way animals abandoned themselves to pleasure without fear of weakness. Somewhere in the evolutionary scheme of things, humans had forfeited that ability, but Marilyn's trancelike gaze confirmed his erotic ownership. She *was* his, to do with what he would, a willing slave to the pleasure he could give her. Nick felt a twitch of that same pleasure riding the curve of his spine. Apparently he hadn't lost his touch. Here was another female hypnotized by the snake's sensuality . . . helpless under the serpent's swaying spell.

In his experience, women always responded to the right stimuli. You just had to have the patience to discover what it was that turned them on. Too often men assumed that their wives and lovers felt what they felt, shared their needs. They didn't bother to find out what was missing, what she dreamed of, what she feared.

He knew what was missing. He knew what they feared.

He had long ago realized that women were good at giving, born to it. They controlled their world with acts of nurturance and support. It was the passive act of reception that frightened them, the letting in. They understood the risks of opening themselves to pleasure, of trusting a man. They had everything to lose by giving a male free access. But once they were persuaded that they were safe in his hands, that all he wanted was what he'd lost, his ability to feel, to laugh, to cry, they were emboldened. And once a woman had accustomed herself to experiencing pleasure with a man that way, both sexual and emotional, she was hooked. She simply wanted more and more and more.

He lifted his hand from Marilyn's throat and watched her eyes fly open, heard her rich, guttural cry of need. Leigh Rappaport had nothing to fear from him . . . nothing except herself. He knew what she liked. He knew what was missing.

CHAPTER
·· SIX ··

GENERALLY WHEN LEIGH wanted to know about a client's sex life, she simply asked. Somehow that didn't seem like the right approach today. Nick Montera was known far and wide as the "sexual sorcerer," but if she put him on the defensive, he would probably feel obligated to defend the legend or explain it away. Either way she would never get to the truth—

The sound of a throat being discreetly cleared brought her back with a start. She abruptly drew her hand away from her face, aware that she'd been fingering the small gold hoop that adorned her ear. She tended to stroke the earring when she was nervous or preoccupied. It had the calming effect of a lucky charm.

"What's up, Doc?" Montera asked softly. "Will I be squinting at large and disgusting ink blots today? Or are you going to shave my head and attach electrodes? I brought a stick to bite down on."

Leigh took note of her client's dark, flashing smile and his magnificent slouch, which was the only way she could think of to describe how he'd arranged his overly long frame in her office chair. He'd draped his arm over the back of the chair and he was absently working the paisley material with his hand, his thumb moving in rhythm with his fingers. The legs he'd stretched out in front of him had fallen open in a rather provocative way, depending on your vantage point.

Leigh's vantage point was excellent.

Perhaps he'd planned it that way.

She forced her gaze to higher ground. Now his smile, she admitted, that was a masterwork of subtlety. It snuck up behind you and whispered, "Gotcha." Leigh might have smiled back if it hadn't been for his eyes. They didn't seem to be in on the joke. They were the same frosty blue as his cashmere

V-neck sweater, which he'd tucked quite neatly into the waist-band of his snug denim jeans.

Rich black hair. Ultra-long legs. And the devil's own grin. He was a fantastically sexy murder suspect. One could almost overlook the fact that he had a penchant for concealed weapons.

"You're not a candidate for shock therapy," Leigh informed him. "You're far too cheeky."

"*Cheeky* . . . cute word. I would have preferred handsome, arrogant, devastating."

"I know." She drew her tablet in front of her and picked up a pencil. "If we've got the BS out of the way—and I sincerely hope we have—why don't you tell me about yourself?"

He tilted his head back, studying her through lashes that were nearly as sooty and thick as her own. "Okay, here's a deep dark secret, Doctor. I'm a photographer and I make it my business to know color. Gray is not yours."

Leigh touched the sleeve of the dove-gray cardigan she'd worn over a matching silk blouse and slacks. She'd never thought of herself as a fashion maven, but she'd actually taken the time to color-coordinate her entire outfit this morning, including her suede T-straps, which was more effort than she normally put into her appearance. "What's wrong with it?" she asked.

"You need more vibrancy. Blue would be better. It would bring out the contrasts in your complexion and the catch lights in your eyes."

"Catch lights?" Leigh was aware of pressure in that sensitive spot near the bridge of her nose, as if her horn-rim glasses were pressing too heavily there. She pushed them up with a touch of her forefinger. She didn't need glasses for anything more than reading, but apparently she'd forgotten to take them off.

"The light sources that reflect in a subject's eyes," he was saying. "Beauty photographers concentrate on them. Of course, it would help if I could *see* your eyes," he added.

She settled back in her chair, folded her arms, and gave him a quelling glance. "Mr. Montera, when I want a wardrobe consultation, I'll go to Nordstrom's, thank you."

"And have some frustrated salesclerk dress you in man-tailored jackets and slacks? Is that what you want? To look like a man?"

"What I *want* is for you to dispense with the mental masturbation and answer my question!"

He rocked back slightly, as if he were greatly enjoying their little disagreement. "It's not working, Doc."

"What isn't?"

"This tough act. You're trying too hard, and it doesn't suit you, anyway. Your strength is your softness. You're a woman."

The way his voice melted around the last word made Leigh want to look away, at anything other than him. Something swelled and turned over inside her like a tidal current. She reached up to remove her glasses, then caught herself just in time. Wait a minute. Wait a minute! She wasn't going to alter her behavior because of him. Her gender was irrelevant. She was a professional and she intended to conduct herself as such.

We'll try this one more time, she thought. If he doesn't answer the damn question immediately, I'm going to end the session and send him packing.

"How did you get into photography?" she asked him.

He gazed at her a moment, as though coming to terms with the fact that he was not going to control the encounter. It was probably a new experience for him, Leigh imagined. He wasn't a client, so empathy wasn't the goal of the session, but she was wondering if she could have achieved a rapport with him if it had been. Despite his casualness, he was a powerfully controlling personality. And she was too much on guard to give up any control of her own.

"It was a woman," he volunteered.

"I beg your pardon?"

"The reason I became a photographer. It was because of a woman."

Somehow that didn't surprise Leigh. Her mind framed an image of a beautiful woman sprawled in a sitting position on a window seat. She wore only a man's trench coat, which she held together loosely at the lapel, exposing her long, naked legs to the camera. The woman might have been gazing out except that her eyes were blindfolded by the coat's sash belt and her neck was arched at an exquisite, almost painful angle. It was the photo of Jennifer Taryn, both living and dead.

"Was it a woman whose picture you wanted to take?" Leigh asked.

"The other way around. She wanted me to take pictures."

"Oh . . . your mother?"

Nick Montera stiffened as if he'd been backhanded. Even his fingers stopped stroking the back of the chair. But in the same flash of time that he froze, he laughed, shaking off the moment. "No," he said, "my fourth-grade teacher. She applied for a grant through the Arts Council. They supplied the cameras, a local photographer gave us a crash course on how to use them, and then the venerable Mrs. Trini Maldonado set us loose— thirty ten-year-olds—armed and dangerous."

"What did you take pictures of?"

"Shoebox houses with clotheslines in the backyard and junk heaps in the front. Mangy dogs sleeping next to winos for warmth, and drug addicts passed out cold in the back alleys. I never realized how ugly my neighborhood was until I had it focused in my viewfinder. There was nothing pretty in San Ramone—no beauty at all—even the red and pink geraniums my mother struggled to grow on our concrete stoop were blighted with black smut."

"How did that make you feel?"

He looked at her as if she'd been born minus an essential organ—her brain. "How do you think it made me feel? I loathed the place. My dad drank. My mother cried. It was the typical barrio scene, except that Faith Montera was Anglo. My mother never fit in. And neither did I—her half-caste son."

"Was the ugliness an incentive to get out of the barrio?"

Again, that look. *Are you really that stupid, woman?*

He came around in the chair and sat forward, gazing at her as if it had become a challenge to communicate with someone so hopelessly naive. "No one needed an incentive to want out of there. I *couldn't* get out. I was ten years old."

"What did you do?"

"What everyone did. I hung out, waiting for something to happen. Some of the other outcasts and I drifted together event-ually, more for protection than friendship. None of the *cholos* wanted us, so we formed our own gang, the Thunderbirds. Our symbol was the feathered serpent, one of the Aztec gods."

"You gave up taking pictures?"

"For a while. But eventually I found something to photograph that even the barrio couldn't destroy."

Women, she thought.

"Light," he said. He glanced out her office window, where midday haze shone in the distance. "I discovered light. Sunlight, lamplight, the flames of a *vago's* bonfire. I caught the blaze in a toothless old man's eyes and the moonlight sheening the rusty chrome bumper of an abandoned car on Serano Street. I took pictures of the sun glistening on raindrops after a downpour."

His voice had softened, but there was something edging through, something nettle sharp. Why did she think it was passion? Or longing? Some needful thing. Suddenly Leigh was straining to hear every word. "I'd like to see some of those photographs," she heard herself saying.

But her comment couldn't penetrate his memories.

"There was a lamp in my mother's bedroom," he went on. "It had a frilly white shade that was torn and ruffles that were yellowing at the edges. She'd had it since childhood, I think. Once or twice I caught her bathed in the glow of that lamp, dreaming about something. She was beautiful then. . . ."

If you want to know about a man, ask him about his mother.

It wasn't anything Leigh had learned in graduate school. It was one of her own mother's many sayings. Kate Rappaport was not a foolish woman, though Leigh had often wished she could dismiss her mother with that one word.

She glanced up in surprise, aware that something had changed. Montera was standing by the room's only window, but she hadn't seen him get up. She forced herself to stay where she was and observe him from the reasonably safe confines of her desk. Was he upset? Had he revealed more than he wanted to? All of her professional instincts were alerted, warning her not to give in to personal curiosity. He'd opened up voluntarily, and if she asked too many questions, he might close up again.

"There was only one kind of light I didn't photograph." He hesitated, a quality of confession in his tone.

"What was that?"

"Morning light," he said after a long moment. "The sunrise. Ridiculous, huh? I couldn't even look at a sunrise without feeling—I don't know what to call it . . . sick at heart, I guess. There was something about that soft pink glow, the way it promised that everything was going to be okay. Maybe even better than okay—perfect, like your dreams."

"It's good to dream. Children need that—"

He shook his head. "Dreams don't come true in San Ramone. Nightmares maybe. Dawn meant another day spent ducking the 'man' and panhandling for pocket change. For fun we watched *adictos* shoot up crystal meth in back alleys. If we wanted a change of pace, we braved the streets and dodged *cholo* bullets. I stayed up all night and slept all day, just so I never had to see the sun come up."

Though Leigh had barely seen his shoulders rise, she knew he'd drawn in a breath and she sensed pain.

"What about school?" she pressed. "You must have had to get up to go to school." She wanted to keep the conversation going. She even repeated the question, but he didn't answer.

Rising, she gave in to an overpowering impulse. She removed her glasses and set them on the desk, then walked across the room to him. His back was to her, and his stillness frightened her a little. Or perhaps it was the powerful set of his neck and shoulders that rang alarms. She was five-four. He was over six feet and his weight must have been nearly twice hers. He would have been a threat even to a male therapist. Now everything about him seemed accentuated by the silence, like that surreal moment in the chair when she mentioned his mother and his hand had stopped moving.

"Nick?" Had she ever used his first name before?

When he didn't answer, she reached out to touch him. She could feel the sensitivity of her own fingertips as they brushed over his sweater. The cashmere was soft, yet prickly against her skin, and the heat of his shoulder muscles penetrated the powder-blue material, triggering her other senses. His hair looked black and glossy, satin soft to the touch. She caught the scent of something minty and familiar. Was it cologne? Mouthwash? The essence took her back, reminding her of that strange erotic incident when she was a young girl.

Leigh was absently aware of a low, rattling sound. Before she could determine what it was, Nick whirled and a dark explosion of movement wrenched at her arms, jerking her off balance. Her feet flew out from under her, but her brain couldn't work fast enough to make sense of what was happening. Dizziness enveloped her, stripping her of everything but the horrible thrill of pitching forward uncontrollably. It was like tumbling down a stairway. She clutched the air, feeling as if she'd been overtaken by a hurricane. Whatever terrible thing was happening, her mind couldn't conceive it, and she couldn't stop it.

Her knees hit the carpet with a soft thud, forcing a moan out of her. The world spiraled madly, sucking her into some black vortex, and then suddenly it was over. The nightmarish blur had cleared. She was on the floor of her office, rearing up on her haunches and clawing at Nick Montera's sweater.

"Stop!" she cried as he thrust her away from him.

He had her by the wrists, a brutal grip. His strength was so overpowering, she couldn't seem to summon any response except trembling shock. There were no reserves of nerve or steel. She hadn't the strength to fight him.

"I don't like to be touched," he whispered, his voice savage and shaking. "Not like that."

He was holding her down with the force of his hands alone. His eyes were incandescent, and he was breathing with the same kind of violence as the day he'd rescued her. Leigh could feel it seeping into her body through his hands, reverberating in her flesh, her mind. She shuddered involuntarily, but for an instant she was caught up in the wild, ringing power of it, utterly cowed by the amazing thing that was happening.

Violence had its own kind of poetry, she realized, its own kind of beauty. It trembled through her like some sweet, irresistible drumbeat, Nature's darkest and most riveting rhythm. It made her remember what she'd felt the day he rescued her— a thrill of release unlike anything she'd known before . . . or since. That man who rescued her could have killed her as easily as looked at her. This one could, too. They were the same terrifying assailant.

"You're hurting me—" She barely got the words out.

There was a flicker of light in his eyes, a triumphant glint of recognition, and then he scowled, as if he'd just begun to realize that she wasn't some new and unfamiliar demon. Searching her face, he seemed to be registering where he was and what had happened. Awareness dawned slowly in his eyes. He glanced at her heaving shoulders, at his own clenched fists with an expression of disbelief. His hands opened slowly, painfully.

Leigh sank to the floor. Reduced to a trembling heap, she had no choice but to stay where she was. Dear God, what had happened? She'd touched him and he'd flung her to her knees? Was that really what he'd done?

"Never come up on a man like that," he said. "Never!"

She shook her head, refusing to look up at him. "I barely touched you!"

"You crept up *behind* me. I thought you'd worked with convicts. I thought you'd been inside a prison."

Anger and fear exploded out of her. "This isn't a prison, for God's sake!" Tears welled in her eyes, stinging like fire. She couldn't blink them away. Burn marks were already beginning to form on one of her wrists. She cradled it in her hand and swore softly.

"Christ—" He stared at what he'd done to her, revulsion in his expression. He seemed torn, as if he wanted to come to her rescue again. Instead, he exhaled another obscenity. "What were you trying to do? How could you take a risk like that?"

Leigh didn't understand his anger. She could barely understand his questions. "How was I supposed to know it was a risk?"

A silence descended that was broken only by the rush of traffic on the street below. It made Leigh realize there was a world beyond the nightmare she'd slipped into.

"Are you all right?" Nick asked her finally.

Afraid he might try to help her, she made an effort to get up, but lost her balance. "Ouch!" she cried as her weight came down on the injured hand. She rocked back and held her throbbing wrist to her chest. Her eyes were wet with tears as she looked up at him.

Pain pierced his vibrant blue gaze. He clenched his fist and took a shaking breath as he saw what she'd done to herself.

Leigh didn't know what was wrong with him. He seemed caught between warring impulses, as if he weren't sure whether he wanted to help her or hurt her. She was frightened of him, but the grip in his eyes sent a stab of empathy through her. Something had ripped him open for a moment, cut away the scar tissue.

And then, just as unexpectedly, it was over.

He shook back his dark hair, catching a lock of it in his hand and forcing it off his face. In the space of one deep breath, he had regained control. He was Nick Montera again, steely cold and deliberate, a man in charge of his destiny, however ill-starred it might be.

Leigh had to ask herself if she'd imagined the other effect, if simple shock had caused her to read into his features—and into his character—what she wanted to see there. But she couldn't have imagined the fierce bite of his jaw or the color of his eyes. His irises were so sharply blue it hurt to look at them.

"What's happening?" she asked. She wanted him to explain himself, but he seemed to misunderstand her.

He fell back, giving her room. She saw little chance of recovering her professional dignity, but she did manage to rise to her feet without hurting herself, smooth her clothing, and walk back to her desk. When she glanced up, he was standing where she'd left him.

"Are you all right?" he asked again. But now his voice was taut, controlled.

"I'd like you to leave," she told him. It seemed the only option. Nick Montera was clearly dealing with some destructive impulses, and she was too scattered to know how to help him. She'd lost all hope of handling the situation professionally the moment he whirled on her—and she wouldn't have had the right to intervene even if she had known what to do. She wasn't his therapist. She'd been hired as a witness for the people.

"If I hurt you—" His chest rose as he uttered the words.

"No, it's all right . . . just go."

He made no further attempt to apologize. Perhaps he understood, as she did, that there was nothing more either one of them could say. He turned away as she looked up, but not before she'd seen a stab of regret in his pale blue eyes.

A terrible sadness washed over Leigh as she watched him leave her office. He moved with dark, brooding grace to her door and opened it. As he disappeared she touched the tender place on her wrist where his fingers had burned her skin. Nick Montera, she thought, what have you done? I know very little more about you than I did before, except that you are a violent man . . . and I will have to tell them.

He probably wouldn't have to worry about the sunrise very much longer, she thought. There weren't a whole lot of pink mornings in prison, and her testimony would surely help put him there. She entwined her icy hands on the desk and bowed her head. She was freezing, cold to the very bone.

CHAPTER
·· SEVEN ··

LEIGH WASN'T AWARE that she was touching herself until the squeal of rubber on asphalt brought her out of her reverie. As she swayed forward against the car's seat belt, she realized two things—her fiancé had pulled up in front of her Manhattan Beach condo, and he was staring at her with an expression that said, "What's wrong with this picture?" Dawson had draped his arm on the steering wheel and cocked his head inquisitively.

"What is it?" Leigh wanted to know.

"Lose something in there?" His gaze dropped pointedly to the way she'd slipped her fingers inside the plunging neckline of her black crepe de chine wraparound blouse.

"Where?" She glanced down, too, and blushed. Dr. Leigh Rappaport had been caught dead to rights in the very sort of autoerotic behavior that psychologists loved to analyze. She'd been absently stroking the softness that swelled from the pink lace cup of her demi-bra. She vaguely remembered that it had started as a tingly sensation that she'd felt the need to investigate, but apparently she hadn't stopped when the tingle did.

"Oh, that?" she said, as if it were nothing. And it *was* nothing, a perfectly normal act of self-stimulation. If one of her clients had been in this predicament, she would have urged that person to tell the truth. Don't explain, defend, or justify, she would have advised. Admit that you're feeling a little foolish. Share your emotions with your significant other. It will strengthen the bond of intimacy.

So Leigh was intrigued to find herself fibbing outrageously. "Cold hands," she told Dawson. "You know how I am, always chilly." She drew her hand from her blouse and began to massage her toasty-warm fingers as if they were frostbitten.

"I could warm you up."

"That's sweet, Dawson, really. But it's been a long day." They'd spent the afternoon at a celebrity polo match, sponsored by the National Charity League, and the evening at a fund-raiser, which, despite its dazzling guest list, had seemed as if it would never end. Leigh was honestly growing a little weary of the social whirl she found herself in as Dawson's fiancée. She'd always been involved with the Arts Council and their functions because of her mother, but Dawson's upcoming bid to be reelected as L.A. County's district attorney seemed to have put the two of them at the very apex of Southland society.

"Did I tell you how much I like your outfit?" Dawson asked. He began to toy with the slinky black skirt's flared hemline, drawing it up on the tips of his fingers, playing peekaboo.

"Yes, I think you may have. . . ." Leigh watched as more and more of her leg was revealed. She was secretly rather pleased at how sleek her calf looked in the sheer black silk hose. Her knee wasn't bad either. She wondered if the sight was turning Dawson on, because it was having an interesting effect on her. Her thigh muscles had drawn pleasantly tight, and the butterflies loose in the pit of her stomach were playing tag with each other.

She let out a strange little sound as Dawson's fingers touched her leg, playing over the sensitive outer curve of her knee and purling up her thigh. Dawson smiled broadly and kept going as if she'd encouraged him. She hadn't meant to. She'd meant to protest, but it had sounded more like a squeak of startled pleasure.

"Dawson, we really should call it a night, don't you think? . . . Dawson, what are you *doing*?"

"Just trying to help your circulation problem."

"My circulation is as good as it's going to get, I'm afraid."

"Oh, I'll bet we can prime the pump a little."

He had begun making languid little circles up her thigh that were so light they tickled like feathers on bare skin. The sensations were fantastically stimulating, and to Leigh's dismay, her body responded involuntarily. Her buttocks shivered and seized. Her nerves tingled in anticipation.

"I have to admit," he said thickly, "you don't look cold tonight, Leigh. Not even cool. You look hot, lady."

"Well, thank you, but—"

"That polo match turned you on, didn't it? Sweaty men and snorting horses. Women love that stuff, right?"

"Do they?" Leigh's voice was getting husky as well. "I suppose it was rather exhilarating, all that horsepower unleashed." All those men in tight pants, their virility on display. All that testosterone running rampant. Perhaps that *was* the reason she'd been touching herself.

Dawson kept hiking up her skirt until the tops of her stockings were revealed. A mutual silence fell over them as they took in the attenuated line of her leg. It ran like a river from ankle to knee, spilling delicately into the curve of her straining derriere.

A sigh slipped through Dawson's lips just seconds before he wet them with a flick of his tongue. He was a starving man eyeing a bountiful feast. When he glanced up at Leigh, his blue-gray eyes had darkened to agates.

"You're hot," he said. "No doubt about it."

Leigh still had enough clinical detachment to be curious about her fiancé's reaction—almost as curious as she was about her own. Her relationship with Dawson had never been driven by passion, and they'd certainly never had a quickie in the car.

Why not? she wondered.

"Come here," he said roughly. He splayed his hand against the small of her back and scooped her toward him. Leigh fell into his arms with a gasp of disbelief. She barely managed to press her hands against his chest to slow him down.

"Dawson?" she got out.

"Shut up," he said, arching over her and pinning her to the seat with a demanding kiss. His hands burned her backside and grazed up her midriff to her breasts.

Leigh was well and truly astonished. His swift passion was a frontal assault on her senses. He'd never been so forceful before, and she almost let herself be carried away by it until she realized that something very bizarre was happening. While Dawson was kissing her senseless, a scene was running through her mind like a slow-motion movie. She could see herself and everything that was happening to her—the impassioned kisses, the half-breathed sighs. But something was wrong with Dawson's face. It was shifting and changing, dissolving into another man's features.

The superimposed image was dark, but the man's gaze shone iridescent. Leigh knew immediately who he was and what he could do. To her. To any woman he touched. She could hear his voice in her mind. It stroked her nerves like a velvet whip, inciting her imagination as well as her body. She could almost feel his hands caressing her with the same sweet sting.

A part of her wanted to resist, but the images were wildly seductive, and her thoughts automatically snuck back to the moment in her office when she had looked up and Nick Montera had seen her tears. For an instant some devastating emotion had thawed his icy eyes to a rich, melting vulnerability. And she had nearly melted right along with them. The image was so real now, so breathingly alive, she wanted to hold on to it, to let it play out for another moment. She reached up curiously and trailed her fingers along his jawline. The curls at his nape were as silky soft to the touch as she'd imagined.

He caught hold of her hand and brought her palm to his lips, capturing some tender flesh between his teeth. And then he bit down gently, sending a thrill spiraling through her.

"Ahhh," she sighed, breathing out her intense pleasure. "Nick, I want—"

"What?" Dawson gasped softly. "What did you say?"

Leigh's eyes flew open. She gaped up at her flushed and panting fiancé. "Oh, my God, Dawson, I'm sorry. I don't know why I said that. It meant nothing, nothing at all. I've just been so preoccupied with—"

But Dawson caught hold of her shoulders and pulled her to him possessively. "Hey, baby, it's okay. It's okay!"

"It is?"

"Yes, I love it when you talk that way."

"What way?"

"You know—*that* way—when you get all hot and bothered." He pushed her hair away from her face, exposing the vulnerable hollow of her throat, and then he began showering that tender spot with sharp little love bites. "You've never used that word before with me."

Now Leigh was truly confused. "What word?"

"Dick." He moaned softly and came up for air, staring into her eyes. "You said you wanted my dick, didn't you?"

"Your di—" She turned a violent red, nearly choking on the word.

"God, you're sexy." His fingers stroked gently over her scarlet cheeks, and then he tilted her chin. "What do they call this? A sexual flush? I've never seen you this excited."

Leigh was appalled. She was profoundly aroused, but it wasn't for the reasons Dawson thought. She couldn't make love to him under these circumstances, not when the man on her mind was a murder suspect that Dawson himself had asked her to evaluate.

Dawson began to unbutton her blouse.

Leigh sneezed suddenly and violently.

"What is it?" he asked.

"I must be catching a cold, probably the chill."

"That's okay. I'll have you hotter than Fourth of July fireworks in no time."

Leigh sneezed again, rapidly, repeatedly. Explosively.

Dawson backed away, apparently discouraged.

Oh, Leigh, Leigh! she thought. Look what you've been reduced to. You've faked poor circulation and now this sneezing? Two bold-faced lies in one night? Was her nose getting longer? Even if it wasn't, this was no way to run a relationship. She'd put a great deal of effort into understanding her own flaws and foibles. Her education had been devoted to quantifying personality types, with the ultimate goal of making human behavior more explainable and predictable. But humans weren't neat and orderly in their motives. They were messy and impulsive. She'd been hoping to tidy things up a bit, to impose some order on the human condition, but somehow she'd miscalculated and landed right in the middle of the mess.

Now she realized that she had never really sympathized with clients who'd been in predicaments like this.

"Maybe I'd better get you into the house," Dawson suggested.

"Maybe you'd better," Leigh agreed, barely getting the words out before she went into another paroxysm of sneezing.

• • •

"Prepare yourself," Nancy Mahoney warned, sotto voce, the moment Leigh entered the reception area of her Santa Monica office the next morning. "You've got a surprise in there."

Her assistant had been on the phone when Leigh came in. Now Nancy had her hand clamped over the mouthpiece and she'd sprung up from her desk as if to stop Leigh from entering her own office.

Leigh could only imagine one surprise that big. "Did you call security?" she asked Nancy.

"No, no—it's not *him*. It's one of his ex-models, Paula Cooper. You know, the sexy redhead they interviewed on TV."

"What's she doing here?"

"I don't know, but she was adamant about talking to you. I tried to stop her, but she helped herself to some coffee and waltzed right past me. Interesting woman. Mind of her own."

Leigh wasn't sure how to proceed. Talking to other possible witnesses in the Montera case wasn't strictly in keeping with her role as an expert witness, but Ms. Cooper was already in her office, and Leigh was curious about having a look at one of Nick Montera's ex-models in the flesh. If the woman said anything that affected Leigh's assessment of Montera, Leigh would simply have to disclose the information to the court.

"Get yourself some coffee," Nancy suggested, going back to her phone call. "You're going to need it."

The coffee corner, as Nancy liked to call it, was a cozy little niche next to the magazine racks, where a fancy European coffeemaker with all the accoutrements sat on an occasional table. The rich dark brew smelled deliciously of macadamia nuts and chocolate as Leigh poured it. Her assistant loved gourmet specialty coffees, and normally Leigh did, too, though this morning she would have preferred her caffeine strong and straight. She fortified the cup with some cream and sugar, then took a sip and closed her eyes. Ready or not, here I come.

When she turned back, Nancy had finished her call and was scrutinizing Leigh's outfit.

"The blue blazer's a nice touch," Nancy allowed. "A little preppy with the khaki slacks, but nice. Too bad you didn't wear something short and tight. And red. Your visitor is a woman who by her mere presence makes all other X chromosomes feel frail and insignificant."

"It wouldn't be the first time." Leigh picked up her briefcase, tucked it under her arm, and headed for her office.

It was fortunate that she had a good grip on her coffee cup as she walked through the door. She wasn't so lucky with the briefcase. It slipped from under her arm and crashed to the floor as she halted in her tracks, astounded.

"What are you *doing*?" she asked the woman on the floor of her office.

Paula Cooper was on her hands and knees, her head arched back dramatically and one leg extended high in the air behind her. A cloudburst of XS flooded the small room. Her perfume, apparently.

"Oh, sorry!" she said, glancing around at Leigh as she continued to hold the extravagant pose. *"Buns of Steel."*

"I beg your pardon?"

"Buns of Steel, the exercise tape. You have it, don't you?" She gave Leigh the once-over, then winked mischievously. "No, I guess not."

Leigh could easily have taken offense—and undoubtedly would have—if her visitor hadn't pulled a grin that bubbled over with engaging warmth. Leigh found herself smiling back. Paula Cooper was going to be hard to dislike, she realized.

By the time Leigh had recovered her briefcase and reached her desk, Paula was on her feet and rearranging her outfit— an exotic mix of black dance leotards, a Hermès scarf, and a clingy electric-blue micromini. She was athletically toned from head to toe, close to five-ten, even in low-heeled blue suede boots, and late-twentyish, but still a photographer's dream.

With one last flourish, she tossed her head and shook out her hair. Her fashionably long pageboy shimmered and flew around her shoulders in a blaze of auburn glory. Her fingernails matched her plum-red lips. Must be a good hair day, Leigh thought. That was reason enough to ask the woman to leave. But Leigh had now gone beyond mild curiosity to the burning variety. What sort of relationship had Paula Cooper had with Nick Montera, besides the obvious sexual thing?

The limits of Leigh's responsibility in the Montera case were somewhat vague in situations like this. She'd been retained to evaluate the defendant and to provide expert testimony regarding his mental and emotional state, as well as his capability of committing the crime. Substantiating interviews were not necessarily part of that obligation as she understood it, but Leigh couldn't resist the opportunity that Paula Cooper presented.

"Ms. Cooper, is it?" Leigh asked.

"Oh, please, call me Paulie!"

Leigh nodded, still reluctant to invite her visitor to have a seat. "You're a dancer?" she probed.

"Dancer, actress, model . . . gypsy fortune-teller." With a sparkling smile, Paulie went to the fan-back chair where she'd left her purse and plucked up the tiny blue suede pouch, its gold chain glittering as she hooked it over her shoulder. "I don't actually have a crystal ball, but there is this fun little thing I do. I seem to be able to predict the future, simply by honing in. Let's see. . . ." She lifted an eyebrow and peered at Leigh. "Oh, yes, absolutely—you're due."

"Due for what?"

"Something major. I'd say within the next four to six weeks, perhaps even sooner. A critical event."

"Should I take out insurance?"

The irony wasn't lost on her visitor.

"Only if you're planning on dying from excitement," Paulie quipped. "On the other hand, if it's insurance you're thinking about, birth control might not be a bad idea. This 'event' involves a member of the opposite sex."

Leigh smiled and sat down in her swivel chair. Okay, she was hooked.

Paulie sat down, too. "The man in your life? Is he tall, handsome, highly intelligent?"

Highly intelligent? Did she mean Dawson? Leigh gave a little shrug of confirmation.

Paulie's nod was knowing. "I see things heating up to a sizzle, Doctor. But if I may, one word of advice? Whatever happens, don't confuse sex with love. That's always fatal for romantics like us. I speak from bitter experience."

Leigh wondered if she was talking about her own relationship with Montera. "Is that why you're here today?"

Paulie sighed dramatically. "I've been on edge for days now, wondering whether or not I should come and speak to you. It's a calculated risk, I guess."

"A risk? Speaking to me?"

"I just thought there were some things you should know about the Nick Montera case. You are the psychologist who's evaluating him, aren't you?"

"One of them. The defense will undoubtedly call their own witnesses."

Paulie glanced at the floor, suddenly pensive. "They'll never get to the truth, Dr. Rappaport. None of them, not even you. No one knows Nick Montera the way I do—" Lacey eyelashes lifted slowly, revealing a cloud-strewn gaze. "And even I don't know him."

"Ms. Cooper, really. This is a murder case, and I've been called by the state to testify *against* Mr. Montera. Perhaps you should be talking to his attorney?"

"Alec Satterfield? I tried, but he wouldn't listen. He saw me on TV and said I did his client more harm than good. Dr. Rappaport, *please* hear me out. I know how this must look, me showing up on TV and then coming here, but I'm not some lunatic fan of Nick Montera's, and I'm not doing this for the attention. I had to talk to someone."

She hesitated, as if waiting for Leigh to stop her, then hurried on. "Nick isn't like anyone you've ever dealt with before," she said. "I can guarantee you that. There are things you should know about him, important things. There are other sides to him, facets no one else has seen."

Leigh felt the tug of something irresistible. She took a sip of her coffee, hoping the lukewarm brew would distract her, but she might as well have been a child lured by carnival music and bright lights. "What do you mean?"

"I know this sounds crazy, but Nick is much more than just a talented photographer. He seems to wield some kind of subliminal power over people. When I answered his ad for a model, I showed up at his studio in the sexiest outfit I could put together. He took one look at me, apologized for taking up my time, and sent me on my way. *Just like that.* Sent me on my way! Can you believe it? I was devastated. I needed the job, so I called him back—several times, as I remember.

Finally he agreed to see me again, but only on his terms."

Her purse lay on her lap and she began to work the gold chain through her fingers as if the links were prayer beads.

" 'When you come to my studio,' he told me, 'come naked. Leave the trashy clothes and the makeup at home. You have no idea who you are, Paulie—or what you can be. I can help you discover who Paulie Cooper is, but if you won't trust me enough to let me do that, then we can't work together'."

She stopped to take a breath, obviously shaken. "That's what he said to me, his exact words. Well, I was scared to death, but I went."

"And what happened?"

"He saw immediately that I was nervous, and it seemed to please him. 'Stay with the fear,' he said. 'The fear is real.' He knelt next to me and talked to me as if I were a child. Well, I fell apart, absolutely fell apart. Pretty soon I was babbling and crying and telling him things I hadn't told my own mother. He took control of everything from that moment on, down to the tiniest detail. He knew exactly what he wanted for the shot, and he wouldn't let his makeup lady touch me. He dismissed her and did everything himself—my hair, my makeup. He even dressed me."

"Dressed you?"

"Yes, in one of his own sweaters—a gray cashmere V-neck. It was huge. I swam in it, of course, but that's what he wanted."

"Cheesecake?" Leigh asked.

"No, no! Nothing like that. I looked like a waif—a frightened, bewildered child all twisted up inside a gray cashmere straitjacket. It was wrenching, really. I felt as if he'd shot me naked—but not physically, emotionally."

She opened her purse and searched through a zippered compartment, pulling out a composite. Leigh stood to look at it as Paulie approached the desk.

"I wouldn't have recognized you," Leigh said honestly. The subject wore no makeup and her auburn hair was loosely pulled back from her face. She looked about fifteen years old, and the sweet misery in her features was heart catching. But there was also something undeniably erotic in the fact that she was naked beneath the sweater. You had to wonder what she'd been doing to get herself in that condition, and all kinds of lurid images came to mind . . . an uninhibited bout of sex play that got out of hand, a tempestuous lovers' quarrel. Had she been mistreated in some way?

"He does that," Paulie said. "He makes you wonder what's happened to the women in his pictures. He makes you feel as if you know them, because you do. You're looking at your own fear, your own secret desires. Your own downfall."

Leigh was no longer uncertain about dealing with Paulie Cooper. She wanted some answers. "Tell me about this power you say he has."

Paulie returned to the chair. "I don't know what to call it, but it's almost a physical thing. I suppose that's because Nick is such a physical man. He's very natural, very masculine. I've been with lots of men over the years, and there's no one who compares in terms of maleness."

She hesitated as if Leigh might want to argue that point.

Leigh didn't. "This power, how does he use it?"

"God, I wish I knew. I'd bottle it. It's nothing obvious, but he has a way of making you feel as if you're the center of his world and his entire focus is you. Just you. He creates a psychic energy field that's like gravity. All I know is, if you're around him long enough, you get sucked in. I can't imagine a woman resisting him, once he's singled her out."

The purse's gold-link chain clicked through her plum-red fingernails.

"You're making him sound like one of those charismatic types with a flock of devoted followers," Leigh observed. "A Jimmy Swaggart or even a Charlie Manson. Are you talking about the kind of man who can influence people's thoughts, brainwash them into doing his bidding?"

"Yes, something like that, only with Nick it's strictly a man-woman thing. He concentrates on his subjects. For me, being with him was a rush, better than alcohol or drugs, I swear. He was addictive. I just lost control."

"How? Sexually?"

"That was a part of it. But there was more. It was the way he took charge. Eventually I became conditioned to everything about him, even the sound of his voice. All he had to do was talk to me in that sexy way of his, and I was turned on, aching for him, dying for him to touch me. It was heaven and hell at the same time. I felt like he'd put me in a sexual trance, and I couldn't bring myself out of it."

She hesitated, shuddered. "At times it was terrifying."

"How did you get out?" Leigh asked.

Paulie didn't seem to have heard the question. "You've noticed his eyes, haven't you?"

"Of course."

"But have you really looked at them? Sometimes the blue is so cold and crystalline you feel like you're getting a glimpse of infinity. You know, one of those tricks they do with mirrors, where the image never stops? You can see it go on forever? There were times when I thought that Nick was my crystal ball. I could look in his eyes and tell the future."

The woman was obsessed, by her own admission, but Leigh couldn't help remembering her own reaction to a gaze so blue-white it had seemed hot.

"He's Latin, you know," Paulie went on. "A Latino with blue eyes. Don't you find that interesting?"

"I believe his mother was Anglo."

"Yes, she died when he was a boy. I didn't know him then, but I think the loss must have ripped him apart. He carries a lot of grief, Dr. Rappaport, and it's made him bitter. He can be cruel. Cruelty comes easily to him."

"In what way?"

"He knew my secrets . . . and sometimes he used them against me. I was afraid of the dark, and he locked me in that terrifying black vault of a room until I begged and pleaded to be let out. I collapsed in his arms afterward, and he swore it was an accident, that the door had jammed."

"Was it an accident?"

"I don't know. I'll never know. Sex became a game with him, too. He knew what excited me, and at times he tormented me with it—the most glorious kind of torture, of course. It was ecstasy, what he did to me. I couldn't get enough of it. *I was hooked on it, totally hooked.* I would have done anything for him, even sell myself, if he'd asked. That's when I knew I had to leave. He was hurting me. He didn't want to, but he was. And I welcomed it. I was a desperate woman, Doctor. I wanted anything Nick Montera could give me, even pain."

"You're not over him yet, are you?"

"I suppose not, but I'll never go back to him."

Leigh had begun to stroke the gold hoop of her earring. God, if only her heart weren't pounding so hard. She hoped Paulie couldn't hear it shaking her voice. "Why did you come here, Ms. Cooper?" she asked. "Was it to tell me that Nick Montera killed Jennifer Taryn?"

Paulie's purse clattered to the floor. "No! I came to tell you that he *didn't* kill her. Nick couldn't take anyone's life. He's capable of many things, but not cold-blooded murder."

"I'm afraid you're wrong. Nick Montera took a life when he was seventeen. He killed a Chicano gang leader and did three years in prison on a manslaughter charge."

If Leigh had been expecting shock or disbelief from her visitor, she got neither. Paulie Cooper was completely nonplussed by Leigh's bombshell.

"That was different," Paulie asserted. "Nick fell in love with the gang leader's girlfriend. She was young and white—a runaway from an affluent family. The gang leader caught them together and came after Nick with a knife. It was self-defense, Doctor. That's exactly what it was, but Nick didn't have a chance of beating the rap. Even the trial was rigged."

"How do you mean?"

"Jennifer Taryn testified against Nick, and she might as well have knifed him herself. She accused him of raping her and attacking her boyfriend. Apparently she was afraid of reprisals from the gang."

Shock registered like a plunge in an icy bath. Leigh clutched her arms. "Jennifer Taryn was the gang leader's girlfriend? The same woman Nick is now accused of murdering? His ex-model?"

"Yes, didn't you know?"

Leigh hadn't known. But if it was true—if Jennifer Taryn was the same girl who betrayed Nick Montera all those years ago—then Paulie Cooper may have just supplied him with a motive for the murder. "Who else knows about this?"

Paulie looked bewildered. "I thought everyone did. It must be part of his criminal record. I know it looks bad, but it doesn't mean he did it—" She shot out of her chair, forceful in her need to make Leigh understand. "He didn't kill her, Doctor. You've got to believe me. He couldn't have, because I know who did."

"You know—" Leigh dropped back in her chair. She couldn't take any more in, but Paulie was impassioned.

"It was Jennifer's boyfriend," she averred. "He strangled her and framed Nick."

"How do you know this?"

"I don't have proof, but Jack Taggart's a homicide cop and a sadistic bastard. Jennifer walked out on him several months ago, and he flew into a rage, especially when he found out that she'd gone back to Nick."

"Gone back? After testifying against Nick? Why would she do that?"

"Because she never got over him—or feeling guilty about what she'd done to him. She showed up on his doorstep one day, begging him to let her explain. She told him all she wanted was his forgiveness, but Nick wasn't sure he wanted anything to do with her. He saw her a few times, took some pictures, but that was all."

"You know what happened between them? How?"

"Nick and I stayed in touch even after our sexual relationship was over. He told me things."

Leigh rose from her chair and walked to the window, hoping it would clear her head. The traffic on the street was heavy and the air was already thick with smog, but a shaft of sunlight penetrated the blue terrarium glass, bathing her two inert turtles in tropical warmth. Neither of them ever seemed to move, and Leigh had wondered more than once if their built-in armor was too heavy to cart around. Was that the price of security? Stagnation?

"Let me see if I understand this." Leigh stood in front of the terrarium, absorbing the warmth that pierced it. "You believe that Taggart, in a jealous rage, killed Jennifer and arranged her body like a photograph Nick had taken?"

"Yes—why not!—if he was trying to frame Nick for her murder."

Startled at the anger in her visitor's voice, Leigh turned. Paulie was flushed and her eyes were glittery. She had retrieved her purse from the floor and she was again pulling the chain to and fro with sharp little snaps. Leigh was amazed that she hadn't yet broken a nail.

"Ms. Cooper, why did you come here?" Leigh asked. "Why did you want to talk to me?"

"I was hoping to convince you that Nick didn't kill anyone. But maybe his attorney was right, maybe I've done more harm than good. Have I? Have I made things worse?"

Leigh shook her head. "I don't know what you've done."

It was a paradox, Leigh realized, touched by the near despair in Paulie Cooper's expression. The more Leigh learned about Nick Montera, the less she felt she knew. She'd come close to removing herself from the case after her last session with him, but she hadn't been able to do it. Like a prism bends light, her memory had refracted that moment of naked vulnerability when he'd knelt down beside her into one burning ray of awareness. She couldn't walk away from the case any more than she could erase the split second of pain from his eyes.

She'd decided that she would limit her evaluation to interviewing and testing him in her own office, but now she wasn't at all certain that would be enough. He'd once told her that if she wanted to know who he was, she would have to go *where* he was. To his studio. His life was photography. Even the murder he was accused of reflected his work in a macabre way. In order to understand him fully, she would have to analyze his pictures. She would have to observe him at work.

She reached up and touched her earring, running her finger around the inside of the hoop. She wasn't required to testify as to whether or not she believed he was a murderer, simply whether or not he was capable of the crime. That level of certainty might be enough for the courts, but it wasn't enough for her. She wanted to know whether or not Nick Montera was a cold-blooded killer. More than that, she had to know.

CHAPTER
·· EIGHT ··

THE STEEP SLOPES and serpentine roads of Coldwater Canyon were host to a startling variety of life-forms. Exotic flora and fauna coexisted with rock stars, movie moguls, artists of every possible bent, and even a conservationist group called the TreePeople. Million-dollar fixer-uppers hung off the side of cliffs and rustic cottages dotted the terraced hillsides. To travel writers the canyon was a crazy quilt, a hodgepodge of humanity and humus. To unwary visitors it was a geographical puzzle of mazelike complexity.

Today Leigh herself was one of those unwary visitors. She'd already negotiated several miles of winding road and had come to the conclusion that the maze had no exits when she spotted the access that led to Nick Montera's place. She could just make out his studio through a small forest of poplars as she pulled her car onto the gravel driveway that knifed through the graceful stand of trees.

The cavernous one-story structure seemed to be made up mostly of windows, skylights, and rustic woodshake shingles. She couldn't detect any activity inside as she drove up and parked, but she'd intentionally arrived a half hour earlier than the appointment time she'd had Nancy set up.

She cut the engine and drew a breath, reaching down to smooth the line of her nylons before she let herself out of the car. She rarely wore skirts and sweaters, but today she'd worn a Dresden-blue, two-piece Joan Vass, perhaps in an effort not to look preppy. Instead of securing her blond hair with combs, she'd let it fall to her shoulders in a swingy pageboy with a part on one side and a few wispy tendrils for bangs.

Kate Rappaport would have approved of her look, Leigh realized with some irony. So would Dawson, but he would not have approved of her making this trip alone. Leigh knew she was taking a risk, but she'd decided against using an escort from the DA's office. She couldn't hope to establish any kind of rapport with a bodyguard lurking in the background. It would alter the relationship and destroy whatever element of trust remained between her and Montera. She also had no idea whether or not the courts would sanction her "home visit," but if she wanted answers to the questions that were plaguing her, she had to take some license.

With that firmly in mind, she grabbed her briefcase and let herself out of the car.

Montera's house was wrapped by a sprawling veranda with trailing bougainvillea in lush shades of orange and magenta, and the front door was made up of eight richly carved wooden panels. Leigh recognized the ancient Aztec influence in the fierce birds and serpents, but a blazing sun and a serene new moon were the door's focal points.

The knocker was an eerie Indian mask in bronze that gave off a brassy echo, like cymbals in a tunnel. No one answered when Leigh tried the knob, but the door gave way with a touch, and as she stepped inside she found herself standing in a circular foyer. Sunlight filtered through the domed glass ceiling, sheening the pictures that hung on the walls.

Nick Montera photographs, Leigh realized. His signature style was all over them. The moody tableaux were studies of women in various states of physical and emotional undress, some of them wounded and watchful, others suffused with erotic yearning, yet all the more difficult to look at because of the searing, melancholy tone of all Montera's work.

She set her case near a table by the door and moved around to look at the display.

The centerpiece was a black-and-white portrait of such strange, haunting beauty that Leigh was drawn to it. The subject, a young woman, sat alone in the shadows in a meditative pose, her legs drawn up, her gaze unfocused. The mood of the piece was desolate. The tones were bleak, yet beautiful, and the picture itself seemed to pulse with unfulfilled longings. Gazing at it, Leigh had a sensation of weight in her chest, of sadness bearing down on her heart. She was reacting to the picture as if it were a photograph of herself. Or of someone she knew.

She couldn't imagine that a man who had produced a work of such depth and power could also take a woman's life. He had captured this woman's soul. Leigh reached up to touch the golden hoop at her own ear, then caught herself and smoothed the shoulder pad of her sweater instead. She was assuming that Nick Montera's motives were artistic, but what if he were driven to do more than unveil his subjects' souls? What if he wanted to possess them?

Men who were pathologically obsessed with control often struck out in violent and violently symbolic ways when they'd been rejected by a woman. It wasn't impossible to imagine that he might have arranged Jennifer's lifeless body in the same vulnerable pose that he'd photographed her, thus creating the illusion that she was inescapably his.

Leigh turned suddenly, thinking she'd heard something. A muffled cry? Several hallways branched out from the foyer. One of them, dimly illuminated with track lighting, looked as if it led into the studio itself. Though she was increasingly uneasy about wandering around uninvited, she followed the corridor to its end, aware of the click and slide of her low-heeled pumps over the gleaming black terrazzo tile. The hallway emptied into a cavelike expanse with an open-beam ceiling and a hardwood floor.

The area was shadow-lit, making it difficult to see, but Leigh could make out lights, umbrellas, and other photographic equipment. The room seemed to be set up with myriad mirrors and reflecting surfaces as if for a photo shoot. Around the perimeter of the studio, tall panels of black ripstop nylon created an ambience of intimacy, and from one of the enclosures, a soft bluish light escaped through an opening between the panels. Catching the murmur of voices, Leigh approached cautiously.

Nick Montera was inside the paneled area. From Leigh's vantage point, it looked as if he were down on the floor on one knee, but she couldn't see what he was doing. She angled closer to the opening, and as her field of vision widened, a scene of unbelievable intimacy was revealed. Only the dazzling white lights with their umbrella reflectors told her there was a photo session going on.

Nick was kneeling next to a low bench where the model sat, a young woman who was barefoot and wrapped in a man's overlarge terry-cloth bathrobe. She was clearly distraught, and he was trying to calm her. His voice had a crooning quality, soft and fatherly as he spoke to her, and finally he drew her into his arms, soothing her muffled sobs with a compassion that was genuinely moving.

Leigh had rarely witnessed such sensitivity in a man, and she'd never experienced that kind of gentleness herself. Her own father left her mother for another woman when Leigh was two. She knew Drew Rappaport from his pictures and little else. Her mother had told her with no apparent rancor that her father was a handsome devil with too much wanderlust to let himself be saddled with the baggage of a small child, causing Leigh to think that she must have been the reason he left. Perhaps that was why the sound of the girl's soft gasps sliced so sharply through Leigh's defenses now. The sudden ache in her throat made it hard to breathe.

The girl's eyes glistened with tears as Nick rose and turned to her, stroking her chin and tilting her woeful face up to him. She called his name and reached out for him urgently as he took a camera from its perch on a tripod. A second later he was snapping rapid-fire pictures and talking to her soothingly.

"It's okay, baby, you're beautiful when you cry," Leigh heard him say.

Leigh backed away from the door in confusion. Had he manipulated the woman into that state of mind? Shock filled her mouth with a brackish taste as she crept out of the studio and hurried back to the foyer, wondering if she should stay or leave. She'd accomplished what she came for. She'd seen him at work.

Moments later, still undecided, she felt a feathery lightness brush through her ankles. She glanced down and saw a sleek yellow creature gazing up at her. With a switch of its blond tail, the cat turned and sashayed across the foyer, then leaped onto a wood-carved Moorish cabinet as if to get a ringside seat.

"Well, where did you come from?" Leigh asked.

"She'd probably like to ask you the same question."

Leigh turned to see Nick Montera standing in the hallway she'd just fled through. She was still shaken by what she'd seen, but it was too late to leave now. She would have to deal with him. "I know I'm early," she admitted.

He shrugged as if to short-circuit her apology.

Leigh hadn't noticed what he was wearing before—which wasn't surprising under the circumstances. Now it was impossible to miss his bare feet, gray sweatpants, and black T-shirt. The latter looked like something left over from football-practice days. The sleeves had been ripped out and the bottom cropped short, revealing a dusky relief map of muscle that ran from his midriff to his belly button, where the sweatpants hung loosely on cocked hipbones.

The T-shirt had a saying inscribed in Spanish with a silver snake coiled just above it: *Si esta vibora te pica, no hay remedio en la botica.* Leigh's Spanish was rusty, but she caught one of the words. Viper.

"If this snake bites you, there's no remedy at the pharmacy."

"I beg your pardon?"

He repeated the saying in fluent *español,* rolling the vowels in the back of his throat as if he took sensual pleasure in the feel of them. "If this snake bites you, there's no remedy at the pharmacy. That's what it means," he told her.

"Oh, I see." Leigh wet her dry lips.

Perhaps it was the way he'd folded his arms over his chest and was very casually taking her measure, but his overall effect was one of such feral sensuality that Leigh wanted to back out of the room. With his rich black hair and pale eyes, he himself reminded her of a mythological serpent, cruel and cunning in its natural habits. Beautiful, yet lethal. He was heir to the kind of dangerous and predatory glamour that women seemed to find irresistible in a man.

Leigh found it distinctly ominous.

"Your assistant told me you were coming," he said. "But she forgot to tell me why."

"I thought it might be helpful if I saw some of your work."

"Really?" He looked intrigued but skeptical. "I've got a few pictures here." He stepped into the room and swept a hand around the foyer, indicating the photographs she'd already seen, then pointed to a table near the door. "There's an unfinished collection behind you."

Leigh turned to a portfolio that lay open on the table. It was another study in femininity, but this work was distinctly erotic. The mood was Victorian and the motif was water. Rose petals floated on the surface of reflecting pools where women waded and bathed nude. Each subject seemed to be immersed in the tremors of some inner awakening, her lush sensuality conveyed in sepia images. But it was the sweetly mournful tone, the air of melancholy, that pulled at Leigh. The subjects' nakedness was more emotional than physical. *What did he do to cause women to abandon themselves in this way?*

Leigh shuddered as if she'd been violated. Somehow he had tapped into their unfulfilled yearnings, their most intimate feminine needs. Sacred things, she thought. Things no man should ever know about a woman, because it would make her too vulnerable.

She turned a page, aware that he had come up behind her.

"They're beautiful," she told him.

"Thank you. Unfortunately, I had to drop the project."

"Why?" The question got lost in her next breath as she turned the page to a young woman standing ankle-deep in a shallow pond. She was gazing at her own reflection and touching her breast with a look of exquisite surprise etched into her features. But it was her other hand that arrested the eye. It arced toward her pubis, the fingers splayed in a delicate, yearning quest.

Leigh was quick to draw her hand away from the page.

"Why did I abandon it?" He laughed. "Because the models I normally use are reluctant to take off their clothes for a photographer with a murder rap hanging over his head. I can hardly blame them."

He moved alongside her and Leigh realized he was watching her as she studied the pictures. The next shot was of a woman on her hands and knees, her back arched as she looked over her shoulder at something behind her. The woman's nightgown was drawn up, revealing her nakedness in a way that was highly charged with erotic suggestion.

"If she stays that way much longer," Montera murmured, "some guy is going to climb all over her."

Leigh caught her breath. She whirled angrily. "How dare you?"

A smile brushed at his handsome features. "How dare I what? Isn't that the way it makes you feel . . . as if she's about to be made love to? Is that bad?"

For a second Leigh was hopelessly flustered. He was purposely trying to obfuscate the point. "I was referring to your remark. It was completely inappropriate."

"We're not in your office, Doctor. This is where I work, and fortunately, your rules don't apply here. If they did, I'd never get anything done. Nothing worthwhile anyway."

"How would *my* rules hamper you?"

"Your rules, anybody's rules. I gave up worrying about what was appropriate a long time ago. It doesn't make for good art. Or good sex. Or good anything."

Leigh slammed the portfolio closed. "I didn't come here to talk about good sex. I came here to look at your work, and perhaps even to watch you work, if that can be arranged."

"What's wrong with sex, Doctor, good or otherwise? That's what my work is about. That's what I'm about. And unless you've been spayed like Marilyn over there—" He flipped his thumb toward the cat, who glanced up hopefully at the sound of her name. "That's what you're about, too."

If he was trying to bait her, he was damn close to succeeding. She would love to have told him what she thought of his sex-as-the-meaning-of-life attitude, which was undoubtedly where he was heading with his argument. But she wasn't going to be goaded into abandoning her professional principles because he didn't believe in them.

"On the surface perhaps some of your work is about sex," she conceded. "But it's more than that." She walked to the nearest photograph on the wall, a picture of a woman whose mood was as bleak and stormy as the sky behind her. "This woman is clearly unhappy, and I don't think it's sex on her mind."

"Don't be so sure." He laughed again, softly. "Maybe she just had a very bad fuck."

Leigh let out a swift and furious breath. "You're an asshole, Mr. Montera. In case you didn't already know it."

Gazing at her indolently, he slipped a hand under his cropped shirt as if to scratch the dark hair that spiraled down his belly. "I like you better when you're angry, Doctor. Your eyes throw sparks."

Leigh was sorely tempted to leave. The man was using vulgarities and scratching himself right in front of her! But

Nick Montera had made her feel like a prig once too often. If she'd been curious before, now she was stubbornly determined to learn what fueled this photographer's dark drives. And if her hunch was correct, the secret was right here in his work—in the photographs that hung on his walls.

"How does it feel when you photograph these women?" she asked him. The question was sharper than she had meant it to be.

He strolled over to where the cat was dozing and began to rake her golden fur lightly with his fingertips. Marilyn uncoiled, stretching out like a small lioness in the sun as Montera stroked her. His snake bracelet gleamed like a primordial symbol of the erotic link between man and animal.

Marilyn's languid purring could be heard across the room. Leigh shifted impatiently. And finally Montera looked up. His expression said that his encounter with the cat was proving to be far more rewarding than his encounter with her, but ever the optimist, he'd hang in there for another round.

"How do I feel? That's a pretty general question, Doctor. Could you be more specific?"

"Well, your subjects open up to you. That's clear from your work. They trust you. Do you ever feel as if you're taking advantage of that trust? Exploiting them?"

"Hell no—I'm immortalizing them."

Leigh's heels clicked against the tile, a startled sound. The way he immortalized Jennifer Taryn? "How do you mean?"

He was still stroking the cat, still mesmerizing her with his sorcerer's touch. "They show themselves to me," he said softly. "They reveal themselves in a way they never have before, or will again. And I give it back to them. That single moment of naked truth. I frame it . . . forever."

Leigh was silent for a moment, watching him lavish attention on the cat. "They never feel exposed? Or violated?"

"Not if they trust me. How could they? I'm their mother, their father, their past, present, and future—" He glanced up at her. "I'm their biographer."

And their lover? she wondered. "But if they don't trust you? What then?"

"Then I don't work with them. They either give themselves over to the work totally, or it's no deal."

"I see."

"Do you?" He stroked the silky underside of Marilyn's chin, but his gaze was trained on Leigh's hand, which had fluttered to her earlobe and the bright golden circle. "I don't think you do," he said.

Leigh squared her shoulder pads with a touch of her fingers. "I understand that you require a woman to subjugate herself completely to your vision. You demand control, total control."

"Subjugate . . . interesting choice of word. It wouldn't have been mine. I would have called it surrender."

"Is there a difference?"

"A big difference. One implies coercion and resistance. The other implies a choice—a captive who willingly gives herself over to the bondage . . . and finds pleasure in it."

"But they're both in bondage," Leigh pointed out. "Isn't that a pretty archaic notion of choice?"

He rose, stretched with a twist of his spine, and sat on the edge of the table, next to the cat. Marilyn's mewl of displeasure was acknowledged with slow, subduing strokes. "We're all in bondage, Doctor," he said. "We can pretend we're not. We can raise flags and shout about freedom, but there isn't one of us who owns his own soul."

"You really believe that?" Leigh found herself staring back at him, struck by his certainty. His gaze was as focused as the lights in his studio, she realized, piercing and soothing at the same time. When he turned it up full force, the effect was hypnotic. She was trying to marshal an argument against his claim, but nothing came. His words had struck some chord in her. She was reluctant to agree with him, yet she knew he'd hit a vein of truth.

"And that's what you give these women," she said, her voice softened by the struggle to understand what it was she was trying to say. "For that one moment? You give them back their soul? Or at least a glimpse of it?"

He nodded slowly. "Yes . . . yes, that's it."

His focus was total now. He was looking back at her as if for the first time she'd said something meaningful, something that actually related to him. A fine vibration fanned out from the center of Leigh's being, some response network that was outside her control. She prayed he couldn't hear the shake in her voice. "I see," she said.

This time he didn't correct her. "Have you ever tried it, Doctor?" he asked. "Have you completely surrendered to anything? Or anyone?"

"We all do, don't we? At one time or another."

"You wouldn't have to wonder if you'd done it. There's nothing to compare. No feeling like it. It's heaven, or the closest we're ever going to get. Physical, emotional, sexual."

Marilyn's throaty whimper confirmed his words. The cat chose that moment to roll over and arch her back, offering him the pink of her belly in a wanton attempt to win back his attention. He stroked her lightly, and her sharp little cry told anyone within hearing distance that she was in complete ecstasy.

"Why don't you let me take your picture?" he said, continuing to mesmerize the cat.

At first Leigh wasn't sure he'd meant her. But then he rose from the table, leaving Marilyn to blink after him in dazed and disappointed wonderment.

"No, that wouldn't be—" She'd almost said "appropriate."

He started toward her. "I promise it won't hurt. And it's the only way you're going to get to see me work. I don't have any more sessions scheduled today."

"No, really. It's out of the question."

"You don't want to be part of my reflecting-pool collection?" His eyes glided over her body, lit from within by male appreciation. He was looking her over, checking her out, both the photographer and the man, art and masculinity commingled until you couldn't tell one from the other.

"You might like posing nude," he said. "I know I would."

"Oh, well—that solves it." She laughed quickly, lightly. "You do the posing and I'll take the pictures." Her heart was beating frantically now. Interesting, Leigh thought that he had two frantic females in the room. One desperate to gain his attention, the other desperate to avoid it.

No, Leigh didn't want to pose, and yet she couldn't help but imagine herself in the beautiful, sensually lit scenes of his collection . . . touching herself, wading languidly in dark, silvery pools. Nude. Free to discover—

She banished the images, her throat as dry as paper, her neck suddenly damp. She never should have come out here. He was dangerous, but it wasn't a threat to her life she feared.

"Do that again," he said, his voice oddly husky.

"What?" She wasn't aware she'd done anything.

"Wet your lips for me."

Leigh wanted to protest that she hadn't, but her upper lip did feel moist and cool.

"Come on, Doctor," he coaxed. "Indulge me for a moment. I'm not asking you to get naked. I just want you to dart your tongue over your lips the way you did a minute ago."

She remembered comparing the rough smoky quality of his voice to a velvet whip. Today there was also a faintly condescending air in his tone, as if he were talking to a jittery bride who needed to be led by the hand into matters sexual. Leigh resented the implication.

"Like this?" She wet the softness of her upper lip with a touch of her tongue.

His smile was rich and wry. "God, yes," he said. "Just like that."

Before Leigh quite knew what was happening, he'd walked over to her and was intently rearranging her hair, drawing one side back behind her ear, coaxing the other side into a deep arc over her face. Perhaps what astonished her most was that she allowed him to do it. There was something utterly natural in the way he took over, as if he had the right to touch her in any way he wanted simply because he possessed some unerring instinct for the hidden female psyche.

"Don't lace it up quite so tight, Doctor," he said, running his finger around the inside of her neckline and opening it up a little. "Everything needs to breathe, even you."

Leigh was having no trouble with breathing whatsoever. If she kept it up, she would hyperventilate.

He touched her earring next, fingering the bright circle as if he were curious about its power. Sensitive to every nuance, Leigh felt his thumb slide along the underside of her earlobe. It was the barest hint of contact, but somehow it alerted every nerve in her body. She barely suppressed a shiver.

Finally he stepped back to analyze the impact of what he'd done. "Good, yes, that's good. Now inch your skirt up, Doctor, slide it up your leg as if you're checking your nylons for a run."

Leigh glanced down in surprise, remembering the incident in Dawson's car, how her skirt had crept up her thighs, how she'd been fantasizing about him, Nick. Now she ran her palm down the clingy material of her skirt, smoothing it. It was more reflex than response, but she didn't expect the sensations her touch elicited. They were riveting. Her stomach muscles fluttered and grabbed. Her skin broke out in dampness. She could feel it through the sheer nylon of her panty hose as she began to do what he asked, to inch the material slowly upward. *What was she doing?* A soft shudder moved through her, and she closed her eyes. Just for a second, she told herself, to catch her breath.

"That would make one hell of a picture," he said.

She imagined the strobe flashing in her mind, Nick moving around her, snapping picture after picture. She could see it with dizzying clarity—

"Ouch!" she cried. Her eyes flew open as she felt a stab of pain at her ankle. *"What are you doing?"*

Nick stared at her in bewilderment. Suddenly they both looked down. Marilyn was strolling away from them, her tail twitching, a glint of triumph in her eyes.

Nick muffled a snort of laughter. "Marilyn . . . shame on you!"

The apparent hilarity of it all was lost on Leigh. The cat had nipped her. It hadn't broken the skin, but her ankle stung and she now actually had a run in her nylons! The nasty thing was creeping up the inside of her $5.95 Evan Picones.

"Are you all right?" Montera assumed an apologetic shrug, but his eyes were sparkling as much with laughter as with concern. "She's a possessive little wench. But she's had her shots."

"There's something to be grateful for," Leigh said dryly. Secretly, she was grateful to Marilyn for much more than that. She'd put a stop to Nick Montera's impromptu photo session. And fortunately for Leigh, a cat had bitten her. Not a snake.

CHAPTER
·· NINE ··

"AN ETHIOPIAN CAFÉ, Mother?" Leigh glanced around, hoping to get a peek at what some of the others among the adventurous lunch crowd were having. Tiled and tented like a Turkish bazaar, the restaurant exuded the savory pungence of garlic and ginger and myriad other exotic spices that Leigh had never before encountered.

"Have you actually eaten here before?" she asked.

"Of course, darling." Kate fluttered her menu reassuringly. "Kenji and I were here just last week. Don't have the camel stew. It's too salty. The green fishball curry is wonderful."

Kenji was Kate's latest discovery, a Japanese multimedia artist who sculpted mobiles out of extension cords and car parts and who needed a patron almost as much as Kate needed to be a patroness. Leigh had often wondered if her mother's liaisons were sexual as well as artistic, but she'd never asked, probably because of her hands-off approach in counseling. For her part, Kate was not nearly so respectful of Leigh's privacy, undoubtedly because of her hands-on approach to everything.

"I thought it might be fun for us to try something new," Kate announced. "We've been having lunch at the Ritz-Carlton every Thursday at twelve-thirty for as long as I can remember. That's just no good, dear. It's like sleepwalking through life. Every once in a while one has to grab hold of one's daily routine like an old rug and shake out the dust. Grab it with both hands, Leigh. Grab it and *shake*."

Leigh nodded at her mother over the menu. *"Nyeleng?"* she asked, stumbling over the pronunciation. "What do you suppose that is? Something with fennel, no doubt."

Leigh knew there was no point arguing with her mother when Kate felt passionately about something. And in this case, Kate happened to be right. Leigh's life had become predictable. She'd cut her client hours drastically in the past year in order to devote more time to her manuscript. There were times when she wanted to have the book done so badly, she could almost taste the publishing-party champagne. That worried her a little. If she were one of her own clients, she would have gently suggested that this drive to see her name on a book jacket was another way to separate herself from an overwhelming mother.

"I think I'll have the stuffed semolina pie," Kate said.

"No club sandwich on the menu," Leigh observed as the waiter brought their *thé à la menthe,* a strong, sweet mint tea with pine nuts floating on top, along with smoking hot ovals of freshly baked bread in a straw basket. "Dawson isn't going to like this."

"Dawson?" Kate said reproachfully. "I wasn't aware he'd been invited. I thought Thursday was our day, yours and mine."

Leigh hoped her smile wasn't too rueful. Thursday was the day Kate reconstructed her week while Leigh listened attentively and applauded at all the right moments, which invariably inspired Kate to do an encore of her greatest hits. Her mother wasn't deliberately insensitive, Leigh had long ago realized. Kate was a born performer who truly believed life was her stage and the "show" her first obligation.

"Darling, why *did* you invite him?"

"I didn't," Leigh explained. "Dawson's been leaving messages with Nancy. He needs to talk to me about something, but we keep missing each other, so Nancy told him where I was having lunch today." She shrugged apologetically. "He may not stop by."

"He will. Dawson wouldn't miss a chance to spoil a lovely afternoon."

"*Mother.*" Leigh gave Kate back her own reproachful tone. "Do you think it's possible that you two might learn to get along? He is going to be part of the family."

"Not until he's been weaned off club sandwiches, I hope. Leigh, the man has no imagination. And frankly, neither do you! What kind of marriage is that going to be, I ask you?"

"A very solid one, I hope."

Kate leaned forward conspiratorially. "A man's eating habits are clues to his libido, my daughter the doctor. If Dawson won't try something new, your sex life will suffer for it. He'll be much too predictable a partner. A man who won't educate his palate is sure to be boring in bed. You didn't know this, dear? You're the psychologist."

Gold bangle bracelets jingled madly as Kate threw off the vibrant green shawl she was wearing. "Your father always loved a good culinary adventure."

"My father ran off with another woman," Leigh pointed out. Kate liked to tell people that her ex-husband shared Paul Newman's sky-blue eyes and mixed ethnic heritage, but lacked the handsome actor's restraint when it came to the opposite sex.

"Drew Rappaport had his failings," Kate admitted. "But he was never boring in bed."

"What are you saying? That it's better to have good sex with a man than a committed relationship?"

"It isn't always a question of what's better. Sometimes it's a question of what's available. You can have a committed relationship with a house pet. Good sex is a little harder to find. That takes a good man."

Leigh set down the menu, her shield. Her mother had an enviable knack for turning an argument in her favor. "You would have made a hell of a politician," Leigh conceded.

Kate clearly intended to pursue the conversation, and probably would have if Leigh hadn't spotted Dawson approaching from across the room. He looked flustered and more than a little out of step in his double-breasted business suit amid the bohemian lunch crowd. Graceful, ebony-skinned waiters flowed back and forth in colorful robes and fezzes, carrying trays of rich, roasted meats, rice and vegetable stews, and flambeau desserts.

"Would someone please tell me why the waiters are wearing bathrobes and slippers?" Dawson asked when he finally reached the table.

"To annoy you, Dawson," Kate said dryly. "It's their sole purpose in life."

"Well, it's working," he retorted, looking around. "If I'd wanted weird, I could have eaten in the courthouse cafeteria. Do they serve malaria pills with the food here?"

Leigh gathered up everyone's menu. "I'm going to order before you two get started and ruin my appetite. The camel stew is salty," she informed Dawson. "The green fishballs are wonderful."

"Do they have a club sandwich?" Dawson asked.

Kate mumbled something about predictable sex, and Leigh moved quickly to change the subject. "Why were you trying to reach me?" she asked Dawson. "Nancy said it was important."

He made a brief and unsuccessful attempt to flag down a passing waiter. "We need your evaluation of Montera so we can dope out our case," he told her. "We've got the lab reports and medical testimony lined up. We've even got a neighbor who saw Montera at the scene. Your report should be the final nail in his coffin, the stake through his heart, as it were."

Leigh discounted the last remark as prosecutorial zeal. Criminal attorneys dealt with so much gore and garbage they often got as morbidly detached as some surgeons. "You sound as if *you're* prosecuting the case," she remarked. "I thought you were assigning someone else?"

"I'm keeping my finger on things. There's an election coming up, and the press is on this one like fleas on a hound. That makes it important."

"Important to the fleas, perhaps," Kate muttered.

"There's something I need to tell you." Leigh reclaimed Dawson's attention and told him about her visit from Paulie Cooper, including Paulie's passionate declaration that Montera was innocent. "She believes Jennifer Taryn's boyfriend did it. Jack Taggart, do you know him? He's a nine-year veteran with the LAPD. Homicide cop—and in Ms. Cooper's opinion, a sadistic brute."

Dawson bumped the table leg with his knee and Leigh grabbed her teetering water glass, steadying it.

"That's nonsense, Leigh," he said with surprising force. "Total nonsense. All this inflammatory crap about brutality is tying the hands of good cops. And Taggart is a good cop."

"My, my, Dawson," Kate murmured. "Such passion?"

Leigh was taken aback as well. She picked up her drink, then set it down without even bringing the glass to her lips. The pressures of campaigning, she thought, must be getting to Dawson.

"How much credibility am I supposed to give some bimbo ex-model of Montera's," he went on. "A woman who's undoubtedly still carrying a torch for him? She wouldn't even be a viable witness for the defense."

"But aren't you going to check out her theory about Taggart?" Leigh asked. "Someone should talk to the man. I called him and made an appointment to—"

"You did *what*?" Dawson rose in his chair.

"I . . . made an appointment."

"With Jack Taggart? Why the hell did you do that?"

"Because Paulie Cooper believes he did it, and she was very persuasive, Dawson. Has it ever occurred to you that you might be prosecuting the wrong man? That Nick Montera might be innocent?"

"It's not my job to decide Montera's guilt or innocence, and it sure as hell isn't yours. That's up to a jury. All I want from you is your expert opinion, Leigh. Tell us whether or not Montera was *capable* of committing the crime. If he was, then tell us why the hell he arranged the body that way. Give us the man's dark side, his motives."

"That's easier said than done," Leigh said, defending herself. "I don't know if he's capable." That wasn't quite candid. She was virtually certain Montera was capable. She just didn't know if he'd done what he was capable of.

"How many times have you seen the guy?" Dawson persisted.

"Twice, I think. Maybe three times."

"You're not *sure*? Have you tested him yet?"

Leigh shook her head, aware that they were drawing interest from neighboring tables. Even her mother was quiet and watchful, a first for one of their Thursday lunches.

"I see," Dawson intoned. "You've seen him three times already, but you haven't tested him yet or formed any opinions about his character. What the hell have you been doing? Posing for one of his calendars?"

Now Leigh was indignant. "He doesn't *do* calendars. And why are you attacking me? All I did was mention Paulie Cooper's name. I don't understand why nobody wants to talk to this woman. The media seem perfectly willing."

Dawson dismissed the remark with a sneer. "It's mutual masturbation. Cooper's a publicity hound, and she's giving the press flacks some sound-bite sex in exchange for a little airtime."

"Well, I hope you're right." A warning singsonged through Leigh's voice. "I hope that's all it is, Dawson. Because everyone's going to be eating public crow if you're not."

Dawson flexed his shoulders and straightened his tie, calming himself, it seemed. "If Paulie Cooper doesn't keep her mouth shut, she may find herself the next dead ex-model."

Leigh's hand hung in midair. She'd been going for the bread, intending to pass it around while it was still hot. "What in the world is that supposed to mean, Dawson?" It had sounded like a personal threat, but he must have meant Montera. "If you're implying that Nick Montera might kill her, why in the world would he want to do that? She's trying to help him."

"Psychos don't need reasons." Dawson picked up the basket, helping himself to some bread as he offered it to Leigh. "You're the one who's supposed to know, only you don't seem to have a clue."

Bewildered at her fiancé's aggressiveness, Leigh passed the basket to her mother. This was more than prosecutorial zeal. Dawson was behaving like a . . . like a what? A jealous suitor? She'd never told him about Montera's advances. Or about her trip to the photographer's studio. Now she was glad she hadn't.

The waiter arrived to take their order, and Leigh noticed that her mother was eyeing Dawson with new interest. Apparently Kate rather liked his bullyboy tactics. Well, Leigh didn't. Not one bit. She didn't know what to make of Dawson's performance, but for the first time in years her own mother's advice didn't sound so bad. *Every once in a while one has to grab hold of one's daily routine like an old rug and shake out the dust. Grab it and shake.*

Paulie Cooper was having one of the best days of her life. She was dressed to kill, coiffed like a Supreme, *and* she was getting paid by the hour to look devastatingly sexy. But better than any of that, she'd just tied a man up with her panty hose.

"I'm not hurting you, am I?" she asked Johnny Wonder, the beefy blond male model whose wrists she'd bound behind his back.

"Are my fingers blue yet?" Johnny inquired sardonically. "They're going numb on me. Think you could loosen the knots?"

Paulie contemplated her own long, red-lacquered fingernails and pursed her lips doubtfully. "Brand-new manicure," she explained with a sigh that was sincere in its regret. "Sorry."

"Whenever you're ready, you two!" the photographer shouted, perching his camera on his hip impatiently. "I'm not interrupting anything, am I?"

Paulie smiled extravagantly. " 'Course not, Stan."

Stan Tidwell was an ace commercial photographer and a royal pain in the ass, but far too important a figure in the fashion industry for Paulie to risk antagonizing. She'd landed this panty-hose shoot only because Stan's Ferrari had nearly mowed her down in a crosswalk one evening on Melrose. He'd had a couple of drinks and he'd been anxious not to have the police involved. Paulie had been anxious for a break in her career. 'Nuf said.

"There's more than one way to trap a man with Ambush panty hose!" Stan bugled the ad's tag line, reminding Paulie and Johnny what they were supposed to be doing. "So *ambush* the man, Paulie. Let's go!"

Paulie was both flattered and alarmed. Tidwell seemed to be counting on *her* to come up with something creative. The ad itself was a photo within a photo of a black-tie affair, set in an elegant Georgian mansion. For the full-page spread, Paulie had worn a hooded, gold lamé micromini that revealed miles of sleek leg, and Johnny, dressed as a hunky waiter, had served vintage champagne to upscale guests while secretly lusting after Paulie's gold-flecked Ambush panty hose.

They'd spent the entire day getting that one shot, an exhausting process that had everyone on edge except Paulie, who had savored every second of the action and the attention. Now, posed near a sumptuous canopy bed in a set designed to look like the mansion's bedroom, they were working on a smaller inset photo for the ad. Paulie, still as radiant as a Christmas ornament in gold lamé and jeweled hair clips, was supposed to be tying Johnny up with her Ambush panty hose for the sole purpose of having her wicked way with him. But so far it wasn't working. Stan wasn't getting the energy he wanted.

Paulie tossed out the first idea that came to mind. "Why don't I get tough with him?" she suggested. "Rough him up a little bit?"

"Rough me up?" Johnny seemed uneasy about that. He already had his jacket off, his shirt undone, and a big, juicy red lip print on his cheek, which Paulie had put there.

"Rough him up?" Stan echoed.

"Sure, like this—" Ignoring Johnny's obvious reluctance, Paulie turned him around and positioned him with his back to her. His hands were already tied behind him with panty hose, so she grabbed the nylon legs as if she were Sheena of the Jungle, subduing her prey, and stretched them as wide as her arms would go. As Johnny swayed backward she propped her spike high heel against his butt for leverage.

"All *riiight,* girl! Go!" One of Stan's female assistants gave out a whoop of approval. Another stuck two fingers in her mouth and whistled.

"Paulie!" Stan exclaimed. "That's completely fabulous! Johnny . . . ? What's wrong now?"

"She's hurting me," Johnny complained in a small, taut voice.

Stan was incredulous. "Christ, man! A stone gorgeous woman is tying you up with the intention of driving you mad with pleasure. This is a wet dream come true. Let's see some excitement!"

"My arms are falling asleep," Johnny persisted.

If Paulie'd had a gun, she would have let the whiny bastard have it. She would have put him out of his misery like a lame horse. Then let him worry about his numb fingers! She didn't have a gun, however, and since there was little chance of anyone slapping one in her hand, it was wits as usual.

"I know an acupressure point inside the elbow," she suggested soothingly, stroking Johnny's arm. "It clears pain and redistributes chakra energy."

Johnny twisted around, leering at her over his shoulder. "I know a better one. It's inside the thigh."

"Go ahead, Paulie," Stan said wearily. "Give the boy a jolt.

Elbow, thigh, wherever. I don't care if you kick him in the balls. Let's just get this over with!"

Paulie cradled Johnny's bound arms gingerly.

"Ouch!" he protested, stiffening as she knuckled a nerve in the crook of his elbow.

"It's supposed to hurt," she explained.

But Johnny didn't seem to care. He shouldered free of her hold, forcing Paulie into action. Grasping the panty hose, she dragged him back, only this time when she leveraged her high heel against his backside, she aimed its pointed toe at an extremely tender spot. Gotcha, she thought, digging in.

Johnny's eyes bugged. "Yeowwww!" he said, lifting off the ground.

"That's it! That's *it*!" Stan squealed as if he'd witnessed a miracle. He began snapping pictures frantically, moving around the two of them, caught up in the frenzy that overtakes a photographer when he has the perfect shot in his camera sights.

Johnny froze in place, a tortured smile on his face, sweat pouring from his brow. Paulie could see his expression in a mirror across from her, and he looked like a bondage freak in chains, pleased, but not sure why. Her own smile gleamed with blissful satisfaction. There *was* more than one way to trap a man with Ambush panty hose. This was going to be the photo shoot of her life! The set fairly crackled with energy.

"That's a wrap!" Stan shouted as he knelt and exhausted the last of his film. "Let's pack up and get out of here."

Moments later, as Paulie stood behind a huge Oriental screen, changing to go home, she gazed at herself in the cheval glass, entranced by the glitter that brightened her eyes and seemed to permeate her entire being. She'd never looked or felt so glamorous. She didn't want to take off the beautiful clothes or the jewelry. She didn't want the shoot to end.

Reluctantly she unzipped the clingy designer dress and let it drop to the floor. Wearing only panties and the pricey costume jewelry Stan's assistant had chosen for the shoot— a faux diamond choker, matching bracelet, and jeweled hair clips—she continued to revel in her own image.

Finally, reluctantly, she removed the bracelet and hair clips and set them on a small mirrored dressing table, knowing someone would be around to collect them soon. The choker she dangled from her fingers, studying its incandescent sparkle with a wistful smile. Her throat tightened with a powerful, impossible longing to have the piece. It would be like taking a little bit of the magical day home with her and preserving it forever.

A moment later, glancing around furtively, she gave in to the irresistible impulse and dropped the necklace into her open tote bag. What Paulie didn't notice as she bent to quickly zip up the bag was the faint whirring of high-tech machinery. Across the room, from the shadows of an alcove that led to an emergency exit door, a man in a nondescript gray suit with a camcorder propped on his shoulder was videotaping her every move.

"Who ate my case notes?" Leigh muttered to no one in particular. Alone in her office, she made another quick pass of the room, visually searching credenzas and tabletops, lifting folders, books, and research journals. She had an appointment with Jack Taggart later that morning, which she'd intended to cancel, if only to mollify Dawson, but when she'd called the Homicide Division, Taggart had answered the phone himself.

"Dr. Rappaport," he'd cautioned in his oddly taut voice, "if there's a doubt in your mind that Nick Montera killed Jennifer Taryn, I'll be happy to send it packing. The man is a monster. I can give you chapter and verse on the sick games he plays with women."

Following up on that bombshell, Leigh had asked Taggart if he'd be testifying for the prosecution, and he admitted that he probably would not be called. "The DA's office doesn't want to give the defense a crack at me," he told her. "They'll claim I was jealous because Jennifer dumped me for Montera. But that's not the way it happened, Doctor. He fucked with her mind."

By the time she got off the phone, Leigh had decided to keep the appointment. If Dawson found out—well, she would deal with that when it happened. He didn't seem to have any trouble setting aside his own personal convictions in order to let a jury decide Nick Montera's guilt or innocence. Dawson probably would have argued that it was the only way to ensure a fair trial. Lawyers defend or prosecute. They leave the verdict to a duly appointed tribunal of the defendant's peers. If it wasn't a perfect system, it was close enough.

Unlike Dawson, Leigh was having a great deal of trouble with that concept. How could she in good conscience give expert testimony that might influence the jury toward a guilty verdict if she herself had doubts about the defendant's guilt? But right now her problem was the missing file on Montera. Both she and Nancy had already done a thorough search of both offices. The only thing left was to mentally retrace her steps. Had she taken the file out of the office?

She walked to her purse and dug her keys from the zipper compartment, hoping to spark some association. Fortunately, she was a creature of habit. She invariably picked up her purse and her briefcase as she left the office. Her briefcase? A glance at the credenza behind her desk told her the soft leather case was missing as well. Another moment of deliberation convinced her that she must have left it in Montera's foyer when she went to investigate the noises coming from his studio.

The keys clinked softly as she turned the ring in her hands. She could have Nancy call, perhaps even send her assistant out to pick it up. But if Montera hadn't already discovered the briefcase, a call would alert him that it was there, and she didn't want him reading her notes. They were much too personal. She would have to pick it up herself on her way to her appointment with Taggart. With luck, she might be able to retrieve it without Montera's ever knowing it was there.

A Jeep Renegade was parked in front of the studio when Leigh pulled up a half hour later. If it was Montera's car, it could mean any number of things. Perhaps he'd already gone out this morning, but he was definitely home now. Damn! She glanced in her rearview mirror, checking her glossy red lipstick and the flyaway wisps of blond that had pulled free of her ponytail.

Her gray eyes were crackling with anticipation, brighter than she'd ever seen them. Even the thought of dealing with him sent her into a tailspin of programmed and predictable female responses. Primping? It was pathetic! At least she had on her uniform, the navy blazer and khaki slacks she'd worn for her meeting with Taggart.

She didn't bother with the brass knocker this time. She was

still hoping to slip into the foyer, grab the briefcase, and disappear before anyone saw her. But when she opened the door, her eye was drawn immediately to the beautiful, inconsolable woman in sepia, the focal point of his showroom. Why did she feel such empathy with that picture? The woman didn't look like her, not really, but there was something. Something . . .

The rise of feeling through Leigh's body was a soft tidal swell, very nearly as urgent as the first time she'd seen the photograph. Certain kinds of imagery had the power to evoke the emotions, to pull up memories of joy and pain with almost as much intensity as the actual moment of experience. The viewer could be brought to tears or filled with wild hope for no apparent reason. This picture held that kind of charge.

The black terrazzo floor caught Leigh's image and rolled it beneath her feet as she turned to look for the briefcase. It wasn't in the foyer, she realized with one dizzy, spinning search of the room. Where would he have taken it? His studio? His living quarters? She had no desire to revisit the studio, but that seemed marginally safer than invading his private rooms.

Leigh's notebook was the first thing she saw as she entered the cavernous room. The area was dimly lit except for a single incandescent beam of light, trained on an altarlike table that had been positioned in the center of the studio. Her notebook was lying open, exposed in the blinding circle of a spotlight.

"What is this?" she breathed, bewildered by the macabre scene. It looked as if her notes were being sacrificed in a pagan ritual. She searched the darkness, looking for Montera, expecting to see his luminous eyes trained on her. But the spotlight had burned itself into her focus. All she could see was a sizzling white dot at the apex of a blue-black hole.

He'd found her case notes. He'd read them and now he was going to force her to acknowledge that. She was alternately afraid to touch the notebook and seized with the desire to grab it and run. What would happen if she invaded that hot circle of light? Would she set off alarms? Would a door slam shut, imprisoning her in the studio?

Damn him! she thought, suddenly angry. He was a master of mind games. He had her spinning in circles, but that's all this was, another game. Out of patience with his tricks, she stalked across the room to the table.

The notebook was within her reach. Her fingers actually brushed over the pages as she heard the creak of door hinges. Her hand closed on air and her head snapped up. Panic overtook her as she tried to see beyond the blinding spotlight. She remembered an assortment of mirrors from her last visit, but now she couldn't make out anything but billowing shadows. An icy breeze crept through her ankles and a faintly acrid smell pierced her awareness.

She was backing out of the circle when she saw him.

Awash in a crimson aura, he seemed to be stepping out of a vault of flames. Leigh's throat locked, strangling off any sound. The hammering was deafening. She barely recognized it as her own heart. What she was seeing had to be a trick of the light. She knew it must be the red glow of his darkroom, but the vision sparked a moment of naked fear. He looked like some kind of *monstre sacré*, the embodiment of evil.

"Nick?" she asked, her voice breaking.

He turned to her, his eyes as bloodred as a demon's.

Good God, she thought. Who was this man? Who *was* Nick Montera? A cold-blooded psychopath? An insane killer? She tried to tell herself it was just the bizarre lighting. It had to be that. She was staring at an illusion, some imaginary fiend who existed only in the darkened corners of her own psyche.

Leigh drew her tongue over her bone-dry lips. She quelled the impulse to run as he moved out of the glow of the darkroom, and to her great relief, she was right. As Nick Montera approached her the red aura fell away like a cape, and the monster materialized into a man.

He flicked the towel he'd been drying his hands with onto the table. "Another surprise visit?"

His sardonic tone of voice cut like a knife. It brought Leigh cleanly out of the twilight zone of her own imagination. "I see you found my notebook," she responded stiffly. "You might have called to let me know."

"I might have . . . but then you wouldn't have come to get it, would you?"

Her notes glowed from the center of the circle. "I did come," she assured him. "And I do intend to get it." She walked to the table, flipped the notebook shut, and picked it up, defying him to try to stop her.

"That won't do you any good," he told her. "I've read every word . . . 'dangerously hypnotic, sexually mesmerizing, animal charisma'? Should I be flattered, Doctor? Are those your clinical opinions? Or is it how you feel?"

"Of course they're my clinical opinions. And I was referring to your work, *not* to you." She stepped back, trying to orient herself as she ducked out of the spotlight. If only she could get closer to the door.

"You're forgetting something, aren't you?"

"What do you mean?"

An object that looked like a fabric belt was draped around Nick's neck. He drew it off, twining the canvas material loosely through his fingers. Leigh recognized it as the sash belt of a man's trench coat. She also recognized it as a potential weapon. Jennifer Taryn had been blindfolded with one like it in Nick's photograph—the belt from the coat she was wearing.

"What am I forgetting?" she pressed.

He let the belt swing toward a dark object propped against the table leg. "Don't you want that?"

It was Leigh's briefcase. She started to say yes, then realized it was a trap. He wanted her to come and get it. "Move away from the table," she told him sharply.

His shrug said sure, no problem.

He stepped back, but it wasn't nearly far enough for Leigh. As she watched him draw the belt through his fisted hand, she realized he had no intention of letting her leave with the briefcase. It was entirely possible he wasn't going to let her leave at all.

"Move farther from the table," she demanded, inching away from him. She'd already decided to abandon the briefcase, but didn't want him to know. If she was going to get out of here, she had to do it now. She crept back and came up against something solid and sharp. Her heel hit first and then a cold metal doorknob dug into her hip. Hinges groaned loudly and the barrier gave way with her weight. Leigh whirled, but it was too late. She had bumped the already moving door with her shoulder and pushed it shut. Clutching the notebook to her chest, she realized she'd trapped herself.

"Change your mind?" Montera asked.

She swung around to face him, prepared to defend herself if necessary. Adrenaline was pumping, but intuition told her he wasn't an immediate threat. He'd twined the belt around his wrist, and he was studying her with the laser focus a man has for a woman who has caught his interest. Casually dressed in jeans and a white cotton shirt, his hair pulled back in a ponytail, Nick Montera could almost fit the cliché of tall, dark, and handsome. Almost . . .

Shadows dominated his Latin bone structure, carving deep relief into the hollows created by his powerful jaw muscles. No, he wasn't handsome, but he was beautifully sinister in the way that only harrowing danger can be beautiful.

"Do you want me to bring it to you?" he asked.

"No—"

He shrugged again. "Whatever you say."

There was nowhere for Leigh to go as he began to approach, nothing for her to do but watch the belt uncoil from his wrist like a living thing. It slithered downward, and she prayed he would let it drop to the floor. She'd worked with hardened criminals. She knew how to defuse dangerous situations, but this wasn't that kind of danger. She'd never encountered the kind of threat he exuded. It was directed at her fears, at her femaleness, at hidden and ungovernable impulses. And until today, it had excited her as much as frightened her.

Until today—

She flinched as he caught the buckle end of the belt and pulled the length of it through his closed hand. With the thoroughness of a professional executioner, he stretched the thing out as if he were measuring her neck for the fit.

"What are you going to do?" she asked.

The glint in his eyes told her he was taking pleasure in her uneasiness. "A little sleight of hand. Would you like to be my magician's assistant?"

She shook her head as he looped the belt into knot after knot after knot. He worked so swiftly, it appeared that he wasn't even touching the thing, and by the time he was done, it looked like a literal can of worms.

He gave her the opposite end with instructions to pull it tight. She complied, and every knot fell out in a graceful, hivering wave. "You do tricks, too?" he observed, his tone droll. "I'm impressed."

Leigh relinquished the belt to him, only this time when he took it, he drew the length of it slowly up her body, letting it slither over her breasts and dangle down her torso.

"Don't let this get away," he said, draping it over her shoulder.

The thing seemed to be moving, crawling with energy. Leigh reached to remove it, then realized that he'd turned and picked up her briefcase.

"Can't let you leave without this," he said.

"I have to go," she whispered. Her heart was pounding so madly, she could hardly hear herself. "I'm in a hurry."

"So am I, Doctor—the goddamnedest hurry I've ever been in in my life."

To Leigh's surprise, he handed her the briefcase, then shifted back as if to let her go. She saw the opening, knew it was her chance. She could open the door and leave. He was letting her go. But she made the mistake of hesitating, of glancing at him when she should have run. Run!

She turned the wrong way—toward him—and he moved in on her. Crowding her into the door, he curved his hand to her throat and turned her face to his. The act brought their mouths within inches. She could smell traces of coffee, rich and hot, traces of a sharp minty flavor that stirred erotic images. She could feel his other hand working the cord, twining it loosely around *her* wrist.

Her book and briefcase clattered to the floor.

Seconds flew by. Charged, pulsating seconds in which Leigh waited for him to do something, to loop the other trembling hand behind her back, *to tie her up.* The reaction of her body was staggering. She felt as if liquid lightning were stroking through her. She felt weakened, blindsided.

His thumb feathered the softness beneath her chin. His breath burned her lips.

"What brought you here, Doctor?" he asked. "What do you want?"

"I came to get my notebook. I thought I could find it and leave without disturbing you."

"Didn't work, did it? You do disturb me."

"I'll leave now! Please! I'll even take myself off your case. They'll assign you another doctor, *please*—"

"I don't want another doctor, I want—"

"What?"

The neckline of her silk blouse had gaped open and he'd noticed it. He touched her damp skin with the back of his fingers, tracing the arc of her collarbone to the place where it met the swell of her breast. Excitement pierced her like an electrical shock.

She made an inarticulate little sound in her throat that was rich with sex. It should have been distress, but it was *sex,* dammit. She couldn't help herself.

Pleasure darkened his eyes as he stared at her. "That's it," he said huskily. "That's all I wanted . . . just to know if it was the doctor or the woman who wrote those words."

CHAPTER
·· TEN ··

LEIGH WAS STILL shaken when she entered the Hill Street coffee shop where she was to meet Jack Taggart. The small diner-style restaurant smelled of bacon grease and onions, and its half-dozen customers were all hunkered over the Formica countertop, doggedly intent on cholesterol loading.

Taggart had told Leigh to look for him in the booth by the emergency exit. He hadn't told her he'd be thirtyish, sandy-haired, and ruggedly clean-cut. Maybe she'd been expecting a grizzly, chewed-nails kind of cop with a clipper cut and a shaved neck, but the man waiting for her hardly looked like the violent personality Paulie Cooper had described.

"Dr. Rappaport?" he asked, rising as Leigh approached the booth. "I'm Jack Taggart."

He seemed a little startled when Leigh offered her hand, but his grip was firm and friendly. Once she was seated, he handed her a menu.

"Tuna melt's not too bad," he said.

The thought of a tuna anything made Leigh want to run for the bathroom. She was still off balance from her encounter with Montera that morning, and the restaurant's various aromas were making her queasy. "I generally eat a late lunch," she explained. "I'll just have some Evian—" She corrected herself as his brow crinkled with disdain. "Water," she said. "Just water, no ice."

Taggart ordered a BLT, American fries, and a classic Coke in the glass bottle. By the time his food arrived, Leigh had the impression that he was pleasant enough, if somewhat rigid. But their small talk waned as she sipped her tepid water and he proceeded with his meal. Lining up his fries like prisoners facing a firing squad, he ran a strip of ketchup down the middle, and ate them from the right side of the plate, methodically, one by one.

It was clearly a ritual, and Leigh wondered if it was meant to bring him gustatory pleasure or a sense of order.

When he'd chewed the last fry thoroughly and washed it all down with Coke, he looked up. "So what do you think of Nick Montera, Doctor? Is he crazy?"

"It isn't a question of his sanity," Leigh explained.

"No, it *isn't*," Taggart said emphatically. "If that guy's crazy, I'm Charlie Manson. He's a snake, Dr. Rappaport. One of those slimy boa constrictors. He wraps himself around women like he's loving them, only he's not. He's killing them. Pretty soon they're too weak to fight, but he keeps squeezing till they're dead."

Leigh set down the glass she was holding. "You clearly think Montera is a dangerous man."

Taggart's neck muscles strained beneath the collar of his red flannel shirt. He pushed his plate away, the double-decker sandwich untouched. "No, I think he's a murdering bastard. He gets off on luring women. He sucks them in and smothers the life out of them. He kills them so slowly they don't know it's happening."

Leigh broke in. "But that isn't how it happened with Jennifer Taryn. Someone strangled her. Very deliberately."

Rage flared through the policeman's steel-gray eyes. "Fucking-A," he bit out. "It was deliberate, all right. It was *revenge*. He wanted her back. He was obsessed with taking her away from me, but not for himself. He wanted to make her pay for what she did to him when they were kids."

"You mean the manslaughter conviction?"

Taggart nodded and took another angry swig of Coke. "Jennifer liked to drink a little, at least when I knew her. She got high one night and admitted that she'd lied on the stand. She told the prosecutor Montera raped her and stabbed her boyfriend to death. The rape charge was dropped, but her testimony put Montera in Chino for three years."

"So he killed her? That was his revenge?"

The Coke bottle clunked against the tabletop, teetering wildly before it settled on its thick round base.

Taggart leaned forward on his arms as if to relieve some sudden, pressing weight. "It wasn't because she put him in prison, Doctor. No man kills a woman over that. He killed her because he was in love with her. He *loved* her, ma'am. And she didn't love him back."

Leigh couldn't suppress a shudder. He'd said it with so much agonized conviction, she was reluctant to press him any further. Her water glass had left wet rings on the shiny tabletop, and she picked up a napkin, working at the dampness.

After a moment Taggart propped himself up and settled back against the maroon plastic bubble that doubled as a seat cushion. "He deserves to die," he said, his voice low, aching with malice. "I'd like to blow him away myself. Better yet, I'd like to get my hands on the woman *he* cared about and blow her away right in front of him."

Leigh was quietly appalled, and more determined than ever to be cautious. "You said that Jennifer didn't love Nick Montera. If that's true, then why would she leave you for him?"

"She was confused, that was all. She couldn't live with what she'd done to him. She thought she could get him to forgive her, but forgiveness was the last thing on his mind. He stalked her like an animal, lured her into his trap, and killed her."

"Sergeant Taggart, do you have any proof of this?"

The policeman fought to smile. "I don't need any proof, Doctor. The DA's got more than enough evidence to convict that bastard—and his mother, too, just for giving birth to him."

Someone had broken into his barrio studio. Nick spotted the signs the moment he pulled his Jeep Renegade into the driveway of the crumbling stucco house. Jagged splinters gouged from the door's wooden frame told him someone had tried to force their way in, probably with a crowbar. The rusty metal knob hung cockeyed, half in, half out of the door.

"Mierda," Nick swore under his breath as he let himself out of the four-wheel drive. "If I get my hands on those bastards, I'm going to kick some *vato loco* ass."

Broken glass crackled beneath his boots as he crept through litter and scrub grass, moving alongside the house toward the back entrance. Whoever had failed with the front door had lobbed a missile through the window of the house's only bedroom, an L-shaped closet the entire family had been forced to share because of space. Neighborhood gang-bangers had been vandalizing the place on a weekly basis recently, leaving behind their used heroin syringes and spent bullet cartridges, and carting off whatever photography equipment they could fence.

Nick hadn't been able to stop the break-ins, but he'd found a way to protect his equipment. He'd stashed the expensive gear in a crawl space between two unfinished walls and left a couple of cheap cameras sitting out to placate would-be thieves. The ploy had worked so far, but he sensed something different about this particular break-in. Homeboys wouldn't have been stopped by anything as puny as a dead bolt. They would have blown the front door off its hinges.

The back door hung ajar as Nick came around the side of the house. He reached for the knife sheathed in his belt, and as always, the awareness of cold steel in his grip—of deadly power—awakened feral instincts. It was a response that had as much to do with lifelong inexpressible rage as it did with gut survival. There was a strange and terrible pleasure to be derived from an act of blood justice. It was a natural thing, man's legacy from the animals. We were all born killers. Nick had learned that as a kid. *A male child born in San Ramone was fated to kill or be killed.* His father had told him that at age six, and Nick had proved the prophecy true at age seventeen. It was machismo poetry, the funeral dirge of the barrio. What his father hadn't told him was that once you kill, nothing is ever the same. *You're* never the same.

With practiced stealth, he eased the back door open and entered the tiny kitchen he'd converted into a darkroom. The house was steeped in gloom, except for a strip of light across the hallway, probably from the broken window. Apparently the vandals had already had their fun and gone, perhaps days ago. But Nick could still smell the stink of their desperation and cunning. He knew what drove them—the same rage for recognition that had driven him out of this barrio hellhole, once he'd found the escape hatch. Maybe they'd given up looking, but that wasn't his problem at the moment. If he ever caught the *fregados*—the fuckups—he was going to relieve them of their balls. First.

He made his way through the kitchen toward the bedroom where his equipment was stashed. The door was open and Nick could see from the hallway that his hiding place was undisturbed. The cameras he'd left on the old wicker dressertop were gone, but the false panel looked as if it hadn't been touched.

He sheathed his knife and entered the room cautiously, making sure he was alone before he knelt to inspect the panel. The weasels had been so busy packing off the cut-rate camera equipment, they'd missed this completely. Another ritual sacrifice to the thunder gods, he thought with a cold smile. At least they'd taken the bait.

The hair on his nape pricked as if he'd heard something. Over the years his senses had become so attuned to any change in the environment that he could often discern another's presence even when there were no sensory signals. There was an unnatural stillness, a hesitation in the normal flow of energy that some sixth sense picked up.

The faint creak of floorboards confirmed his intuition. He wasn't alone. The urge to go for his knife was strong, but he knew better. Never fight a ghost.

"No haz fregadas!" a voice hissed. "Don't do anything stupid!"

Still on his knees, Nick pivoted and found himself face-to-face with the outstretched arms of the Virgin Mary in miniature. Before he could react the Holy Mother arced down like a battering ram, exploding savagely against his forehead. Firecrackers popped inside his skull and a burst of pain radiated up from the base of his neck. He reeled backward, falling heavily against the wall.

Through a blizzard of white plaster flakes and dizzying pain, Nick fought to bring his attacker into focus. He'd expected to be staring up the barrel of an automatic weapon, but the boyish features gaping at him looked more like a frightened animal's than a gang-banger's. Whoever the kid was, he'd hit Nick over the head with a religious statue, perhaps not realizing that plaster of paris would shatter. The tiny barrio bedroom looked like winter in the fucking Alps.

The boy dropped the cameras he was clutching and lurched around as if to run, but Nick reered up and collared him. "Not so fast, *pendejo!*" he said, hauling the kid back. The hot, stitching pain of his efforts brought tears to Nick's eyes.

A deep throb at the base of his neck told him the mother of all headaches was on its way. His skull must be in more pieces than the statue.

"Chingate!" the kid bellowed, trying to kick himself free. "Go fuck yourself!"

"Oof!" Nick doubled with a direct blow to his pelvis. The crazy little bastard was trying to castrate him. Ducking flying limbs, he sprang to his feet and wrestled the kid into an armlock. "What's your name?" he huffed, unmoved by the boy's quick cry of pain. "How old are you?"

"I'm fifteen, asshole!"

Nick snorted at the punk-ass bravado. He couldn't have been more than nine or ten. Except for his blazing brown eyes, he was a skinny, grungy little drowned skunk of a kid. "Fifteen? That's great. *El bandido notorio!* They'll try you as an adult and throw your bony ass in San Quentin."

"Go ahead, call the cops!" the kid flared defiantly. "What the fuck do I care? My brother, Jesus, he's already in San Quentin. Death row." He tossed his head proudly, as if that were the highest badge of honor a homeboy could hope for.

"Hey, that's swell," Nick said sarcastically. "What did he do? Ice a cop?"

"Yeah! How did you know?" The kid seemed genuinely startled, even pleased. "You read about Jesus in the papers?"

Nick released the kid and shoved him toward a steel cot, the room's only other furniture besides the rotting wicker dresser. The kid stumbled and broke his fall against the mattress, but refused to sit on the bed. He slid into a scowling heap on the floor and swung up his arms as if to ward off a blow.

"Your brother's no hero," Nick told him, shaking plaster snow from his own dark hair and swacking it off his faded denim shirt and jeans. "Your brother's a stinking corpse, *pendejo!* He's dead already! You shoot a cop, they make an example of you."

The kid glared up at Nick, but it wasn't anger fueling his wild-eyed stare, it was some kind of strange and defiant glee. "They can't make no example of Jesus," he crowed. "He didn't do it! He shot up some *vatos locos* that night, but he didn't kill no goddamned cop."

"What's he doing on death row?"

"Fuck if I know. The cops, maybe they frame him. Maybe they want him dead. Jesus is bad, man! *El mero chingón,* the top dog."

Nick swore softly, more from frustration than anger. Scare tactics didn't work with barrio kids. He knew that from personal experience. They were wiry little garbage rats who grew up with a fatalism no outsider could ever understand. You had to be born here to know the soul emptiness. Even ten-year-old gang-bangers had nothing to lose. Nothing. They had no future. To live well meant to live outside the law, dealing dope or fencing contraband. The alternative was minimum wage or welfare. Their strange, twisted sense of personal honor was the only thing no one could ever take away.

Nick knelt to pick up one of the cameras the kid had dropped. "What were you going to do with this?" he asked. It was a casual question, made even more so by the way he scooped up the lens cap and refitted it. "Sell it for drug money?"

Nick glanced up, aware for the first time that his hostage's expression had turned calculating.

"The money's for *abuelita mia,*" the kid said, doing a bad impression of a Boy Scout. "She's sick."

"Yeah, sure, and your sick gramma runs guns, right?"

"Up yours, *bastardo!*"

Nick lunged toward the boy, thrusting out the camera. "You want out of here? You want out of San Ramone?"

"Shit, no." Hunkered over, proudly sullen, he glanced up. "I like it here."

"You like this stinking cesspool of a neighborhood? You like junked cars and filthy winos and dead bodies."

"Yeah . . . maybe I do. So what, asshole?"

"You're the asshole, kid. And you're going to stay an asshole if you don't listen to me." Nick held up the camera, shoving it in his face, forcing him to acknowledge it. "You don't need guns or drugs. This is your weapon. And it's powerful. It can get you out of here. It got me out!"

The kid stared at him suspiciously. "Whatchu doing? You giving me that camera?"

"Yes, I'm giving you this camera—on one condition. You have to use it, not fence it."

"*Q-vo?* Use it for what?"

"To take pictures. You take pictures of this place, and I'll pay you for them."

The kid's shoulders jerked with mute laughter. "You said this place was a cesspool, and now you want pictures? Pictures of addicts and dead bodies. You think I'm stupid? Maybe you're stupid, huh?"

Nick set the camera on the floor. He rose and looked out his bedroom window, staring through the broken fragments of glass at the rows of ugly stucco shacks, patched together with weathered wood and chicken wire, that was Salerno Street. The neighborhood stank of beans and car fumes and homemade brew. His reasons for hanging on to his parents' home weren't sentimental. The place was decaying on its foundation, but he'd resisted fixing things up. He wanted it this way, damaged.

He'd promised himself that one day he would photograph the hellhole he grew up in, rusty car parts, dead bodies, and all. The squalor of San Ramone had become a habit for Nick Montera. He barely saw it anymore. But they would see it. He'd promised himself that, too. One day he would open the complacent eyes of his affluent patrons and show them how the other half really lived. And died.

"Yes," Nick said finally. "I want pictures of this place." When he turned around, the kid was staring at him with undisguised curiosity.

"I think I see you before," the kid said, scrutinizing him. "I think I see you on TV. Aren't you the hombre who's up for murder? They talk about you in the hood. They say you offed some woman, some beautiful *chica*. You going to death row, too, huh?"

Nick nodded. "Looks like it."

"Hey, that's great, man. You gonna be a hero, just like my brother, Jesus? Maybe the cops framed you, too?"

Nick sucked in the room's moldering air. "Cut the crap and get out of here, okay?"

The kid sprang to his feet like a jack-in-the-box. He snatched the camera from the floor and sidled toward the door, clearly calculating the odds of his making it out of the room.

Impatient, Nick waved him away. "Get me some pictures," he growled. "Or I'll come looking for you, *bandido*. You can leave the exposed film in the kitchen. I'll pay you for the shots I use." He jerked his thumb toward the bedroom's broken window. "You know how to get in."

The kid tried to smile but couldn't manage it very well. "I'm Manuel Ortega," he said. "They call me Manny, and I come from a long line of brave hombres on my father's side. My family, we're revolutionaries, you know, Mexican *bandidos*, like Pancho Villa and Emiliano Zapata."

Nick's throat muscles tightened. For the first time the kid had sounded almost desperate. Nick had liked him better defiant. Groping for pride, for anything that would make him more than he was—a mangy little garbage rat from San Ramone—Manny had somehow diminished himself. Nick wanted to cry.

"Get out of here," he snarled.

The kid clutched the camera and ran.

Some time later, when Nick wrenched himself out of his self-imposed loathing and looked around the bedroom, there was anger in his heart, fiery rage. Across the L-shaped room on the rotting wicker dresser in a tarnished heart-shaped frame sat a wedding picture of Armando and Faith Montera, his parents. What went wrong? he thought bitterly.

Memories twisted his smile into a grimace. His father's family came from Veracruz, a seaport on the Caribbean side of Mexico. Armando Montera had been a proud young man, a teacher of *la raza,* Mexican history and culture, when he met the lovely Faith. The sweet-natured *gringa* secretary had come to the "fiesta city" for a vacation and promptly fell in love with the forbidden—a foreign port, a handsome fiery Latino.

Though Faith spoke only *turista* Spanish and was a virgin in matters of romance, they had married the night they met. It was a crazy, impulsive thing, a grand passion. God had made them complete opposites—dark and light, fire and rain. They were archetypal male and female, the sun and the moon. But if they fell in love with their differences, it was that, the differences, that killed their love.

Nick was born in Veracruz the first year of their marriage. But Faith couldn't live in Mexico. She was wasting away from homesickness, so Armando wrenched himself up by his roots and brought her to Los Angeles, thinking it would save her.

Instead, it destroyed them both. He couldn't find work in the schools, and he was too proud to ask for help. Eventually they ended up in the barrio, in San Ramone, where Faith did ironing by the pound and Armando toiled as a day laborer.

Armando had started drinking even before his young wife's tragic death, but it was different afterward. Embittered and belligerent, he lashed out at everything, and especially at his son, the living symbol of his failure. Nick had worshiped his father once, but love couldn't survive the onslaught. It was soon twisted into fear and loathing.

Armando Montera had succumbed to cirrhosis of the liver just two years ago, but Nick hadn't gone to the funeral. He didn't hate his father by then. He just didn't care. He'd had that beaten out of him by the time he was a teenager.

Now a jagged shard of glass caught his eye. Giving in to an impulse, he stooped, picked it up, and began to sketch at random on the bedroom's cement floor. He hadn't escaped this place. All his fine photography and his canyon studio space didn't mean shit when the chips were down. Like Manny, he was still a garbage rat from the hood.

Cold, angry laughter twisted in his gut.

Nick Montera was living out his father's prophecy. If they convicted him of murder and gave him the gas chamber, he would have fulfilled it. Just as Jesus Ortega was fulfilling his destiny. Just as Manuel Ortega would fulfill his. But Nick Montera wasn't going to jail. He wasn't going to die. He fucking wasn't going to let that happen.

He sketched steadily, obsessed with the details of his subject, determined to get them right. He wanted the swan curve of her long neck and the cold perfection of her lovely mouth. He wanted the remote beauty, the princess who taunted all men, but was available to none. As he traced the pale pink scrollwork of her ear to the lobe where the golden hoop would have pierced her soft flesh, he felt as if *he* were being pierced.

Dr. Leigh Rappaport, he thought, glaring down at his rough creation. The golden girl. The society psychotherapist. Now there was a woman he could have tortured with pleasure. There was a woman he could hate . . . *or love.*

His hand fisted on the jagged glass and fiery agony flared up his arm. He dropped the shard, a guttural cry in his throat. As he stared at the blood pouring from his hand, he knew what he had to do. If he couldn't convince the courts of his innocence, he would have to convince them of someone else's guilt. And this woman, this beautiful, inaccessible doctor, who looked like every other woman who had ever made him bleed—she was going to help him do that.

CHAPTER
·· ELEVEN ··

"Leigh! How's the book coming along? We're all terribly excited about it here!"

"Fine—" Leigh cleared her throat discreetly, trying to eliminate the telltale crack from her voice. "Just fine, Val!" Her right hand was occupied with the phone receiver, so she reached for her coffee cup with her left. She'd been expecting a call from Dawson. Just her luck it was her book editor instead.

"Things are moving right along here." Coaxing the coffee cup around, Leigh curled her fingers through the handle and tried to glance at her watch at the same time. What time was it? Seven P.M.? That meant it was ten in New York. Val must be calling her from home.

"Great!" Val exclaimed. "The sooner you can get the manuscript to us, the better, Leigh. We've already got *Forbidden Urges* scheduled for the spring of next year. I know *I* can't wait to read it!"

"Oh, no!"

"What's wrong? Leigh? Leigh!"

Coffee had sloshed all over Leigh's brand-new desk blotter. The cup was still teetering, half on, half off the fabric border as she grabbed for the Kleenex box on the credenza behind her desk. Struggling to keep the phone at her ear and pulling out handfuls of tissue was a logistically impossible task!

"Leigh? What's wrong?"

"I spilled my coffee!" she snapped, blotting frantically. "I'm just so damn right-handed!"

The silence at the other end of the line made Leigh's shrill tone all the more glaring. She sounded like a victim of raging PMS. Swearing softly, she threw a wad of coffee-soaked Kleenex into the wastebasket.

Val cleared her throat. "Leigh, *dear one*," she said. "This call was meant to be good news. If there's a problem at your end, I think we should talk about it, don't you? We're planning a major-markets promotional campaign for the book, and time is of the essence. Is there going to be a problem delivering the manuscript? Leigh . . . ?"

Leigh tilted the phone away from her ear and stuck her tongue out at it. Dear one? Take that, insensitive, unreasonable New York editor-person. Art is not slave to your publishing schedule!

The very idea of making a show of temperament caused Leigh to smile. She was, after all, a therapist and a clinician, writing a book about unlocking the secrets of the psyche through the analysis of personal drawings and sketches. Someone of her professional ilk was expected to set an example of responsible adult behavior—role-model stuff—not give in to the forbidden urges she was documenting. No wonder sticking out her tongue had felt so damn good. She would have to do it more often.

"Leigh? Are you still there? Were we cut off?"

"There is a problem, Val," she admitted.

"Surprise, surprise. What's going on?"

"It's the Montera trial." She tipped up a pile of sodden tissues to inspect the coffee stains—and wished she hadn't. She would never get the foul brown stuff out of the paisley fabric, and her office smelled like a catering truck. "I have the feeling I may be getting too involved. I've been thinking about taking myself off the case."

"Good God, Leigh, why? The country is completely fascinated with Nick Montera and you're the one who's been tapped to evaluate him! It's more than a plum. It's the whole damn pie. I can't imagine a forensic shrink in the country who wouldn't love to take the case off your hands. It's tailor-made for a book!"

"Yes, I suppose it is."

"Sup*pose*? Having Montera in *Forbidden Urges* could bounce it right out of the self-help category into mainstream best-sellerdom. You could do the whole book about him if you wanted to. You could do the man's life, go all the way back to his barrio childhood! Believe me, Leigh, the audience is there. This could be as big as the Menendez trial."

Leigh thought about how much that kind of recognition would have meant to her as recently as a few weeks ago. There was a time when she would have done almost anything to escape the chill of her mother's shadow. It wasn't that she wanted Kate's fame and fortune. She simply wanted to separate herself somehow, and to do that, it had always seemed necessary to achieve something in her own right. Her advice to a client would have been to look within for self-acceptance, to find personal worth in the small deeds rather than the great achievements. She would have told that client to accept herself as she was. But doctors were notoriously lousy patients, and Leigh was no exception.

"Let me think about this, okay, Val?"

"What is there to think about?"

Leigh removed her reading glasses and rubbed her burning eyes. "Well, I'm concerned about the ethics, for one thing," she said. "Montera's on trial for his life, and I've been called in to serve the interests of justice, not to gather material for a book. Besides, I haven't even tested him yet. Other things keep . . . happening."

"So get busy. Chop, chop, Leigh. Test him already, then call and tell me all the little nasties, every steamy detail of his fabulous sex life."

"I can see you're terribly concerned about my moral dilemma."

"Leigh, seriously, you can't *not* write this book. It's the opportunity of a lifetime. Whether he's guilty or innocent, women all over the country are riveted by this man. You owe it to us to tell us why we're mesmerized."

I think I know, Leigh thought. He's dark and beautiful and sexy, with a flashing white smile. And he's afraid of the sunrise.

Reluctantly then, she admitted that there was another side to the issue. "If he is guilty, then women should be alerted to how that sort of man works, how he draws victims into his web."

"That's my girl!" Val cried.

"Of course, I'd have to delay his portion of the book until after the trial was over, and even then, I'm not promising anything, Val."

As her editor continued to pep-talk her Leigh thought about

her other concerns, even bigger ones than the ethics issue. It
bothered her that no one, not even her fiancé, would follow up
on Paulie Cooper's suspicions about Jack Taggart. She knew
there was no point in involving Val in any of this. Her editor
couldn't be counted on to be objective at the moment. She
wanted a book and damn the torpedoes.

"So why *do* women everywhere want to have this man's
baby?" Val inquired, breaking into Leigh's thoughts. "I hope
you're going to explain that in your book. Is it the danger?"

Leigh laughed out loud. "Is this anyone we know, Val?
Come on, confess! Oops, got to go! There's someone at the
door."

It was true. Someone was thumping vigorously on the door
of Leigh's office, and it sounded urgent. She hurriedly promised Val that she wouldn't abandon the project, then hung up
the phone and headed for the front office.

The surprise that waited for her on the other side of the
door was the anxious smile and quick little wave of Paulie
Cooper.

Alec Satterfield had decided to give full rein to his hedon-
istic desires tonight. Swathed in a robe of rich purple silk and
arranged on his pedestal lounge like Caligula, he'd surrounded
himself with a bacchanalian feast for the senses—deep-frozen
vodka, scrambled eggs, and *rosti* with Sevruga caviar, lemon
soufflé, a Schubert sonata playing languidly on the stereo,
and a Buñuel video loaded in the VCR, if he couldn't fall
asleep later.

He didn't imagine sleep would be a problem, though. The
one-hundred-twenty-proof booze was already making him
pleasantly woozy. Dipping his finger in the sterling-silver
pail of caviar, he hooked a dollop of the pungent black stuff
and transported it to his mouth. "Ambrosia," he murmured,
groaning softly.

He was a man who enjoyed his sybaritic pleasures, and the
only thing that could possibly have added to tonight's menu
would have been a good old-fashioned blow job. Unfortunately, he was too relaxed to pick up the phone. Even calling his
favorite service seemed an effort, though a visit from one of
their male escorts would have been an interesting diversion.

Alec considered himself fortunate to have eclectic tastes

where sexual fulfillment was concerned. He was picky about the looks of his partners, but not about their gender. As long as they were dark, dusky, or exotic, he could happily make do with male or female.

"Who's there?" he murmured thickly, roused by shadowy movements near the door of his bedroom. His housekeeper, a wraithlike Cambodian woman in her fifties, tended to hover when she wanted to catch his attention.

"Am I disturbing you?"

The voice was barbed with sarcasm and unquestionably male. It jolted Alec out of his warm stupor and brought him up to a sitting position. "What the hell are you doing here?" he croaked as his latest client walked into the room.

Nick Montera was the incarnation of every WASP male's worst nightmare. Coming out of the shadows as he had, he looked more than anything like a true barrio savage, ready to eviscerate the cringing Anglo, simply for his wallet. His head was wrapped with a red bandanna, street-gang style. His tattered jeans were ripped out at the knees and his shirt hung open, a St. Christopher's medal gleaming in the darkness that caressed the muscularity of his upper body. Even more menacing was the knife sheathed in his belt, which he casually exposed as he tucked his shirt behind his hip.

If Alec had had a gun handy, he would have emptied it by now. "Who let you in?" he asked, his voice shaking.

"Your housekeeper."

"Looking like that? I'm surprised she didn't set off the alarm and run screaming."

A smile flared, undoubtedly as dark as Montera's spic soul.

"Actually, I think she likes me," he said. "I promised I'd talk to you on her behalf, counselor. She tells me she hasn't had a raise since she started working for you. I've heard the BAR Committee takes a dim view of their members employing illegal aliens. I've heard they like to *reprove* them publically."

This time Alec recognized the heat that warmed his neck for what it was—anger. His client had the manners of an animal. If Alec's instinct for self-preservation hadn't been so strong, he would have set off the alarm system himself.

"I don't do business at home," he informed Montera abruptly. "Call my office tomorrow and make an appointment. And have the decency to wear some civilized clothes."

The bedroom door slammed shut behind Montera as he strode into the room. "This won't take long."

Alec swung off the lounge and jerked his robe together hurriedly. "Get out of here, you crazy SOB! I should have your ass thrown in jail!"

"What you *should* do, counselor, is listen to me for about ten minutes." Montera moved into the glow of the bedroom's track lighting, his eyes as chrome cold as the mirrored sunglasses that hung from the pocket of his shirt.

"Why?"

"Because I know who killed Jennifer Taryn."

Alec couldn't suppress a sneer at that news. "And I presume it wasn't you?"

"It was her ex-boyfriend, Jack Taggart."

"You have proof of this?"

"Taggart's a cop—Homicide, LAPD. He had the motive, the capability, and the opportunity."

Alec fished the fifth of vodka from the ice bucket and swilled down some of the explosive liquor straight from the bottle. His eyes stung with tears and he could barely talk as he glared at his client. "What are you talking about, Montera? Explain yourself—and make it good."

"Who better than a homicide cop to stage a murder and frame someone else for it?"

"You're saying Taggart set you up? He strangled Jennifer Taryn and made it look like you did it? Why would he go to all that trouble? Why would anybody?"

Montera briefly described the tangled history of his teenage relationship with Jennifer Taryn and how years later she'd taken up with Taggart, then dropped him because she was determined to win Montera's forgiveness.

"She told me he threatened more than once to kill her if she left him," Montera explained. "He was a violent SOB—abusive, insanely jealous. She gravitated toward men like that, men who dominated her."

"Including you?" Alec plunged the fifth into the ice, plucked up a napkin, and blotted a line of moisture from his upper lip. "Your prints were all over the body. You admitted to having a physical encounter with the woman."

"I explained that. She was drunk. She didn't want me to leave."

Alec nodded at the silver snake entwining Montera's wrist. "That bracelet matches the ring you claim was stolen, doesn't it? I'm surprised the police didn't confiscate it."

"They confiscated the original bracelet. I had another one made."

"Why?"

"It holds special meaning."

"Was it an heirloom? A gift?"

"Not exactly. The meaning is symbolic."

Alec eyed his client narrowly. "What happened to the ring, Nick? Your claim that it was stolen is a bit convenient."

Montera ripped the red bandanna from his head and shook his springy black hair as if freeing himself. His jaw muscles jutted like wires. "I told you what happened," he said.

His voice was so soft it made Alec shiver. Everything about the man frightened the holy hell out of him. He was a dynamite-filled dam, primed to blow. Alec yanked at the ties of his robe, cinching it uncomfortably tight as he rose from the lounge. He wanted another shot of vodka, but he needed his wits about him.

"Okay, let me see if I understand this," he said, careful to avoid Montera's unnerving stare. "It was Taggart who stole your ring, is that what you're saying? He deliberately, deviously, and with malice aforethought plotted to murder Jennifer by strangulation, mark her with your ring, and then arrange her body in exactly the way you photographed her?"

Montera stuffed the bandanna in the back pocket of his jeans. "That's right."

Alec sighed. "Was it luck or more brilliant planning that she was murdered the very night you had a fight with her?"

"Taggart's a cop. He was waiting for the right time. He knew it would come."

"He did. Really? How did he know that?"

"He knew Jennifer. She was an emotional basket case. She pushed everything to a confrontation eventually. All it took was some simple surveillance on his part. He watched us. He *waited*."

"And his motive?"

"Jennifer dumped him for me. His motive was revenge—against both of us. What better payback than to murder her and frame me?"

"You're describing a full-blown psychopath."

"I'm describing Jack Taggart. Check out his police record. He's been up twice already on charges of unwarranted force."

Alec paced the room, not terribly happy with this bit of information. He was toying with several different defense strategies, including the possibility that Montera had been framed, but this wasn't a version he preferred. "So why didn't you tell me this theory of yours before?" he asked.

"Because I was hoping you'd figure it out on your own. Stupid of me, huh?"

Alec bristled. "You really believe you can do this job better than I can, don't you? How was it you were stupid enough to hire me if you thought I was such a schmuck?"

Montera's eyes blazed softly, fueled by unspoken disdain. "You're not a schmuck, Satterfield. You're just not motivated. I am. My life's at stake. I want you to defend me as if *your* life were at stake. Can you do that?"

Alec wet his lips and eyed the vodka. The son of a bitch was turning him into a drunk. "I've got some ideas," he said. "Diminished capacity, for one. We could argue that you weren't responsible, that you'd been drinking, that she went crazy and goaded you into it—"

"Por el amor de Dios!" Montera breathed. "Why bother to defend me at all? Why not just hand me over in chains? A diminished capacity defense says I did it, you asshole!"

"Easy!" Alec raised a warning hand. "I said it was one possibility. I've got others."

"Such as?"

"I'll go after their evidence, discredit their witnesses—"

"Go after their forensics people," Montera cut in. "Show their witness a blowup of a woman's neck with a snake's head bruise on it. Ask him if it could be the bruise on Jennifer's neck. When he says yes, show him how the mark was made—with a hand-carved Aztec necklace, the kind Jennifer always wore."

Alec stared at him in shock. "That's good," he admitted, managing a weak nod.

"You're fucking right, it's good. You, on the other hand, are incompetent. The only reason I haven't cut you loose, Satterfield, is because we both know you need this case and that means you can be controlled. Just don't make any moves without me, and we'll be fine."

Montera walked to the ice bucket and helped himself to the blue-chip booze. The dripping bottle of vodka swooshed from its icy depths like a torpedo and was thrust high in the air. The defiant salute was Montera's last word as he swung around and strode out of the room.

Alec stared after him, disbelieving. As the front door slammed shut he whirled toward the empty bucket, wild-eyed. He'd been robbed! He scooped out some ice with his hand and shoveled it into his parched throat. Crunching down, he perused the remains of his meal with genuine despair—cold eggs and caviar, a sunken soufflé.

Montera's scheme for discrediting their forensics expert was nothing short of brilliant. But why the hell was the bastard insisting he was framed by a cop? It was a defense strategy out of a *Mission Impossible* rerun. It would bring down the wrath of the entire law enforcement community on their heads— the LAPD, the DA's office. Christ, why not the governor! Worse, Taggart's motives weren't convincing, not unless the policeman was straitjacket crazy.

Alec became more and more indignant as he pondered the ramifications of Montera's plan. It wasn't Jack Taggart's mental health that concerned him now. He was beginning to think his own client was either a madman or guilty as hell. And quite possibly both.

CHAPTER
·· TWELVE ··

"OH . . . HELLO." LEIGH'S surprised response had reluctance written all over it. Poised awkwardly on the threshold of her office door, she tried to think of a polite way to discourage her visitor. "Paulie Cooper, right? Is there a problem? I was just getting ready to lock up and leave."

Paulie checked her watch, its huge black numbers on a luminous green dial confirming that it was after seven P.M. "It is late, isn't it?" she agreed quickly. "But I'm so glad you're still here. I was down the street having dinner at that little northern Italian place. Have you tried their minestrone? They make it with mussels and saffron. *Magnifico!*"

She laughed, magically produced a paper napkin from the pocket of her gold brocade vest, and touched it to the sides of her mouth with the mock fastidiousness of a gourmet. "Anyway, I saw the light in your office window and hoped you'd still be here."

Leigh smiled despite herself. Paulie Cooper had a disarming way about her, but Leigh was determined not to become embroiled in another conversation about Nick Montera. "Bad timing," she apologized. "I was just finishing up. I've been snowed under with work, trying to meet a deadline."

"Oh, of course." Delicate fingers curled around the napkin as if Paulie were about to discard the thing. "Otherwise, why would you be here this late? I just wondered if you were able to follow up on what I told you about Jack Taggart?"

Leigh was aware of something different about her visitor, but she couldn't decide what it was. Her brocade vest, man-tailored slacks, and loosely knotted tie were the perfect contrast to her rich auburn hair, which drooped seductively over one very blue eye and was tucked behind her ear on the other side. If anything, she looked even more beautiful than before, but Leigh had an artist's eye for details . . . and something was off.

"I spoke with someone in the prosecutor's office about it," Leigh explained, hoping that would suffice as an answer.

"Yes . . . and?"

"Nothing so far. I passed the information on. That's all I could do, really. It's up to them to act on it."

"But they *won't* act on it, Dr. Rappaport. Taggart is law enforcement! It's a brotherhood. You know how they protect each other." The napkin fluttered in her grip, as if trying to escape before it was crushed. "Who did you talk to in the prosecutor's office?"

"I don't think that's an appropriate question, Paulie. I really shouldn't discuss the case with you any further. I've done what I can." It was a weak argument, but Leigh saw no alternative. "We'll just have to let justice take its course."

She stepped back as if to shut the door, but Paulie moved quickly into the empty space and flattened her hand against the frame. "Dr. Rappaport, you can't be serious. Nick Montera is an ex-con from the barrio. He's a Hispanic man accused of killing a white woman from a prominent family. If we leave this to *justice,* he'll end up in the gas chamber!"

"I'm sorry. There's nothing more I can do."

"Yes, there is! You're involved with the district attorney, aren't you, Dr. Rappaport? I read somewhere that you were engaged to him."

"Where did you read that?"

"A newspaper—the *Times,* I think. The two of you were at a polo match for some charity. If you're engaged to the DA, then you must have some pull."

Apparently not, Leigh thought. Dawson hadn't seemed the slightest bit interested in Paulie's theory when Leigh brought it up at lunch. "Using my relationship with Dawson to influence the outcome of the trial would be a serious ethical breach. As far as legal proceedings go, expert witnesses are supposed to be neutral. They state their findings, interpret them for the jury, and that's it."

Paulie's crumpled napkin had long since dropped to the floor. "Is your fiancé actually the district attorney?" she asked. "Is his name Dawson Reed?"

"Yes . . . why?"

Paulie's darting gaze met Leigh's, then dropped away as if she were trying to decide whether to proceed. "Were you aware that Dawson Reed once had a relationship with Jennifer Taryn?"

"What?" If Leigh hadn't touched the door frame to steady herself, she would have stumbled back in shock. "What are you talking about?"

Paulie twisted at the points of her vest. "It's true," she said. "They knew each other—well."

"Knew each other *well*?" By now Leigh was more than astonished, she was getting irritated. "How could they have?" What kind of trick was Paulie pulling now? She was desperate for some way to help Montera, that much was clear, but it didn't excuse her muddying things up by trying to involve Dawson. It was preposterous.

"It's true," Paulie insisted. "Jennifer and I roomed together for a while several years ago. We couldn't get enough work as models to pay the rent, so we took temp jobs, found an apartment in the city, and shared expenses."

Leigh cut in impatiently. "You said she had a relationship with Dawson? What did you mean by that?"

"Well, maybe that's the wrong word. I never actually saw him at the apartment, but he left messages on her phone machine. I heard her play them back. I even heard her return the call and make plans to meet him."

Leigh was torn between an impulse to pepper Paulie with questions and a powerful desire to dismiss the whole thing. "I'm sure my fiancé is not the only Dawson Reed in Southern California."

Paulie shrugged. "It's a pretty unusual name. How many others could there be?"

"You must have misunderstood," Leigh said curtly. She was not going to allow this thing to take root and grow the way Paulie's other seeds of information had. What she really wanted was for her visitor to leave. Paulie had done nothing but complicate her life.

"She told me about all the men she'd been involved with," Paulie revealed. "Including Nick and that whole fiasco. She even admitted to me that she'd lied about Nick on the witness stand and felt guilty. But she never mentioned Dawson. She was keeping him a secret, for some reason."

"No—" Leigh shook her head. "It was someone else. It had to be. Now, really, I do need to go."

"Sure." Reluctantly Paulie began to back down the hall. With a quick, despairing smile, she made one last attempt to change Leigh's mind. "They're going after the wrong man, Doctor. Talk to your fiancé, please! Tell him you know about him and Jennifer."

Torn, Leigh shut the door and fell against it. Her hand was still on the knob as she pressed her forehead to the lacquered wood. She felt disconnected from the floor and the walls and everything that supported her. Her heart was pounding. She needed a moment, just one moment.

But it was considerably longer than that before she was able to draw back and breathe in some calmness. Paulie Cooper's napkin lay at her feet and she knelt to pick it up, trying not to tip over. She was off balance, and the tattered piece of paper didn't help her equilibrium any. It had Nick Montera's name scribbled all over it. Her visitor was still in love with Montera, Leigh realized. To the point of obsession.

As Leigh studied the word on the napkin she suddenly knew what had been different about Paulie Cooper. Her fingernails! They'd been filed down—or bitten—nearly to the quick. The other time she'd been confronted by Paulie, her fingernails had been long and lush and painted to match her plum-red lipstick. Maybe they'd been false, but they'd looked natural to Leigh.

That discrepancy led her into another more disturbing line of reasoning. From the first she'd suspected that Paulie's motive for coming to Montera's aid was the publicity she would get from being associated with him. Nick Montera was the "dark darling" of the media, a mysterious Latin lover whose allegedly total power over the women he photographed was widely gossiped about. Several publications, including *Newsweek,* had picked up on Paulie's "supernatural sex" reference and quoted it. What struggling model wouldn't be tempted to take advantage of such a golden opportunity for national attention?

Leigh wanted to throw the damn napkin away. The ideas were stimulating, and they were coming faster than she could consider them. Was it possible that Paulie herself had a motive for the murder? Jealousy, the age-old green-eyed monster? It had driven women to crazier acts than murder, and if Paulie had wanted to clear the way for a relationship with Nick . . . ?

As Leigh studied the model's intricately looped and exaggerated handwriting, she realized there was a glitch in her theory. If Paulie had wanted Jennifer out of the way so she could have Nick for herself, why would she have framed Nick for the crime? It made no sense if her motive was to get him back. You couldn't have much of a relationship with a man on death row.

Leigh crumpled the napkin in her hand. She had an uneasy feeling in the pit of her stomach, a lightness that bordered on dread. The Montera case was getting too complicated. It seemed to have tentacles that were reaching out from everywhere to draw her in, no matter how determined she was to escape them.

She wanted to think of it as a situation that could be resolved once and for all in a court of law. She would testify and that would be the end of her involvement. Either Nick Montera was guilty or he wasn't. But it wasn't that simple. There were other people involved in ways that she didn't understand, including her own fiancé. If Dawson had once had a relationship with Jennifer Taryn, why hadn't he ever mentioned it?

Keys jangled down the hall, and a door banged open. The start-up whine of a vacuum cleaner told her the janitorial service had reached her floor. It was late and she was exhausted. As she headed back to her office she passed her assistant's desk and paused, torn. Finally she dropped the crumpled napkin into Nancy's wastebasket.

The act briefly restored Leigh's sense of control, but it did nothing to discourage the concerns that were piling up in her mind. What else did Paulie Cooper know about the Montera case that she hadn't revealed?

Nick pulled off his disposable gloves and dropped them in the darkroom's trash receptacle. Several sepia-toned prints, still wet from the final wash, hung on the line in front of him. The room reeked of sulfur from the processing, but Nick hardly noticed as he studied the shots one by one. He was pleased with his latest efforts. He'd caught her in another pensive mood, caught the rich sunlight that shadowed half her face and made her look wary and vulnerable, caught the smoky hints that clouded her gray eyes when she was troubled. Or gazing at kittens.

She'd been walking her bike on the boardwalk that morning, and at one point she had turned suddenly and looked right into his camera. She couldn't have seen him, of course. He'd been hidden on the deserted patio of a beachfront restaurant over a hundred feet away, a telephoto lens on his camera. But his heart had taken forever to force out its next beat.

He'd wanted her that way, in a mood.

Half-sunny, half-shadowed.

He'd felt an impulse to reach out and touch her lovely, solemn face with his hands, just a feather stroke, something fleeting that would have heightened the pain of wanting. It was hell, that wanting, a sharp blade turning in his gut, but it was all he had that morning. The need to punish her that had sustained him was gone, or at least dormant, and so he'd let himself go with this feeling, with this agony. After all, she had made him forget who he was for a moment. That day in her office when she'd encouraged him to talk about his work, he'd felt like a boy again, full of hunger and hope. *Christ, that alone was reason enough to hate her*.

Now, staring at her pictures suspended in the lurid red sea of his darkroom, he felt the knife turn, a sweet, cutting pain. Eyes closed, he slipped his hand beneath his cotton T-shirt, absently rubbing the scar that split the dark whorls of hair on his belly. He had to touch something, and if it couldn't be her . . .

As he ran his hand up his abdomen, over the hardened nub of his nipple, and onto the ridges of his biceps, he allowed the longing to rip through him one more time before he cut it off.

"Jesus," he whispered harshly.

He knew what would happen when he cauterized the wound. Once he had sealed it off, the energy would run straight to his groin. It would pool there like fire, and he would be hard. God, the nights he'd lain in bed, dying for a woman, but unable to imagine himself inside anyone but her.

Her . . . the insane pleasure of her . . . he knew every tender thing there was to know about that kind of insanity . . . the parted thighs, the strangled sighs, the small, shapely breasts that rose delicately from her rib cage. Her softness had called to him in his dreams, but when he'd reached out, he'd found nothing but his own swollen excitement, and so he'd given his body what it craved. Release.

Now the temptation to slide his hand inside the loosely tied band of his sweatpants was nearly overpowering. The worn, downy-soft cotton caressed his uncoiling erection as lightly as a woman's hand. In another state of mind, he might have been able to enjoy that feeling, but he was a dying man . . . dying to touch her, dying because of her.

A sharp yowl jolted Nick out of his erotic distractions. The thunderous crash that followed brought him careening back to reality. The darkroom rocked with red-and-black light. He'd hit the safelight as he whirled around, and it was swinging wildly.

A chaotic sight greeted him as he wrenched the door open. Marilyn, the cat, was skittering across the room in wild flight, ears flattened, claws bared against a gleaming wood floor that mirrored her every move. Estela was in the studio, too, circling tipsily, trying to get a bead on the fleeing cat. At the other end of the room, a storage cabinet had been upended, with maintenance equipment, extension cords, clamps, and gaffer tape strewn everywhere. A couple of packed cases holding cameras had fallen too.

"Ay, Dios mio!" Estela cried, cursing the cat as she shook her hands at the mess.

"Oh, my God is right," Nick muttered. Apparently Marilyn had been exploring the rickety storage cabinet where he stashed spare parts and extra equipment, and she'd dumped the whole thing.

Nick flinched as Estela began to kick at the debris that was scattered around, herding it into a pile. *"Que pendejade!"* she moaned as she laboriously bent to pick up a Nikon F4 camera. "Look at this! *Que desastre!*"

"Estela!" Nick thundered. "Leave that alone!"

She lost her grip on the camera and staggered backward, dropping to her knees. *"Esta loco?"* she whispered. "Has everybody gone crazy?"

"I'll clean up," Nick said, striding toward her, menace punctuating every step. "Go on—get out of here. You must have other things to do."

She slapped at him as if he were going to strike her, but he gripped her arm anyway and lifted her to her feet, perhaps more roughly than he meant to.

"Bastardo!" she screamed, scurrying for the door the minute she could pull free. Her trembling, indignant snorts filled the room, and as she reached the threshold she swung around and defiantly flipped him the finger. All of her Catholic moral outrage was contained in that one obscene gesture. Seeming to be pleased with herself, she flashed him a glare that damned him with all the intensity of a *bruja's* evil eye.

Once she'd turned her back, Nick allowed himself a smile that was as quick as it was cold. He watched her stalk off down the hallway, and when he was sure she was gone, he shut the door to the studio, locked it, and went to the camera that had been lying at his housekeeper's feet, the one she'd been about to pick up.

The Nikon had been damaged in the fall, though that wasn't what had him concerned. The aperture ring on its 400mm telephoto lens hung loosely, dropping into Nick's hand when he touched it. He tipped the lens at a sharp angle and a bubble pack about the size of a baseball card rolled into his palm. A silver snake's head was clearly visible through the clear plastic.

A red light danced before Nick's eyes, harbinger of another deadly headache. His hand closed, crushing the bubbles. The sinew of his forearm contracted as he concealed the packet in his grip and swore softly. This was the piece of evidence everyone was searching for, the one that could hang him. He would have to find a better hiding place for the ring.

CHAPTER
·· THIRTEEN ··

A SHARP BURST of static over the intercom announced
Leigh's assistant. "Dr. Rappaport?" came Nancy's breathless
rasp. "It's Mr. Reed on line one, returning your call."

"Thanks, Nancy." Leigh's finger hovered over the flashing
button.

"Hold it!" Nancy interjected. "Your client's here, too. Nick
Montera. Shall I ask him to wait?"

Leigh tapped the button. This was the call she'd been waiting for. She and Dawson needed to talk. She was swamped
with work, as was he, undoubtedly, but something had to be
arranged. She hadn't been able to connect with him since her
talk with Paulie Cooper yesterday.

The light blinked insistently. Leigh could almost feel
Dawson's impatience at being kept waiting, but she drew
her hand away. This wasn't the time for a discussion that
might become complicated—not when she needed to focus
her energies on the upcoming session. "See if Dawson's free
for dinner tonight, would you?" she asked Nancy. "And set
something up at that northern Italian trattoria down the street
if he is. Thanks."

"What about your appointment?" Nancy asked.

"Give me a minute before you send him in."

As the intercom clicked off Leigh touched the pad of her
thumb to her little finger and pressed firmly, employing a
technique of posthypnotic autosuggestion designed to summon calm. Within seconds she felt her breathing deepen, her
shoulder muscles relax. She hadn't used the technique in years.
Fortunately, it still worked. She felt ready now, even for Nick
Montera.

She'd narrowed down the battery of tests she intended to
give Montera to a standardized personality inventory and two

projective tests, one of which was the Johnson-Rappaport Art-Insight Survey, the diagnostic tool she and her mentor, Dr. Carl Johnson, had developed at Stanford. Nancy would administer the personality inventory since it was multiple choice and computer-scored.

"Psssst," Nancy whispered over the intercom. "Ready or not, here he comes."

Leigh rested her elbows on the arms of her chair and gazed expectantly at the door, pleased at how relaxed and professional she felt. She barely registered any surprise when Montera opened the door and walked in. Her first impression was of height and power, of vivid contrasts. He wore a dark suit, double-breasted and expensively cut, with a creamy white turtleneck underneath that curled upward to caress his strong, angular jawline.

The suit, which looked like something by a European designer, should have had a civilizing effect, but instead it emphasized his strong bone structure, blue eyes, and long black lashes. His lush dark hair was drawn loosely into a ponytail, which made him look suave and sinister, a gangster with savoir faire. He was the kind of man women crawled on their knees over broken glass to get to, Leigh acknowledged reluctantly, though she wouldn't have admitted it to him under threat of torture.

She was mildly curious about his dress-for-success outfit. He seemed to change personae with the naturalness of a chameleon, but was it simply an instinct for protective coloration, or was it an indication of some deeper dysfunction, like sociopathy? He could be charming when it suited him and he was clearly intelligent. His early criminal behavior was the key, as was his apparent aversion to authority. Many of the distinguishing traits were there, but Leigh had decided not to draw any conclusions until she had the test results.

"If you'll have a seat," she said, slipping on her tortoiseshell horn-rims as she double-checked the materials for the first test. "I'd like to get started."

"Good . . . so would I."

She glanced up warily, peering at him over the rims of her glasses and fully expecting to see a sardonic twist or something more expressly sexual in his smile. But there was no such thing. He was smiling with the kind of civility one adult shows another in a potentially awkward situation. She blinked in surprise and smiled back. Apparently they were going to play model patient and august psychologist. That promised to be a refreshing change.

"I'm going to show you some pictures, Mr. Montera," she told him. "And I'd like you to write a story about each one of them, a short story that fits the picture, so to speak. . . ."

She was very much aware that he was observing her as she went on, instructing him to describe what led up to the event in the picture, what was happening at that moment and the outcome. "Put down whatever comes to mind," she said. "Don't stop to analyze it. I need your first reaction, all right?"

"Your earring," he said.

"What?" A nerve sparked in Leigh's hand.

Nick settled back in the chair as if to observe her. "You haven't touched your earring. I always thought it was something you did when you felt threatened, a security thing. Does that mean you're feeling secure today?"

The chameleon had changed his clothes, Leigh realized, but not his approach. "I'm the doctor here, Mr. Montera. Please try to remember that as we go along."

She whisked off her glasses and set them on the desk, then held up the first card, a picture of a boy contemplating a violin, which rested on a table in front of him. "What comes to mind when you look at this picture?"

His eyebrow flattened, lending him a faintly pained expression. "You could have found an artist with some imagination."

"You get to supply the imagination, Mr. Montera. Here. Write about what you see." She handed him a clipboard with a legal tablet and a sharpened pencil. "But don't focus on aesthetic considerations. I am not measuring your artistic taste. Describe how the boy feels, what he's thinking."

He wrote swiftly and with a spontaneity that surprised and pleased her. He didn't ask questions or make comments about what he saw, he simply wrote whatever scenario came to mind just as she'd asked him to. By the time he'd finished with the set of cards, the rich scent of freshly brewed coffee had crept into the room, and Leigh suggested a break. "How about something to drink before we start the next test?" she asked. "I think Nancy made a pot of coffee."

He smiled. "Smells like chocolate truffles."

"Macadamia nut . . . her specialty."

Leigh went to get the coffee, and when she returned, Nick Montera was standing by her window, studying her terrarium of turtles.

"You like animals, don't you?" he said as she approached him with the steaming cup of coffee.

"What makes you think that?" Leigh took elaborate care to make sure their fingers didn't brush as she handed him the coffee, then retreated immediately to the vicinity of her desk. Her goal was to keep the exchange cordial, but professional.

"Just a hunch," he said. "You look like the type who collects strays. Which is it? Cats or dogs?"

Leigh took a sip of her coffee, unsure what direction he was going. "No pets except the turtles," she said. "But I do love animals. You're right about that."

"Any particular kind?"

"All kinds, I suppose."

His black hair caught the glow of light from the window as he studied her. "Narrow it down for me, choose one."

"Okay, then . . ." Anything to keep the subject happy, Leigh thought. Especially since he still had one test to go, and she wanted to encourage a mood of cooperation and trust. "Hawks, I think. Yes, hawks—I like the way they soar on air currents. They're not earthbound. They're totally free."

"Interesting . . . how about horses?"

"What about them?" she came back, laughing. "Are you doing marketing research for horse chow?"

"Thankless job, but—" He shrugged a yes.

"I like horses fine." She perched on the edge of her desk and held her coffee cup in both hands, enjoying the warmth that seeped into her chilly fingers. "But when it comes to four-legged animals, I'm rather partial to the lioness."

"Queen of the jungle?"

Leigh inclined her head as if revealing a long-held secret. "Nobody messes with mother lion."

"Hawks, lionesses, and . . . ? What else?"

"Are we compiling a list here?"

"Humor me. One more."

"Okay," she said, heaving a sigh. "Probably a shrew mole."

"A shrew mole? Why, for God's sake?"

"They're just such homely, wretched little things. I can't imagine who loves them, even their mothers."

His smile told her she'd intrigued him.

"Did I pass the test?" she asked.

"I don't know, Doctor. You tell me." He mirrored her stance, settling onto the credenza behind him and cradling his coffee cup in both hands. "Your first choice, the hawk, is how you want others to see you. Your second choice, the lioness, is how you see yourself. And the shrew mole, well—sorry, but that's the real you."

Leigh tugged at her jacket, only half aware that she was attempting to button it up. Her laughter was rather too sharp. "I see . . . so I aspire to be a hawk, or perhaps a lioness, but at heart I'm really a shrew mole?"

His blue eyes narrowed with wry awareness. "Funny, you don't look like a shrew mole."

"I'm afraid to ask what I do look like."

"You don't have anything to be afraid of, Doctor."

She was aware that he was studying her hairdo as if he were curious about the way she'd gathered up her blond tresses with combs on each side, leaving a white-gold sweep of bangs to soften the severity. She could almost feel the subtle heat of his interest as his gaze flicked over the prominent shoulder pads of her houndstooth jacket and down the length of calf revealed by her short black skirt.

She'd taken extra care to look feminine today, wearing a skirt instead of slacks. She'd told herself it was because she was expecting to meet Dawson, but now she was beginning to wonder. Was there another more compelling reason? Had she worn a skirt so that Nick Montera would look at her in exactly this way, so that he would check out her legs and then do what any number of other men might do, under the circumstances—imagine himself *between* them?

She promptly crossed her ankles, aware of a deepening flutter in the pit of her stomach. *What was wrong with her?* Was she so starved for male attention that she was reduced to tempting her clientele? As much as that idea disturbed her, she couldn't deny that Montera's remarks about her "look" had an impact on her. She was not indifferent to his approval. That much was clear. Somehow his masculine values had insinuated themselves into her thinking over the last few weeks. He had subtly, yet powerfully, worked his sorcery, until she'd become so accustomed to the pleasure of a man's interest—of *his* interest—that she'd begun to expect it, to seek it.

"Trust me, Doctor," he said. "You're beautiful. If I could photograph you . . . if I could pose you, dress you, arrange your hair exactly as I wanted to—" He didn't finish the sentence. He let his eyes do it for him.

Leigh resisted the urge to touch her earring, though the impulse raged through her. She had felt like a shrew mole for most of her childhood, and she'd never completely outgrown the image, despite her outward appearance. As an adult she'd simply become one of the homely little things in disguise. Until very lately, that is . . . until him.

Being around Nick Montera had put her in a state of conflict she'd never experienced before. She'd never been the object of a focus so intense, except once in her life, and that was when she was a girl. Was that what made her vulnerable to him? Because she yearned to be noticed, to be special in someone's eyes? He made her feel as though he saw things in her that no one else had ever seen, qualities invisible to the human eye that he alone had some magical ability to decipher. She was a Christmas scene encased in a plastic bubble. Only he understood that you had to shake the bubble to make it snow.

That was all fine and good, she told herself. Fine and good for some other woman. But not for her. Having some guy shake you up was great, but not if you'd been hired to assess his criminal inclinations.

"Is this a scientific test?" she asked, knowing it couldn't possibly be. "Have you done reliability studies?"

"I made it up just for you. Is that scientific enough?"

She slid off the desk, tugged her jacket straight, and went around to sit in her chair. "Back to business," she said, all very bright and professional, once she'd settled herself.

Montera made no move to accommodate her. He continued to sit exactly where he was, observing her. "I'm waiting to hear what you thought of my test," he said.

Leigh gave it five beats before she returned his wry amusement. "I think you may have made a major breakthrough in the field of behavioral sciences."

Their gazes locked, and though Leigh would like to have won the stare-down, the color of his eyes was so intense it seemed to stain her field of vision. When she looked away, at the papered walls of her office, at the testing materials on her desk, she saw them as if through a blue filter. The room seemed to be underwater, five fathoms deep.

"In other words, I nailed it," he averred softly.

"That's one way of putting it." Leigh dropped her hand into her lap and squished her thumb to her little finger, determined to stop the perturbations in her stomach. The deep, erratic pulse that coursed through her fingers told her it was already too late. Calming techniques would no longer work.

"If we could continue," she said abruptly, indicating the chair he'd vacated. "I have a few more pictures I'd like to show you. These are paintings. Rather good art, actually. I think you'll enjoy the artists' imaginations."

As he sat down Leigh turned on the tape recorder she kept on her credenza and then joined him, taking the other chair that faced her desk. This particular test required a level of implied trust and interaction that couldn't be achieved from behind a desk, but that also put her, the administrator, at some risk. Perhaps that was why she was feeling nervous.

Leigh herself had tested the technique with convicted felons in prison settings. She'd shown them art that included a group of paintings chosen specifically to elicit unconscious sexual and/or violent impulses toward women. Those were the paintings she would be using today, some of which were highly erotic in content.

"Tell me about these women," she said, handing him a copy of *Leaf Drift,* a turn-of-the-century work, depicting three slender nudes sprawled ecstatically in a bed of fallen leaves. The women's backs were curved like archers' bows, their arms thrown up, their faces contorted with either torment or bliss. It was difficult to tell which.

Montera settled back in his chair to study them, his thumb pressed to his lips as if to stop from smiling. "Where's Smokey the Bear, when you need him?" he quipped. "These babes look hot enough to set fire to the woods."

"Hot as in sexual arousal? Or as in anger?"

"Hot as in it's going to be a long, hard night." He looked up, his gaze burning into Leigh's. "Surely there can't be any question about that, Doctor. This isn't about anger. It's about fucking."

Leigh's chair creaked as if she were going to stand. Again the room swam with blue lights, and her elbows pressed sharply into the stiff leather arms of the chair. She reminded herself that his answer was typical and not at all surprising. The test was designed to disinhibit subjects by giving them the most obvious and explicit paintings first. Crude responses were commonplace, especially among male respondents. It was the reaction to the later paintings, which were more subtle in their latent meanings, that was significant.

If some other subject had said what Montera just did, it wouldn't have fazed her. "If you were to come upon these three women in just this state, what would happen next?" she asked him, pressing on. "Paint that picture for me."

He emitted a husky sound. "If I were a vibrator salesman, I'd hold an auction and get rich."

His response was equally irreverent to the next few paintings, which included a portrait of a sitting woman and a gigantic, adoring wolfhound standing alongside her with its head in her lap. Its muzzle, certainly the world's longest, was buried intimately in the folds of her skirt.

"Wonder what her second and third choices would have been," Nick murmured, apparently referring to his animal test.

It wasn't until Leigh showed him a Hermann Moest painting, *The Fate of Beauty,* that he sobered. The haunting soulscape pictured a lovely young nude, lying lifelessly on a bed of white sheets, with a young man prostrate across the blanket that covered her legs.

"What has happened here?" she asked Montera, offering him the print. "Can you tell me their story?"

Montera moved to take the painting, then hesitated as he saw what it was. The flesh of his cheeks sucked in, carving deep grooves in the contours of his face as he stared at the tragic scene.

"What's wrong?" Leigh asked.

His eyes had narrowed to slits, but something hot and terrible flared in their depths as he looked up at Leigh. "Why did you show me this?"

Leigh very carefully secured her grip on the painting. Hold it still, she told herself, but her wrists were like water. Once again she was witnessing the darkness that lived inside him, the black passion that was so infused with pain, it was frightening.

"It's part of the test," she said, controlling the shake in her voice. "Please, try to give me an answer. What do you think has happened between these two people?"

He lifted his head, as if he could hardly bear to look at the picture, yet he never took his eyes off it. "The man is in agony," he said.

"Why?"

"Because he believes he killed her."

"And did he . . . kill her?"

When he finally responded, his slow nod made Leigh's heart jerk with such painful force she could hardly think. She had no idea what that simple, deliberate gesture meant. Was he simply responding to a disturbing work of art? Or was he, himself, confessing to something?

"I don't understand," she said. "If he's in agony, then he couldn't have wanted her dead."

"He didn't."

"How did it happen?"

"Stupidity."

"Stupidity? Then it was an accident?" Leigh wanted him to agree. She was waiting for him to agree.

"No. He lost his head. He gave in."

"To what?" she asked.

"To rage, to greed . . . to his own insane ego."

The picture weighed a thousand pounds. Leigh fumbled it into her lap and was silent a moment. Her nerves were firing, but she had to proceed cautiously now. She felt as if she'd just stumbled upon some arcane knowledge that held great power, and she didn't know how to wield it, or if the power was for good or evil.

"This man in the painting?" she said. "Tell me about him. Would you say that he feels great remorse?"

"I would call it great, yes. I would call it unbearable."

"What will he do now? What will happen to him?"

"I don't know. Die for his sins, I suppose. In his own way, he'll die."

There were more pictures. Leigh was just getting to the group selected to elicit unconscious responses, but she couldn't go on. There was a war raging inside her. Montera had been informed from the first interview that the testing sessions would be taped, and unless the defense found some way to block the recording as evidence, it might even be used against him. A really clever prosecuting attorney would find ways to construe it as an admission of guilt, and a jury would undoubtedly be influenced by it, just as she had been. Her impulse was to stop Nick now, not to let him say anything more. She could destroy the tape—

A frantic clicking sound made her realize what she was doing. She was tapping her glasses against the desk blotter as if she could somehow drum up a solution to the dilemma she was in. Destroying the tape would be as unethical as it was unprofessional, and though it made her nearly ill to think of turning it over to the DA's office there were things that had to be considered. If the session contained what could be construed as an admission of guilt, she would have contributed immeasurably to the state's case. What was more, her test would have been validated in ways she couldn't even have imagined. All her years of struggle and self-denial—the drudgery her mother accused her of—would have been worth it. She was on the brink, it seemed, of either ruining her career or advancing it.

When she looked up, Montera had turned to look out the window, and Leigh found herself wondering where that steely gaze of his took him when his attention wandered off.

"Perhaps we should stop," she suggested.

"No," he said evenly, "I think we should go on. I want to do the next painting."

Leigh had placed the box of materials in the space between them. The picture he was referring to was set in a spring garden, wild with flowers, where a Victorian woman was disrobing in front of a mirrored pond. She was clearly intent on taking a dip without being discovered, and to that end, she had a ferocious black Doberman standing watch over her clothing, and perhaps her virtue.

"Why that one?" Leigh asked.

"Because she looks like you."

The woman's heavy golden hair was secured with combs and her milk-white skin and slender, full-breasted figure were discernible through the delicate lace shift she wore. But it was her expression as she undressed, one of cautious reserve giving way to guilty pleasure, that was most striking. She clearly wanted to shiver with the delicious excitement of her secret, and the thought made Leigh want to shiver with her.

"I don't see it—" Leigh was firm in her pronouncement. "Other than her blond hair, she looks nothing like me."

"Really?" He bent and picked up the picture, studying it with a knowing smile. "Perhaps then I was identifying with the beast that's guarding her."

"What do you mean?"

"Look at him . . . he's aroused."

Montera handed her the picture, and though Leigh was reluctant, she had little choice but to accept it. The gleaming black Doberman was tensely alert, every muscle rigid with the promise of physical action. He was coiled steel. His sleek loins rippled with sensuality as he watched his mistress and awaited her bidding. And those loins were quite clearly male.

"He does look fierce," she admitted, "but not in the way you mean."

"What way is that? Are you suggesting that he's not aroused because he's not physically . . . stimulated?"

Leigh flushed. "Yes, that's exactly what I mean."

"I wonder if it would be different if he were a man, say the lady's driver—a brawny young fellow, forced to stand guard and watch while she undressed?" Montera rubbed his lower lip thoughtfully, dragging at the softness with his thumbnail. "What's your clinical opinion, Doctor? Would a young man get physically stimulated in that situation?"

Leigh felt a sharp tug at her vitals. The conflict rising inside her told her to stop this line of questioning. As a woman, she felt compromised and threatened. And yet her clinical experience compelled her to pursue it, to draw him out and see where he was going. "Perhaps, but not all men would take advantage of that situation," she said. "Some would find it morally—"

"But every man would *want* to," he cut in. "Especially if the woman looked like her . . . like you."

Leigh rose and walked to the window, unwilling to let him see the effect he was having on her. She turned to him. "I really wish you wouldn't—"

"You wish I wouldn't what, Doctor? Talk this way? Isn't that what I'm here to do?"

"You're not here to talk about me."

"Why not? Why can't I talk about you if that picture reminds me of you?" His voice dropped off, forming a hush, as if something had constricted his breathing. "Have you ever wondered what it would be like to have a man want you that badly, Doctor? To have a man get hard just because he looked at you?"

Leigh clasped her hand at the wrist, holding herself that way as she turned to look out the window at the city skyline. She didn't answer him. She would let silence do that for her. She would let it buy her time and bring the tension down while she tried to figure out how to end this session.

But a moment later she heard the creak of a chair and then a sharp click warned her what was happening. Nick Montera had just turned the tape recorder off.

CHAPTER
·· FOURTEEN ··

LEIGH HADN'T HEARD Nick Montera come up behind her, but she could see him reflected in the glass of her office window, and the image was mesmerizing. As his features materialized in the slanting light the angles of his face sharpened and deepened until he looked as hauntingly compelling as the sorcerer everyone accused him of being. More than that, he looked like everything Leigh had ever secretly fantasized in a man . . . like demonic passion and dark fire.

"You didn't answer my question," he said.

"I'd like you to leave. The session is over."

"Have you ever wondered—"

"Don't," she whispered.

"What it would be like—"

"No!"

"To have a man want you that badly?"

"Stop, please!"

But he didn't stop.

"I want you that badly," he said.

I want you that badly.

Leigh let out a muffled sound as his impossible declaration struck her. "No," she implored softly. Finally she turned on him, furious. "I'm a doctor!"

He held out her notebook.

"What are you doing?" she asked, realizing he must have taken it from her desk.

"Open it," he said, "to the last page."

She stared at the book for a second, then snatched it from him and began to leaf through it frantically. The pages flew through her fingers, some of them ripping partially free of the spiral rings. She was dangerously close to losing control, and once she had, she knew there would be little hope of regaining it. Her own words blurred past, and as her fingers began to stiffen and shake, she was forced to acknowledge what her physical body already knew—that something was going to happen between her and Nick Montera today. Something that would inexorably change her life.

"The last page," he told her.

She breathed out a shocked word as she reached that page and saw the sketch he'd scrawled in pencil point. A woman was pressed up against a wall, her head turned away as if she were either frightened, or aroused. The man with her was made of shadow more than flesh, but his hand encircled her throat in an erotic caress that made Leigh empathize with the woman's tremulous response. She wanted to turn away, too.

Leigh stared at the illicit tableau Nick Montera had created, absorbing its dark, wild mood as if through her pores. There was no question who the woman was. Or the man.

"When did you draw this?" she asked him.

"You left your book at my studio." He touched the page that was crumpled in her hand. "Tell me who this woman is, Doctor," he demanded softly. "Tell me what she's feeling."

"No—" Leigh tried to close the book, but he stopped her and took it away from her.

"Then I'll tell you," he said, dropping the notes on the credenza. "She's never been more excited. The emotions pounding through her are making her feel wild, electric, immortal. She could do anything. She could spar with the gods. But she doesn't want immortality, Doctor. She wants life, sweaty and hard, just the way life is. She wants heat. Animal heat. And she wants it with him, the man who's backed her to the wall."

"You have no right," she whispered.

"I have every right. I'm the one who made her feel that way."

He caught her arm as if he'd sensed that she was about to back off. Leigh stared at his hand, at the way his long dark fingers encircled her slender wrist. She'd never seen anything quite so breathtaking as the contrast in their skin tones. It was as if she were seeing their differences for the first time, and the clarity of it mystified her.

As she glanced up, her gaze locked with his, and the entire world seemed to telescope into the charged connection that held their eyes. The knowledge that passed between them was too pure, too carnal, for her to comprehend. It overwhelmed her. He was speaking to every forbidden impulse she'd ever had. He personified everything that had ever frightened her, a level of risk beyond anything she'd experienced. She knew intuitively that surrendering to her desire for a man like him was to enter the realm of the flesh and the senses. It would be a sweet sexual hell for the uninitiated.

His other hand came to rest on her throat.

"Stop this," she warned, refusing to look at him any longer. "If you don't, I can't continue to work with you. I'll have to take myself off the case."

"Then do it," he said, bringing her back to look at him and staring into her eyes so intensely it made her weak. "Take yourself off the case. You want this more, don't you? This thing that's happening right here in your office? Right now in your life?" His voice roughened. "I want it."

"Please," she begged. "You have to leave."

"Leave?" He laughed, disbelieving. "Look at me, Leigh— Doctor—whatever the hell I'm supposed to call you! Take a good look at my face, and then tell me you don't know what's going on. Tell me you don't know what you're doing . . . to me."

He held her with his gaze, boring through every attempt she made to deny him. His eyes were black with frustration and desire, with sudden anguish. They held the banked rage of a man who was marked as different—as doomed—from the moment of his conception, a man who would never have what the sunrise promised.

Tears welled, swift and uncontrollable. "I'm sorry—"

She barely understood the apology or the emotion that came with it, but somehow she knew that she was the cause of his deepest frustration, that just by the fact of her fair skin and her privileged existence, she represented everything that was unattainable. Not to the photographer, who could undoubtedly have had any woman he wanted. She reminded Nick Montera of his past, of who he really was, the ex-con, the half-cast *vato* from the streets.

She blinked and a tear slid down her cheek.

He halted its path with his thumb, then scowled at the shiny wet streak it made as he drew it across his fingers. Some inner violence knotted his jaw muscle. "Is this for me, Doctor? Did I say something that touched your heart? Because that's all I need to know. All I *ever* need to know . . . is that I touched your heart."

His own eyes glittered, and Leigh knew the anguish of defeat. She couldn't fight this. There weren't any weapons known to mankind, not against this. His vulnerability was infinitely more powerful than his anger. "I can help you," she said. "But not this way."

"No, *this* way, goddammit. Just this way . . . Leigh, please."

He caressed her face and she closed her eyes for an instant, overcome by flaring tenderness. She could feel him shudder, and the longing that cut through her made her want desperately what she had no right to want. Him. It took her breath away, the wanting. It made her shake.

On impulse she feathered his lips with her fingertips, afraid of what he might do, yet unable to stop herself.

"Jesus, you touch me and I get hard," he admitted, his voice savaged by emotion. "I think about you and I get hard."

Leigh wasn't prepared for the ferocity of his response. His pain and desolation were shadowy, beautiful in the same way that his photographs were. With no more warning than a soft groan, he cupped her under her arms and lifted her to him, and though every right-thinking instinct she possessed shouted at her to resist, she couldn't. He was too swift, too strong. He seemed empowered by a bodily force that wanted to dominate everything else in his world—and hers—all other concerns. He had taken control in some wild, thrilling way, and he wouldn't be denied.

"I want you," he whispered. "Like that fierce black animal in your test. And I want you that way, the way he wanted her."

He pinned her to the wall, and she responded involuntarily. Her spine arched deeply as he bent to kiss her. The feel of his fingers curving her throat brought a sigh to her lips and filled her mouth with his name. His thighs burned into hers.

His mouth was the softest thing she'd ever known, his body the hardest. But it was his touch that dominated her senses. She couldn't think, she couldn't do anything but soften under the steel will of his hands.

There were sounds outside, traffic noises coming up from the street below—horns and engines revving. Traces of macadamia-nut coffee lingered in the air, on his breath. But Leigh was so absorbed in the sensations generated by the touch of their bodies, she couldn't focus on anything else.

The rough rhythm of his heart commanded her total concentration for a moment. His biceps crowded her breast, and she wanted to know—suddenly she *had* to know—if it was possible for human flesh to be that hard. When she touched him, the soft snarl of his pleasure echoed in her head.

"I've been waiting all my life," he said.

His movements took on an urgency as he tugged her blouse free of her skirt and insinuated his hands inside her clothing. His touch brought gooseflesh to her bare skin. She followed it avidly with her mind, aware of every new incursion. When he stroked down her back and cupped her buttocks, she felt a wild surge of desire to have him inside her. She wanted the initiation that only he could give her. She wanted the sweetness, the *hell,* all of it.

"Have you ever done it against the wall, Doctor?"

Leigh flushed. The question was crude, and as she struggled to answer it he pressed his fingers to her lips. "Don't," he said roughly. "Don't say it. I don't want to know. I can hardly stand the thought of you with anyone else. Jesus!"

Confusion tightened Leigh's throat.

"I can't share you." He gripped her face, his thumbs curving into her cheeks. "I have to be the only one."

She shook her head, bewildered.

"Say my name, Leigh . . . call me Nick. *Say it.*"

"Nick—" She caught her lower lip between her teeth, refusing to reveal any more of the turmoil that was welling inside her. "Why are you doing this? What's wrong?"

"Nothing's wrong. I want you . . . I've always wanted you. From the moment I saw you. God, you were beautiful, but so far beyond my reach. I was a stupid, romantic kid—"

Leigh braced her hands against his arms. "What are you talking about?"

"What is it?" His expression clouded as he returned her searching stare. "What did I say?"

"You said you were a kid. You've only known me a few weeks, Nick. How could you have been a kid?"

She pressed back, and he gripped her tighter.

"Wait a minute," he said, seeming confused. "I didn't realize I'd said it. Maybe I got lost in time for a moment."

His awkward smile brought her a twist of pain. And though she didn't say it aloud, the question that tore through her thoughts was a damning one. *What other woman did you want all those years ago? Who, Nick? Jennifer?*

"Leigh, wait," he said, catching hold of her wrists. "Let's talk about this." His silver bracelet flashed in the light from the window.

"Let me go—" She tried to twist away, but a tearing pain made her lurch toward him. The bracelet was caught between their arms and the raised head of the snake dug into her flesh as she struggled to free herself.

"Look what you've done!" Her arm flew up as he released her. There was a reddened weltlike mark where the bracelet had gouged her inner wrist.

"Leigh?"

He reached for her, but she rebuffed his attempt to help.

"I'm all right," she insisted, clutching herself and moving away from him. She'd just begun to realize what had happened and how serious it truly was. She'd been moved by his pain, and she'd responded to him in a human, empathetic way. But she'd gone dangerously beyond the bounds of her professional duties. She was the trained therapist and that made her responsible for whatever happened between them, even if he initiated it. It was her obligation to safeguard the subject's welfare, even if that meant fending off his inappropriate sexual overtures. She should never, ever, have allowed Nick to think she would respond to his advances. She had failed in her duties, and if this incident were to be reported to the Committee on Ethical Standards, she could have her license taken away.

"Go, please," she told him. "Right now, do you understand? I want you to leave."

"No, Leigh, not this time. I'm not leaving you this time—"

His voice was jagged with emotion, but a sharp burst of static cut him off.

"Dr. Rappaport?" Nancy called over the intercom. "It's Mr. Reed on line one." Leigh stared at the blinking phone machine, aware that she was thoroughly disheveled and breathing heavily. A cold shudder ran through her as she walked to her desk.

"Nancy," she said, depressing the intercom button, "Mr. Montera is leaving. If he isn't out of this office by the time I hang up this phone, I want you to call security."

"Leigh, are you all right?" Nancy called back.

"I'm fine, Nancy. Just do as I say, please."

Leigh's finger was still jammed against the button when she heard her office door open and slam shut a moment later. *He had gone.* She should have been relieved, but the only thing she felt was a shaking lightness in her limbs and a crushing pressure in her chest. The horror of her professional lapse had already given way to a personal response, a tight, aching awareness of what he'd said and done. All that pain and passion inside Nick Montera was for some other woman, she realized, some romantic obsession from his past. It wasn't Leigh Rappaport he wanted. She was simply the current incarnation of the fantasy, but probably any well-bred blonde would do.

Sometime later, still standing alongside her desk, Leigh realized that her pain was turning to anger, but it was mostly directed at herself. She could hardly breathe she was in such agony. He'd done it to her again, and she had allowed it. He'd lured her like a starving child to a feast and then sprung the trap. She had sensed his deep hostility toward her from the beginning, and yet she'd opened herself to it, to him. How could she have let that happen? Was she having a breakdown? Was she crazier than Nick Montera himself?

She quelled the shaking in her throat, summoning whatever reserves of strength she had left. She had to resolve this situation immediately and there was only one way to do it. The blinking light on her phone reminded her that Dawson was still on hold. If he was unhappy about being kept waiting, she was sure he would be even less pleased with the topics she had in mind for their dinner conversation.

How did one talk to a naked man without looking down?

Leigh pondered that predicament as she sat on the edge of Dawson's bed, trying to avoid eye contact with his nether regions while he toweled off from a quick shower. It wasn't that she hadn't seen her fiancé naked before. But with her being so busy lately and Dawson embarking on his reelection bid, their relationship had taken a platonic turn.

She'd almost forgotten what his private parts looked like, and it was a little disconcerting to be reminded so blatantly now. Especially when she had other things on her mind.

"Are you sure you don't have time, Dawson?" she asked as he dried his sandy-blond hair with a plush black towel. "Not even for a cup of coffee? I was hoping we could talk."

"Can't, Leigh. I told you I'm keynoting the United Way fund-raiser tonight. I'm late as it is." He flung the towel away, reached for his hair dryer, and bent over.

Leigh averted her eyes. She needed his attention, not an anatomy lesson! She had several crucial things to talk about, one being her conversation with Paulie Cooper and the other her disturbing encounter with Montera. She was not looking forward to discussing the latter. She had no intention of conveying the details, but Dawson would need adequate notice that she wanted to be taken off the Montera case so that he could replace her.

Leigh's sigh reflected the heaviness that had settled on her from that afternoon's ordeal. While the hair dryer droned like a hive of angry bees, she glanced around Dawson's newly redecorated bedroom suite. The bath was set off in a huge open alcove where a Jacuzzi tub and shower sat rather grandly on a black marble pedestal, backed by a dramatic wall of glass bricks.

Leigh ran her hand over the bed's goosedown comforter, a silky fabric with a gold-and-black plaid design. Dawson had recently had his entire condo redone in neo-moderne. He'd picked out all the fabrics and designs himself, and Leigh had to admit that he'd done a beautiful job. The furnishings were in black and cream, accented by sprays of red poppies and warm gold picture frames. He had exquisite taste for a man, much more sophisticated and avant-garde than her own. She gravitated toward low-maintenance houseplants and garage-sale terrariums, populated with dozing turtles.

"How's the Montera evaluation coming?" Dawson asked as he switched off the hair dryer and traded it for his Water Pik.

"I tested him today," Leigh answered.

"Great! Pray God he checks out a raving psychopath. We're going to need plenty of firepower going into the trial. The press will have a field day if my office loses another big one, especially with an election coming up. They're still kicking my butt over the Menendez thing."

"Actually, I was going to talk to you about Montera."

"Hold it, Leigh!" Dawson stabbed his toothbrush toward the TV, which was flickering soundlessly in the Mute mode. "It's the stock reports. Would you check Equinox for me while I brush my teeth? Thanks, babe."

"Equinox?" Numbers and symbols scrolled by on a black band at the bottom of the screen. Leigh squinted at the set. "What do you want me to check?"

"The close."

"Would Equinox be shortened to E-Q-N-X, Dawson? Looks like, hmmm—twelve and five eights? Does that sound right?"

Dawson jackknifed up from the sink, his mouth full of foaming green toothpaste. "Twelve and five eights?" he gurgled. "I just dropped a bundle!"

Leigh was apologetic. "Maybe I read it wrong?"

"Keep watching," he spluttered. "It'll come 'round again."

She cast a baleful eye toward the TV set, absently aware of what looked like a camera lens protruding from the open drawer of a cabinet in Dawson's entertainment unit. Mildly curious, she might have investigated further if she hadn't been so intent on what she'd come to speak to him about.

"Dawson, this is *important,*" she said, determined to get his attention one way or another. Since Nick Montera didn't seem to interest him, perhaps someone else would. "I had another visit from that woman—Paulie Cooper, the model."

Dawson took a swig of water, rinsed out his mouth, and spit. "I took care of it," he said, grabbing a hand towel to blot away the remaining dobs of green. "I put an investigator on the Jack Taggart thing, and the guy checks out. He's got an alibi for the night of the murder that's watertight as a frog's ass. He was on duty."

Leigh felt a quick clutch of despair over that news. Apparently she had very much wanted to believe that Jack Taggart was the culprit. Well, of course she did. Everything would have been less complicated that way, she told herself. She could have set the case aside, dismissed it from her mind.

Dawson was now giving his jawline a quick once-over with an electric razor while he kept one eye on the TV. It rather surprised her that he had so little modesty about his body. They'd met at an Art Council function and started dating seriously three years ago, but she'd never known him to parade around naked. Maybe he was just distracted.

"Why don't you put something on?" she suggested.

"Why don't you take something off?" He winked at her. "You know my motto. Always room for Jell-O."

Dawson had once jokingly equated the squishy, squeaky sounds of congealed gelatin to sex, and since then any reference to the rubbery stuff usually meant he was in the mood. Not terribly romantic, and Leigh was reasonably certain he was kidding now, but just to be on the safe side, she held her forefinger to her nose and sneezed delicately.

"Not again?" he said in mock terror, briefly wrenching his eyes from the TV set. "Maybe you should get an allergy test, Leigh."

"Maybe I'm allergic to you," she murmured, knowing he wasn't listening. He'd already refixated on the tube. "Dawson, I didn't come here to talk about Jack Taggart." She left the bed and raised her voice for good measure. "Paulie Cooper said something that disturbed me a great deal."

"Really? What was that?"

Having dispensed with the razor, Dawson turned to his portable valet, where he'd laid out his clothing. He slipped on his briefs and a T-shirt, then seated himself on the cushioned bench to pull on his argyle socks. "Where the hell is Equinox?" he muttered, peering at the TV screen.

Leigh was momentarily distracted by the object she'd seen in the open drawer of his cabinet. Standing had given her a better vantage point. It wasn't a camera, she realized. It was a camcorder. She wasn't aware that Dawson had ever used one, or that he even owned one. "Dawson, when did you get—"

"Shhhh, Leigh, just a minute."

Leigh drew in a breath, preparing to take her life in her hands as she stepped in between him and his pipeline to Wall Street.

"Leigh! What are you doing?" He craned his neck to one side, then the other, trying to see around her. "If I'm about to be a pauper, at least let me watch it happen."

Leigh stood her ground. "Paulie Cooper said you'd once had a relationship with Jennifer Taryn. Is that true?"

Dawson yanked on one sock, then the other, clearly disgruntled. It wasn't until he stood to put on his shirt and had one arm in a sleeve that he stopped suddenly, jerked around, and stared at her. "Paulie Cooper said *what*?"

Congratulations, Leigh. You got his attention at last. She repeated the model's comment, watching carefully for Dawson's reaction. When it came to body language, she knew the signs of evasiveness. And even if she hadn't, her intuition was telling her there was some connection between the murder victim and Dawson that went beyond the bounds of this case.

"I knew her," he explained, shrugging into his formal shirt, "but only in a professional way." Taking particular care, he lined the starched placket up and snapped his shirttails into place before starting to button up. "I was clerking for the DA's office when she testified against Montera. I interviewed her, several times."

"I had no idea you'd worked on that case. Why didn't you tell me?"

"I didn't realize I hadn't told you. It was tried twenty years ago. I can't talk about them all." He finished with his shirt, reached for his suit slacks, and moved around her to put them on. "Now, if you don't mind, I'd like to know if I'm going to be standing in a breadline tomorrow."

But Leigh did mind. "Paulie lived with Jennifer, Dawson," she said, moving once again into his field of vision. "They were roommates. She said you called at the apartment."

"I may have called her. So what? That wouldn't have been unusual. She was an eyewitness to a crime."

"No, this would have happened later, several years after the trial. Jennifer was working as a photographer's model. Why would you have called her then?"

He stepped into his pants, pulled them up swiftly, and fastened them before confronting her. "I wouldn't have," he said hotly, "and I *didn't*. What are you suggesting, Leigh?"

"I'm not suggesting anything. I'm just trying to find out why Paulie Cooper believes you had a relationship with Jennifer."

"Paulie Cooper is a woman who desperately wants publicity."

"Yes, perhaps—"

"You'd take her word over mine?"

"I'm not taking anyone's word, Dawson. I'm just trying to understand what happened."

"*Nothing* happened. Oh, shit, Leigh, get out of the way! There it is! Equinox, twenty-four and a half." He ducked around her and let out a groan of relief. "I'm still solvent! You must have been reading something else, maybe Equintex?"

He walked to the valet, whisked his tux jacket off the valet, and put it on. Grinning raffishly, he stepped into his patent leather dress shoes, took a look at himself in the mirror, and threw out an arm. "So what have we learned from this little adventure, Leigh? That we mustn't jump to conclusions until we have all the information, right?"

What we've learned from this little adventure, Leigh thought, is that Dawson Reed is not being entirely forthcoming on the subject of Jennifer Taryn.

He fastened his tux jacket, straightened the lapels, and walked to her, affection brimming in his gray eyes. "Can you stay until I get back? I miss you, Leigh, I do. We haven't had much time together lately."

She was surprised and touched, but the day's events had exhausted her. "I don't think so, Dawson. I'm dragging."

One of the combs that held her hair had come loose. He gave it a little nudge to secure it, then caressed her face. "Sorry about dinner," he said. "There's some sushi in the fridge. Help yourself. And I picked up some of that ice cream you love, the green stuff. Gotta go."

As he dove into his trench coat and headed for the door, Leigh smiled bleakly. That was Dawson—rushed, but thoughtful. It was impossible for her to believe that he was keeping anything really serious from her, though she felt quite sure he hadn't told her everything. Still, if she was unsettled about how quickly he'd dismissed Paulie Cooper's remarks, she was far more concerned about the news she hadn't yet given him.

Leigh found the television remote on Dawson's nightstand and switched off the set, glad to darken the thing. She didn't even glance down on her way out of the bedroom as she passed the open drawer of the cabinet with its curious object. Her thoughts were firmly fixed on Frango Mint ice cream, refuge of the troubled mind.

CHAPTER
·· FIFTEEN ··

LIFE'S A BITCH and then you die.

Deep stuff, Nick thought, contemplating one of the many placards that framed a neon beer sign behind the bar of the Goat Hill Tavern. The Reseda watering hole was a veritable toxic dump of bumper-sticker wisdom. The coffee was just plain toxic. Nick had been taking up space on one of the faux goatskin barstools for the better part of the evening, nursing a mug of the stuff that looked and tasted like it had been drained from the fossil sludge of the La Brea Tar Pits.

At least he could take some small comfort in the knowledge that he was in the right place. If you were searching for the meaning to your sorry existence—or just wanted to get sideways—you could do either with impunity at the Goat Hill.

Tonight Nick didn't give a rat's ass about the meaning of existence, but the idea of getting sideways—now, that held some appeal. There was a fist beating against the inside of his skull that felt as if it could crack bones. As always, the pain had started at the base of his skull and flared out like a football being drop-kicked. He could remember times when it had spiked so violently, he'd blacked out.

Grimacing, he dug his thumb into the excruciatingly tender muscles at the base of his neck—and thanked Los Coyotes, phantoms of his tortured youth, for the pain. His parents had moved to San Ramone from Reseda when he was six, and from the day they arrived, he'd been stalked by the Coyotes, one of several *vato loco* gangs in the area. His father's boozy pride about the Monteras being descended from Spanish conquistadores and his Anglo mother's blond hair and blue eyes had made them objects of suspicion, and eventually hatred, in the barrio. Nick had taken the brunt of it.

It had all come to a head with his mother's tragic death. Grief and guilt had driven Nick to confront the gang, a reckless act that nearly got him killed. He would have died on the streets of San Ramone if not for the mysterious old man who had called the paramedics. When Nick woke up in the hospital, he was clutching a silver snake bracelet in his hand and the old man's words echoed in his head: "The serpent will save you."

Nick had taken several vicious kicks to the head during the brawl, one of which had nearly broken his neck. His father had tried to tell him he'd hallucinated the old man, that the bracelet must have belonged to one of the gang members who attacked him. But Nick had believed the silver snake was a talisman. Perhaps he still did. He'd worn it religiously ever since.

Nick glanced at the beautiful, evil thing coiled on his wrist with a sense of irony. The serpent was supposed to save him? More likely it would be his ticket to hell, and the hoary old man would be there to greet him. Satan himself.

"Warm that up?" the bartender asked, hovering with a fresh pot of prehistoric ooze.

"Sure." Nick swung his cup the man's way. "Goose it with some Gold, would you, Harve?"

Nick could easily have waded his way through a fifth of Cuervo Gold by now, and probably would have if not for one of the conditions of his bail. He'd been ordered not to imbibe. The presiding judge hadn't bothered to explain his reasons, but Nick suspected it had as much to do with his ethnicity as with his criminal record. To the majority of blue suits in the legal system, a former barrio kid was automatically perceived as either homicidal, larcenous, or a liquored-up loser. Often, all three.

A vintage Motorola hung in the space just above the bartender's head. The eleven o'clock news was playing, and Nick's attention was drawn to a noisy group of reporters clustered in the lobby of the Biltmore Hotel. They were jostling for room and shoving their microphones at a sandy-haired, square-jawed type, who looked suspiciously like the district attorney.

"Mr. Reed!" one of the reporters shouted. "Any truth to the rumor that you're going for the death penalty in the Montera case?"

It *was* L.A.'s esteemed DA, Nick realized. Dawson Reed flashed a cosmetically bonded smile that spoke of desperation masquerading as supreme confidence. Another crooked politician up for reelection, Nick concluded. Poor dumb schmuck actually wanted to be a civil servant, apparently.

"I never comment on rumors," Reed said with his characteristic dispassion. "But I can tell you this. If the trial were held today, we would have more than enough evidence for a resounding conviction. Nick Montera is as guilty as original sin, folks, and the people can—and will—prove it."

"Your win/loss ratio's taken a beating lately," one of the pack called out. "What about the Michael Jackson fiasco?"

"And what about the Menendez brothers?" another shouted. "Is this a political maneuver? Are you going after Montera to save face and win back voter confidence?"

Reed's smile lost its warmth. "The criminal justice system is not a popularity contest, ladies and gentlemen. My office tries every case on its own merits. Whether we'd lost the last ten cases, or won the last twenty, we would still be pursuing a vigorous prosecution of Mr. Montera."

The reporters had mentioned a couple of highly visible celebrity trials, cases that Reed's office had screwed up royally—and very publically. Nick might have been pleased to see Dawson Reed take the heat under other circumstances, but he didn't want a bloodletting at his own expense. The prosecutor was obviously under tremendous pressure to get a conviction, and Nick didn't relish being a sacrificial lamb on the altar of Dawson Reed's career.

The crowd turned restless again. Heads began to swivel. Shouts went up. "Mr. Satterfield! Over here!"

Nick watched as his own attorney was rudely summoned by the pack of reporters. Interesting that Satterfield and the DA traveled in the same social circles, Nick observed. Interesting, but not surprising.

Microphones were launched like missiles toward the defense attorney. "The DA says he's got an open-and-shut case against Montera. Can you comment?"

Alec Satterfield perused the pale moons of his manicured fingernails before answering the slavering pack. It was a delaying tactic that allowed the throng time to lob more deafening questions, but he ignored them all. Eerily cool in the midst of chaos, he looked as if he'd been born in black-tie apparel with a headful of wavy raven hair, and not a one of those hairs out of place.

Nick wished the man was half as good as he looked.

"With all due respect," Satterfield said, "I've seen the prosecutor's ammunition, and he's shooting blanks. His evidence is circumstantial, his eyewitness is on probation for driving under the influence. I'm not worried. I'm eager."

Nick's head lifted. Satterfield clearly loved the opportunity to shine—and to attack the prosecutor's case. In Nick's opinion, it was a lowest-common-denominator approach, the strategy of last resort when you didn't have a good defense. If your own evidence sucked rocks, throw stones at theirs. If your witnesses were drunks, throw bottles.

Nick didn't like the plan, but at least it kept them in the game. He rubbed his thumb against his mug, caught a whiff of the coffee, and wondered what the hell the bartender had spiked the stuff with. Paint thinner?

"Why do they call you the vampire bat, Mr. Satterfield?" someone was asking.

Nick glanced up just in time to see Satterfield's eyes gleam with malicious intent. "Perhaps you should ask Mr. Reed. He's come up against me before. My client is innocent, and that's all that matters. We will prove that beyond a shadow of a doubt."

Satterfield's disembodied smile lingered, ghostlike, as Nick's own image flashed up on the screen. It was a piece of video taken the night of his arrest. Nick was inside the police car, peering out through the window, and the camera was focused on his face. His eyes were metallic silver, gleaming with rage at the world. His hair spumed around his face, as dark and swollen as a rampaging river.

"*God.*" The word was harshened with disbelief. Nick stared with narrowed eyes, observing himself as if he were someone else, an innocent bystander at the scene of an accident. That creature on the screen had some kind of frightening inner life, an aura that made him look capable of anything. Even truly evil people rarely thought of themselves in those terms. Charlie Manson didn't believe he was a monster, and certainly

Nick had never thought of himself that way. But for that one instant he had seen evil. He'd seen a monster—and so would everyone else who saw it. If that piece of footage continued to run, he was a dead man. He wouldn't have a chance with a jury trial.

Fortunately none of the bar's dozen or so customers seemed to be aware of the television, or of their doomed fellow patron, Nick discovered as he glanced around. He'd always managed to feel anonymous at the Goat Hill, which was why he was hanging out here now instead of going home. His canyon studio looked like a public campground since the paparazzi had figured out where he lived.

He took a drink of the spiked coffee and had to bite down to swallow it. The stuff was foul, but then so was his state of mind. The damned had little reason to be charming. And even less reason to be charmed. Life was a bitch and then you died, according to the wall. But if he really was going to die, there were a few things he wanted to do first. He'd never walked naked into the sea or eaten a pomegranate. Hell, just once he wanted to be able to face a sunrise.

A wave of longing hit him, colliding with the breath he was trying to take. Sweet Christ, there were so many things he wanted to do. He wanted to run a marathon and sing opera in the shower. Crazy things. But there was only one wish that really mattered. He wanted to steal a woman's heart before he died. Her heart: Leigh's.

Somewhere in the background, a button was depressed on a jukebox and a record dropped. It was a song from the eighties that had always made him think of a woman being stalked by her lover. The male singer vowed to watch every move the woman made, every breath she took. Every *heart* you break, Nick thought, paraphrasing the lyric. I'll be there, watching you.

She'd thought he meant someone else. Maybe he had. Maybe she was more fantasy than reality to him—Snow White, Cinderella, and Claudia Schiffer all rolled into one. But it was Leigh's blond hair that had streamed like silk through his fingers. And it was Leigh he could still taste on his lips. She was macadamia nuts and gourmet coffee and sweet fuckable woman. It tore at him that he would never know the pleasure of having her naked in his arms. That he would never feel her beautiful legs wrapped around him, her body melting into his.

As he bowed his head and rested it against his fingertips, he was aware that someone had moved onto the barstool next to him. Without looking, he knew it was a woman. He could tell by her scent, the swish of her clothing, the click of her fingernails on the bar. At least the serpent hadn't failed him there. He still had his perceptual powers when it came to the opposite sex. Women were a sixth sense to him. He absorbed their presence as if they were made of essence rather than flesh, he felt their needs as an empath would, responding from intuition and viscera more than reason. He knew them through and through.

And he knew this woman. There were many clues, including the fragrance she wore, a rose geranium oil. He'd chosen it for her. But it wasn't perfume that convinced him of her identity. It was the fact that she hadn't yet spoken. And more importantly, she hadn't touched him. She knew how he reacted to someone coming up behind him, someone touching him without warning. She knew what the monster was capable of.

She would wait until he acknowledged her, which told him that her presence next to him on the barstool was no accident.

His first impression as he turned to her was that she had changed the color of her hair. Then he realized it was the lights that made her fiery red tresses look black. "I thought we agreed not to do this, Paulie," he said.

Her smile was rueful. "I had to see you, Nick. Just to assure myself that you were okay."

"Are you assured?"

"No, you look like hell."

Paulie Cooper reached up and feathered her fingers through his hair, brushing it lightly off his forehead. Her expression was a revelation of tenderness, naked vulnerability, and pure female calculation. He knew she would do anything she could to save him, whatever it was in her power to do. He also knew she had no intention of honoring their agreement to keep some distance between them. She would cross the line he'd drawn. She already had in countless ways, and that meant only one thing . . . she couldn't be trusted.

• • •

"Leigh, the man is dangerous. If his test scores are any indicator, he not only killed Jennifer Taryn, he probably killed ten more like her."

Nancy Mahoney had tucked herself into the chair facing Leigh's desk. Her knees were drawn up to her chin and her feet crisscrossed at the ankles, creating a pretzellike configuration that most advanced yogis would have found challenging.

Leigh was too busy pacing the length of her small office to appreciate her assistant's flexibility. She had come in this morning with just one thing on her mind—to resolve her dilemma about Nick Montera. She'd been up all night, reliving the prior day's incident and torturing herself with the need to explain her behavior. Her breach of conduct might have been human, but it was grossly irresponsible. She was a licensed therapist, but she wasn't acting like one. The only recourse she had left was to determine what her professional obligations were in this case and act accordingly.

Fortunately Nancy was a terrific sounding board. Her assistance on Leigh's manuscript had been invaluable, and she was a grad student in psychology, familiar with a wide range of diagnostic techniques. But even though Leigh felt comfortable discussing Nick's test results with Nancy, she had not revealed the true nature of her encounter with him. That information was too explosive to share with anyone at this point.

The room began to feel smaller as Leigh paced, and the carpet's paisley pattern seemed to writhe, snakelike, beneath her feet. "I know what the scores indicate," she said, turning to her assistant. "But tests are fallible, especially the projective techniques."

Nancy perked up, suspending an eyebrow in mock horror. "Fallible? Not the Johnson-Rappaport Art-Insight Survey!"

Leigh smiled, aware that it was the first time she'd let down her guard in days. Her work with Carl Johnson had been aimed at establishing quantitative norms for their test as a basis for interpretation. But their true goal had been to design a diagnostic technique that could distinguish between latent fantasy wishes and the overt expression of those wishes. In other words, they wanted to do what no other psychometric test had been able to do with any degree of accuracy—label and predict behavior. They had succeeded in the former, to the accolades of their colleagues in the field. Whether or not they had succeeded in the latter was still a matter of debate, but their work was widely regarded as the standard against which other such tests were measured.

"Okay, but what about the personality inventory?" Nancy countered. "That's an objective test. It's standardized and computer-scored, so there's no chance of interpreter bias or error. He came out with elevated T-scores all over the place—paranoia, sociopathy, and two of the three validity scales. That's about as deviant as you get, Leigh."

"True, but those scores can be skewed by life experiences—" Leigh was responding more passionately than she'd meant to, but some sense of injustice had set her off. "Nick was raised in a barrio. He did time in prison—not exactly an environment conducive to the development of social skills, you have to admit. A convict survives by his wits, and for him, paranoia is completely justified. People *are* trying to kill him."

Nancy slid down in the chair. "I don't care, Leigh. I think the guy's a clear and present danger."

Leigh resumed her circling, her gaze drawn again to the carpet's hypnotic design. *Vipera,* she thought, remembering the Spanish word for snake. She could have been walking over a sea of vipers, yet she was strangely attracted to the coiled power. Some things in life were irresistibly compelling—erotic signs and symbols, archetypal men. What dark part of us did they call to? she wondered. And why did we have to answer?

Finally she stopped and sighed, unable to deny what had become painfully apparent. "So do I, Nancy."

Nancy unwound herself. "You think he's dangerous, too? Then how can you not testify? It's your ethical duty."

"For the very reason that you and I are debating. I no longer trust my objectivity where Nick Montera is concerned. I'm afraid I'm becoming . . . emotionally involved."

A smile crept into Nancy's worried expression. "I'm with you there. He is sinfully attractive."

Leigh went to push up the sleeves of her burgundy cardigan, then remembered the bruise on her wrist. "Yes, sinful," she agreed softly, "and perhaps very sick."

"I'm with you there, too. What are you going to do?"

"I don't know." Leigh's intuition was at war with the over-whelming evidence of his guilt. The courts strongly preferred evidence over hunches. So did she.

"He's not psychotic," she said, talking more for her own benefit than for Nancy's. "He has no difficulty distinguishing right from wrong, but all of the tests indicate sociopathic tendencies. And who else but a sociopath would try something as reckless as arranging a murder victim's body the way he did?" She drew in a breath. "So why don't I believe it?"

"What do you mean?"

"I just don't believe he did it, Nancy, I never have. Despite his tests, despite the evidence, despite everything."

Nancy was staring at her oddly. "Are you sure?"

"Yes . . . why?"

"Didn't you hear yourself? You said only a sociopath would arrange a victim's body the way he did. *He* did. That is what you said, isn't it?"

Leigh looked away from the carpet, her vision swimming with the dizzying design. She felt as if she were floating. Suddenly she needed to get out of this small, suffocating room. She needed air.

"Are you okay, Leigh?" Nancy sprang up as if to help her. "What's wrong? You look like you're about to faint."

"Exactly," Leigh agreed, fingertips pressed to her damp forehead. "And that's why I'm taking myself off this case. I'm falling apart."

"Have you told Dawson?"

"Told Dawson what?" a man asked.

Startled at the sound of her fiancé's voice, Leigh lurched around. Dawson was standing in the doorway of her office, his overcoat hanging loosely on his shoulders, as if he'd put it on in a hurry. How much had he heard? she wondered. She couldn't decide if he looked angry, or if she was simply projecting her own guilt.

"What are you doing here?" she asked.

"We had a lunch date, didn't we?"

Leigh checked her watch, astonished at how much time had passed.

"Did I hear you correctly, Leigh?" Dawson asked. "You're going to take yourself off the Montera case? Why would you do that at this late date?"

"Uh . . . excuse me?" Nancy waved the way a child might who was trying to get her feuding parents' attention. "Why don't I leave and let you two discuss this?"

"No, Nancy—stay!" Leigh insisted. The smile she flashed at Dawson was apologetic. "Nancy and I aren't finished yet."

Dawson looked Leigh up and down, taking in her pale, moist skin and the way she'd clasped her hands. "What's wrong?" he asked. "Are you having a problem with the evaluation? Is Montera giving you trouble?"

"No, it's not that. We were just discussing his test results. I think they may reflect his deprived background more than any truly deviant behavior."

"His deprived *background*?" He gaped at her as if she'd lost her mind. "Are you serious?"

"Yes." She clipped off the word. "Very serious."

"And that's how you'd testify?"

"Yes, possibly—I just don't know, Dawson." She steadied herself against the credenza behind her, aware that lack of sleep was catching up with her. She was exhausted, running on nerves. "That's the point," she told him. "You need someone who can testify with conviction. Someone who believes in their interpretation, and I'm not that person."

"What about your own test? Did you give him that one?"

She indicated she had, although it wasn't entirely true. She couldn't very well say that she'd become too flustered to finish the test. "It indicated some eroticized thematic content."

"Eroticized as in sexual? That's all?"

"Well, there were some indications of problems with impulse control."

"Impulse control? What does that mean? Violent tendencies?"

"Yes, perhaps." Perhaps? She almost laughed aloud. She'd witnessed the man's violent tendencies. She'd been the *object* of them. Why was she downplaying them now?

As she glanced at the rug again her mind flashed an image of a huge snake coiling itself around a woman's limbs, climbing up her body. Perspiration filmed the back of her neck and a cold chill shivered across her shoulders.

"Dawson," she said abruptly, "do you think we could postpone our lunch? Nancy and I really do need to finish up here. She wants to leave early today."

Leigh felt a moment's panic as Dawson glanced at Nancy as if for confirmation. She had just lied to him and made her assistant a co-conspirator. Fortunately, Nancy's noncommittal shrug seemed to satisfy him.

Dawson whipped off his raincoat and draped it over his arm. His hand, just visible beneath the material, had curled into a fist. "I seem to have lost my appetite anyway."

"I'm sorry," Leigh said, immediately contrite.

"Hey, don't give it a thought. I shouldn't be wasting my time on things like food anyway. I have to find another expert witness, don't I?" His smile was brittle and sarcastic.

Leigh didn't know what to say. He glanced at both her and her assistant as if they had somehow betrayed him, then turned and walked out of her office. Nancy, who'd fallen into the chair and curled into a ball again, was looking very perturbed.

After a moment Leigh turned to the window, to the terrarium with its thick glass walls. Her pets, as Nick had called them, had an amazing ability to withdraw and protect themselves. It might be a rigid strategy, but it worked for them more often than not . . . as long as no one upended them.

She had done the right thing, she told herself.

CHAPTER
·· SIXTEEN ··

A GLASS OF blush zinfandel and her trusty television remote. Those were Leigh's only friends at two in the morning on this long and lonely night. Somehow they would have to get her through the rest of it. Ensconced in her "commodious, turned-wood Victorian four-poster," which was how the antique store's ad had described her one and only indulgence in bedroom furniture, she was tuned to *In a Lonely Place,* an old favorite with Humphrey Bogart and Gloria Grahame.

Exhausted as she was, the film classic should have lulled her to sleep the moment she settled her head into the decadent luxury of red panne velvet pillows, piled three deep. But even combined with wine and tasseled cushions, Bogart couldn't do the trick tonight.

The television remote was cradled in Leigh's open palm and her thumb roamed the buttons restlessly. For the last hour she'd been Ping-Ponging between the movie and the news channel, but she had just this moment ordered herself to stop. She didn't *care* whether or not they were talking about the Montera trial on CNN. She'd taken herself off that case, and all she really wanted to do was lose herself in this excellent old movie. She loved it when Grahame lit two cigarettes on the same smoldering match and handed one of them to Bogart. . . .

Or was that *Now Voyager* with Bette Davis and Paul Henreid?

Apparently she had her old movies confused.

All the more reason to watch this one, she told herself. She plumped the pillows behind her and snuggled determinedly into the bedding in search of a cool spot for her feet. It spoke well .of her new goosedown comforter that she was almost uncomfortably warm, especially since she felt as if she'd spent most of her life in cryogenic suspension.

Just as Leigh was getting herself perfectly arranged and reasonably content, the station broke for a commercial. First a breathless bevy of "party girls" tried to persuade her to call their 900-number, and then Slim Whitman serenaded her with the latest collection of his all-time greatest hits.

"Shit." Leigh's arm sprang up as if it had wires attached. Aiming the remote, she relegated Slim and his quivering falsetto to microwave oblivion. The Channel button rocketed her back to CNN.

"What efforts are being made to locate Paula Cooper?" the news commentator was asking as the camera panned to a heavyset fortyish man Leigh recognized as one of Dawson's deputy district attorneys.

"There is no formal effort to locate her as such," the deputy DA said. "We'd simply like her to make herself available to testify. Of course, we'll track her down and subpoena her if we have to."

Leigh held down the volume button with her thumb. Something had happened to Paulie Cooper? She couldn't determine what it was. She'd come in too late in the interview, but it was clear that Dawson's office now wanted Paulie to testify when they hadn't seemed terribly interested before.

"What if you can't locate her to serve the subpoena?" the reporter probed.

The attorney brushed off the question with a bland smile. "We'll find her."

Leigh listened as the reporter quickly summed up, but all she could make out was that the DA's office had been trying to find Paulie Cooper and couldn't track her down through normal channels. The news report must have been taped earlier that day, Leigh realized, because the men were standing in front of the L.A. County Courthouse in what looked like broad daylight.

Perplexed, she threw back the covers and sat up. No point trying to sleep now. She might as well have taken a cold shower. There didn't have to be anything sinister about this, she reasoned, reaching for her robe. Paulie could have gone away for a few days without telling anyone. That was possible, but Leigh had her doubts. Paulie was too involved in Nick's upcoming trial—and very vocal about it. Perhaps someone didn't want her to testify?

Now, that was sinister.

I'm off the case, Leigh reminded herself as she buttoned up her robe. The white eyelet material was as wispy and insubstantial as her nightgown, but she'd decided to go down to her office to work and dressing seemed a wasted effort. If she was going to be up all night, she might as well get something done.

By the time she reached her office, her concern about Paulie Cooper had already been supplanted by a more immediate problem. She'd tried to reach Dawson all day, but he hadn't been available to take her calls, nor had he returned them. She regretted the way he'd learned of her decision not to testify. He was clearly disappointed and deeply concerned about the case, but her decision had been a professional one. It should have been respected on that basis. At least she knew it was the right choice. Almost any other expert witness would be more effective than she.

Once she'd stationed herself at her desk, she faced the problem of where to begin. Her personal and professional lives were hopelessly entangled, and the confusion had affected everything, even her manuscript. Her editor had wanted the book's focus to be on Nick, but that no longer seemed possible.

Absently she began to leaf through her case notebook until she found herself at his intake page. It was the first time she'd interviewed him and her notes brought it all back vividly. "What kind of game are you playing?" he'd asked her. She hadn't realized what he was doing until he'd drawn a snakelike circle around that very question in her notes. He was reading what she'd written about him.

The drawing had transfixed her that day, and now as she stared at it, she rotated her arm until she could see the vibrant bruise on the inside of her wrist. Pink and violet against her pale skin, it was oddly beautiful, more a flower than a serpent.

Fear touched her, raising gooseflesh. He had marked her, just as he had marked Jennifer Taryn. It was as distinctive as a signature. His signature. Leigh forgot to breathe as she stared at it. She was remembering something . . . a painting, a drawing? The answer forced a soft sound of recognition out of her. Wasn't there a picture card that she and Carl Johnson had decided not to include in their test because they couldn't agree on the symbolism?

She rose from the desk and went to her files. The unused cards were in a box at the back of the drawer, and she found the picture in question almost immediately. It was a charcoal drawing of a woman suspended in space, her head falling forward as if she were unconscious, her nude body ringed by a silver snake that was biting its own tail. The drawing was dated 1896, the artist was unidentified, but the picture had been titled *Woman*.

At first glance the image was ethereal, even lovely, and yet there was something disturbing about it. Leigh felt uneasy just looking at it. One detail in particular struck at the panic building in her heart. The snake was almost identical to Nick Montera's bracelet.

She dropped the picture in the box, shut the drawer, and stepped away from it. It had to be a coincidence. There was no other explanation, but she couldn't bring herself to go back and sit down at her desk. The agitation gathering inside her was familiar, like soft rain pattering against the roof, only now it was as noisy as a hailstorm.

Ghostlike, her reflection bounced back at her from the windows that made up one wall of her office. As she gazed at the phantom in white eyelet, she began to walk toward the image, hesitant, yet wanting to see herself more clearly, to resolve the distortions. But as she approached the mirrorlike surface she had a premonition that there was someone on the other side, someone watching her.

Her heart went crazy, hammering so hard it brought her to a stop. She couldn't go any closer. She'd had the feeling of being watched before, in this very room. And before that. The awareness of an unseen presence had been with her for years, since childhood. But it had been an increasingly powerful fantasy since she'd come to know Nick Montera. It *was* a fantasy, of course, only her imagination, but that didn't stop her vital signs from reacting as if the threat were real.

She turned from the window, wanting to stop the physical sensations—and knowing exactly what was at the root of it. Her erotic flashes were the product of a much earlier time. She couldn't have been more than thirteen, a budding adolescent, when she discovered one of her mother's male "protégés" watching her as she slipped out of her nightgown to take her morning shower. He was a young South American artisan to whom Leigh had been secretly attracted.

The bathroom door was a slider that wouldn't close all the way, and she realized he could have been watching her for some time without her knowing it, and perhaps on many other occasions. Her first reaction was paralyzing shock, but by the time she'd slipped inside the shower to hide herself, she'd already begun to quake with a strange and painful excitement. When she turned on the water, the faucet rattled and gave out a huge sigh, and the warm streams of water touched her body in ways she'd never noticed before.

He appeared at the door several times over the next few weeks, and his presence always left her trembling with confusion and inner turmoil. His watching awakened her imagination in countless ways, until the morning when she finally mustered the courage to look back at him. Nearly crippled by shyness, she raised her head and saw what he was doing, the way he was touching himself, the raw need glittering in his eyes.

The excitement had frozen inside her that day, its energy bound up in terrible conflict. She had never seen an aroused man before, and the sight of his exposed flesh, the carnality of it, was too much for her. The fragile flowering of her sensuality was replaced by shock, by guilt and shame. Her cry had brought her mother running, and the young man was booted unceremoniously from the great Kate Rappaport's studio.

"Why in the world would he want to spy on a gawky thirteen-year-old when there was an adult woman in the house?" Kate had wondered afterward, laughing with her artist friends. She was greatly perplexed and undoubtedly more upset at him for his preferences than for the way he'd violated her adolescent daughter's privacy.

Leigh had tried to block the incident from her mind, but she'd never been able to shut out the erotic flashes that still intruded on her thoughts at the most unlikely of times. In college she'd been drawn to the study of psychology initially to learn more about herself, but she'd soon found it easier and safer to lose herself in the analysis of others' problems.

Her learning-theory classes had taught her that the human nervous system was clever in the way it sought equilibrium, discharging excess impulse potential as if it were water overflowing a damn. Eventually she'd rationalized the libidinous flashes as nothing more than trapped energy seeking release, and she'd dismissed the entire incident as one of those childish episodes of experimentation, like playing doctor. It had eased her mind, but she'd never been able to deny that those forbidden thoughts had taken possession of her in a way that nothing else ever had in her life.

A quick shudder made her realize that she was standing exactly where she'd come to a halt, with her back to the window. It startled her that her foot was pivoted to the side and her hand was splayed across her stomach, almost as if she'd been caught in midflight. Very creative, Rappaport, she thought ironically. But enough procrastinating for one night. Get back to work.

The first thing she did as she sat down at her desk was to close her case notes and set them aside. That accomplished, she took a deep breath, opened the bottom drawer, and pulled out her abandoned manuscript. Nick Montera was no longer under her observation, so there was no justifiable reason to have him as the focus of her book.

Her only option now was to return to the original focus, which was to make the Art-Insight Survey accessible to the lay public through a simplified version of the test. She had initially balked at the idea, fearing all her painstaking work with Carl Johnson would be turned into some kind of party game, but her publisher had assured her that it would be an invaluable tool for those seeking personal insights, who didn't have the skill or the training to wade through an academic textbook.

She began to sort through the stack of manuscript pages, searching for where she'd left off in her revisions. But even as she found her place and set to work, she was unable to shake the feeling of another presence. Now it was more than the sense that she was being watched. Her awareness had taken on qualities that were almost physical. She could feel the pressure of the watcher's gaze, the heat of his interest. And she could feel one more thing, a kind of familiarity. Somehow she knew that he wasn't a stranger. What was more, she sensed all this with the same childlike certainty she'd had at thirteen, when her instincts had been purer and largely untouched by adult reason.

Back then she had looked at him. She'd given in to the impulse, and like Lot's wife she'd been turned into a pillar of salt. This time she wouldn't let herself break the spell.

Closing her eyes, she imagined that she was rising to her full height, her back delicately curved, her shoulders sloped forward as she unbuttoned her robe and let it fall into the chair. Cool air crept through the eyelet openings of her nightgown, awakening her bare skin like tiny fingers, soothing and exciting her at the same time.

She'd never been so aware of fabric, of texture. The wispy cotton billowed and fluttered against her body parts as if it were made of breezy air currents. The densely stitched eyelets brushed tender skin, abrading ever so slightly. It was wonderfully stimulating. A tiny shiver started in the base of her spine and fanned out gently, raising the soft hairs of her back and causing her breasts to tighten.

As the sensations deepened and intensified Leigh let go of the breath she was holding and opened her eyes. Her imagination wasn't enough, she realized. She wanted to do it. She wanted to live out the fantasy, to experience the sensations while knowing someone was there, watching her. The impulse was so powerful it was all she could do to resist it.

She reached for her book as if it were a lifeline, her fingers rigid as manuscript pages fanned through them and fell back into place. She had no idea what to do next. Her neck was filmed with perspiration, her mouth powder dry. She'd forgotten how to move. And even if she hadn't, the links of her spine were so tightly fused, she couldn't have.

She was as rigid as the day Nick Montera had come up behind her in her office . . . the day he'd whispered those insulting things, baiting her, waiting for her to respond to him. He hadn't known about her erotic experience as a young girl, but it wouldn't have mattered if he had. It didn't count.

It wasn't like this, like him. That boy wasn't a man . . . .

Have you ever wondered what it would be like to have a man want you that badly, Leigh?

Had he called her Leigh? Had he said that, her name? She couldn't remember now. But yes, she had wondered . . . all her life.

. . . to have him want you so badly he gets hard just looking at you?

No! She didn't want that. Why did he feel the need to use that kind of language, to shock her? She didn't want a man to respond to her that way. Not *any* man—There was only one man she wanted to look at her, to get hard for her. Just one.

I want you that badly. . . .

"Oh, God," she whispered.

Somehow, despite the unsteadiness of her limbs, Leigh rose from the chair. She could hardly catch her breath and she was trembling in every fiber, but the tiny pearl buttons of her robe seemed to fall away under her hopelessly clumsy fingers. And when she'd undone them all, the robe slid down her arms and fell to the chair in a graceful heap.

The sensations were exactly as she'd imagined, only much more powerful. She would never have believed her body could contain this much feeling. She felt as if she might fly apart from it. The cool air stealing through the eyelets of her gown teased her overheated skin and stung her senses awake. The fabric itself caressed her like feather boas, fluttering about her breasts until they were heavy with sensation and pleasurably tight at the nipples.

But it was the deeper tightening that compelled her.

She was being plucked and pierced in the most tender parts of her being. It could have been a needle stroking the soft, swollen lobe of her ear, searing her with hot excitement, filling her with the unbearable anticipation of being very gently pricked. Yes, it could have been that kind of sensation, but this was much deeper, much lovelier. With every breath the intensity built until she felt as if she were riding the crest that separated pleasure from its opposite.

Another guilty impulse overtook her and she reached down as if to touch herself. I'm not going to do anything, she assured herself as she drew up her nightgown, cool fingers whispering over hot skin. She just wanted to know what it felt like to be so aroused, to experience the physical sensations that were triggered when the body was this exquisitely responsive.

Her hand stole toward the soft blond curls, fingers searching. And then, all at once, she did know, and the sharp pleasure of it made her head snap up. She nearly choked on the sound that quavered in her throat. Her legs didn't want to hold her up, and the sweet, hot throb at the center of her being demanded that she do something more, whatever she could, to release the tension. Her fingers curled into her palms, and she doubled over in sweet agony. If there was a threshold that separated pleasure from pain, she had crossed it.

"This is crazy," she breathed. She was perspiring like a long-distance runner, shaking like a shock victim, and she didn't understand any of it. She was familiar with the physiology of sex, but this was much more profound. Adrenaline was flowing as if she'd barely averted an accident. She couldn't have been reacting to the man. That would make no sense. She hardly knew him. This was a response to something unresolved in herself. Nick Montera was a symbol, that was all. He represented some rite of passage she had yet to undergo.

As her breathing began to ease she tried to analyze what had happened. She wanted to analyze it, because then maybe she could stop feeling it! In many ways she was still that gawky thirteen-year-old, frozen in time, her sexuality held hostage by an encounter with the stark reality of an excited boy.

The fantasy about Montera was forcing her to deal with that blocked expression, to admit that it was something more than trapped energy. She was reexperiencing the young girl's feverish awakening because Leigh, the woman, had to relive that aborted experience before she could open herself to a woman's needs.

It wasn't him. It was what he represented—a way to free herself with someone as dark as the impulses that frightened her. It all made sense, perfect sense. She should have been able to set it aside . . . but none of her brilliant reasoning seemed to matter because the man himself and things he said to her kept flooding her senses.

Look at me, Leigh. Look at my face and tell me you don't know what you're doing to me.

What had she done to him? What could a gawky thirteen-year-old do to someone like him? All she could remember was what he'd done to her, how he'd lifted her to his mouth, the steel of his hands. All she could see in her mind was the picture he'd sketched, his hand caressing her throat, his lips at her ear, whispering to her, setting fire to her mind with the terrible things he could do to her.

Her legs had begun to shake and the dampness gathering on her skin was condensing, forming droplets. A tiny silver stream trickled down her throat, collecting in the heat between her breasts before it rolled down her midriff.

As she lifted the damp fabric of her nightgown away from her body, she realized that what the papers were saying about Nick Montera was true. He was a sorcerer. He was capable of totally beguiling a woman through some combination of sensitivity and sexual mastery. He had done it to her.

A chill took her, forcing a quick, violent shudder. Her body was wet, her nightgown damp. She let out a moan of despair at the condition she was in, and the sound startled her into laughter. What in the world had possessed her? Look at her!

Without a second thought, she stripped off her nightgown, tossed it away, and reached behind her for her robe. As she picked up the clothing she heard a tapping noise, like tree branches hitting a windowpane. Her head came up and she caught sight of something that left her dizzy with shock. There was a man standing at her office window, watching her.

Leigh dragged the robe up to cover herself, unable to believe what she was seeing. It was a delusion. The fantasy had been so powerful, it was tricking her senses. But as the man moved closer and she realized who it was, nothing could stop the scream that forced through her lips. "Dawson!"

"I'll be all right in a minute." Leigh was shivering in her living room, wrapped in an afghan she'd taken from the couch. She'd managed to get her robe on before letting Dawson in the front door, but she hadn't been able to stop trembling. He'd come over thinking she might still be up, and they could talk, Leigh knew they needed to, but her only goal right now was to gently convince him to leave.

"How could you be all right?" Dawson questioned, pulling off his white shawl scarf and offering it to her. He was standing across the room, dressed in the tuxedo he'd worn to some evening affair. "You're dripping wet and your eyes are feverishly bright. If I got close enough, I could probably hear your teeth chattering."

Did that mean he thought she was physically ill? That he hadn't seen what she was doing? Hallelujah! "Don't get close," she warned. "I don't want you to catch whatever it is I've got."

"Should I take you to a clinic?"

"They'd only tell me to take some aspirin and go to bed, which is exactly what I need to do." She shuddered, wrapping the afghan tighter. "Make me one of your famous hot toddies before you go, would you, Dawson? That and a warm bath should fix me up."

As he turned to the wet bar Leigh sank to the couch in relief and exhaustion. This made two close calls with Dawson. Much too close.

Nick Montera was on the brink of doing something that would result either in his salvation or his suicide. As he stared through the partially shuttered front windows of his studio at the three-ring media circus that had set up its tents on his property, the circus analogy took on a disturbing reality. Suddenly he knew why the animals in a sideshow paced their cages and glared at tourists with that flat, deadly gaze. He also knew why they went savage and attacked their keepers.

Something warm bumped his bare shin and he looked down to see Marilyn butting her head against his leg. A sharp yowl gurgled in her throat, and from its slightly frantic quality, he assumed she must be hungry. Despite his attempts to apologize, his housekeeper hadn't been back since the day he'd verbally roughed her up, and without Estela's stabilizing presence, everything had pretty much gone to hell. Nick had barely remembered to feed himself.

"You're interrupting my suicide mission," he told the cat, scooping her up as he headed for the kitchen. "But what the hell, first things first."

He deposited Marilyn on the countertop and went in search of some food for her, brushing at the strands of orange hair she'd left on his black tank top and shorts as he banged through cabinets and drawers. Where had Estela hidden the cat food? The refrigerator yielded some KFC hot wings, but Nick wasn't sure how his picky pet would take to those.

Marilyn's nails clicked against the ceramic tile as she serenely cleaned her paws in preparation for the meal.

Moments later, having picked the wings to the bone, Nick set a plate of tender white chicken morsels on the countertop. Marilyn attacked it greedily, but with great daintiness, reminding him that cats were complicated creatures.

As he watched her eat, eschewing the fat and the spicy sauce in favor of pristine tidbits, he was struck by how much she reminded him of the various females he'd known. Beautiful and self-absorbed, many of them attached to their pristine tidbits to the point of dependence, yet never, *ever,* to be taken for granted. One woman in particular came to mind. Paulie Cooper's appearance last night had surprised him, though it probably shouldn't have.

She was an artist at vulnerable womanly wiles, but in her case the vulnerability was real, and his sense of self-preservation was too keen these days to involve himself in anything that didn't contribute directly to prolonging his life expectancy. No emotional sinkholes for Nick Montera. He'd been there, done that. His top priority now was expediency, eliminating obstacles, and Paulie Cooper, he had assured himself, would not be one of those.

In fact, their brief, clandestine meeting had resulted in a windfall for Nick. It had given him a whole new angle on beating the murder rap. It was a reckless idea to be sure, but then *el que no arriesga no gana.* Nothing ventured, nothing gained, as his absent housekeeper liked to say.

"Sweet Mother of God." With a hand to his head, Nick contemplated the disaster area his life had become since Estela walked out. Dirty dishes were piled high in the sink, the garbage was overflowing, and the stack of newspapers in the corner had become a fire hazard. He'd even dug his shorts and tank top out of a moldering clothes hamper. He had to get her back. That was his first order of business this morning—just as soon as he'd put on some coffee and made the phone call that would seal his fate.

The coffee was perking when a moment later, portable phone in hand, he rested a shoulder against the refrigerator and tapped out the number of his attorney. Satterfield's receptionist answered on one ring and put Nick immediately through to the lawyer.

"Nick?" Alec's voice was warm and cordial. "What can I do for you?"

"Funny you should ask," Nick said. He paused, not so much for effect as to be sure his voice was absolutely even. He didn't want to reveal anything the attorney might be able to use against him, particularly emotion. "I want you to subpoena Leigh Rappaport as a witness for the defense."

An indrawn breath resounded through the phone wires. "Are you crazy?"

"Of course, just ask the doctor."

"She's the prosecution's headshrinker! Why would you want to call a hostile witness?"

"I'll explain later." Nick wasn't sure his telephone was safe, or that Satterfield himself wasn't taping their conversation. "Certain information is better conveyed in person."

"Explain now or I won't do it!"

"Do it," Nick replied coolly. "Or you're fired."

Satterfield's answer was succinct. "Fuck you," he muttered, seconds before the phone line went dead.

As Nick replaced the receiver he saw that Marilyn had finished her snack and was looking at him as if she expected him to wave a wand and magically replenish her empty plate.

"I'm good, Marilyn," he said, laughing softly. "But I'm not that good."

The cat strolled toward him, and he leaned over the countertop to knuckle her silky golden ruff. She smelled of chicken and hot wings sauce, and as she leaned into his touch a purr of feline pleasure trembled in her throat. Nick smiled.

Now all he had to do was get Estela back.

CHAPTER
·· SEVENTEEN ··

THREE WEEKS LATER . . .

Television weather gurus liked to call it a February heat wave, but diehard Angelenos scoffed at such timidity. When the sun went vertical and the air stopped moving, they were dealing with the dog days of winter. Terms like heat wave couldn't touch it. The city of lost angels turned into a blistering breeder reactor. Given the choice, most of the angels would rather have had their breakfast coffee in hell.

This morning the temperature outside the Los Angeles County Courthouse was approaching meltdown, and the crowds cluttering the entrance were showing signs of wear and tear. The fourth estate had already begun to strip down to shirt-sleeves, shells, and in some cases, T-shirts. The Nick Montera groupies pressed enormous plastic Super Sippers, dripping with condensation, to their flushed faces and fanned themselves with the FREE NICKY! signs they were carrying.

They were all waiting for a shot at their boy, and as Leigh made her way through the throng of newspaper reporters and television journalists, she was glad for once to be anonymous. She'd worn a lightweight, blue linen suit in deference to the weather, but she was still perspiring freely, undoubtedly as much from nerves as from the heat.

She'd been subpoenaed by the defense, but Dawson's office had put up a fight, claiming that her evaluation of the defendant was privileged information. The defense had charged the prosecution with trying to suppress findings important to their client's defense, and the judge had ultimately ruled in favor of the defense. So here Leigh was, a "reluctant" witness, as they called it. Only they had no idea *how* reluctant.

Nick's attorney seemed to believe her testimony would help his case, although she couldn't imagine why. The psychological tests had indicated that his client was capable of committing the crime of which he was accused. If pressed, Leigh would have to acknowledge that yes, Nick Montera appeared to have the emotional makeup of a murderer. But she could also add that almost anyone, under the right conditions, was capable of a violent crime of passion. Was that what Satterfield wanted to hear?

She was surprised to see Dawson coming toward her as she entered the courthouse. She'd expected him to avoid this scene like the plague, especially since he wasn't trying the Montera case and had sidestepped any direct association with it. If the people won, however, she was sure he would be willing to come forward and accept the responsibility—and the glory.

He looked terrific in an ultraconservative gray suit and burgundy tie. He even appeared to be smiling as he walked her way, but Leigh wasn't looking forward to an encounter with him. He'd been furious when he learned she was being subpoenaed. He'd gone into a bizarre tirade, suggesting that she was conspiring against him and warning her that she was behaving recklessly, as if she were to blame for the defense's move. He'd even threatened to break off their relationship. Leigh had found his behavior so outrageous, she'd barely spoken to him since.

"How are you?" he asked now, genuine concern in his voice as he reached her. "Time for a cup of coffee before court convenes?"

She lifted her briefcase. "Thanks, but I'd like a moment to review my notes."

He stepped back as if to get a better look at her, and she flushed self-consciously at his obvious approval.

"You look wonderful," he told her.

She tried to shrug it off. "Big day in court."

"I think we should talk, Leigh."

"I've been subpoenaed, Dawson," she said quickly, determined to forestall another argument. "I have no choice but to testify. Would you prefer I be held in contempt of court?"

He touched her elbow, drawing her aside. "Just be careful, Leigh, please. Once the press hears that you're a hostile witness, they'll be hanging on your every word. I know you'll be sensitive to what's important—our engagement, of course, and well . . . the primary. It's only a few months away."

"Don't worry. I couldn't *possibly* forget that you're up for reelection."

As she glanced at her watch he caught hold of the sleeve of her jacket, tugging on it affectionately. "I just don't want you to be embarrassed in there, okay? These guys play rough. They won't spare you, Leigh. Not even our relationship will help. In fact, it could make things worse. The prosecution may feel the need to be tougher on you in order not to be accused of favoritism."

"I'll take my chances. My testimony won't be any different than it would have been if I'd been called by your people."

"But they'll make it sound different. They'll twist it around, have you saying Montera's some kind of Boy Scout, that he helps old ladies and little kids across the street."

"Maybe he does, Dawson."

Dawson's voice dropped to a quick, angry whisper. "For Christ's sake, Leigh! The man's a predator. I'd hate like hell to think your testimony was going to set him free to prey on other innocent women."

Leigh quelled the desire to rush to Nick's defense. She knew what Dawson was getting at. Tests and psychological profiles aside, she had never been, and still wasn't, convinced that Montera was guilty. Dawson knew that, but he didn't want her saying it for the record. Today his agitation seemed so great that Leigh felt a compelling need to reassure him that she would never do anything to hurt him. He *was* her fiancé, after all, and up to now their relationship had been mostly a happy one.

Dawson had always been supportive and caring, and she had returned those feelings unreservedly. She would have bet her life on their future, until recently. Normally he was a rock, solid and dependable, but she didn't know how to account for his sudden paranoia. He was acting like a threatened man, both personally and professionally. She'd suspected for some time that he might be jealous of Nick Montera, but other things concerned her as well. She hadn't forgotten the way he'd brushed her off when she'd questioned him about Jennifer Taryn—

A sudden explosion of activity whirled Leigh around just as

the courthouse doors burst open and the throng that had been hovering outside swarmed in. The reporters were fighting for position and thrusting microphones at the half-dozen people caught in the eye of the storm.

One of those people was Nick Montera.

Leigh's fingers tightened on the handle of her briefcase. She lifted the case to her midriff. He'd been on the newsreels of course, but that had always been videotape, old footage. This was real, very immediate. This was Nick Montera, accused murderer in the flesh, entering the hallowed halls of justice. He was about to be put on trial for his life, and Leigh was totally unprepared for the impact of seeing him.

He was wearing a clay-colored double-breasted suit and a seafoam-green shirt that contrasted beautifully with his tawny skin tones. He hadn't bothered to have his hair cut short, as most defendants in a capital offense trial would have, but the effect of his longish, glossy black mane was fabulously appealing. He looked wounded and artistic and moody, a man apart. It was a potent mix if the jury was predominantly female, as Leigh had heard it would be.

Alec Satterfield walked at his right side. Leigh didn't recognize the attractive thirtyish woman flanking Nick on the left, but her first instinct was a competitive one. The woman had long legs, dark hair, wrapped in a sexy French roll, and as far as Leigh was concerned, she was a good deal too glamorous to be a lawyer. Still, she looked totally professional, and Leigh could only assume that Satterfield, wisely, had decided to have one of his female colleagues do some of the actual arguing.

Nick was protective with the woman, Leigh noticed, fending off the jostling reporters, drawing her close. The thought that he might be involved with someone else was a surprisingly painful one to Leigh. It bothered her terribly that he might be opening himself up to this woman, telling her the things he'd revealed to Leigh in their sessions . . . that it was his fascination with the play of light that had drawn him to photography, yet he'd never been able to face a sunrise. She didn't even want to think about the possibility that there was something more than that between the two of them.

On impulse, she glanced back at Dawson and saw that he was observing the procession, too. But what struck her about him was his expression as he stared at Nick Montera. His eyes were burning with undisguised malice.

"That's him." The elderly man's voice quavered and broke as he pointed out the defendant for the benefit of those assembled in the courtroom. "That's the man I saw going in to Jenny's apartment that night." He was pointing at Nick Montera.

Carla Sanchez, the statuesque deputy district attorney who was prosecuting the case, swept a hand toward Nick as she walked to the defendant's table. "This is the man, Mr. Washington? You're absolutely certain of that?"

"Yes, ma'am, I am."

"How can you be so sure? Couldn't you have made a mistake? You said it was evening, around six o'clock? It would have been dark outside."

The witness, a spindly man who appeared to be in his sixties, shook his head vigorously, loosening a wiry strip of hair that looked as if it had been shellacked to the bald spot on his crown. "Wasn't that late. Wasn't dark either. I like to sit out on my porch and digest after supper. Do it every night. That's when I saw him."

He grinned broadly and went on. "Had pork chops that night, with a little applesauce and prunes. My memory's probably sharper'n yours, ma'am."

Titters broke out in the courtroom.

"I'm sure it is, Mr. Washington," Sanchez agreed, laughing. "I'm sure it is. But eyewitnesses make mistakes all the time."

"No mistake," he insisted indignantly. "I've seen him before. Plenty of times. He was her boyfriend, she told me that. She said he had a bad temper. Said he was mean to her. That's the word she used—*mean*."

"Objection, Your Honor!" Alec Satterfield shot out of his chair. "That's hearsay. What Ms. Taryn might or might not have said to Mr. Washington is not admissible. I move to have it stricken from the record."

"Your Honor," Sanchez countered, "I submit that Mr. Washington's testimony shows the victim's state of mind regarding the man who stands accused of murdering her. That makes it an exception to the hearsay rule."

The judge, a slender black woman with a deceptively soft manner, took a moment to make her decision. "I'll let the reference stand, counselor," she said finally. "You may proceed."

"Thank you, Your Honor, I'm done." Carla Sanchez looked positively triumphant as she walked to her table and sat down, pausing for effect before she turned to Alec Satterfield. "Your witness."

All eyes were on Satterfield as he took a snapshot from a folder on the table in front of him, rose, and walked to the witness stand. An attorney of his repute not only commanded absolute attention, he also generated burning curiosity in the minds of his audience. What would the vampire bat do now? they were wondering. How would he discredit a charming old man without losing sympathy for himself and, by association, for his client?

"Mr. Washington, do you drink?" Satterfield asked as he approached the old man.

"I beg your pardon?"

Satterfield handed the snapshot to the witness. "Is this a picture of you, Mr. Washington? And if it is, would you be so kind as to tell the court what you were doing when this picture was taken?"

Washington's face drained of color as he stared at the photograph.

After several awkward seconds of silence, Satterfield spoke up. "Maybe I can help you, Mr. Washington?" he asked. "It's a picture of you sitting on your porch swing, drinking from a fifth of eighty-proof Popeye vodka, is it not, sir?"

Washington nodded, wetting his cracked lips with a flick of his tongue as he handed the snapshot back.

Moving quickly, Satterfield gave the picture to the judge and asked that it be marked as Defense Exhibit A and admitted into evidence. "You do drink, don't you, Mr. Washington?" he asked, turning on the witness, bearing down. "You drink every night. Nearly a full fifth of vodka, isn't that right?"

Sanchez sprang up. "Objection! Leading the witness."

"Sustained," the judge said. "Mr. Satterfield, you will confine your cross to questions, please."

"Your Honor," Satterfield explained, "I was attempting to establish that Mr. Washington's drinking habits are of a severe enough nature that they would seriously interfere with his ability to make a positive identification. Your Honor, I submit to the court that Mr. Washington is a full-blown alcoholic."

Satterfield approached the witness, his eyes gleaming, his voice soft. "Is that true, Mr. Washington? Are you an alcoholic?"

Washington bowed his head, several more wiry hairs falling forward. His nod was nearly indistinguishable.

A bleak smile touched Satterfield's lips. "And do you drink a fifth of vodka—or the best part of a fifth—every night as you sit in your porch swing and 'digest'?" Without waiting for a reply, the attorney nodded to the judge. "Thank you, Your Honor, I'm through with this witness."

Satterfield returned to his seat amid buzzing admiration from the onlookers. Obviously pleased with himself, he accepted the congratulations of his tablemates, a pat on his sleeve from his young female colleague, and a smile from his client, Nick Montera.

"Not . . . anymore," Washington said shakily as he struggled to stand in the witness box.

The whispering stopped. Heads swiveled and the press leaned forward as the old man turned to the judge imploringly.

"Is something wrong, Mr. Washington?" she asked him.

"I don't drink anymore," the old man said, clearly mortified at having his moral failings revealed so publicly. "I jus' like to pretend I'm drinking, that's all. I s'pose it's dirt stupid, isn't it? But every once in a while I get the urge so bad, I jus' fill that fifth up with tap water and take a few swigs. Sometimes I sift through the neighbor's garbage and sniff their wine corks, too," he admitted sheepishly.

The judge bent over her bench, peering down at the elderly man. "Are you telling the court that you *don't* drink alcohol, Mr. Washington?"

"That's right. I'm clean and sober, ma'am. Have been for six months now."

"And this picture?" She picked up the photograph Satterfield had submitted as evidence and held it out so that the witness could see it.

He nodded proudly. "That's me, all right, with a fifth of H-two-0. I've been dry now for one hundred eighty-two days and"—he glanced at his watch—"ten hours. And I was stone sober the night Jenny got killed." He began to fumble through his coat jacket. "Would you like to see my A.A. six-month pin, ma'am? Just got it a week ago."

The judge settled back and smiled. "No, thank you, Mr. Washington, I believe you . . . and my heartiest congratulations on your sobriety."

The courtroom broke out in a smattering of applause, and Mr. Washington waved at his admirers before carefully making his way out of the witness box. The crowd had found a hero, and Alec Satterfield had lost the first round.

Nick Montera was hot news. His name garnered worldwide headlines, and his face automatically guaranteed a feature story, not only on the local five o'clock news, but on all four networks, the independents, and cable. CNN had done an in-depth profile that included an interview with his housekeeper, who'd recently returned to work for him and spoke emotionally on his behalf. *"Un hombre terco, pero grande de corazón,"* she said, her eyes glistening as she displayed the gift he'd given her, a crucifix on a delicate gold chain. "A stubborn man, but a good heart." The news channel also had videotape of his blond cat scaling a huge sycamore tree on his property.

The Fox Network hired a prominent radio talk-show psychologist to analyze the appeal of the "ladykiller," one of many labels invented by the media. The Latino community rallied, throwing support behind a brother in trouble. Men were curious about his "fatal appeal." Women everywhere were fascinated by it. They had found their dark prince, a man whose redemption had become their personal dream and their private fantasy.

As the case against Montera mounted, and it seemed increasingly apparent that he would be found guilty, the public debate took on feverish proportions. Those who believed him guilty called loudly for the death penalty. Religious groups in particular denounced him as a "disciple of Satan," pointing at his icy eyes and snake bracelet as evidence. His supporters called for justice, and if not that, then mercy. The court had to hire bodyguards to protect him from the crowds who wanted a glimpse, a touch, or a piece of the condemned man.

Leigh could do nothing more than watch it all from a distance. As a sequestered witness, she wasn't permitted in the courtroom, except to give her own testimony. Normally she would have been left to fend for herself in the hallway outside the courtroom, but because of the intense media interest, she was being kept in a small, cell-like room, where her sense of isolation rose with every hour of every day that she waited to be called. It was difficult not to imagine the worst. Paulie Cooper had predicted that Nick couldn't possibly get a fair trial, and now those dire warnings seemed to be coming true. If he was found guilty and sent to San Quentin—to death row— how would she feel? *What could she do?*

When she went home at night, she pored through newspaper accounts of the proceedings and hung on every word of the television news, aware that she was becoming what her fiancé had accused her of being, a Nick Montera groupie. She had little choice. The media's coverage was sensationalized and exploitative. It fed her fears, but it was her only source of information. She couldn't rely on Dawson for feedback, and she didn't like or trust Alec Satterfield especially after having been interviewed by him at some length.

On a personal level, her conflicts about Nick remained unresolved. He still frightened and disturbed her, yet thoughts of him had pushed everything else out of her mind. She'd tried to block them, only to be haunted by a recurring dream that always began in exactly the same way, with the drawing he'd sketched. Her back was to the wall, his hand at her throat. His touch was fatal, an irresistible force that sucked the air from her lungs and spiraled her down into depths of feeling too powerful to escape. *He held her under. He drowned her in dark, dark excitement.* She always woke up gasping for breath.

Her responses were sharpened with physical longings that should have warned her how deeply she was getting involved. Instead, the dream's potent energy fed her fears *for* Nick rather than of him. Perhaps she even understood that it was because he was condemned that she felt safe enough to acknowledge her fantasies about him. If Nick Montera had been a free man, she would have run the other way. Or tried to. But he wasn't free. He was on trial for his life, and she couldn't run away from her sense of responsibility or her concerns about the outcome. To her he was much more than the media's hunk of the moment, a fascinating, but passing curiosity. He was her personal cross to bear, the man she had intuitively believed innocent despite all evidence to the contrary, the man she could have saved . . . if she'd been given the chance to speak.

She had never wanted to testify, and now, ironically, with the trial running into its third week, she had begun to think she would not have the opportunity. The prosecution had already brought on their experts, a criminal profiler among them, who'd made a devastating case against Nick with his behavioral description of the ritual murderer. Leigh had followed the criminologist's testimony on the news, and it had frustrated her greatly that she'd been helpless to counter the damage he'd done. She couldn't defend Nick against such attacks, except silently, in her head. And in her heart.

Both the defense and prosecution were still looking for Paulie Cooper, who had vanished without a trace. Leigh had done her own private search, first securing Paulie's home phone number through Dawson's office and then leaving messages on her machine. She had hoped Paulie might trust her over the law or the media, but she'd had no response so far.

The DA's office was already suggesting foul play, and Leigh strongly suspected Paulie's disappearance was not voluntary. It no longer seemed possible that she'd gone off on a vacation. The Montera trial was big news. She couldn't have missed it. Someone didn't want Paulie to testify, or at least that was what Leigh believed.

In the final days of the trial, as the defense was winding up its case, Leigh took advantage of an unexpected opportunity. The judge had called a recess just as Leigh was visiting the ladies' room, and several of the women spectators were engrossed in a conversation about the latest turn of events. Leigh avoided their discussion, but as they returned to the courtroom she slipped in among them, unnoticed.

Now, as she stood at the back of the room, Leigh realized what an impulsive thing she'd done. If the judge discovered her, she would certainly disqualify her as a witness. She might even toss her in jail for contempt. As she studied Nick's profile her hammering heart forced her to examine several things, including her preoccupation with the trial and with him. She'd abandoned work on her manuscript altogether, and she'd been avoiding her editor, at great risk to that relationship. Her relationship with Dawson had also deteriorated to the point that they'd only seen each other twice in the passing weeks, and one of those times had been arranged by Kate, Leigh's mother, who suddenly seemed concerned now that the engagement was in trouble.

What was happening to her? Leigh wondered. *Was* she having a nervous breakdown? Was she becoming one of those women who attach themselves emotionally to dominant and dangerous men? Nick Montera could be either, or both, when he chose to be, and in a haunting way, he was also like the photographs he took. He seduced you into the dark corners of your own imagination, whether you wanted to go there or not.

The judge's gavel rapped sharply, bringing Leigh out of her thoughts. The clerk walked forward, preparing to make an announcement. Leigh had lost track of the proceedings, but her scalp tightened with animal caution, and she moved surreptitiously toward the exit as if she could somehow predict the immediate future.

The door was swinging shut behind her just as the clerk's voice boomed through the microphone. "The defense calls Dr. Leigh Rappaport to the stand."

CHAPTER
·· EIGHTEEN ··

NICK MONTERA WATCHED with a concentration that bordered on the superhuman as Leigh Rappaport was sworn in. She looked cool and composed in her slim black rayon suit with its stylishly fitted jacket. He didn't like that. He wanted to think she was suffering. He wanted to think her heart was hurting under that perfectly tailored jacket of hers, and that this whole stinking mess had shaken her up good.

Suffer, baby—His throat tightened as he watched her take her place in the witness box. There was a grace to her movements, a delicacy that reminded him of candles, long slender tapers in crystal candelabra. *I'm not asking for much, Leigh. Suffer just a little so I'll know you care.*

Once she was settled, Alec Satterfield rose and approached the witness box. Nick had advised his attorney on how to proceed with the doctor, and if Satterfield screwed up this time, Nick was going to fire the lawyer's ass, even if it meant he had to represent himself.

"Dr. Rappaport," the attorney said, rearranging the gold signet ring on his little finger, "would you please cite your credentials for the court."

Leigh briefly described her academic background at both UCLA and Stanford University, her clinical experience, including the extensive fieldwork she'd done and the scholarly papers she'd published, as well as the psychological test she'd developed with Carl Johnson.

"Very good, Doctor. And now would you please tell us more about this test you spoke of. The Art-Insight Survey, I believe it's called."

"Of course," she said, beginning a description that covered the basic contents of her technique, but kept them simple and succinct enough for the jury.

She was the very picture of professional behavior. There was just one little slip in her brilliant guise. Nick smiled as she absently reached up to stroke her gold earring. Someday he was going to take those earrings away from her and give her something else to play with . . . if he lived that long.

She went on to describe the survey, saying that it was an assessment test that required subjects to create stories about actual pieces of art, chosen for their symbolic content. "It's considered a projective test," she explained, "which means that the survey itself is largely unstructured to allow the subject to give free play to his fantasies, inner conflicts, and fears, and to 'project' them onto the test materials."

Satterfield nodded. "You used the word *unstructured*. How can you draw valid conclusions from such a test?"

"Our test is unstructured, but our scoring system is not. It's both objective and standardized. Dr. Johnson and I developed measurement scales and quantitative norms that allow us to compare a subject's responses to a base group of over a thousand respondents."

"And is this test especially designed to measure violent tendencies?"

"The test has several applications. One version was developed specifically to assess aggressive and/or sexual impulses. Quantitative norms were based on the responses of over five hundred prison inmates, all convicted of felonies involving violence."

"And that was the test you gave to Nick Montera?"

"It was."

Nick had put his hand over the bracelet on his wrist and now he rolled it back and forth beneath his palm. The doctor had neglected to mention that they never finished her vaunted test. Somehow or other they got hung up on a quaint little guard-dog scenario. Didn't we, Doctor? he thought, gazing at her, willing her to look his way, just once. Didn't we get hung up?

"Under whose authority?" Satterfield asked Leigh.

She seemed startled. "I beg your pardon?"

"Who directed you to administer the test?"

"Oh, the district attorney's office. They contacted me and asked me to evaluate Mr. Montera."

"I see. Why is it, then, that you're not listed as one of the prosecution's witnesses?"

She reached up to touch her earring, then caught herself. "Because I asked to be removed from the case."

"You asked to be removed from the case?" The defense attorney glanced over his shoulder at Carla Sanchez and her prosecution team as if to say, Listen carefully, my esteemed colleagues. You are about to get fucked and I don't want you to miss the experience. "How interesting, Dr. Rappaport. You took yourself *off* the case. Why did you do that?"

Leigh drew in a breath, revealing just the faintest bit of hesitation. Were the edges fraying? Nick wondered. He wanted to applaud. Very little would have given him greater pleasure than to see the doctor come undone.

She went on, speaking a little faster than before and with less than total composure. "For reasons of clinical comparison, I gave Mr. Montera an entire battery of tests, including my own. For the most part, the results were uniform enough to draw preliminary conclusions, but there were discrepancies, and after taking Mr. Montera's history into consideration, I began to question the validity of some of the scores."

"Discrepancies? Can you tell us what those were? In simple terms, Doctor." Satterfield flashed a brilliant smile at the twelve jurors. "I'm sure the ladies and gentlemen of the jury understand you perfectly, but I'm having some trouble."

The laughter and nods of appreciation from the jury were exactly what Satterfield was after.

"Of course," Leigh assured them all. "Mr. Montera's scores were elevated on several scales, indicating antisocial tendencies, overcontrolled aggression, and paranoia, but that's not at all unusual for someone of his background. He was raised in a barrio known for its gang warfare. His environment would have demanded he develop those tendencies simply to survive."

"I see. So if we're living under constant threat of attack, we need traits like paranoia and control, is that what you mean?"

"Exactly. Mr. Montera also tested out highly intelligent, which mitigates against violent behavior in subjects with elevated sociopathy scores."

"Elevated sociopathy scores?"

"Sorry—subjects with antisocial tendencies. Studies have shown that those who score low on standardized intelligence tests are more likely to be violent. Beyond that, Mr. Montera is an artist, and creative types view the world a little differently from the rest of us. That factor alone tends to invalidate the norms on which mine and the other tests were based."

"That's all very interesting, Doctor, but still a bit over my head, I'm afraid. So let's see if I can make this simple." He paused for effect, glancing at the jury again. "Dr. Rappaport, based on your evaluation of Nick Montera, do you believe he killed Jennifer Taryn with malice aforethought and premeditation as the prosecution's case against him claims?"

"Objection, Your Honor!" Carla Sanchez's hand flew up. "The witness isn't here to state her beliefs."

Satterfield approached the bench. "Your Honor, I'm asking for an opinion based on Dr. Rappaport's evaluation of the defendant."

The judge nodded. "You may answer that," she told Leigh.

Conflict clouded Leigh's beautiful gray gaze. She hazarded a glance Nick's way, and their eyes connected just long enough to completely tense him up. His stomach muscles tied themselves in a thousand knots. His neck muscles turned to rock.

"That's a difficult question," she said at last. "If you're asking me if I think he's capable of such a crime—"

"No, I'm asking you if you believe he killed her," Satterfield clarified. "As a professional and in your clinical opinion, Dr. Rappaport, do you *believe* that Nick Montera killed Jennifer Taryn?"

She flushed slightly and looked away. "No, I don't."

"Ob*jec*tion!" Sanchez was aghast. "The witness's beliefs are not expert testimony!"

"Overruled," the judge said firmly. "The doctor was asked for her clinical opinion, and she gave it."

The tension at the base of Nick's neck dissolved like water. Sweet Mother of God, he thought, wanting to laugh out loud. He'd been right about her. A woman who longed to rescue baby kittens would fight at the drop of a hat for the rights of the oppressed, the downtrodden, and the truly needy. The doctor had done exactly what he hoped she would. She had come down squarely on his side.

Satterfield turned to Carla Sanchez, a smile curving his lips. "Your witness."

Sanchez looked for a moment as if she might pass. She tapped the papers in front of her with her pencil, then sighed, tossed the pencil aside, and rose. "Dr. Rappaport, are you in love with Nick Montera?"

Gasps could be heard throughout the courtroom.

"Objection, Your Honor!" Satterfield came out of his chair as if he'd been ejected. "The counselor's question is not only irrelevant, it's insulting."

Sanchez glared at Satterfield, then wheeled around and approached the bench. "Your Honor, there is reason to believe that this expert witness may have formed a relationship with the defendant that went beyond the bounds of her professional duties. On that basis, the question is totally relevant, and I ask your permission to continue this line of questioning."

"I object!" Satterfield sputtered. "Dr. Rappaport is not on trial here!"

"But her clinical opinion is," Sanchez insisted. "The people have the right to establish the doctor's credibility as an expert. Your Honor?"

The judge looked as if she'd eaten something that tasted bitter. "I don't like this turn of events, counselor," she said. "I don't like it at all. I'll allow another question or two, but make your point and do it quickly."

Sanchez didn't seem to relish the situation either. She caught her lower lip between her teeth, studying Leigh for a moment. "Dr. Rappaport, how many hours did you clock in during the evaluation of the defendant?"

Leigh lifted her shoulders. "I don't know exactly. I wanted to be thorough. In fact, I informed your office that I wouldn't take on the case unless I could give the evaluation the time it deserved. After all, a man's life is at stake."

Sanchez nodded. "Yes, that's true. And that concerns you greatly, doesn't it, Doctor? The fact that Nick Montera's life is at stake."

Again, Leigh flushed. "Of course it does. As a professional and as a licensed therapist, I take very seriously the responsibility for evaluating a client's mental state, no matter who the client is. If a life is at stake, I'll stop at nothing in my search for the truth. I wouldn't be sitting up here in this box if I hadn't done a completely thorough and painstaking investigation of Mr. Montera. That's why I took myself off this case, counselor."

Nick found her indignation totally captivating. The deputy DA, however, looked as if she were about to open fire.

"That's very good, Doctor. Very impressive, but I'm curious just how thorough and painstaking you were. I understand that you made several trips to Mr. Montera's private home, did you not?"

"His private home *is* his studio, and yes, I went there to evaluate his photographs and his working habits."

"How many times?"

"Two, maybe three."

"Against the advice of the prosecutor's office?"

"I felt it was necessary—"

Sanchez cut Leigh off, insisting that she answer the question, and when Leigh finally admitted that she had gone against the advice of the DA's office, Sanchez moved in for the kill. She brought up Leigh's reluctance to test the defendant, even after repeated prodding, and her abrupt decision to take herself off the case. She ended by dropping a bombshell.

"Dr. Rappaport, didn't you admit to your own office assistant that you found Nick Montera very attractive. Didn't you say you were afraid you might be getting emotionally involved with him?"

"No! Not in those words, I—"

"Objection!" Satterfield shouted. "Leading the witness!"

"Overruled." The judge turned to Leigh. "The witness is instructed to answer the question."

As Leigh tried to explain Nick fought with his own powerful desire to come to her aid. The stunned look on her face told him she'd been betrayed by someone, and he was reasonably sure it wasn't by Nancy, her assistant. Somehow her own fiancé must have given his people that information—and the go-ahead to use it. Dawson Reed clearly wanted desperately to win this case if he was willing to humiliate Leigh to do so.

"Doctor," the deputy DA continued, "remember that you're under oath now, sworn to tell the truth. Can you honestly say that the sole reason you took yourself off the case was

because you weren't convinced of the defendant's guilt? Or
was it because you became emotionally involved with Nick
Montera during the course of your evaluation?"

Leigh was obviously going through a terrible struggle. She'd
been blindsided, but she seemed to be searching her conscience
for the answers. Watching her, Nick was torn. On the one hand,
he'd never wanted more to hear a woman admit her feelings.
On the other, she could so easily destroy them both.

"That depends on how you define the term *emotionally
involved*," she said. "I was no more involved with Mr. Montera
than I would have been with any client I worked with extensively. You do come to care about a person's welfare."

A little white lie in the interests of self-preservation, Nick
thought. At least he hoped she hadn't become involved with
all her patients the way she had with him.

"You 'come to care'?" Sanchez pressed. "Interesting choice
of words, Doctor. I'll use them, if you don't mind. Having
come to *care* for Nick Montera, as you did, do you really
believe that you could have been objective in your evaluation
of him? Hasn't everything you've said here today been skewed
by your feelings for him?"

"No," Leigh said emphatically. "My evaluation was based
on extensive hours of interviewing and testing, not on my
feelings—"

"Thank you, Dr. Rappaport."

The prosecutor was attempting to cut her off, but Leigh
swung around to the judge. "Your Honor, may I be allowed
to continue? It isn't just my credibility in question here, it's
my professional reputation."

"Your Honor—"

The judge raised a hand, silencing the prosecutor. "Go
ahead, Dr. Rappaport," she said.

Impassioned, Leigh turned to the room. "My life's work
with Dr. Johnson was devoted to making the field of psychological assessment more scientific and reliable. I'm cur-
rently writing a book documenting the Art-Insight Survey and
making the test available for personal use. What's more, I'm
a trained therapist. I went through many years of schooling
and countless hours of supervised counseling to learn how
to be objective and caring at the same time. I know how to

separate my feelings from my clinical opinions. I do so on a daily basis."

She stopped abruptly, and Nick thought the place was going to break out in applause again. She was magnificent, fiery and righteous. His heart was pounding, watching her. But unfortunately for both of them, no one seemed to be buying her story. As he looked around, Nick could see it in the constrained expressions of the jury as they watched her. They wanted to believe her, but they didn't.

Christ, he didn't know whether to laugh or cry. In Dr. Leigh Rappaport's flushed denial that she was in love with him, she'd as much as admitted it to the world. She'd certainly rocked *his* world. But she'd also sealed his fate.

"Dr. Rappaport, over *here*!"

"Doctor! Are you another one of Nick Montera's victims?"

"How about your fiancé? How does the DA feel about this?"

Pandemonium broke out in the courthouse hallway as Leigh tried to make her way out of the building. She wasn't prepared for the press's onslaught. They came at her from every angle, a blizzard of anonymous faces, shoulders, and arms, viciously elbowing and shoving each other in their attempts to get at her. The crush was terrifying.

"Please!" she said, hugging her briefcase to her chest. "Let me through. I have no comment at this time."

A woman thrust a microphone in her face. "Are you in love with Montera, Doctor?"

"Is your engagement off?" someone shouted from behind.

"No comment," Leigh said imploringly. The entrance was less than twenty feet away, but she couldn't get to it! A security guard was stationed by the door. Using her case as a shield, she ducked her head and pushed through the jostling bodies. If she could get to him, maybe he could help her.

"This way, ma'am."

Someone gripped Leigh's upper arm firmly and jerked her around, pulling her in the opposite direction. She couldn't make out who it was at first, but the voice and the unyielding hold on her arm were male. He was guiding her out of the commotion, and it looked as if he were heading for another exit door.

"Where are we going?" Leigh asked, once she got close enough to be heard. She didn't recognize her rescuer, and she wasn't reassured by his trench coat and sunglasses or by his steely-jawed lack of emotion.

"I was told to get you out of here safely, ma'am. Come right this way."

The lesser of two evils, Leigh decided as she glanced behind her at the mob scene. She had a better chance against one than a hundred. The man opened the door and urged her through it, simultaneously holding off the press as they tried to crowd into the narrow corridor behind her. The slam of the exit door cut off the shouting, and if there'd been time, Leigh would have let out a relieved sigh. She'd forgotten what a blessed relief quiet could be.

The hallway was dimly lit and the sunlight was blinding as Leigh's rescuer opened the door at the other end. The ninety-degree-plus heat hit her like a wall.

"That taxi, ma'am," the man said, pointing her toward a Yellow Cab that was idling at the curb. As the back door of the taxi flew open, Leigh saw several reporters coming around the corner of the courthouse. She made a run for the car, and by the time she reached it, she was dripping with perspiration.

"Doctor!" someone bellowed at her. "Were you sleeping with Montera?"

Leigh barely got herself and her briefcase inside the taxi before the driver took off. Somehow in the scramble, she shut the case's leather strap in the door, but the car was already moving too fast to do anything about it. Worse, by the time she got herself turned around and saw who her companion was, it was too late. They were accelerating down Hill Street, and the one man in the world she did not want to see at this moment—or perhaps ever—was in the backseat with her.

"I'm sorry, Leigh," Dawson said. "I tried to warn you what might happen in there."

If Leigh could have freed her briefcase, she would have slammed it into the space between them. The cab stank of dirty carpets and human sweat, but it smelled better than the man. Dawson's skin was pale and moist, his eyes were huge behind his round Armani glasses, but Leigh had no sympathy. Her face was flushed with anger as much as heat.

"You tried to warn me that you were going to make a public joke out of me?" she asked him. "That you were going to drag my professional reputation through the mud? Dawson, this is going to hit every paper in the country! I'll be a laughingstock. My publisher will probably cancel my book contract!"

With a swashbuckling flourish that was totally uncharacteristic of him, Dawson reached down and produced a bouquet of flowers.

Leigh was so astounded she pushed the ridiculous peace offering back in his face. "Are you out of your mind? How can you think flowers would be anything but an insult? I don't like being ambushed, Dawson, particularly by my own fiancé!"

"That isn't how it was, Leigh. I told Carla not use it."

"Well, she did use it! Which gives you the perfect reason to fire her. She went against direct orders." In some more rational lobe of her brain, Leigh knew she was being petty and vindictive, but she didn't care. Firing was the least of what she'd like to do to Carla Sanchez.

Dawson couldn't quite meet her gaze. Leigh watched his Adam's apple bob as he swallowed, and she knew she hadn't heard the worst of it yet. "What is it?" she asked, warding him off as he reached for her hand. "Tell me, Dawson."

"I told Carla not to use it unless she had to, a do-or-die situation, do you understand? I told her under no circumstances was she to use it unless the world was coming to an end. I don't know what happened. Your testimony must have been so persuasive she felt she had to drop a bomb."

A bullet of sweat rolled down his temple.

Leigh was too furious to speak. Tears welled in her eyes, and for one utterly rash second she contemplated jumping from the moving cab. When she finally found words, they trembled with anger and disbelief. "So that's how it is? My career and my peace of mind were all expendable, just another nail in Nick Montera's coffin?"

"Nothing is expendable, Leigh, least of all our relationship. I've got it all figured out. We'll hold a press conference, you and I, a show of solidarity. I'll raise questions about Carla's tactics. I'll state, categorically, that I didn't believe any of it, not a word she said. We'll announce our wedding date, our plans—"

"There isn't going to be a wedding, Dawson."

He moved toward her, stricken. "Leigh, *please*. You don't mean that."

Suddenly Leigh knew what the problem was, what it always had been. The regret in her fiancé's eyes had little to do with guilt or remorse about what he'd done. He wasn't seeking forgiveness because he'd caused her pain. He was trying to avoid his own pain, the pain of losing her and the social status that came with her. A sociopath operated in his own self-interest, often without conscience or regard for others' welfare. At least Nick Montera's background had given him an excuse. She wondered what Dawson's was.

"I do mean it." Her tone was softened and sad as she realized how deeply she felt. "Even if I could forgive you for this, Dawson, it would never work between us. I'm not cut out to be the district attorney's wife. I don't have your priorities. I'm not willing to sacrifice everything for your career."

Anger kindled in his eyes, gathering heat. "But you'd throw it all away for him?"

Now she understood what else was driving him. Jealousy, just as she'd suspected. "I've thrown *nothing* away for him. I took the case because you pressured me into it. That was my first mistake, and it was a fatal one. I should have seen the rest coming. Stop, please!" she told the cabdriver. "I want to get out."

Leigh had the car door open before the taxi had reached the curb.

Dawson snagged her by the pocket of her jacket as if to pull her back into his arms. His voice was harsh with regret. "I'm not going to let you do this, Leigh."

"It's done, Dawson. And you did it."

She fended off his attempt to stop her, scooped up her briefcase, and stumbled out of the taxi, glancing around her in bewilderment. She wasn't even sure where she was.

"Leigh—"

The door slammed shut with a kick of her foot, cutting off his voice. Resolved to escape him, Leigh clutched her briefcase in both hands and hurried toward what looked like a business plaza. A flight of steps took her to a large open courtyard, where she hesitated at a small fountain. Two pigeons splashing amorously in the water made her shake her head and tear up again. She couldn't even do this right! She couldn't even break up with the world's biggest jerk.

The misery she felt seemed to move her, to spin her in a circle until she was facing the way she'd come. She was looking for him, she realized, looking to see if he was going to follow her. What was worse, she felt lost and vulnerable enough that she might have capitulated if he had. Her career and her private life were in shambles. Everything she'd pinned her hopes and dreams on—her name, her reputation— the things she most valued and cherished in life, they had all been jeopardized in the course of one afternoon.

A moment later, standing at the head of the cascading steps, she saw that the taxi had already pulled away from the curb and disappeared. Dawson was nowhere to be seen.

CHAPTER
·· NINETEEN ··

HER LIVING ROOM was as dark and funereal as a morgue, and Leigh wanted it that way. She had purposely left off the lights, the television, and anything else that might remind her that life raged on as usual outside her door. She had even pulled the plug from the brass pendulum clock on the wall because she wanted to think the entire world had stopped that day . . . the day her world stopped.

She'd come home the afternoon of Nick Montera's trial and Dawson's betrayal, her only thought to make the horror go away, to wipe out the grievous mistakes and start over. But the rest of the world was reveling in her grief, she realized, and after an evening of seeing her own face splattered all over the television screen and listening to dire predictions about Nick's fate, she had pulled the plug.

He was going to be found guilty and sentenced to death.

Why did it feel as if *she* were going to die?

For the last hour she'd been sitting in her nightgown on the looped Burman carpet, resting against the sofa, her bare feet straight out in front of her. For entertainment she'd been listening to the telephone ring. Her message machine tape had already filled up with calls, and the phone's volume switch had broken when she'd tried to turn off the ring. This wasn't the kind of instrument you could silence by unplugging a handy little jack. Apparently she was going to have to rip it out of the wall.

That thought pleased her. She'd already counted thirteen rings. Two more and Ma Bell's infernal machine would go the way of yesterday's trash.

"One," she said, pushing stiffly to her feet. A second and third ring had already sounded by the time she reached the occasional table, but as she fumbled in the darkness to find the cord, she knocked the telephone off the table.

"Leigh!" someone shrieked as the receiver bounced and rolled across the floor. "Leigh, are you there?"

Leigh shuddered reflexively. She'd developed such an aversion to the phone's incessant ringing that she didn't want to touch the thing. Instead she dropped to her knees, bent down, and put her ear near it, listening. As the woman continued to jabber, she realized it was her assistant.

"Nancy? What's going on?"

"*Leigh!* Oh, my God, Leigh! Where are you? I've been calling all night. Did you see the television? Were you watching the trial?"

The trial! Leigh tucked into a near-fetal position. If the proceedings were over, and he'd been found guilty, she didn't want to know.

"He's *free,* Leigh. Nick Montera is free!"

Leigh stayed put, unwilling to allow in what she'd just heard. She didn't believe it. She was afraid to believe it!

"Leigh, for heaven's sake! Are you there? Turn on the TV. They're playing a clip of Paula Cooper's testimony. She was a surprise witness for the defense today!"

Leigh bolted upright, first to her knees, then to her feet. She couldn't find the TV remote in the dark, but she managed to open the panel on the set and stab at buttons until the screen lit up. In shocked silence, and with Nancy still yelling at her over the phone, Leigh watched as Paulie Cooper's tear-streaked image materialized. She was in the witness box, being questioned by Alec Satterfield.

"Another woman nearly died the night Jennifer Taryn was killed," Satterfield was saying. "Can you tell us who that woman was, Ms. Cooper?"

"It was me." Paulie's color was ashen, her eyes huge and sunken. "I tried to kill myself that night." She went on to explain that her boyfriend had left her and she'd become despondent. She'd cut her wrists, then panicked and called Montera, who'd picked her up and taken her to an emergency clinic. Afterward he'd driven her to his place and sat up with her the entire night while she slept, keeping vigil.

"I made him promise never to tell anyone," Paulie said. "My modeling career was finally taking off after years of struggle.

I'd just signed a promotional deal with a cosmetics company for a new shampoo, and I was afraid they'd fire me if there were any scandal."

She shook back her long, luxurious red hair as if she were advertising the shampoo now. "I knew Nick didn't kill Jennifer. He couldn't have. They did argue, but he left long before she was murdered. He was with me when it happened."

She turned to the jury, her expression pleading with them to understand. "I kept hoping he'd be exonerated without my having to come forward, but when I saw how badly the trial was going—"

The newscaster broke in then, explaining that the next witness the defense had called was a clerk from the emergency-room clinic. The young man had confirmed Paulie's story and testified that he'd admitted her that night. He also identified Nick as the man who was with her.

"And that makes Nick Montera a free man tonight. When we caught him out in front of the courthouse after the trial, he had this to say."

The screen flashed to Nick and his legal defense team trying to make their way through the crowds. A reporter yelled out, "Where are you going now, Mr. Montera?"

Nick managed a faint smile. "Not to Disneyworld," he said. "It feels good to be exonerated, but we never got to the truth of who killed Jennifer Taryn. I'm going to find out who did it."

As the camera zoomed in on his face his eyes dominated the screen like two cobalt stars. Leigh wanted to look away, but she couldn't for a moment. It seemed as if those eyes were telepathic, as if he were looking directly at her. When at last she averted her gaze, the darkness of her living room was misted with blue. He was free.

It sounded like the roar of a distant helicopter coming in for a landing. Stirring from a deep sleep, Leigh fought to rouse herself as the low-pitched sounds vibrated through her temples. There was a muted, rumbling quality to the noise, like bass drums and thunderstorms.

She rolled to her side, still groggy, yet shivering from the film of perspiration that coated her skin. Gooseflesh crept up her bare arms and legs. Apparently she'd pushed off her covers while she slept because of the sticky heat. The dog days had lived up to their reputation in the last twenty-four hours, turning the weather still and sultry.

It didn't occur to Leigh that there was anything to be frightened about as she rose from the four-poster. She was too busy trying to get her bearings. The shutters were drawn so tightly she couldn't tell whether it was day or night, but the room smelled deliciously of the Raspberry Royal iced tea she'd left unfinished on the night table.

The rumbling had already stopped when she opened the bedroom door and entered the hallway, but her curiosity had been piqued, so she slipped on the robe she was carrying and went down to investigate. It was four A.M., according to the bedroom clock. The house was shadowed and heavy with heat, but it was the quiet that made her uneasy. It was possible she'd imagined the noise, but she didn't think so.

The table lamp sitting on her tea wagon flared to a soft amber glow as she turned it on, illuminating the living room. Nothing seemed out of place. The black porcelain dog her mother had brought back from a trip to the Orient sat in the tiled entry hall next to the Kentia palm. A silver tray on the coffee table held decanters of brandy and amaretto. Even the crimson decorator pillows on her watchman's plaid sofa were aligned exactly as she'd left them.

But now there was another noise, a soft pattering that took her to the front door. It sounded as if someone were knocking. She left on the chain lock and opened the door a crack, peering out. A gentle downpour lent the spring night a translucent sheen.

So that was it, she thought, smiling. A thunderstorm. This time of year electrical storms were often as violently noisy as they were short-lived. Satisfied she'd solved the mystery, she shut the door, hesitating as she was about to turn the dead bolt. A premonition made her stop and reflect on what she'd just seen. There was something unresolved in her mind, an image sensed more than seen.

She walked to the window and looked out. The moon shadows cast by the sycamores that lined her driveway made it difficult to see, but it looked as if there were a man standing in the road. Her fingers froze on the windowpane.

There *was* someone out there. He was leaning up against a four-wheel-drive vehicle parked at the curb, his hands plunged deeply in the pockets of his duster coat as he gazed at her doorway.

Standing in the rain . . .

Staring at her doorway.

How long had he been there?

The trees shrouded his features, but she didn't have to see them to know who he was. Every detail of his face was there, fully realized in her mind. The tension that spread through Leigh's jawline had an aching quality to it. Nick Montera was standing in the rain outside her door at four in the morning. She should not have understood that, but she did. From their first explosive encounter in the parking garage, there'd been an inexorable quality to their relationship that she couldn't explain away with tests or psychological profiles. It was intuitive, primitive, and powerful.

Leigh, the clinician, knew everything there was to know about Nick Montera. He was the embodiment of every dark dream she'd ever had, a beautiful, sensual aberration, sprung fully formed from her id. Nothing else could explain the power of her obsession with him. Leigh, the woman, knew only one thing about him. He was a man. Male, virile, animal. That truth pulled at her feminine center like gravity. Nothing else mattered . . . and therein lay the danger. Her obsession was more than a dark dream. It was sexual, chemical. He was out there. And everything about him drew her, even her fears.

Her front door creaked softly as she opened it, and the sound danced in her belly, plaintive and fearful. The rain had lightened to a sparkling mist. It enveloped Leigh like gossamer as she stepped out on the porch. She hesitated, but only long enough to breathe deeply before she started down the walkway. Her bare feet splashed in a pocket of cool rainwater, startling her. The night was sultry and close, yet she was aware of gooseflesh tingling up the back of her neck, biting at her arms and legs.

He didn't move as she walked toward him, just watched her approach. His stillness frightened her. It made her wonder if she was safe. There was a wounded part of Nick Montera that wanted to lash out, and she wondered if that was the part that had brought him here. The times he'd erupted in violence had all been directed at her, which made responding to him now feel like a terrible risk. But something inside her, the very fear dancing in her belly, seduced her into continuing.

He was wearing a black duster coat with jeans and a white T-shirt underneath. The cowboy boots on his feet had silver tips that glittered like stars when the light hit them. He was drenched. She could see that now. When he lifted his head, the water running down his face dripped off his jawline. Droplets quivered on his lips. They glistened in his hair and clung to his dark eyelashes.

He looked like a mystic, some sort of modern rainman.

Leigh had never seen anything so beautiful as the rain shimmering on his face and darkening his hair. It had the effect of detailing his features while doing nothing to soften them. Instead, the wetness spiked his lashes and sent shadows searching across his cheekbones.

She hesitated on the walkway, twenty feet from him. The movement he made, a slight lift of his head, awakened her as if from a trance. She was filled with awareness—of him, of her own situation, of everything around her. The air smelled pungently of wet earth and freshly mown grass. The night was as silent as a vault in the aftermath of the rainstorm. And all she had on was a linen nightgown and robe.

She was wet, too. Wet and trembling in the moonlight. "What are you doing here?" she asked him.

"Besides making it rain?" Fires kindled in his blue eyes. Even his slow, sardonic tone couldn't dampen them. "Sobering up, I suppose."

"You've been drinking?"

He shook back his hair, his hands still thrust deeply in his coat pockets. "Celebrating is the way I'd put it."

"Then, are you . . . ?"

"No, not drunk. Not the way you think." He stared at her, taking in the moisture pebbling on her face and throat, the quicksilver rivulets that purled toward the open lacing of her nightgown's drawstring bodice. Her robe hung open and the linen material of her gown was starting to cling to her damp skin and go transparent in places. She could feel the tightness gathering around her breasts. She could feel the material pulling, and as she reached up to free herself his eyes flared with hunger. It was visible, even in the darkness.

"I'll leave if you want me to," he said. "Just tell me to go."

He sounded as if he might want her to do that.

A muscle in his jaw strained, signaling something held in check. But the raindrops on his cheeks and his long wet lashes made it look as if he'd been crying.

Leigh felt her heart catch. She knew better than to give in to the sudden emotion, but she *was* relieved to see him, terribly relieved, and so grateful he was free. The impulse was crazy, but she wanted to brush the raindrop tears away, to touch his mouth and make him smile. She longed to do those things.

"Nick, what are you doing here at four in the morning?" she asked him finally, unable to think in terms any more subtle than that. "What is it you want?"

"God—" His laughter was quick, hoarse. "Lots of things. I want to eat a goddamn pomegranate, and let's see, what else? I want to sing opera in the shower and walk naked into the sea." His jaw tightened another notch. "And there's one more thing, Leigh. One more thing I want . . ."

She couldn't look at him.

Water glittered on the pavement between them and dripped heavily from her gown, forming a pool at her feet. It sluiced through her toes when she moved them, arresting her for a moment. She was amazed at the way it felt, cool and squishy, startlingly sensual, yet terribly urgent. Her insides could have been that rainwater, pooling and sluicing, glimmering with energy.

A sharp shiver ran up her arms. Suddenly the mist was ice-cold, the night swelteringly hot. Her thoughts were quick and jumpy.

"Leigh . . ."

She was startled to see him drag his hands from his pockets and push off the car. "No," she said, trying to think how to stop him. He began to walk toward her and her body reacted as if to a physical threat. She was short of breath, her mouth dry, too dry even to swallow. The signals were instantaneous. She went into a fight-or-flight response every time he got near her, only this time the threat was real. She wasn't his doctor anymore. There were no ethical or legal barriers, nothing to stop him from whatever he had in mind, unless she could find a way— That irony brought her up short. Not much chance of that!

A strange, thrilling helplessness stole through her as she averted her eyes. What *did* he have in mind? Her imagination reached for the possibilities, but there was no time to grasp them. A warm sensation near her breast drew her focus.

"They gave you a rough time on the stand," he observed.

"Yes," was as far as she got with her answer. He was touching her. His fingertips brushed her collarbone through the sheer material of her gown.

"You were good up there."

"No, I fell apart." If it had been anyone else, if he'd been touching any*thing* else, she might have stopped him. But he was as casually intent as an artist exploring a new medium, and after all, the collarbone was a fairly innocent thing.

She counted his brush strokes, measuring their length and breadth, the infinitesimal changes in pressure. She did all this with the feverish precision of her nervous system. She even ticked off the seconds between them, counting one one thousand, two one thousand . . . waiting for the next caress.

But when his fingers stopped, when they slid to her throat, she made a quavering sound. By now the furor of her responses was so disorienting she could no longer track them. There was no way to step back and monitor what was happening. Her head was spinning too fast. Her heart had gone mad. Everything in her immediate world, even her next heartbeat, seemed geared to the ultimate destination of his hand.

She turned away . . . and felt him at her back.

"Leigh—" His voice dropped low, rustling with passion. "Don't turn your back on me. Don't ever do that."

She closed her eyes, shuddering the length of her spine. A film of cool perspiration mingled with the sultry rain. She was drenched from her head to the bottom of her feet. There wasn't a place on her body that hadn't been violated by sweet, rank moisture, including the warmth between her legs.

Why shouldn't I turn my back? she thought. What will you do to me, Nick? Murder me? Fear rose inside her, but it wasn't fear for her life. She'd heard something in his voice, an echo of the longing that lived inside her. For some reason, it frightened her to think that he might hurt like her, that he might *need* like her. Perhaps because she didn't know who it was he really needed. Was it her or some unattainable dream girl from his past? Was it Leigh Rappaport he wanted? Or would any well-bred blonde fulfill the fantasy?

"Leigh . . . turn around. Look at me."

His fingers drifted along her bare arm, electrifying her. Though she tried to stop it, her mind flashed a vision of the two of them making love, his powerful body moving over hers. It was muted and indistinct, but the dark imagery set a torch to her imagination. There was hunger, a beautiful animal passion to their coupling. His nakedness was terribly arousing and, in her mind, terribly explicit. Somehow she knew exactly what he would look like, exactly what he would *feel* like. And that knowledge made itself felt deep inside her. It turned her to shimmering rain again. Bright, burning rain.

She wanted to turn around, but now he wouldn't let her.

"Don't move," he said. "Just tilt your head."

She was confused until she felt him lift the damp hair from her neck. His hands were cool and silky against her flushed skin. As she bent forward slightly something feathery brushed her nape. She wasn't sure if it was the man or the mists, but it was surprisingly pleasurable. She inclined her head further.

As his fingers purled up and down her skin, she was aware of his deep respiration and his warm, humid breath in her hair. He smelled faintly of wintergreen and smoky, expensive booze. Scotch, she imagined. Her thoughts were becoming as soft and languid as her muscles. Whatever he was doing, it was terribly sexy. She would soon be as limp as a kitten—

"Ouch!" Pain stabbed, freezing her for an instant. The stingingly sharp sensation took her breath away, and if Nick hadn't caught her, she might have dropped to the ground. She felt as if she'd been pierced by something—needles or fangs—and it made her think of the saying on his T-shirt. *If this snake bites you, there is no remedy at the pharmacy.*

"What happened?" she asked, turning dizzily in his arms.

He was blocking the light, and with the moon glowing behind him, he looked shadowy around the eyes and sharp at the edges. She couldn't see his expression, but she imagined it as piercing, like the fangs. What had he done to her? She felt woozy and light-headed.

The back of her neck still stung. She touched it, but couldn't feel a puncture wound. "Was that you?"

"Ummm . . . the snake."

He was holding her arm, and his silver bracelet gleamed on his wrist. A strange aura encircled the serpent's head. Was that what had bitten her? What else could it have been . . . except him. She felt as if an intoxicant had been introduced into her system, and it was fuzzing her senses. Her focus was hazy, her ankles wobbly. Or was she just reacting to him, to his closeness? She ought to move away. She thought about it.

"Stay with me," he said, his voice encircling her, a sorcerer's invitation.

"I can't. There's something wrong, I'm dizzy."

"You're excited."

"I am?" She looked up at him.

"Yes." He curved his hand to her face as if she were a wild creature who could be subdued by his touch. Her eyelids fluttered, weighted by nerves and languor. Her hips seemed to sway beneath her. She had dreamed of being subdued by Nick Montera, of having her heart calmed by his expert handling. She had dreamed fearful things about him, too, that he was capable of killing. That he might even kill her. That was all right, she decided, her thoughts sliding woozily from one thing to the next. She was ready to die. It was better than being numb, and that's what she was without him.

"I like you this way," he told her. "Dizzy. Excited."

His thumb curved into the soft flesh of her cheek as he bent toward her. The pressure of his hand beneath her chin would have prevented her from looking away if she'd tried. But she didn't try. She tilted herself willingly. With an abandon that was unlike her, she offered her mouth to him, and so much more, everything that was in her power to give. When he bent to take it, she caught back the sound in her throat. A breath took its place . . . soft, frantic, sweet.

The first light pressure of his lips was perhaps the most intimate connection she'd ever had with another human being. It was as elemental as the thunder that had awakened her— simple, yet profound. He plunged his hand into her hair and gripped her head. His other hand closed on her wrist and swung it behind her back, locking it there. He'd imprisoned her, but the play of his lips over hers was as hushed and tender as a whisper in the dark. She felt as if she were being kissed by the mists. It was tormentingly exciting, like dandelion fluff dancing over her parted lips, tickling her, gliding down her cheekbones, and breathing in her ears. His lips were dandelion fluff. But she longed for more. For his whole mouth. Hard against hers.

He broke away, sliding his fingers across *her* trembling lips. "Now that I have these," he said, "I want the rest of it. I want to be in your mouth."

Yes, she wanted that, too, though she wasn't quite sure what he meant.

"Don't make it easy for me," he said.

She pursed her lips then, bringing a smile to his.

Sliding his hands to her throat, he gently coaxed her to look at him. When she did he traced the periphery of her mouth with his fingertips, sending rivulets of pleasure through her. He stroked its fullness until she moaned. Leigh could hardly bear the heightened sensitivity. She compressed her lips, trying to resist him as he kissed her lightly, tasting and probing until he found an opening. He pierced her with his tongue, a succulent invasion that made her feel penetrated everywhere. She recoiled in the deepest part of her.

But he wasn't done with her, not nearly done. He seduced her curling pink tongue and filled her slender throat with searching heat. By the time he withdrew, she was reeling with pleasure and barely aware of his wicked intent as he bent his head and bit the soft flesh beneath her lower lip.

"Oh!" The nip had the same stinging intensity as the snakebite. It brought tears to her eyes, and her fingers to the spot. He was marking her, she realized. He was placing little signs of his possession all over her body. She would be black and blue before he was done . . . and she loved it.

Dizziness washed her.

He drew back to look at her and his intensity made her want to hide her head. "What have you done?" she asked softly. "I can hardly stand up."

"Good," he whispered. "I'll hold you."

"Kiss me?" she entreated, wishing he would. She felt as if she could kiss him forever and that might even be enough for her, just his delicious lips. Would it be enough for him? she wondered. The dark pleasure flickering in his eyes implied that it would be. But when she brushed her hip up against him, she realized that he was fully aroused.

"You *know* what you do to me," he said.

Not only did she know what she'd done to him, she knew exactly what she wanted done to her. And by whom. There was nothing more he had to say or do. She'd been seduced by the mere feel of his hardness. A second ago his kiss had been everything, her consummate pleasure. Now nothing would satisfy except that he make love to her. She simply had to have him inside her. It was as imperative as breathing.

His hand had slipped beneath the collar of her robe.

"I want to make love to you in the rain," he said, his fingers cool against her skin. "And then I want to drink every raindrop off your body."

She flushed with pleasure, and a truly crazy impulse took hold of her. Stepping back from him unsteadily, she began slowly to raise the delicate white linen of her gown, revealing herself to him a little at a time. Her thighs were slick and moisture-sheened, and by the time she'd inched the material up their gleaming length to the golden shower that crowned her pubis, she was feeling rather bold.

He studied her for a long moment, gazing at the quite wanton display of her nakedness as if he wished he could capture it on film. The desire kindling in his eyes had begun to burn very hot indeed, and Leigh was just beginning to understand what kind of blaze she'd started. Unwilling to give in, she fluttered her nightgown a little, giving him peekaboo glimpses.

He lifted his head, tilted it. Another angle.

"This isn't a photo shoot," she pointed out.

"Oh, but it is," he corrected. "And I've got you in my sights. In my mind, I'm shooting you."

"With a camera?"

He smiled. "One shot after another until I'm out."

"Of film?"

His hand dropped to the button fly of his jeans. "Of everything, Leigh. I want to give it all to you."

"Wait a minute," she said. "What are you doing?"

But he'd already begun to walk toward her, and the slow sensual menace of his approach warned her that she was in trouble. She dropped her nightgown and stepped back, moving swiftly to make sure he didn't close the distance between them. She crept toward the house, successfully evading him until she bumped up against the wall of the porch and couldn't go any farther.

By that time he had the top buttons undone.

"What *are* you doing?" she repeated.

"Turning to rock, Leigh. It doesn't take much . . . just you."

Muscles fluttered madly in the pit of her stomach. *Just* me? she thought. Was it her he wanted, only her? As much as she craved the answer to that question, she couldn't ask. Her body was too urgently excited, and the parts that were calling out for relief didn't care whom he wanted. They wanted him!

He backed her to the wall, flattening his hand alongside her head. He didn't look like a sorcerer at the moment, or anything supernatural at all. Even with his duster coat flaring around him like an evil black cloud, there was no question about his Y-chromosome count. He was one-hundred-percent aroused male.

She was well aware that his other hand was engaged in some questionable activity in the vicinity of his nether regions, but she couldn't bring herself to look. God, she hoped he wasn't stroking himself or anything. She would faint. As it was she was frozen in place, cringing beneath him and wondering where her boldness had gone.

"I think you should take a look at what you've done, Leigh. Maybe you could put me in your test." Irony lent his voice a razor's edge. " 'Make up a story to go with this picture. Tell me what the nice man is doing, how he came to be that way, and what the hell he's going to do next.' "

Holding her gaze, he very deliberately reached down to free himself from his jeans. This time there was no question about what he was doing.

Curiosity, perhaps the lowest of human impulses, made Leigh hazard a glance. All she got was a glimpse, but that was more than sufficient. *As was he*. Her impression was of darkness and power, of rampant energy and steamy, thickening muscle.

With a soft groan, Leigh let her head fall back against the wall. Witnessing Nick Montera's full-blown erection was like staring at an eclipse of the sun. One more second, and she would certainly have gone blind. Maybe it was her background—the shock of a thirteen-year-old girl confronted with male sexuality before she was ready—but she had never been comfortable with the sight of an aroused man. Fascinated, but not comfortable. *Not at all.*

"You don't have to look—" He seduced her in tones that were grindingly soft, with words that seemed to be caught in the vise grip of his throat, strangling there. "You can touch. I've got this thing for you, Leigh. Only for you."

The snake was going to have to bite her again, Leigh realized. It was the only way she could go through with this. She needed to be woozy and crazy and bold. She closed her eyes and felt his fingers graze her cheek, his thumb pad feather her lips invitingly. If her mind resisted the sensual overture, her body's response was lightning hot. A bolt of excitement shot straight for her groin. Her mouth opened eagerly, pursing, sucking as he dipped inside. He was a stick of cinnamon candy, burning sweet, tantalizing her taste buds, her salivary glands, making her mouth water freely. She was woozy by the time he took the candy away.

Her eyelids fluttered, then opened.

Enough, little girl, his expression said. Enough playing.

Leigh answered him recklessly. She reached down and discovered him with her fingertips, discovered the burgeoning virility that sprang from his thighs.

"So big," she breathed as she trailed her forefinger along the entire length of him. He was as smooth as the pool of rainwater beneath her feet, as solid as the pavement. He was also very generously proportioned, but most remarkable were the changes in his eyes as she touched him. They were already dilated almost to blackness, but when she cradled him in her palm and gently squeezed him, his pupils shrank for an instant, turning his gaze a beautiful, pulsing blue.

His smile twisted into a grimace of pain. "Christ, I could devour you. I could chew and suck and eat you alive, and never get enough."

Leigh had barely released him before he caught her under the arms and lifted her to the wall. He held her there like a child's plaything, held her in the fierce glare of his eyes until she thought she would melt from the heat. Air streamed from his nostrils as he bent toward her, then hesitated.

He was making her wait too long! Her head fell back and she spoke his name, her breasts straining toward him.

She could feel him shaking, holding off, holding her off. A word slipped from her throat, so passionate and obscene it broke his control.

"Fuck—" He jerked her toward him savagely.

All restraint gone, he took her mouth with sudden and hungry ardor, cursing her, devouring her. Leigh had never been bombarded with so much passion. He was venting his rage and his uncontrollable desires at the same time. He wanted her dead and gone, out of his life. He wanted her in his bed, tonight, every night, his woman, his! She quaked under the assault, but it wasn't from pain or fear or cold. She could feel none of those things. His duster coat covered them both and her nerves had long ago insulated her from any trauma. She quaked from the soul, from the place that knows its mate and quickens instinctively. She quaked with naked, elemental need.

By the time he'd settled her on her feet, he was breathing and shaking as hard as she was. "I need to be here," he said, sliding his hand to her sex, fondling her through damp and delicate linen. "I came for this. I exist for this."

"Take it, then—" She sobbed more than spoke. *"Hurry."*

He lifted her leg high, imprisoning it between the swell of his bicep and the damp heat of his ribcage. Leigh's gown rolled up to her hips, exposing everything to his eyes. He swore softly and cupped her with his hand, pressing into the soft golden curls that sheltered her womanhood, and then he took her with his fingers, two of them, plunging deeply, thoroughly, until she cried for him to finish it, to make her come.

Apparently he liked her that way, needing him, rocking urgently against him. Apparently he knew *she* liked it, too, because he ignored her broken-voiced pleas to stop. Fluttering his fingers deeply inside her, he began to caress her with his thumb as well, stroking the rosy flush of her swollen lips, the distended button, until she writhed and moaned, an addict tormented by the madness that had ensnared her mind and body. When at last he pulled out, she was so aroused, his fingers glistened with her wetness. The sight seemed to move him to near violence.

"This now?" He cupped his own sex.

"Yes," she gasped.

She wanted it fast and deep, all at once. But she was still tight from his fingers, and her body wouldn't permit any such sensual violence, no matter how desperately she needed it. He could do nothing more than gentle her with hot, tender touches and coax her trembling muscles into taking him a little at a time. Leigh groaned as he entered her, delving into the heart of her, groaned as if she would die. By the time he was where she wanted him, deeply embedded, the root to her flower, she was again on the brink of orgasm. But he only thrust a few beautiful times before he stopped moving altogether and began to withdraw.

Her body clutched painfully, and her hands echoed the loss, gripping his shoulders. *"What are you doing?"*

"I'm taking you inside."

"Inside the house? Why?"

He stroked her hair and pressed a kiss to her lips, smiling at her through the pain of his own frustration. "Because you're a noisy wench, Leigh—my sweet, dignified Leigh—and they won't let me finish making love to you if we're in the city jail."

By now she was sobbing openly, though she barely understood why. Sweet and dignified? Noisy wench? Was she any of those things? Who was this woman he'd driven half-mad? Who *was* Leigh Rappaport? She wept copious tears as he wrapped her in the warmth of his clothing and brought her with him into the house.

But he barely had the door shut before the duster coat hit the floor and she whirled in his arms. "Finish," she implored. "Finish me, dammit."

"An impatient wench, too?" He led her to the coffee table that sat in front of her couch, leaving her just long enough to clear it. He took the time to set the silver tray and decanters on the floor, but the rest of the table's surface was emptied of magazines and paraphernalia with one powerful sweep.

"I'm insane for you." He drew her down, positioning her on wood polished to the high gloss of a mirror. "Insane. You know that, don't you?"

Leigh's nightgown curled wetly in her lap, and he ran his hands over the material and down her glistening thighs before he opened them. His skin was as dark against hers as the sycamores had been against the moonlight. Her mind flashed an image of a faceless man in a black coat, kneeling before her, drawing his finger down the middle of her body, opening her to his touch.

The musky smells of warm human flesh and wet clothing swirled all around her. She wanted to close her eyes as he bent his head to the gold between her legs, but she was still riveted by the contrasts in their coloring. His black hair ran with blue lights. His skin was as rich as brandy. But when his tongue darted out and touched her, when it slid across the surface of her desire, she forgot all about contrasts and screamed.

"No, please—" She roped her fingers into his hair and tried to yank his head back. "You promised!"

He caught her by the wrists, holding them tightly. His laser-blue eyes were piercing. "I promised you nothing—"

"You did!"

"Nothing." A muscle wrenched his jaw, harshening his voice. "But I'll give you what you need, Leigh, everything you need and more. If you'll give me one thing in return . . . just one thing."

Suddenly she understood, and terror gripped her. "No," she whispered. "No!"

His hands were iron cuffs. He held her wrists so tightly she couldn't move them, and when she tried to close her legs, he forced them apart with his shoulders. Moving against her fervent pleas, he dipped down into her secrets again, and she screamed with the raw, wild pleasure of it. This truly was insane. Torture! He was forcing pleasure on her. If this was his revenge—to put the demented doctor in an asylum, to have her straitjacketed so she couldn't abuse herself—it was working!

His tongue stroked and teased her in ways no finger ever could, nearly lifting her off the table. Her body tautened against the gentle suction of his lips, against his sweet, tugging kisses. The soft, sensual ache that invaded her knotted thigh muscles drained her of strength. She could feel another wild cry rising inside her, she could feel the pressure building like a wave, but it never broke. Instead she shuddered and slumped forward in abject surrender, yielding to his power over her—giving him what he wanted. "Anything," she sobbed. "I'll give you anything."

He slid his tongue into the heat of her then, plunging it so deeply she could do nothing but sway above him in mute wonder. The sharp nip of his teeth made her gasp for breath. He had marked her again. Even there.

Within seconds he'd brought her to a climax with his mouth that was so explosively beautiful, she lost touch with the world. Sweet, dignified Leigh Rappaport, who barely knew who she was, or where she was, flew apart at the seams and came back together again like sorcery. Somewhere a celestial magician was waving his hand in the air and bowing extravagantly to the cosmos. She could hardly believe such intensity existed. It had never been a part of her existence. Never. There was only one thing wrong, one thing missing. She didn't have him.

Her body began to tremble and clutch again. "Nick—"

She reached for him, and as he lifted her up they came together. Suddenly he was there, in her arms, moving inside her, filling her with the deep pressure and pleasure she needed to close the circle of ecstasy. She reached for him, and he was there, again and again, part of her body, the voice in her mind, the harsh cry of her heart. He was there, holding her, loving her, whispering her name with a reverence that brought the tears spilling back. He gave her everything he'd promised, everything and more. He made her fantasy a reality, and all he wanted in return, all he wanted in life . . . was her.

Leigh shivered in his arms.

Somewhere in her soul she had responded as if to a mate. This union was her destiny, but had she coupled with a man or a sorcerer, a dark hunter of souls? Whatever he was, Nick Montera had well and truly taken possession, for she bore the tender marks of his ownership, inside and out.

CHAPTER
·· TWENTY ··

THE LIVING ROOM was dark except for the lazy orange flames undulating in the gas fireplace. The soft patter of rain on the roof was the only sound that broke the silence, and the shadows leaping against the walls made the room look as if it were submerged in the cascade of an amber waterfall.

They were lying on the floor, still entangled. Nick was stretched out nude on his back, his eyes closed, his face and body offered to the flames, and Leigh, curled up next to him, had found herself meditating on the way the firelight sheened his burnt caramel skin with rich shades of gold. Earlier she had taken a crocheted afghan off the couch to cover them, but somehow she'd ended up with most of it, perhaps because she'd gradually inched it off him.

Apparently she was cured of her fear and loathing of the naked male body. Not only that, she hadn't sneezed once. Her ex-fiancé would have been proud. Well, perhaps not, she admitted with a quick mental headshake. It was the first time Dawson had come into her mind that morning. It was also the first reminder of the world she'd been trying to block out.

She couldn't seem to grasp the full impact of everything that had happened over the last few days, either privately or professionally. It was still too soon to know the effect on her career, although she'd already collected a few anxious telephone messages from her publisher and one from the psychological association's ethics committee informing her a complaint had been filed against her.

She hadn't responded to any of them. She hadn't been able to think past the wreckage of her personal life. Was it really possible that she and Dawson were no longer together? That she and Nick *were*? Even more bizarre, it felt right with Nick. How could that be? She didn't understand it, given the ambivalence she'd harbored, the suspicions and fears. Conflict couldn't be canceled like a dinner reservation, not even by a night of astounding sex. Leigh's world had shrunk to a population of one since the trial. Tonight she had expanded the tiny circle to include Nick, but their encounter had seemed more dream than reality, as it still did now, *especially* now, lying in a firelit room with this "dark prince" of a man.

She smiled ruefully. That reference had popped up recently in the press, among other places. To Leigh's surprise even a comic on late-night cable had complained about his girlfriend's obsession with the "fucking prince of darkness." More than once Leigh had thought about the emotional price of surrendering to her feelings for Nick Montera, that it would be a sweet sexual hell for the uninitiated. She'd never felt such raw turmoil or known such naked pleasure. The tiny wounds on her body where he'd marked her were still hot and tender. For once the media had been right. He *was* a dark prince. He was everything people thought he was—except a murderer.

A sigh brought her back to the present. His sigh.

Stirring, still more asleep than awake, he acknowledged his physical body with a touch that ran from his chest to his groin. It was an unconscious act, apparently born of some atavistic desire to connect with his own flesh, and perhaps even a way to bring himself back to consciousness. His fingers curling, he raked them lightly through the sable fur that swirled his pectorals, palming one of the muscles briefly before following the shaft of hair that rode down toward his belly, where a knife scar whitened brown flesh. It was over in a matter of seconds, but not before he had cupped the darkness between his thighs.

Watching him, Leigh felt a thrill that nearly stood her honey-blond pageboy on end. It was a totally spontaneous thing, she knew, and the most natural of gestures, but it had left his nipples taut and another strategic muscle visibly thickened. The final blow to her composure was the way his silver bracelet glowed in icy contrast to his warm sienna skin.

She was still recovering when he turned toward her, his eyes just flickering open, dark lashes at half-mast.

"It was a good dream," he said, his voice faraway and coarsened by sleep. "But this is better."

He reached up as if to touch her hair, and she tilted her head, making the blond tresses available to him. Closing her eyes, she allowed herself to savor the ripple of his fingers as they moved through the loose tumble of gold, to enjoy the tender possession of his hand as he cupped her head and massaged her neck. He had no trouble giving pleasure, or receiving it. She wanted to be that free, too.

"Do you want my full-service massage?" he asked, shifting to his side as she opened her eyes. "More importantly, are you going to share that thing?"

"What thing?"

"That blanket you're hoarding. I'm feeling slightly exposed here."

There was no way to cover herself and him as well. Something was going to have to show, so Leigh lifted up to turn the narrow blanket sideways, intending to drape it over them both from shoulder to thigh. What she didn't intend to do was dangle her breasts in his face, but that's exactly what happened.

She felt a darting sensation of pleasure, and when she turned back to him, she caught his faint smile before his lips closed over the rosy softness of her nipple. He hadn't given two tender pulls on her breast before she was wet between her legs and ready to climb on top of him, to climb all over him! She was so ready, so instantly aroused, that she ran her hand down his torso to his loins, caressing him just the way he'd touched himself.

"You're bad," he said. The words sizzled in his clenched jaw.

"You make me that way."

"I want you that way."

She reared back as if to get up, some wickedness making her want to stretch the tension even tighter, to tease him until he was driven to ravish her with his beautifully hard body, to punish her for her sensual transgressions. It was a feminine impulse she'd never experienced before, much less given in to.

Instantly he gripped her wrists and brought her back to him, holding her suspended as he searched her sparkling gaze. "And just where the hell are you going, Leigh?"

"There's something I need to do," she told him, breathless laughter on her lips.

"You and me both, baby."

"Sorry, buster, save it for later—"

"Buster? You bet you're sorry."

She'd already pushed him to the edge. The heat flaring in his eyes told her that much. But she reared back again anyway, tossing her blond hair, brazen in her defiance as she dared him to try and stop her.

"Bitch," he said softly. He pulled her down to his chest with a grip that rivaled a professional athlete's, then rolled her onto her back and loomed above her. "I'm going to fuck you now, you sweet little blond bitch. Because that's exactly what you want me to do, isn't it?"

She didn't have to answer him. She was writhing, tied up in lovely little knots of desire. Her hips were undulating against his locked thighs, and the sound that quavered from her throat was a whimper of pure sensual need.

Within seconds they were sexually entangled, and Leigh was fighting not to crest even as he entered her. She'd never known such crazed, tortured lust to be with a man. There was a purity about it, the fierce spiritual quality of a water baptism or some other ancient rite of cleansing. She climaxed several times, a wild rippling, seemingly never-ending series of them as he moved powerfully within her, each tiny implosion leaving her limp beneath him before it built to another. If their coupling was spiritual, it was also primal. She felt as if she were being swept into the same dark world of aching eroticism that fueled his work.

She was emotionally and physically spent when it was over. Exhaustion was her protection, her cocoon. The lassitude was as sweet as it was profound, like emerging from a coma, and when she finally opened her eyes to the world, he was sitting next to her, his coat draped over his shoulders, a snifter of brandy in his hand.

"You called for a Saint Bernard?"

She was too weary to return his smile. "I can't move," she told him, moaning as he lifted her into his arms. She tried to sit up, but couldn't manage it. Grateful for his strength, she let him cradle her against his chest and tuck the afghan around her. She had never been enfolded so gently in a man's embrace. He stroked her hair, his voice murmuring against her temple. He was father, lover, priest, and healer, everything the hungry heart longed for. Letting her head loll in the crook of his shoulder, she gave herself permission to feel the way she never had as a child—cherished. A sigh welled in her chest. It was a new experience, this tender, loving care. It was frightening how much she liked it.

"How are we doing?" he asked, holding the snifter to her lips. "Can you handle some of this?"

As Leigh sipped the brandy she realized there was pink light seeping through the curtains. It was dawn, and she was with the man who couldn't face a sunrise. If she could keep him occupied, he might not notice.

"How did you ever find the brandy snifters?" she asked him.

"I keep them in a china closet in the hallway."

"Now she tells me."

She couldn't see him, but his voice had the wry quality that she associated with masculine helplessness.

"You're lucky I'm persistent," he said, laughing. "I searched every nook and cranny of this place, doctor. The real payoff is that I now know all your culinary secrets. For example, this particular snifter was hidden in the last place a bachelor would look, your dishwasher."

"I'm into organization," she admitted, loving the toasty warmth of his arms and body. He was a regular heat machine.

"I may be able to arrange to have you forgiven for the sin of organization, but you'll have to stay naked and messy all weekend."

"That shouldn't be a problem as long as you're around." She glanced over her shoulder, expecting a raffish smile. Instead she got mock seriousness and a kiss on the corner of her lips. Her insides quivered and twisted expectantly. No, not *again*. What a frightening thought. She couldn't want to do it again! A soft groan reverberated through her.

He laughed softly and nuzzled her, gently biting her earlobe. "You *are* a sweet little blond bitch. I can't believe how hot you are."

"Neither can I!" Leigh wasn't finding it funny anymore. Her thighs ached as if she'd been doing calisthenics, and another part of her was throbbing with sensitivity. She felt as tender as a bruise. She *was* that tender. "Don't kiss me anymore, okay? Do something brotherly."

He lifted her hair and caressed the tiny wound on her neck with his lips. "This is as brotherly as I get."

Leigh sighed, determined not to give in to the quivering in her depths. "I hope you didn't have any sisters."

Taking pity, he began to sway with her and croon as if she were an unhappy child, petting and cajoling, sweet-talking until finally she could do nothing else but relax in the circle of his sheltering arms. Unfortunately, as her nervousness subsided, other doubts and concerns were there to fill the void. So many things had been said in the heat of passion last night. He'd made it sound as if she were the only woman in the world, the center of his existence, and as much as she wanted to believe him, she remembered Paulie Cooper saying Nick had made her feel the same way.

Leigh did not want to be one of Nick Montera's conquests, photographically or otherwise. She would not be relegated to his studio wall, a half-dressed, melancholy female in his photographic harem. Nor did she want to be the realization of an adolescent fantasy. "Why did you come here last night?" she asked him, her voice tellingly soft.

He sifted her hair through his fingers as if weighing the silky threads for gold. "I thought we covered that."

"You said something about eating pomegranates, I remember that, but you also said there was one more thing you wanted to do."

"Be with you, Doctor. I thought I made that clear, but if there's any doubt in your mind—"

She ducked away as he bent toward her. "That much is clear," she assured him, wrapping the afghan around her as she curled herself into a ball and sat up. She wasn't willing to face him quite yet. There were several things she wanted explained, and it would be easier if she didn't have to stare into the world's most seductive blue eyes while she did it.

She heard him get up and slip on his jeans, the zipper being the telltale clue. She was ready for him when he returned and sat down. "Why me, Nick? That's what I want to know. What's the attraction?"

"You are a homely little thing, that's for sure, but I think Groucho said it best—I never met a shrew mole I didn't like."

"Be serious, Nick. Is it because I'm blond?"

"Do I have any other choices?"

Damn him! He was determined to make a joke of this. "Then is it because I'm a doctor? Is that what attracts you? Or is it because you believed I was inaccessible to you?"

"All of the above?"

She stiffened.

He laughed. "You're an inaccessible blond bitch of a doctor. What more could a man want?"

She turned her head and glared at him, hurt by his insensitivity. "How much does *any* of this have to do with me, Nick? Could you tell me that?"

The pain must have come through in her voice because his smile faded. Chastened, he reached out and drew her around to face him. "It has everything to do with you, Leigh, and nothing to do with blond hair or doctoral degrees or anything else."

"Then this isn't about Jennifer? Or some other dream girl from the past?"

"Is that what you think you are to me? Wish fulfillment?" He gazed at her in amazement. "At first maybe you did remind me of things I thought I could never have, but that's not what this is about, Leigh. You took an incredible risk for me. You jeopardized your career, broke off your engagement. I know what those things must have meant to you, and you put them on the line. I should be asking you why—" He sat back, rubbing his arm. "Why *did* you do that, Leigh?"

"I didn't believe you could get a fair trial."

"So it had nothing to do with me personally? It was all about justice?"

She looked away, the answer in her eyes.

"That's what I thought." He was silent for the space of a deep breath. "You're not wish fulfillment, Leigh. My teenage dreams couldn't do you justice. They weren't even close."

If he'd known what her heart had wanted to hear, he'd just said it. His fingers touched hers and she took his hand, grasping it tightly, but she wouldn't allow him to pull her into his arms. There was too much emotion welling inside her. If he got any closer, she might break down and reveal how vulnerable she really was. She might even say words she could barely believe were there on her lips.

"Thank God Paulie Cooper came forward at the trial," she said. "If she hadn't . . . you wouldn't be here now."

"Right." He laced his fingers through hers. "Thank God for Paulie."

His tone suggested a reluctance to pursue the topic, but there were so many things Leigh still didn't understand about the trial or his relationship with his former model. She decided to try again. "I caught the newscast where you said you were framed. Who do you think did it?"

His continuing silence drove her to press forward a little. "Or shouldn't I ask?" she said, pulling up the afghan to more fully cover her breasts. She found it hard to believe that he wouldn't share his feelings with her after the things they'd just done, the talk they'd just had, but men were often reticent about subjects women opened up to automatically. The key factor was usually pain. Very often a man's defense against it was to avoid it altogether.

"Jennifer had a boyfriend," he said.

"Yes—" She offered what she knew, hoping to keep the conversation going. "Paulie told me. He's a policeman—Jack Taggart. Is that who you think did it?"

Nick's lip curled back in disgust. "I know the bastard did it. I just haven't figured out how to prove it."

"Maybe I can help. I spoke to Taggart once."

His reaction was instantaneous. "What the hell for?" He gripped her with sudden force, his fingers closing over hers as if he could stop her from doing something reckless. "He's a maniac, Leigh. I don't want you anywhere near him."

"It's all right, I won't be," she promised, anxious to reassure him. "I think it's smarter to let the police take care of these things anyway."

"The police? He *is* the police."

She was beginning to be sorry she'd brought the subject up. It was ruining what had otherwise been a beautiful interlude. The intimacy she'd felt between them was slipping away, and reality was intruding again, bringing with it the unresolved problems—her career, her editor, her mother. What were those people going to say when they found out who she was with? What would Dawson say? She was reasonably sure he didn't consider their relationship over, even if she did.

Nick's sudden change of mood confused her. Apparently the trial was a taboo subject, but she didn't understand how the event that had brought them together and changed both their lives could be off-limits. She would have liked to broach it again, but she didn't want to test his feelings for her. If she pushed him, he might do something drastic, like close off altogether, or worse—walk out on her. The latter would make things a great deal easier for everyone concerned, she supposed, but the possibility left her feeling bereft. She couldn't risk it. Perhaps tomorrow or the next day, but not now, not while she could still remember every detail of the way he'd held her, every word of the sweet declaration he'd made.

Leigh drew her hand away from his, despairing of any way to bridge the gap between them. There was another reason she'd been trying not to think about the future. The odds against happiness with Nick Montera seemed impossibly high, so why court failure? It wasn't just the outside forces working against them, it was the man himself. He was confoundingly unpredictable, a moody bastard if ever one existed. He was forceful, arrogant. Controlling, too.

A sigh burned through her lips. Oh, Leigh, Leigh, she thought. Those were just exactly the reasons she couldn't keep her hands off the man! She'd had the wretched luck and worse judgment to fall for a knife-throwing, neck-biting ex-jailbird. A fucking prince of darkness in the inimitable words of some TV comic.

She drew her legs tight against her chest and pulled her hand into the confines of the afghan. Once she'd curled the wrap around her as tightly as she could get it, she felt like a mummy who'd returned to its case. The only thing showing was her blond head and all ten of her toes.

"What do you think about this weather, huh?" she remarked listlessly. "The pits, isn't it?"

He didn't answer her, but there was something about her mummified state that seemed to have caught his attention. He was contemplating her exposed toes as if they ranked among the most fascinating things he'd ever seen. Apparently her little toe held the most appeal, because he ventured a forefinger over to examine it.

She watched in disbelief as he coaxed it back and forth in a tiny arc, then lifted and wiggled, as if product-testing for flexibility. Eventually he began to amuse himself with her other digits as well, and soon Leigh was biting back a smile.

His hand stilled. "Leigh? Are you okay in there?"

She looked up at him imploringly, all caution forgotten. "Just promise me one thing, Nick, okay? *One* thing?"

He gazed at her through dark lashes, surprise kindling in his features. If he'd been about to say something, her passion to express herself had cut him off.

"I don't want you to take on Taggart by yourself," she told him, determined to get through to him somehow. "Figure out another way, okay? Hire a detective to investigate him or something. Whatever. Just don't do it yourself."

As he registered the depth of her concern the distance seemed to melt from his expression.

"Really, Nick, can't you leave it alone?" she persisted. "Going after a man like him would be terribly dangerous."

His smile was a little slow in coming, but it was worth the wait.

"What do you think I am, Leigh, crazy?" he said. "On second thought, don't answer that."

They both laughed. It was their joke, the doctor's and the patient's.

The gloom seemed to lift from the room, and yet he grew sober, as if some awareness had come to him for the first time. "You asked for a promise. I've never made you one of those before, have I?"

"No, you never have."

"Then I guess that makes this a significant occasion." He rapped the knuckles of her toes lightly with his fingertips, as if he were making a drumroll. "You can take my word on this, Leigh. I'm not going to do anything to endanger myself."

He hesitated, his fingers going still as he glanced up at her. There was a hint of sadness in his smile. "Not now," he averred softly. "Not after tonight . . . after you."

She pulled a quick breath, but couldn't seem to get it past the stitch in her throat. Her heart had already begun to make itself heard. It sounded like the drumroll he'd made with his fingertips. Gazing at him, she was almost afraid to smile. Some emotion was stealing into his expression, but she couldn't decide what it was. Hope? By any chance was that a glimmer of hope in his eyes? Or was she only imagining what she wanted to see? God love her. God *help* her! He'd made a promise, a solemn oath. If he broke it now, if he did that to her, she would die.

"This isn't like you, darling. You've always been so sensible."

Ice cubes clinked madly as Leigh stirred artificial sweetener into her passion-fruit iced tea. She shouldn't have been enjoying this so much, but today's lunch with Kate was a milestone. Her mother was sternly cautioning her to be more prudent in her behavior. In the annals of the Rappaport mother-daughter relationship, this was a first.

"I thought that being sensible was the problem." Leigh took a sip of the tea and wrinkled her nose. She added a squirt of lemon to cut the sweetness, then plunged the entire wedge into her glass. "Didn't you tell me I needed to grab hold of my life and shake it like a rug?"

"Yes, but you've thrown the rug out the window, Leigh. You've thrown every rug in the house out the window."

Leigh was intrigued by her mother's uneasiness. She didn't want to call it a gulp, but Kate had just taken the latest of several healthy swallows of the white wine she was drinking, and now she was reaching for the bottle of Pouilly-Fuissé to refill her glass. At Kate's suggestion, and in order not to cause a public stir, they were lunching in today, on the sunporch of Kate's home, the Pasadena mansion where Leigh had grown up.

"As for Nick Montera," Kate went on, "you've exposed yourself to scandal and ridicule for his sake. Don't you think that's enough? Is it necessary to date him, too?"

Leigh sat back in the creaky wicker chair and gazed past her mother at the moss-green arbors of the hanging gardens, her favorite place to play as a child. The air smelled of tender green sprouts and damp, fertile earth. Spring was upon them with its frenzy of growth and procreation. "I decided to take your advice and try a man with eclectic tastes," she said. "You were right, by the way. He isn't boring."

Kate snorted. "I'm sure Nick Montera is anything *but* boring. However, when I recommended a man with eclectic tastes, I wasn't thinking about a man with a taste for murder."

"He was acquitted," Leigh stated calmly.

"Yes, I know." Kate waved her hand, determined to draw Leigh's attention away from the gardens. "But didn't you think it was odd the way that ex-girlfriend of his popped up? It seemed convenient to me. If Dawson isn't checking it out, he should be."

Leigh turned on her mother angrily. "Checking *what* out?" she demanded to know. "Don't you think Dawson's office has harassed Nick enough? A jury found Nick innocent. It was due process. His only crime is being with me, your daughter."

Leigh had been getting anonymous phone calls recently, though she didn't want to frighten her mother with that information. Most of them had been ominously silent, nothing more than a breathing presence on the line, but one time Dawson had announced himself and asked how she was doing. Before she could end the conversation, he'd tried to talk her into coming back. He'd also left messages on her machine, dire warnings about Nick, as if he were determined to convince her she'd made a mistake.

"Well, that may be true," Kate was saying. "But you can't deny that Nick Montera has a dangerous reputation with women." She strained forward, pursing her lips as she scrutinized Leigh. "What is that mark near your mouth? He isn't manhandling you, is he?"

"Yes, he is, Mother. He is doing exactly that. Nick Montera is manhandling me—and I like it."

"Leigh! Have you lost your mind?"

Leigh touched the tiny welt near her mouth and sent a thrill buzzing through her lips like a live current. She pushed her iced tea away. Enough of this fruit punch, she wanted some of Kate's wine. She wanted to banish all her fears and concerns, to laugh out loud. It was nearly spring, "the cruelest and fairest of the seasons," and the man she'd taken up with had a dangerous reputation with women. Was that perfect? Or had she lost her mind as her mother believed?

• • •

The anonymous calls persisted in the days that followed. Every time the telephone erupted, it set off warning bells in Leigh's mind, disturbing what might otherwise have been an halcyon existence. She hadn't told Nick about the calls yet. She didn't want to break the intimacy that was building between them or to trigger his suspicions of Jack Taggart. She'd already decided it must be either Dawson or Taggart making the calls, and she was virtually certain that Nick would have gone after either man—or both.

She dealt with the situation by letting the messages pile up on her answering machine. It was an avoidance technique that allowed her to ignore the anonymous caller and everything else she didn't want to deal with. She made only the briefest calls to her mother and editor to say that she was hard at work on her "project" and would talk to them when she could break away. She didn't bother to explain that her project was Nick Montera.

In the meantime she and Nick became fugitive lovers, living on dreams and borrowed time. They both understood that their halcyon days were numbered. The media hadn't yet discovered their whereabouts, so they took full advantage of their freedom, knowing it couldn't last. They disguised themselves with caps and sunglasses, rode bikes on the beachfront sidewalk, visited the shops, and went to art movies.

Leigh introduced Nick to Frango Mint ice cream and he returned the favor, sneaking her into his studio one night and whipping up Veracruz margaritas and fresh shrimp drenched in lime, his favorites. Nick's housekeeper, Estela, whom Nick admitted to bribing with devotional objects and vows of good behavior, had left some flan, a delicate Spanish caramel custard, in the refrigerator. Leigh ate with abandon, drank too much, and afterward she seduced Nick right there on his kitchen table with Marilyn watching. If she'd done it to bug the cat, she'd succeeded. Marilyn had stalked off, nose in the air, tail twitching, not to be seen again that evening.

Leigh wasn't entirely sure what else she and Nick had done that night. Her memory was a little fuzzy on the details, but she did recall swirling madly in his arms through the carnival set he was creating in his studio, a fantastic display of glass and mirrors, and ending up in his waterbed, where she'd plummeted into one of her exhausted sleeps and dreamed of a mermaid washing ashore on the crest of a silvery-blue wave.

By the following morning the dream was over. When she and Nick returned to her condo, they were greeted by tabloid reporters and mobile television crews. The media had found them. Within twenty-four hours they were featured on every local newscast and the front page on all the major Southern California newspapers, including the *L.A. Times*. EXPERT WITNESS RENDEZVOUS WITH SEXUAL SORCERER, the headline blared.

"Nick!" Leigh cried the next evening, listening to the messages on the telephone machine. "*Vanity Fair*? Nick, come here! *Vanity Fair* called you today!"

She found him in the shower and dragged him out, naked and dripping. While he wiped down with a towel she played back an astonishing number of inquiries about him and his work. Leigh had feared the publicity would be the deathblow to her career, but ironically it was turning out to be a windfall for Nick.

"You've been made like a bed," she teased him softly.

"Climb in," he coaxed. "Let's have a slumber party." He looped the towel over her head, creating a swing for her hips, and hootchy-kootchy'd her to him.

In the days that followed he was flooded with offers from art dealers all over the country. They gushed about the dark power and cathartic emotion that permeated his work. They talked of launching his career on a grand scale nationally, of prestigious showings and worldwide recognition.

Everyone wanted a piece of Nick Montera. Calls from top magazines like *Vogue* and *Gentlemen's Quarterly* continued to come in. Hollywood was interested in the story of his life, and MTV wanted to talk to him about rock videos. Leigh was staggered by the onslaught. It was a once-in-a-lifetime opportunity for Nick, and though she harbored concerns for her own predicament, she was thrilled for him, as well as grateful that all the hoopla seemed to have distracted him from the Jack Taggart situation. Still, she couldn't help wondering how Nick's phenomenal success would affect the two of them.

When she expressed her fears to him, he literally swept her off her feet with his reassurances. Carrying her in his arms to the Victorian four-poster, he confessed his need for her, how he wanted her with a sweet rage that overrode every other consideration in his life. Leigh was virtually helpless to resist him. Their lovemaking was a fever dream played out in slow motion, deliriously intoxicating. Sex with him had become a pleasure drug injected directly into the vein, she realized. She was mainlining Nick Montera.

But all too soon the time came for him to make a decision about his career. The asking price for his photographs had already quadrupled and was predicted to skyrocket from there. With that in mind, he'd hired a top agent to help him field the offers.

Tonight Leigh was unaccountably nervous as she waited for him to return from an appointment with his new agent. A rich turkey-and-okra gumbo was bubbling on the stove, and she'd started sipping the dinner wine as soon as she realized Nick was going to be late.

"Known the man for less than a week in the biblical sense," she said under her breath. "And already I'm a widow to his career."

She was seated at the kitchen table, wearing nothing but one of Nick's huge denim shirts, her legs crossed, her foot tapping as she eyed the empty wineglass. The front door slammed just as she was rising to revisit the bottle of chardonnay.

"Am I late?" Nick asked, appearing in the doorway.

He was wearing jeans and a camel suede jacket that Leigh particularly loved, with an open-necked white shirt underneath. Sometimes Leigh wished he didn't look so damn sexy. More and more often, quite honestly.

"What happened?" she asked, cutting right to the heart of things. She didn't seem to be able to do much of anything else lately. The media had her trapped inside. She hadn't been to her office in days, and cabin fever had set in. Besides, there was so much at stake, or at least it felt that way to her.

"I'm going away," he said.

"Oh, God—" It spilled out of her, so much emotion she couldn't contain it. She turned away, her fingers at her mouth.

"It's all right," he said. "It won't be for long. I told him five days, no more."

"Where are you going?"

"The East Coast, New York. I'll do a couple of showings, we'll talk to some magazine people. Why don't you come along?"

"No—" He sounded as if he really wanted her to, but they'd already agreed that they wouldn't feed the media frenzy by being seen together in public. It was damage control for her career.

"Leigh, it's okay," he assured her. "I won't be gone long, and I've brought something to keep you company. Have a look."

His coaxing tones finally made her turn.

"Oh, Nick!" He was holding a tiny gray kitten in his arms, and the sight of him cradling the forlorn little thing brought tears to her eyes. It made her want to fall to her knees and weep with joy. She knew then that it had happened, that she'd already stepped off the cliff and was hurtling through that nerve-shattering void that means you no longer own your own soul. She was crazy in love with both of them. The kitten *and* the man.

CHAPTER
·· TWENTY-ONE ··

THE PHONE WAS ringing and Leigh couldn't get into her condo to answer it! Most of the press had followed Nick to New York, so she'd chanced a quick run to an all-night convenience store for some cat food. Fortunately she hadn't been spotted, but now she seemed to have jammed her door key in the lock! Of course, it had to be Nick calling her. She *knew* it was Nick.

The groceries hit the cement doorstep with a metallic clunk. Cans rolled out of the bag. Leigh twisted the key furiously, wincing as its notches cut into her fingers. If she missed him, she'd die! He'd been gone three days and she hadn't heard from him yet. It was nearly nine o'clock, so it must be after midnight in New York, but he'd been on a whirlwind schedule. This was probably the first chance he'd had to call.

"Ahhhh!" she cried, half pain, half relief as the key gave and the dead bolt rolled back into its groove. She threw the door open and the first thing she saw was Bashful, the gray-and-white bundle of fur who was named for the shy dwarf. The kitten was fleeing down the hall.

"Bashful, it's okay!" Leigh made a dash for the phone and caught it on the last ring before the answering machine took over.

"Hello?" Her voice echoed in a hollow tunnel. There was no dial tone, but there didn't seem to be anyone on the other end. Was it another anonymous call? Normally she wouldn't have answered the phone. Now she hung on for a moment longer, still thinking that it might have been Nick. He must have hung up just as she answered, trapping her in the eternal void—that flat, dead space where no one could call in or out.

"Hello? Anyone there?" Disappointed, she hit the disconnect button, but the silence pressed back like an opposing force. The line was in limbo.

"Dr. Leigh Rappaport?"

Leigh jumped. "Yes?" The man's voice was hushed, yet crystal clear, as if he were right there in the room with her. She glanced around, trying to collect her wits. It wasn't Nick, but it might be his agent. "Who is this?"

"You're in danger, Doctor."

Leigh fell silent, listening to the caller. It didn't sound like Dawson, but some of the other anonymous messages hadn't either. She couldn't tell whether this was someone she'd heard before, but the man's voice was uncanny. He could have been behind her, whispering in her ear. The resonance on the line was that sharp.

"If you don't believe me," he said, "go to Nick Montera's studio. Look in his darkroom."

"Who is this?" Leigh's suspicions had been piqued. He'd tipped his hand with the reference to Nick. It was either a reporter with some ploy to scare up a sensational story, or perhaps Dawson had put someone up to this sick joke.

"Do you want to die like Jennifer Taryn, Doctor?"

Leigh made no attempt to hide her irritation. "If you don't identify yourself immediately, I'm going to hang up."

He went on as if she hadn't spoken. "The studio has a side door. The key is in the porch light. Go there, Doctor. Go and see what your lover has done."

The line disconnected with a burst of static.

"It must be a crank caller," Leigh said firmly as she hung up the phone. "Some nut who has no life except preying on people's fears. Either that or it's a reporter desperate for a story." But as she glanced down the hallway and saw Bashful peeking at her from the crack of a doorway, she could relate to the kitten's blinking fearfulness.

There was no door key in the porch light.

There wasn't even a porch light. Leigh groped in the darkness, searching for some way to open the side door of Nick's studio and feeling foolish that she'd taken the caller's bait. At least the press hadn't been waiting for her when she arrived. The paparazzi had disappeared the moment Nick left on his trip, though they could be hiding in the bushes, videotaping her forced entry.

And it *was* going to be a forced entry, she realized, twisting the doorknob. The door didn't appear to be securely locked. It wasn't even hanging quite right on its hinges, so she ought to be able to manage it. The weather had turned chilly recently, and she'd worn a quilted coat for warmth.

Now, bracing herself to ram the door, she hoped the shoulder pads would provide some cushioning. She hit tentatively the first time, testing her own strength and the door's resistance. With the next blows, she applied more and more force until she heard something crack in the frame. After that it was no more difficult than unjamming a warped door. She gripped the knob with both hands, levered a foot against the outside frame, and wrenched until it gave.

The door creaked open onto nearly impenetrable blackness. Wondering why she hadn't thought to bring a flashlight, Leigh groped along the walls, searching for a light switch. She never found one, but by following the shelves that lined the walls of what seemed to be a storage area, she got to another door. To her great relief this one was not locked, and it led her into the studio itself.

The area was dimly lit by intermittent spotlights on the ceiling. At the center of the room, several spidery, scaffoldlike objects were arranged like the dark maze of a circus funhouse. Mirrors dominated the huge, eerie set, every kind imaginable. They studded the scaffolding, floated from the ceiling, suspended by wires, and dotted the floor, freestanding. She and Nick had danced through the half-finished set the night he brought her here for shrimp and margaritas. She could see now that it was almost done. He'd been working on it at every opportunity in preparation for the upcoming shoot.

There was plenty of light for Leigh to navigate, but she held off long enough for a quick visual search of the room to be certain that she was alone. Nick had said his housekeeper was only there during the day, and no one had appeared to be on the premises when Leigh drove up. The entire place was dark, including the living quarters. Estela had undoubtedly gone home long ago.

Leigh found the darkroom almost immediately. The safelight saturated the room with a lurid red glow that made her uneasy, but seemed a necessary precaution. She knew very little about the developing process, but she didn't want to take the chance of damaging any exposed film.

Someone had been busy, she realized, scanning the lines of prints that had been hung to dry. Nick had told her he was anxious to get back to work, but she hadn't realized he'd been taking photographs recently. The first group appeared to be candid outdoor shots rather than carefully arranged studio work, but something about the pictures disturbed her.

She was having trouble focusing, and at first she thought it was the light giving them a bloodstained quality. But on closer inspection, she saw that they were photographs of terrible carnage. A man, who appeared to have been viciously stabbed, was lying in a busy intersection as cars zoomed by. A toddler was screaming over another dead child, who might have been an older sibling. A driver was slumped over the steering wheel of a crashed car, and a mangy dog had been shot through the head.

Leigh's stomach was churning. Was this what the caller had meant? The pictures were grotesque, but she didn't understand why he would have associated them with danger to her. She turned to the prints hanging behind her. They all seemed to be of the same woman in progressive close-ups. She was lying on a bed, nude, her arms flung out, and though she appeared to be sleeping, the shadows crisscrossing her body made it look as if she'd been tied down.

The shots were riveting, frightening, and Leigh found herself moving closer to inspect them. "Oh, my God," she breathed as she realized what she was looking at. The woman sprawled nude on the bed was her! The first shot was of her entire body, but he'd isolated her upper torso in the remaining shots and blown each one up progressively larger. The last print contained nothing but her head and neck in the frame, and the shadows swathing her throat gave the illusion that she'd been strangled.

Washed in dirty red light, the scene looked particularly horrific. And the woman, dead. Leigh stepped back, wanting to run from the room. A tray clattered to the floor. She whirled and bumped into something else, the countertop. Her flying arm knocked over an electric timer, and a glass beaker exploded against the tile floor. The entire room was falling down around her! Rolling red shadows created an alien landscape, and the smell of ammonia rose like a cloud, piercing her nostrils.

She pulled one of the enlargements off the line and rushed out of the room, crushing the print in her grip. She couldn't seem to breathe right, even in the huge hangarlike studio. When had he taken that picture of her? It could only have been the night they'd stayed here. The night she'd gotten high on margaritas and lovemaking.

The darkroom door became her support system as she fell against it. She felt as if she'd been violated. No, she didn't believe it, not this. He wasn't capable of something as obscene as this—taking nude photographs of her without telling her. He would never have invaded her privacy that way. He would never have taken advantage of their relationship.

The studio's shadowy lighting made it difficult to see details, but she began to search the room for a phone. She felt as if she were drunk again as she tried to navigate the room. She would call Nick and tell him what she'd found, let him explain all this to her. It had to be some photographic trick.

There was a small office across from the storage area where she'd entered. The cubicle was sparsely furnished and didn't look as if it had seen much use, but there was a telephone on the desk, and she had memorized Nick's itinerary. If nothing had changed, he would be at the Meridien, a hotel in Manhattan.

A moment later a hotel operator put her through to his room. His voice was heavy with sleep as he answered, but it was a tremendous relief just to hear him. He sounded so reassuringly normal that her fears began to dissipate.

"I'm calling from your studio," she told him. Discarding the crumpled print on the desk, she hurriedly explained what had happened. "When did you take the photographs of me, Nick? And why didn't you tell me?"

His silence rushed at her. It frightened her. "Nick, are you there?"

"What are you doing in my studio, Leigh?" he wanted to know. "How the *hell* did you get into my studio?"

His voice was harsh, so brutally cold, Leigh couldn't answer him. Pain shot through her arm, nearly fusing her hand to the phone as she stared in shock at the print—at the close-up of her own symbolic strangulation. Swaying in mute agony, she dropped the receiver back into its cradle.

Leigh couldn't bring herself to drink more than a sip or two of the pot of chamomile tea she'd brewed to calm her nerves. She'd been home over an hour, but the agitation building inside her had left her spinning and sick at heart. She couldn't slow her racing thoughts or stop the torturous replay of what had happened tonight in Nick's studio. He might as well have struck her. That was the impact of his cold fury.

The telephone rang as she rose from the table to put her dishes in the sink. The china pot and teacup clattered into the stainless steel basin, abandoned in her haste to get to the cordless phone. She was certain it must be Nick calling, and that there'd been some misunderstanding.

"Dr. Rappaport?"

"Yes?" Leigh's fingers closed over the edge of the countertop. Very carefully she lifted herself onto one of the barstools. It was him, the man who had warned her about Nick. Her impulse was to hang up the phone, but she resisted it, aware that there was something vaguely familiar about his voice. If he was trying to disguise it, he might slip. He might say something that would help her identify him.

"Do you believe me now?" he asked her. "I warned you that your life is in danger. He'll make an attempt on you soon, perhaps even tonight."

"Who will?"

"Nick Montera."

Leigh released the countertop, her fingers bloodless. "Nick is in New York! I just spoke to him."

"He's coming back—"

"This is *absurd.*"

"You're in his way, Doctor. You know too much."

"In his way? What—"

The line clicked in her ear. It was dead before she could complete the thought. What *had* he meant? She stared at the handset as if it had turned into a weapon, and in fact, it had.

Over the past few weeks the machine had assaulted her privacy and her sanity. More recently it had turned the assault on her sense of safety, putting her in fear of her life.

She placed the unit in its cradle and crossed her arms tightly over her chest, anchoring herself as she held on to her own shoulders. She felt as if she were pinwheeling in space, at the mercy of wild winds and tides. Every tie in her life seemed to have been severed in recent days and weeks. And now the last one, Nick, had been cut, too. She had nothing left.

Her training in crisis intervention was of little help to her now. Not only was she the victim instead of the caregiver, she'd lost touch with what was real, and more fundamentally, with *who* was real. Everything that was happening fell outside the bounds of rational behavior. It was a psychic earthquake that left her with no footholds and nowhere to turn for help.

She couldn't call Nick. He'd become one of the tormentors. Dawson was out of the question, too. There was her mother, but Kate would probably insist that she go to the police, and Leigh didn't want to bring the law into it, not with the media screaming at her heels.

If only she could have identified the caller.

A soft mewing at her feet drew her attention. "Bashful!" She dropped to the floor to scoop up the kitten she'd forgotten all about. Swallowing thickly, she knelt on the kitchen floor and clasped the tiny bundle of warmth to her body. "Thank God for you," she said. Her fingers were clumsy as she stroked his silky gray ears and the white markings on his forehead.

The kitten's body began to vibrate softly and Leigh choked up at the sound. She threw back her head, tears in her eyes. The ache that filled her throat held a glimmer of relief. Praise God, something was normal. Kittens could still purr!

An idea came to her a short time later, while she was feeding Bashful a bit of tuna on a paper plate. She'd been letting her phone messages accumulate for some time, especially in the days before Nick left. The tactic had caused her some guilt, but now she was glad she'd done it. She wanted to hear every message that had come in prior to tonight, all of the man's calls. Perhaps there would be a clue to his identity, or something that would tell her whether or not the calls had all been made by the same person.

She played back the entire tape, cringing at some of the tabloid reporters' crude attempts to get her to return their calls. The messages from her mother made her feel guilty, and the ones from her editor made her wonder if she would still have a book contract when all of this was over. There were also long, silent stretches with nothing more than a breathing presence. But it was a call from Paulie Cooper that brought her up short.

The model's voice was soft and urgent. "Dr. Rappaport, I need to talk to you," she said. Unfortunately, she hadn't dated the call, so Leigh didn't know when it had come in, but she had left a number.

It was a local call, but Leigh wasn't familiar enough with the first three numbers to identify the town. She tried the number several times, but no one answered and there was no machine to leave a message on. Finally Leigh called an operator, who verified that the line was not out of order and told her it was a West Hollywood exchange. There were no other listings for Paula Cooper, so Leigh continued trying the number into the night, then gave up, promising herself she would start again in the morning.

Exhaustion set in as the night wore on, but Leigh knew she would never be able to sleep. She wasn't worried about the caller's threat. No matter what Nick had done with the photographs, she did not believe he would try to hurt her. It made no sense. If she was in his way, he could simply walk out of her life. He owed her nothing. And she knew nothing about him that she could, or would, use against him. At least nothing she was aware of.

Toward dawn she went back to work on her manuscript, a decision that enabled her to feel as if she were regaining some control over her life. In order to avoid the feeling of being watched she'd had in her office, she brought the book and everything else she would need upstairs to her bedroom and closed the shutters tight. Once she was arranged on the bed, with the kitten snoozing at her feet, she forced herself to block out everything else and concentrate on the work.

It wasn't an easy task, but it went reasonably well until sunshine began seeping through the shutters. Her first thought as light struck was that he'd been wrong. The caller had warned her of an attack, and though she hadn't believed him, the possibility had been preying on her mind all night.

She removed her glasses, laid them down on the nightstand, and went to open the shutters with a sense of profound relief. After a quick shower, she fed the kitten and tried Paulie Cooper's number again. There was still no answer, but the moment she hung up, the phone rang. The decision about whether or not to answer it had her poised on the balls of her feet.

The machine came on. A long, taut silence told her someone was on the line.

"Doctor," the caller said at last, whispering the words "I was wrong. The attempt will take place tonight."

Leigh's sharp intake of air was the only sound in the hushed room. She hurried to the machine and played the message back several times, listening for clues. Though the volume was soft, the resonance and clarity of the man's voice made her think of someone speaking into a microphone. Had she ever heard this voice before?

When she gave up at last and tried to go back to work, she could no longer concentrate. The call had truly frightened her. Her thoughts kept straying to Nick Montera, and they were macabre. Images of the violent photographs she'd seen in his darkroom came back to her, bathed in red. Was it possible that he was indulging in a form of fantasy aggression in order to suppress his real impulses? Or could the prints be exactly what they appeared to be—precursors to violent behavior?

Perhaps it was exhaustion, but she was having flashes of recall—remembering the explosive way he'd reacted when she'd come up behind him in her office and the black wrath she'd witnessed the day he'd driven off the two gang members. He was a volatile, dangerous man. She'd never doubted that, but she'd never seriously believed he would turn his anger on her in a murderous way.

Why hadn't she considered it? she wondered now. Being a doctor did not make her exempt. Therapists had often become targets of their hostile or paranoid clients, and Nick's history of violence would have been enough to give anyone pause. Yet she'd searched for every way possible to excuse it, along with his test results.

A wave of light-headedness washed over her as she slid

off the bed and walked to the windows. Fatigue, certainly. She rubbed her burning eyes, but only succeeded in blurring her vision and making her stomach desperately queasy. She hadn't eaten anything except some cereal for breakfast, and now it was late afternoon. Still, she could hardly tolerate the thought of food.

Bashful mewled at her from his perch on the bed. She'd woken him up apparently, and he needed some reassurance. But she couldn't even manage that right now. How could this be happening? she asked herself. She had years of training and fieldwork. Her specialty was psychological evaluation. It was her job to assess and predict behavior, yet she'd discounted the quantitative findings in favor of her intuitive feelings about the subject. It had "felt" right at the time. Now it was beginning to feel like a drastic error in judgment.

The kitten yowled again, startling Leigh into a near stumble. She was staggering on her feet. She had to get some rest. "I just need a little nap," she told Bashful as she approached the bed and fell across it, rolling to her side.

With a sigh that sounded almost human, the kitten rested his head on his paws and joined her.

Leigh drifted off immediately, falling into a troubled, half-conscious state, and though she told herself she would only close her eyes for a minute, she felt as if she'd been given anesthesia. She was floating in a strange twilight sleep where she had some vague consciousness of what was going on around her, yet was helpless to do anything about it.

At some point later she realized it was getting dark, but she didn't have the strength to get up and close the shutters. The thumping sound she'd heard was the kitten jumping off the bed, she told herself as she dozed off again.

She continued to wash in and out of conscious awareness. In her waking moments she found herself struggling to remember what she knew about ritualistic murderers and their pathological need for control. She had once wondered if Nick had struck out against Jennifer Taryn in a symbolic way, killing her and arranging her lifeless body in the same vulnerable pose that he'd photographed her, thus creating the illusion that she was inescapably his.

Had she been right?

"Doctor . . . ?"

"What? Who is it?" Leigh tried to rouse herself. She couldn't tell if someone was speaking to her or if she was dreaming.

"The attempt will be tonight . . . ."

The phone—had the phone rung? Was it the machine taking a message. She raised her head and realized the entire house was dark. Stuporous, she lay back down, struggling to get her bearings. She had to wake herself up and turn on some lights. She had to find the cat.

"Leigh?"

That was Nick's voice, but it sounded as if it were coming from a distance. She tried again to push herself up when something slammed against her shoulder. The crushing blow knocked her back to the bed. Pain gripped her like talons, and a cry echoed in the darkness. Leigh couldn't tell if it was human or animal. Had *she* screamed? Was she dreaming this, too?

Her head snapped back as a suffocating weight pressed down on her face. It snuffed out her vision and her breath. A pillow, she realized. Someone was trying to suffocate her! She swung up with her arms and smashed into the form that was climbing on top of her. She couldn't move. She couldn't *breathe*. Her attacker's hands pinned her to the bed and his knees gouged deeply into her thighs.

The pillow pressed her into the mattress with lethal force, as if her attacker meant to push her through the bed. Instinctively she fought to suck in air, but her throat spasmed painfully against its own walls. There was no air. Her lungs were empty, burning. She was suffocating in her own spent oxygen.

Rainbow colors exploded behind her closed lids. Panic galvanized her. She wrenched up from the middle of her body, trying to buck her attacker off. And then she got an arm free. Swinging it back and forth furiously, she grabbed hold of the first thing she connected with, the heavy brass extension lamp that sat on her nightstand.

She brought the metal base down savagely, aiming for her attacker's skull. The crack of brass against bone was muted by the pillow, but Leigh heard a roar of pain. The suffocating weight lifted off her, and she flung the pillow away, lurching to her feet. She made a frantic dash for the bedroom door as the intruder staggered backward.

There was no time to find the kitten. She prayed he'd hidden under the bed. Her only thought was to get help, but as she fled down the stairs and ran out of the front door of her condo, she realized the neighborhood was asleep, and she couldn't risk taking the time to wake someone. She had to get to her car.

She kept a spare car key in a magnetized case under the driver's side fender of her car, but she'd never had to use it in the six years she'd owned the Acura. She had no idea if it was still there. When she reached the carport, she turned back to see if she'd been followed. There was no sign of her attacker, so she dropped to her knees and groped for the key case. Her throat and lungs were burned so badly, it was torture to breathe, and when her fingers touched the rusted case, she nearly collapsed from relief.

The smell of gasoline permeated her nostrils as she backed the Acura out of the garage a moment later. She'd nearly flooded the car trying to start it. Oblivious to any other traffic, she wheeled the car onto the street and floored it, but she only had a few seconds to enjoy the taste of freedom. Headlights flashed in her rearview mirror as she reached the corner.

She glanced behind her, terror rising in her heart. Was she being followed? There was only way to find out—try to lose the car. She would have to drive as if her life depended on it. If he stayed behind her, he was either a policeman or the man who'd attacked her.

Five minutes later Leigh hit the 405 freeway going ninety miles an hour. There was no doubt in her mind now that she was being followed. The headlights had been with her since she left her street, and it wasn't a black-and-white. She would have been pulled over for speeding by now. This car had the high, blinding beams of a truck.

A horn sounded behind her. She glanced in the mirror and saw that he was moving up on her rapidly. Sweat from her hands slicked the surface of the wheel, forcing her to bear down and grip it hard. There was an exit coming up. She couldn't take it at this speed. She had to slow down, but if she could find a gas station or a convenience store, she might be able to get help.

The car was on top of her before she ever got to the exit.

Rattled by its blaring horn and blinding headlights, she slowed up and felt something hit her from behind. Her head snapped back, and she braced herself for another concussive blow, but suddenly the car was alongside her on the left, ramming her fender. Within seconds, it had forced her off the road onto the shoulder.

Leigh had her foot on the brakes, but the engine was still running as she reached frantically to lock the car doors. The door was ripped open just as her finger touched the button. She shrank back, a scream on her lips as she saw who it was.

"What the fuck are you doing?" Nick snarled.

"No!" she cried as he reached in for her. But she was no match for his strength or determination, and he pulled her bodily out of the car.

CHAPTER
·· TWENTY-TWO ··

THE DOOR HANDLE dug into Leigh's thigh as she braced herself against the passenger door of Nick's Jeep. He was driving with a cold-blooded vengeance that terrified her. But even if his recklessness didn't get them killed, she wanted as much distance from him as the cab could give her.

She'd put up a fight when he tried to take her from the car, and she'd landed a brutal kick to his shin. In a rage, he'd pulled her out by her ankles, thrown her over his shoulder, and carried her to the Jeep. After depositing her in the passenger seat, he'd warned her that if she tried to escape, he'd bind and gag her. Leigh had taken him at his word.

He'd also accused her of making him force her off the road, and he'd demanded to know why, but Leigh hadn't responded. She hadn't wanted to provoke him further especially since her greatest concern was where he was taking her. It looked as if they were headed back to his place, and she didn't know how to stop him. She'd already discarded one escape plan after another. There was no way to jump from the moving car without killing herself or to grab the steering wheel without killing them both.

She tightened her grip on the hand strap as he negotiated the corkscrew canyon road. The sharp turns were making her ill, and she ducked her head, trying to reduce the physical stimuli. Trees were rushing at them, houses whipping by. The headlights of moving cars streamed endlessly, yet seemed to stand still.

She had her eyes closed by the time he drove up to the studio and cut the engine. The driver's-side door slammed and gravel crunched under his angry footsteps as he came around the car. Her hand snagged in the leather grip before he swung the passenger door open and pulled her into his arms.

She made no attempt to fight him this time. She had been coaching herself to relax, knowing any resistance would trigger more aggression. With her hands tightly clasped in the hollow of her throat, she let herself be carried into the house like an invalid and set down on a cordovan leather sofa in his vast living room.

The area was dark except for two low-lit hexagonal lanterns, one on each side of the fireplace. A bronze panel by the door had several rows of what looked like intercom buttons. Nick hit one of the buttons and a hanging Tiffany lamp beamed to life, casting yellow light in a wide arc. Leigh was absently aware of the Spanish influences in the room's decor. Of glazed pottery and hand-loomed wall tapestries.

Of black terrazzo flooring . . .

And of Nick, staring at her from across the mirrored expanse of tile, anger smoldering in his expression. He was wearing a khaki trench coat over a black shirt and jeans, and other than the slow blue burn of his eyes, he bore very little resemblance to a ritualistic killer.

"Now are you going to tell me what the *hell* is going on?" he asked.

She gathered herself up protectively, tucking a leg beneath her. "What do you mean?"

"Why did you take off when I pulled up behind you? You floored the damn car, Leigh. You were going at least ninety miles an hour. Why?"

"Why were you chasing me?"

"Chasing you? I was trying to get you off the road before you killed yourself."

Leigh brought a hand to her mouth, watching him as she rubbed her knuckles along her lips. He sounded as if he knew nothing about what had happened to her. Did she dare believe that? "You're supposed to be in New York," she said.

"I came back early. You sounded upset on the phone. You hung up on me—"

Remembering what he'd done to her, the pictures he'd taken, she was suddenly furious. She'd been through twenty-four hours of hell because of him. She'd been forced to reexamine every ghastly second of the last weeks, to search her heart for impossible answers.

"Someone attacked me tonight," she said, her voice taut.

"Someone did what?"

She tried to stand and couldn't. A stabbing pain shot through her shoulder as she moved to steady herself. Her blouse sleeve was ripped out, she realized, and there was a gash on her arm. In all the chaos, she'd forgotten about that first painful blow to her shoulder.

The wound throbbed hotly, but it was the sudden fierce ache in her heart that made her blurt, "Someone attacked me!"

Weakness washed over her. The adrenaline was wearing off, and she was beginning to quake. "Stay away from me," she pleaded, falling back on the couch.

"Leigh? What are you doing?"

"Stay away!" She waved him back as he broke toward her. "The man who called me. He said it was you, that you wanted me dead."

Disbelief seemed to hit him in the gut. "Someone told you I was going to kill you?"

She stared at her arm, at the injury.

"Who attacked you tonight, Leigh?" His voice was suddenly, achingly hard. "Who did it?"

He would not be put off this time. He strode over and knelt down next to her, examining the laceration on her arm. It had stopped bleeding, but there was a nasty bruise.

"Who did this?" He laid open the torn material of her blouse with his fingers. "Tell me!"

"I couldn't see him."

"But you knew who it was, didn't you? Or you *thought* you knew."

She would never understand what had made him force the issue. Perhaps it was the same impulse to inflict damage that took hold of her. Something made her say what must have been locked up inside her the entire night, the accusation she should have known she was going to make.

"You." Her mouth twisted with pain. "I thought it was you!"

His hand gripped the sofa arm as if a collision had rocked him from the inside, some horrible, internal impact. And then a wave of fury broke over him, and he rose up in a rage.

"I don't prey on women!" he snarled.

He walked away from her, shoulders rigid, looking around him as if for something to smash. His trench coat flew as he moved. His black hair glowed and swung in the light. It was eerie watching him. Haunting. His reflection flared out across the terrazzo like something alive, the sorcerer incarnate, railing against forces even darker than himself.

There were no clocks in the room that she could see, but some internal clockwork was ticking at an accelerating rate, and Leigh could feel every stroke. Each advance of its hand, every quiver of its spring-driven energy, told her that time was her enemy now, that it was speeding both of them toward catastrophe.

"No, don't—" she whispered.

He'd swept up a pottery jug from a pedestal. It looked like an antique of some value. She thought he was going to heave it through the windows as he strode toward them. Instead he gripped it in the white web of his hand for several seconds, then abruptly set it down and turned around.

Leigh thought it was over, that he'd come to his senses, but her relief died quickly. His eyes seemed to ignite from within as he stared at her. They were fiery with some conflict she couldn't analyze, but there was pain in the mix, terrible pain. She was struck by their glitter.

"Fuck it," he breathed suddenly, and swung back. His arm sliced an arc through the air. His entire being seemed bent on destruction. The jug flew across the room and smashed against a liquor cabinet, vaporizing in clouds of dust and shards of clay. Advancing on the wreckage, he ripped a painting off the wall and impaled it on a table lamp.

The sound of canvas being rent and torn was sickening.

It made Leigh shudder in horror.

He spun around as if looking for something else, something priceless and irreplaceable. But there was nothing . . . nothing but her. Defeat seemed to burst from his lungs in a shaking fury. He picked up a chair and dropped it, letting it clatter to the floor and topple over.

Violence had a sound to it, Leigh realized. It was a sharp reverberant song that sprang from the wound. The melody was pain, the lyric was fear. And it was echoing now in the teetering wood of the chair, the groaning canvas of the painting. It was echoing in her own flesh.

In the midst of that song, Nick Montera stood silent and shaking, his head bowed. All the anger seemed to have drained out of him.

Leigh wanted to say something, but she was frightened.

"It wasn't me," he said at last. He seemed to be speaking to his own reflection, gleaming up at him from the terrazzo tile. "One death on my conscience is enough."

One death? Did he mean Jennifer? The court had acquitted him of that crime, but Leigh wasn't sure of anything anymore. She asked him.

"No," he answered. "It wasn't Jennifer. For Christ's sake, I never *touched* Jennifer. It was her."

Leigh followed his line of sight to a framed photograph that was sitting on the floor next to the fireplace. The picture was facing the wall. She couldn't see it, but she could guess what it was. Glancing back at Nick, she saw the mute desolation in his expression and realized that she was right. This picture was the source of it all, his black rages, his deepest grief.

A moment later Leigh was on her knees by the fireplace, the photograph in her hands. It was the portrait that had transfixed her when she first came to the studio, the dreamy, sad-eyed woman who'd been the centerpiece of his showroom.

But someone had destroyed the woman's moment of vulnerability. The picture had been slashed diagonally, cleaved into two triangles by a knife blade. There was no question in Leigh's mind who'd done it. Nick had clearly meant to destroy the photograph for some reason. Perhaps he'd set it by the fireplace, intending to burn it and then found he couldn't.

"This isn't Jennifer?" she asked, still not understanding.

"No, her name was Faith. She was my mother."

"Your mother?" Leigh tore herself from the damaged portrait to look at Nick. "Did you take the picture?"

He shouldn't have tried to smile. It was heartbreaking to watch his mouth twist, to see the uncontrollable bitterness and grief. Leigh looked away quickly, but he had seared her focus like a too bright image. She would remember him that way for a long time, she feared.

In the silence that followed, the only sound she heard was the ticking of an omnipresent clock.

"When I was in grade school," he said at last, "a camera manufacturer sponsored a scholarship program for underprivileged kids. I was one of those kids."

"You were good even then," she assured him. It was his mother's wistfulness that made the photograph memorable, but the play of light and shadow was surprisingly skilled for a child.

"Your mother died when you were ten, didn't she?" Leigh broached the subject carefully, trying to ask the question in a conversational tone.

"She didn't die, she was killed." On the next soft breath, he added, "She was shot."

Leigh found that information shocking. He'd admitted he was responsible for her death. What was he saying now? That at ten years of age he'd shot his own mother? It had to have been an accident, but what a terrible trauma. She was beginning to understand the rage. If he had been the cause of her death, he must be driven by the blackest kind of passion, the need to punish himself for something he believed unforgivable. He must have been eaten up with guilt and self-reproach his whole life.

"Can you talk about it?" she asked.

"There's nothing to say."

There's everything to say, she wanted to tell him. Your mother is dead, but you're dying right there where you stand, dying every day because of whatever it was you did.

"How did it happen?" she asked.

"Pretty much like any other cold-blooded murder committed on a Sunday afternoon at a kid's birthday party. She was serving cake and ice cream in our front yard. I was ten years old. I was happy. It was one of the few times in my life."

"But you said she was shot."

"Yeah." He dragged his thumb down his cheek, creasing the flesh. "Los Coyotes blew her away. *Vatos locos* from the San Ramone barrio. It was me they wanted."

"You? Why?"

"I stole their cache of drugs and guns. I was desperate to prove myself to the Alley Boyz, a local gang. I figured if I ripped off the Coyotes and got away with it, I'd be in. They'd have to accept me."

"But you didn't get away with it."

"My mother saw the low-rider pull up, and she told me to go in the house. If I'd done it, she might be alive today. But I made a run for it, and Los Coyotes opened fire. When she saw their guns, she threw herself in front of me."

"And that's how she died?"

He touched his breastbone. "The first bullet killed her. It lodged in her heart."

Leigh watched helplessly as his jaw muscles locked with the fire of unshed tears. She understood now. When his mother had seen the guns, she'd tried to shield him. Faith Montera had risked everything for her child. It was an impulse as ancient and instinctive as nature. But when she gave up her life, her ten-year-old son took on a debt he could never repay. He lost more than a mother that day. He lost his soul.

"I fell to the ground with her," he said. "I had her in my arms. Her blood was everywhere."

Leigh didn't want him to go on, but he didn't seem to have any choice. In a voice that was toneless, crushed by the weight of his memories, he told her the rest of it—how his mother's last wish was that he get out of the barrio alive, how she'd wanted him to make something of himself.

"I got out." He lifted his head. "She didn't."

His pain was so raw, Leigh ached for him. "You couldn't have known what she was going to do. You were ten years old."

He seemed not to have heard her. He'd buried his hands in the pockets of his trench coat as if they somehow symbolized his crimes. "Nothing mattered after that," he said. "I went insane for a while, I tried to get myself killed."

Leigh rose to her feet. "Is that why you got involved with Jennifer? A gang leader's girlfriend?"

"That was later, but yes, it was one death wish after another. Even prison—that stinking hole—wasn't punishment enough." He looked up at her, his eyes emptied of light. "Nothing is."

Leigh didn't know what to say. Nick Montera, the photographer, was larger than life, in some ways, a contemporary legend. The man himself was powerful, unassailable. She had felt the steel in his hands—and in his will. Perhaps that was what made this so difficult. It was almost unbearable for Leigh to see him suffer this way. The grieving ten-year-old still lived inside him, and she had to do something, say something, speak to that sadness. It was her job to offer counsel, but she couldn't play therapist. She was reduced to basic human instincts in dealing with him. She always had been.

"What is it?" she asked him.

Some painful recognition flickered as he stared at her.

"You remind me of her," he said. "You even resemble her physically in some ways. She was remote like you, beautiful like you. It's in your nature to be kind, I think. But I can't touch you. I can't reach you. She was like that, too, always withholding a part of herself."

Leigh could hear her own breathing. She had drawn in a soft, inaudible gasp of surprise. Sweet and total surprise. "Let *me* touch you, then," she said.

His head lifted and his eyes washed to a shade of blue so dense they reminded her of sapphire shards. He didn't seem to be quite prepared for her as she rose and walked toward him, but that only aroused Leigh's compassionate nature more. She was unsteady herself, and she found it poignant that he was off balance, too. He had always been the one in control, and perhaps for that reason, it gratified her tremendously to know that she could affect his breathing the way he had hers, that she could make him tremble with surprise.

He watched her with disbelief as she came up to him.

His gaze was so sharp and wild, it would have been easy to lose herself in it, to forget what she was doing. But as she reached up to touch his face, he closed his eyes. A shudder moved his body. Warm air jetted through his nostrils, bathing her, and his muscles tightened to knots beneath her fingers.

She loved what was happening to him. Loved and feared it. She didn't want to hurt him anymore, there was no question of that. But she didn't quite want him to stop hurting either, sweetly hurting in response to her actions. His vulnerability was mesmerizing.

"There's tenderness in your mouth," she told him, though she didn't touch him there. It seemed too much of an invasion. "It's part of your male beauty . . . and sensuality."

His jaw was sandy and textured from a five o'clock shadow, but she liked the roughness of it against her skin. His lashes were spiky with a dampness that made her wonder what it would be like to press her lips there, to comfort him tenderly. She had never tasted a man's tears before. She had never responded to a man's pain the way she had to his. Every nuance struck at her heart.

He arched his throat as she trailed her fingers down it.

He breathed something, a word she couldn't hear. She knew it must be profanity, but it had sounded holy.

The cords of his neck stood out like knives against her caress. His Adam's apple was a small stone.

"Let me be kind," she heard herself whisper.

She saw his hands curl into fists inside the pockets of his coat, and she felt as if parts of herself, parts deep inside, were doing the same thing, curling as uncontrollably as his fingers. Yes, she was touching Nick Montera, yes, she was reaching him, but what was she doing to herself?

Longing sang out. Like violence, it had a sound, only this was the lonely shiver of bells, the searching cries of birds. It called to her sweetly. In all the craziness, she'd lost touch with how powerful her feelings ran. How deep.

Somewhere in the play of her hands over his face, the contact had begun to take on a new quality. Leigh could feel the tension in her fingertips, a tingling centered in her palm. Her hand had curved itself from his jaw to his cheekbone, and she was fighting the impulse to draw her thumb over the fullness of his lower lip. As she imagined how hurt and tender it would feel, her fingers curled into the warmth of his cheeks.

And then suddenly she was doing it, caressing his mouth.

Moisture sheened the soft curves, making them shiny from the trembling strokes of her thumb. He caught her flesh between his teeth, and when he bit down, the longing spoke to her again. It sang out softly.

"I won't hold anything back," she whispered. *I won't hurt you the way your mother did.*

His eyes flew open, pale irises bleeding into the black velvet of his lashes. A new kind of pain burned in his breathing now, the pain of desire. But he didn't move to touch her. He didn't even take his hands from the pockets of his trench coat. He simply watched her watching him. And breathed.

She was almost afraid to move.

His shirt had pulled free of his jeans on the side, and she made entry there, stealing inside the cocoon of cotton-knit warmth, seeking the intimacy of his being. Smooth skin invited her to explore as she gingerly ran her hand around to his back. The graceful, powerful cord of his spine was nearly lost in overlays of muscle, but she glided down its length and felt his back arch as she reached the place where his waistband stopped her, just inches above his tailbone.

"Christ," he said, "what are you doing to me?"

"I don't know . . . being kind?" The sound of her own voice startled her. It was full of sexy, throaty passion. She sounded terribly aroused. She expected to be stopped at any moment as she eased her hand around to his rib cage. His muscles quivered and seized under her touch, but he didn't intercept her. He left his hands where they were. He let her roam.

"Just being kind," she insisted.

His breathing was deep and profound as she laid her palm against his belly. It rose to a gasp when she rode upward over his nipples. They hardened to diamonds, and his body lifted as if he were in pain.

She was awed by his reactions and by her own ability to trigger them. Her experience of cause and effect had rarely been so immediate, or so thrilling. And she'd never seen a man transported like this. A touch made him tremble, the scrape of her nails brought a ragged moan. He was rigid with something that must have been agony, but it was very different from the pain of his childhood loss, and she couldn't have spared him these feelings if she'd wanted to. They brought her too much aching wonder, too much breathless trepidation.

A long, raised scar spiraled gracefully from his rib cage into the depths of his blue jeans. It led her eye and her mind and her hand. Proud flesh. Something grabbed deep in Leigh's belly as she touched this magical wound. Something gripped and held her tightly, making her want to shudder with him.

She could feel the wound's sensitivity under her fingertips, the grainy ridges, the tender heat of puckered flesh. Again, it seemed as if she were touching something equally tender within herself as she explored him, something that compelled the senses inexorably toward torment, an anguish as sweet as it was nerve-strung.

If she followed the wound's path, it would take her to the seat of his agony. Would he allow that? Did she dare? His beautifully contorted face told her that anything was possible, that he might even have suffered this injury for her, borne the cutting weight of the knife blade so that she could discover the flesh and the pride and the pain of his being. The scar was a symbol, a sinuous snake, taking her down the path of life's mysteries, leading her into temptation.

He seemed to stop breathing altogether as her fingers floated down its ridges. When the scar dipped into his jeans, she followed it, sliding her fingers into the waistband. Before he could stop her, she began to undo his button fly.

With every button she visualized him tearing her hands away and pulling her to her feet. She understood that he had given up a great deal of control. Perhaps that was why it was so terribly important that he not stop her now. He was surrendering to her with every touch, becoming aroused as she worked. By the time she had the last button undone, she was down on her knees.

His hipbones were locked, his pelvis clenched.

Leigh heard him groan as she released him from his briefs, but she was barely aware of it. Nick Montera was aroused. He was hard. His entire body was an extension of the quivering muscle that sprang from the center of his being. Horrible and beautiful at once, it seemed to have nearly as much power over her as it did over him. But instead of being repelled, she was fascinated by what his body had done, by its gift for bringing a man both pleasure and pain, for altering his consciousness with unreasoning sexual urges. Her heart was pounding, her thighs aching and straining. Her mouth was watering.

She touched him with her hands first, stroking lightly along the sinewy hardness, aware of the powerful vibrations that ran from base to tip. The raised ridge on the underside and the flaring head were ultrasensitive, she discovered. He jerked when she caressed him there.

When she finally took him in her mouth, she glanced up and saw that he was watching her. His hands still imprisoned in the pockets of his trench coat, he watched silently as she made love to the most intimate part of his body.

Leigh wondered fleetingly if he might come to a climax that way, if he might explode with his hands fisted in his pockets. The thought excited her somehow, but it wasn't to be. As she explored him with her mouth and her tongue, discovering his slick, swollen contours, she felt his hands on her at last. They roped through her hair, gathering it up and compelling her to take him even more deeply.

"Be kind to this," he breathed raggedly.

His voice was constricted with need. His hands were rigid on her head, gripping her fiercely as he probed the limits of her mouth and throat. She could feel him shuddering deep in her throat, and the shocking pleasure of it left her weak. She had never thrilled to this kind of sex before, never wanted a man to engorge her mouth and send his fluids rocketing down her throat. She did tonight.

She wanted to touch him everywhere, to caress the firm, downy balls, swollen with the heat of his body, to feel his naked buttocks flexing beneath her hands. She wanted to make him cry with pleasure, to drain him dry. But as she reached out for him she felt him pulling away, withdrawing from her warmth.

"Why?" she asked as he lifted her to her feet.

Pain harshened his features. "You could kill a man with that much kindness."

He was shaking as he curved his hand to her throat and drew her to him. He held her in a soft, dangerous caress, tilting her head back until all she could see was him—the wild radiance of his eyes, the savage power of his constricted jaw. His hard face was her only focal point. She would have fallen if he hadn't locked his arm to the small of her back.

"It's my turn," he whispered. "To be kind."

She closed her eyes as hot breath touched the corner of her mouth. His parted lips trembled, whispering so lightly over that tender, shivering part of her, she wasn't sure she'd been kissed. He dragged his mouth over the softness, touching and murmuring, creating the most incredible friction. But he didn't quite kiss her, and the waiting tantalized her. It made her strain toward him hungrily.

"Don't hold anything back, Leigh," he warned, his fingers encircling her throat.

"How could I?" she responded faintly.

Leigh's stomach dipped into oblivion as he took possession of her mouth. He swept past her defenses, leaving her weak with surprise as he gently assaulted the softness of her parted lips with a deep and powerful kiss. He burned his way into her being, his mouth a firebrand, his teeth sweetly punishing, and then he filled her up with his tongue, reminding her what he had just done to her moments before, what he would do to her again. She had to grip the sleeves of his trench coat to anchor herself, but nothing could have lessened the impact of the shock wave that hit her. It inflamed her need. She wanted him now, immediately, and everywhere, in the heat of her mouth, her body. She was wet. She ached.

"Be kind," she told him, pulling free of his arms.

She began to unsnap her jeans and back toward the couch, imploring him with her eyes as she undressed. In her rush she managed to get out of the jeans, but she didn't bother with her blouse. It was a wise choice. By the time she hit the couch and toppled backward, Nick Montera—the man, the photographer, the sorcerer—was already between her legs.

He fell onto her, his hands on either side of her head as he entered her with one long, deep thrust. Leigh let out a sharp cry of pleasure and bent toward him, rising almost instantly in the grip of a glorious crisis. She had no control with this man! All he had to do was enter her, and she was gone, lost. Her back arched like a bow and she shuddered uncontrollably as the ripples began to cascade through her in a seemingly endless chain of sensation.

His thrusts were strong and perfect, an arrow impaling the target. Dropping back to the couch, she sprawled beneath him helplessly, her legs flung wide, her arms limp above her head, utterly abandoned to the sorcerer's dark spell. She had never felt anything so beautiful as the way his body plunged and dove into hers. The ache deep inside her was sweeter than life itself. It rolled and soared, some fabulous internal tide over which she had no earthly power. Would she ever be still again?

And then suddenly, sensing the final throes, she reached up to grip his powerful shoulders and was taken on another rocket ride as he bent to kiss her lips. She curled into a knot, entwining her legs around him, rising toward him in a vibrant coil of pleasure. The joy that shook through her was strange and wild. Primal. But the tension didn't abate completely until she felt him release inside her, until she was filled with his hot, searing juices. Then they fell together in a shuddering heap, clinging and exhausted, complete.

Luxuriant. That was the sensation, the feeling, the word that filled Leigh's mind as she lay in his arms afterward. She felt luxuriant in his warm, strong embrace as she would have in the hot steaming water of a bathtub. A warmth spread through her that penetrated to the bone, promising she would never be cold again. It was so deeply fulfilling, such a balm to her spirit that she drifted off for a moment, her head curled into the hollow of his neck, her shoulder tucked into the warmth of his armpit.

She had never trusted, never loved this way before.

Some time later, rising drowsily, she realized he'd built a fire for them, that he was offering her Calvados and a warm flannel throw to wrap themselves in.

She roused herself and took the cordial glass from him, smiling dreamily. "You're almost as good as a hot bath," she told him, feeling wicked. "I'm so relaxed I may never move again."

"Just what the doctor ordered?"

"Yes . . . oh, yes."

The room was drenched with the pungency of burning pitch and the liqueur's fragrant perfume. He dropped to the couch and pulled her into his arms, wrapping the blanket around them, building a cocoon. They sat in silence that way for some time, sipping Calvados and watching the fire burn down, until it slowly dawned on Leigh that the portrait of his mother was missing. He must have removed it while she dozed.

Reality intruded with an abruptness that made her pull away from him. Sadly she remembered the nude pictures she'd found in his darkroom. Sadly she asked him why he'd taken them.

He seemed surprised that she didn't understand. "I'm a photographer, Leigh. When I see something beautiful, I take a picture. We'd just made love, actually we made love all over the house that night, if you remember. You fell asleep on my water bed afterward, and I'd never seen anything like it. My first instinct was to capture you that way, with the lamplight flowing all over you like a river."

If his motive flattered her, it also concerned her. He didn't seem to realize that he'd invaded her privacy. "Some of the shots were blown up. Why?"

"I didn't notice the shadows until I'd developed the negatives. They fascinated me, and I kept blowing them up to see what they were."

"What were they?"

He smiled at her apologetically. "Shadows."

"Really? Nothing more sinister than that?" Still, Leigh wasn't satisfied. "What about those other shots?" she probed. "The violence?"

He seemed perplexed. "Oh, you must mean Manny's pictures. He's a protégé of mine."

"A photography student?"

"No, Manny's a grungy little barrio rat who broke into my place in San Ramone. I made him a deal. If he'd take pictures of the hood for me, I'd pay him for any shots I could use. That was his first roll."

She set her glass down on an end table. "But all the carnage, Nick. Should a child be exposed to that?"

"Leigh, he *lives* in that carnage. I'd rather have him taking pictures of it than getting involved in it. His stuff is rough—he lacks any kind of technique, of course—but it's real."

"Can you do something with it?"

"Maybe." He shrugged and took a sip of the Calvados. "I've got a show in mind. I haven't figured out what to call it yet—a boy's photographic diary of everyday life in the barrio. Something like that."

Studying him as he sipped the liqueur, Leigh wondered who Nick Montera really was. No amount of training, no textbook, could help her delve deeply enough to solve that mystery. He had an artist's complexity, an outsider's rage. But he was not a killer. He'd offered help to a desperate kid. He seemed to care more about exposing violence than committing it.

Nick set his cordial glass down, too. "Are you really that concerned about the photographs? I'm sorry, Leigh. I didn't think, I just acted."

She wet her lips, not certain how she felt. "It's okay."

"No, it isn't, but there's a much bigger problem here. Someone attacked you tonight." He sought her hand inside the blanket that covered them, lacing his fingers through hers and making a bridge. "Who would have wanted to hurt you?"

"There's only one person I can think of."

"Dawson?"

"No . . . Jack Taggart. I think it *was* Taggart," she said suddenly, remembering something the policeman had said.

"Did you get a look at him?"

"No, but the day I had lunch with him, he said he wanted to blow you away, and then he changed his mind. He said he'd rather get ahold of the woman you loved and blow her away right in front of you."

"Jesus, the guy is insane."

"Think about it, Nick," she pressed. "It makes sense. If Taggart believes you stole his girlfriend, his twisted idea of retribution might have been to come after me—and frame you again."

Things were beginning to come together for Leigh. Thoughts were whirring so fast she didn't hear the click of nails on the terrazzo, the sharp little cry. But when Marilyn strolled into the room from the hallway, Leigh pressed her fingers to her lips. She'd forgotten about Bashful.

"The kitten! Oh, my God, Nick, the kitten. We have to go back to my place. I left him there!"

CHAPTER
·· TWENTY-THREE ··

STANDING AS CLOSE to the flames as she dared, Leigh rubbed her icy hands together. Nick had been adamant about her not going with him to get the kitten. She'd argued that Bashful wouldn't know Nick, that he would never come to a stranger, but Nick's argument had been more persuasive. "I don't know what to expect at your place," he'd said. "Whoever attacked you might be hanging around, waiting. You'll be safer here at the studio."

Leigh had suggested they call the police, but she hadn't pressed it. Now she wished she had. It was going on two hours and Nick still hadn't returned. Waiting was torturous, but it wasn't herself she was worried about, it was him. If someone was lying in wait for her, what would stop him from going after Nick? She was concerned about the kitten, too. The commotion of the attack must have terrified Bashful.

A telephone rang somewhere in the house. Leigh spun around, searching the area. She remembered seeing a phone in the kitchen, but she wasn't sure which way that was. She'd only been in the room one other time, and she could barely recall that night.

Following the sound of the rings, she crossed the living room and entered the darkened dining room. By the time she reached the kitchen, the phone machine had already clicked on. It was taking a message. She could see the illuminated digital readout in the darkness.

"Nick?" a woman's voice pleaded angrily. "You can't avoid me forever. I took a huge risk for you. I lied for you, Nick. At least you could pick up the phone!"

Leigh stared at the machine in disbelief. It had sounded like Paulie Cooper. Leigh was virtually certain it was her voice, but she didn't understand why Paulie would be calling Nick, or what she'd meant about lying for him.

In the next moment Leigh realized what it must have been. Only one thing made sense . . . Paulie's testimony on the stand had been a lie. Leigh rushed to pick up the phone, but all she got was a dial tone. She replaced the receiver with a sense of rising dread. Paulie had been trying to reach her, too, but Leigh had no idea why, and something was telling her she was better off not knowing, that this phone message was just the tip of some deadly iceberg. Paulie had testified that Nick was with her the night Jennifer died. If she'd lied, then Nick had no alibi for that night, which meant *he* could have been the murderer.

Was that why Paulie called? Had she been trying to warn her about Nick? Leigh stepped back and turned, searching the shadowy room. Her mind rushed in two directions at once— her immediate safety and Nick's imminent return.

Paulie hadn't left a number, which told Leigh that Nick knew how to reach her. That raised several frightening possibilities in Leigh's mind, including the question of whether or not he and Paulie still had a relationship. He had implied that they didn't, but no woman would take that kind of risk for a man casually. There had to be something enormous at stake for Paulie. Why had she done it?

Standing frozen in the gloom of the kitchen, Leigh found herself contemplating a nightmarish scenario. As far as she knew, Paulie and Nick had known each other for several years. Perhaps things between them had gone beyond the relationship stage. Perhaps they'd been co-conspirators. Was it possible that they'd plotted to get rid of Jennifer for some reason, knowing that Paulie could provide Nick an alibi? The motive for implicating Nick was obvious enough, and the use of his photograph of Jennifer a brilliant stroke. Nick's career had skyrocketed. He was a cause célèbre, the media's barrio success story poster boy—

Leigh stopped herself, aware that she'd wadded the collar of her blouse into a damp stub. She was terrifying herself! She left the kitchen in haste and got herself back to the living room, resolving to calm down. The last several days had been a harrowing experience. She was emotionally and physically exhausted, which must be why she was letting her imagination run away with her. She'd just made a nightmare out of one unexplained telephone message.

Her Calvados sat unfinished on the end table. She picked it up, holding the tiny glass in both hands as she took a deep swallow. The fumes burned her nose, and the liqueur snagged in her throat, nearly choking her. She sank to the couch and set the glass down, blinking away tears. She had to get a grip on herself. She had to think what to do before Nick got back.

A hot bubble of resin popped, startling her as she returned to the fire. The strong piney scent sharpened the air, seeming to clear her head. She had no transportation, but she could always call a taxi to take her to her car. Still, what would she do then? Where would she go? The thought of dealing with Nick when he returned frightened her, but she had little other choice. If she cared about the man—if she was in *love* with him—then the least she could do was give him a chance to explain.

Hinges creaked softly, drawing her attention. "Nick?" She called out his name, her heart rocketing. Was that a door she'd heard? Had he returned? Looking around for something to defend herself with, she cautiously made her way into the showroom.

Wrapped in shadows, the entry was ominously quiet, yet it seemed undisturbed. Nick's gallery of women gazed down at Leigh with sad, knowing expressions on their faces. Was she to become one of them after all? The next victim to hang in his gallery? He'd already taken the photograph, a picture that looked as if Leigh Rappaport had been strangled in her sleep.

Leigh turned toward the studio, alerted by a soft meow. Marilyn! It was the *cat* making the noises she'd heard.

"Marilyn? Where are you?" Leigh looked around for a light and found a brass panel of switches on the wall. The first several she hit provided illumination for his photographs, but none of them lit the hallway. Concerned about the cat, she decided to investigate anyway.

The studio looked exactly as it had the night she'd gone into his darkroom. It was dimly lit, with mirrors everywhere, some suspended from the ceiling, others with funhouse glass, creating bizarre distortions. She could see herself dimly reflected across an array of glowing surfaces. Leigh Rappaport was everywhere, even staring down anxiously from the ceiling. Nick had imagined every aspect of the set, from the design to the carpentry. He'd always needed to have total control over his work, and he'd outdone himself with this vision.

A scuffling sound came from the area of the darkroom.

"Marilyn?" Leigh picked up a hammer from a worktable as she passed it, intending to have something in hand when she nudged open the darkroom door with her foot. Her own voice echoed in the silence of the cavernous room as she called the cat again. Was Marilyn taking her on a wild-goose chase?

The door creaked softly as she eased it open. Leigh's heart went crazy. She felt like a frightened child waiting for a bogey-man to spring out at her. But it was only darkness that came at her when she peered inside. It seemed to pour through the crack in the door. She'd never seen such an endless black pit. She could imagine stepping over the threshold and plummeting endlessly, freefalling toward the center of the earth.

"Marilyn?" Leigh inched into the room just far enough to search for the safelight switch. The ammonialike smell of developing fluid was still chokingly strong. It must have been the container that shattered the night she'd found the photographs.

"Who's there?" she asked.

She'd heard someone moving in the darkness. She prayed it was the cat. Groping around the darkroom paraphernalia, she hit the light switch. The glow blinded her for a moment as the safelight came on, and then, through a wet blur of red, she saw Marilyn at the far end of the room, arched over something on the floor. The cat seemed to be playing with a small metal object.

Before Leigh could move, she had to recover from a bout of trembling relief. She had never been so glad to see Nick's cat. She had never been so glad to see anything in her life.

"What is that?" she murmured aloud.

The small cylindrical object seemed to absorb the room's light, gleaming so brightly Leigh couldn't make it out until she went over to the cat and crouched down. She reached to touch the object and froze, her hand suspended in midair. It was a man's ring.

Marilyn looked up proudly, then batted the ring toward her. Leigh leaped away as if it were poisonous. The coiled silver snake had its tail wrapped around it head. It was Nick's ring. The one he'd sworn had been stolen. She shrank back in horror.

Her first and only thought was to run. She had to get out of this place to somewhere safe. She rose to her feet dizzily, appalled at Marilyn's apparent delight with her evil plaything. Leigh didn't want to touch the ring, but she couldn't leave it. Scooping it up, she tucked it in her jeans pocket and headed for the door.

A flashbulb exploded in Leigh's face as she came out of the darkroom. She staggered backward, blinded by the brightness. The staccato click of a camera's shutter sounded like machine-gun fire to her dazed senses. Punctuating the snaps, brilliant flashes of white came at her like bombs.

"Who is it?" she cried, shielding her eyes. The incandescent light penetrated the flesh of her hands like X rays. She backed up against something solid, then turned into the wall for protection.

"Turn your head, baby. That's right. Give me a smile."

"Nick?" Leigh screamed his name. She couldn't turn around. The light was too blinding, but she'd heard his voice. "Nick, what are you doing?" she sobbed.

She crept along the wall, trying to escape the punishing explosions. The shutter clattered incessantly and there was a horrible screeching noise, as if a tape recorder were being played at the wrong speed. It sounded like the laughter of demons.

"You're beautiful, baby. You just fucking knock me out you're so beautiful."

It was Nick's voice, but what was he doing? Did he know she'd found the ring? Was he going to kill her now?

"Please, Nick, *don't!*"

As he bore down on her, his camera blazing, she ducked and made a run for it, but she couldn't get to the doorway. He was there, blocking her way. Instead, she whirled and broke blindly toward the mirrors.

Her own horror ricocheted across a million reflecting surfaces, darting in every direction. She saw herself coming and going, running madly in circles, sprinting directly at herself and racing away. Every time she turned her head, hundreds of heads spun like gyroscopes. She hesitated, reeling in confusion, trying to stop the merry-go-rounds.

But she couldn't stop them. A simple eyeblink stuttered forever. A tendril of hair flew like so many whips. She was lost in a sea of images. There was no way out. A flashbulb exploded into eternity, and her vision spiked as if she were staring at a chain reaction of lightning bolts. Every surface lit up, bouncing the jagged white wires like an electrical storm.

"Hold that pose, bitch! Do it or you're dead . . . you're dead . . . you're dead . . . you're dead . . ."

His threat roared in her ears, careening off the studio walls. Leigh threw up her arms to shield herself. It was Nick! He was going to kill her! His gleaming silver sunglasses danced wildly in the mirrors. His red bandanna unfurled like a crimson flare, streaming across the studio.

Leigh spun around, searching for a way to escape. Somewhere a strobe light came on, and then another and another. One flashcube had turned into an infinite string and the studio erupted with a nightmarish fireworks display. The popping lights stung her eyes, fouling her vision. The acid stench of sulfur seared her nostrils, but she was desperate to know where he was. He seemed to be coming at her from all directions. His red bandanna and silver glasses were everywhere.

He had a gun!

"No! Nick—no!" Leigh screamed wildly. The weapon shimmered on every surface of light. She could see the gleam of cold metal, the smooth round barrel, the wooden butt clenched in his gloved hand. In a gleaming arc, the revolver came around until it was pointed at her. Frozen in place, Leigh stared up the barrel of a million handguns, stared into the unblinking eye of her own life and death.

"It's been fun, baby," Nick's soft voice taunted. "Don't think it hasn't been fun."

A metallic click told her a bullet had just been chambered.

She dropped to crouch, desperate to avoid the mirrors. If she kept her eyes on the floor, she could find her way out. If she was blinded, he must be blinded, too!

The hardwood surface burned her skin, bruising her hands and knees as she searched for the way she'd come in the night before, through the storage-room door. It was a frantic, flailing attempt to escape, and in her desperation, she knocked over one of the mirrors. As it crashed to the ground and shattered, she slammed into something solid, a man's legs.

She hit him hard enough to make him stagger.

His voice shrieked at her from every direction. "You're dead! You're dead! You're dead!" He lurched toward her, and she grabbed for the first thing she could get her hands on, a small stool on wheels. She rammed it into him furiously. He toppled backward, and the gun hit the floor, skidding in a wide arc. Leigh tracked it frantically, trying not to become confused by the mirrors. It hit the metal base of a stand and ricocheted back toward her.

"Leigh! Where are you? *Leigh?*"

Leigh scooped up the gun and whirled in shock. It was Nick's voice, but it had come from another direction. Her searching face flashed back at her, turning and twisting. Now she was lost in the mirrors again, hopelessly bewildered, her sense of direction gone.

The red bandanna and silver glasses beamed at her from every plane and surface, but another face hung there, too. Nick's face, his black hair streaming, his blue eyes wild. It was a separate image, but both men seemed to be turning and strobing endlessly in the darkness. Leigh couldn't distinguish one from the other.

"Bitch!" someone snarled.

Leigh could hear him coming up on her, thundering at her from behind. She didn't know how to use a gun, but she whirled as the snarling form rushed at her and squeezed the trigger automatically. A body dropped at her feet and high, screeching demonic laughter filled the room. Silver glasses rebounded in the mirrors, dancing wildly, jubilantly.

"You stupid *bitch!*" a voice shrieked. "You just killed the wrong man!"

Leigh sank to the floor in horror, staring at the man sprawled out there, his trench coat billowing around him. There were no silver glasses or red bandanna. This was Nick, the man who'd made love to her tonight, the man who'd gone to get her kitten. She'd just shot him. Blood was oozing from his beautiful mouth.

"You're dead now!" the voice shrieked repeatedly. "You're dead, bitch!"

A shard of glass sliced open the sleeve of Leigh's blouse, grazing her skin. Another missile razed her face, narrowly missing her eye. As her own bleeding image appeared in the mirrors, she screamed in terror. He was throwing the broken glass like knives.

"I'm going to cut your throat!"

A glittering stiletto slashed at her, ripping and tearing. An agonized sob broke from Leigh's throat as her assailant plunged toward her. It took all of her strength to hold the gun up, all of her battered courage to use it. She gripped the weapon with both hands and closed her eyes, firing into the void again and again. Mirrors shattered in an endless cacophony of exploding glass. And Leigh's soul shattered with them. She had taken a life, and she was dying inside, as helpless as the body lying at her feet.

A cry rang out, but Leigh couldn't open her eyes. She heard the impact of someone falling and shuddered. The gun fell from her hand and she sagged into a heap. Death was all around her, but she did not understand its finality. She barely understood its power.

When at last she did open her eyes, she saw the silver sunglasses lying in the middle of the floor. The sightless, staring body of her tormentor was crumpled next to them. Leigh let out a bleating sound. Neither laughter not tears, it was the helpless whimper of a trapped animal. What kind of cruel, sadistic joke was this?

The demonic creature who'd attacked her with such vicious intent was stretched out on the studio floor as gracefully as a ballerina. In repose, Paulie Cooper's face was a study of feminine beauty and serenity. She was as peaceful as Leigh had ever seen her. She would have made a stunning Nick Montera photograph.

"Dawson!" Leigh rushed toward her ex-fiancé as he appeared in the doorway of the hospital waiting room.

"How is he?" Dawson asked.

"No word yet." She took the hand he offered and gripped it hard, trying to stop the terrible shaking inside her. Her voice broke with emotion. "He's in surgery. He's been in there for hours."

Dawson steadied her with a touch at her elbow, as if sensing her profound fatigue. He looked oddly unkempt with rough blond stubble shadowing his jaw, but his blue Nike workout suit and the Canoë cologne he'd splashed on were familiar, and a welcome balm to Leigh's nerves.

"Do you want to hear about Paulie?" he asked. "It can wait until later. Maybe now isn't the time."

But Leigh insisted on hearing. "Please tell me everything. It will take my mind off . . ." She'd been about to say Nick's name. With an uneasy glance at her ex-fiancé, she let the sentence hang unfinished.

Dawson searched her face, pain flickering through his expression. There must have been many things he wanted to say, Leigh realized, but he simply pulled a breath and guided her to a quieter corner.

A beleaguered mother had just herded her three small children into the waiting room, and she wasn't having much luck controlling the youngest boy, a squealing toddler, as he made a beeline for the candy vending machine.

"Paulie's in the county hospital in a guarded ward," Dawson explained. "She won't be doing any shampoo ads for a while, but she should recover fully. The bullet pierced her rib cage and punctured one of her lungs, but it missed any other vital organs."

Leigh pressed Dawson's hand in relief. Paulie's death on her conscience would have been more than she could bear, no matter what the woman had done. Leigh had enough to deal with knowing she'd shot two people, and that one of them— the one she loved—might die.

A Naugahyde couch against the wall beckoned to her. It was exactly the same color as everything else in the spartan room, institutional green, but decor was the least of her concerns now. She felt too shaky to stand.

"Why did Paulie attack me?" she asked as she and Dawson sat down. She released his hand, grateful for his support. "Was it because of Nick?"

Dawson took off his glasses and cleaned the lenses with the lining of his workout jacket. "She wanted him back," he explained, "and her scheme to get him made Machiavelli look like a piker. You were never one of her original targets. She attacked you only because you'd foiled her grand plans. Unfortunately, Jennifer Taryn was the bull's-eye."

A child's cry of surprise and moral outrage echoed Leigh's feelings almost exactly. The exploring toddler was being dragged bodily from the candy machine by one of his older sisters.

"It was Paulie who murdered Jennifer?" Leigh asked, astonished.

"She murdered Jennifer *and* framed Nick for the crime."

"I thought she wanted Nick back?"

"She did. That's what made her scheme so twisted and, in a weird way, brilliant. She believed Nick was madly in love with her, but he just hadn't realized it. She thought if she saved his life—at great risk to herself, of course—he'd be so grateful he'd have to stop denying his true feelings for her."

Leigh was beginning to understand the frightening scope of Paulie's plan. "My God," she said, her voice soft with shock. "She must be completely delusional. Are you saying that she killed Jennifer and framed Nick, knowing that she was going to come forward at the last minute and save him?"

Dawson shrugged a yes. "She thought Nick didn't know his own heart, and it was her destiny to show him that they were soul mates. People have done stranger things for love, but not much."

"Then she was lying about the alibi?"

"When you've killed someone, a lie is a small thing, even under oath. It turns out that Nick did take her to an all-night clinic after a botched suicide attempt—that much was true—but it happened weeks before Jennifer was killed. Apparently Nick had wanted to put some distance between him and Paulie, and suicide was her way of trying to hold him. When it didn't work, she put her grand plan into action, which included seducing the not-too-bright young male clerk at the clinic. She bought the kid a car, gave him sex, and God knows what else."

"Done stranger things for *love?*" Leigh touched her earring. "That's not love, that's pathological obsession. She needs help."

"Have no fear." Ever the prosecutor, Dawson's tone was cynical. "The woman was barely out of recovery before she'd started mobilizing her forces. I'm sure she would have held a press conference from the hospital bed if they'd let her. She's even announced who's going to head her defense team."

Leigh waited expectantly.

"Satterfield." Dawson grimaced. "The bat is back."

"Oh, God! Bet you can't wait to prosecute that one."

"It won't be me."

Leigh was aware of a finality in Dawson's tone, but she didn't take the time to question it. There were too many other things unresolved in her mind. "Was it Paulie behind the phone calls warning me about Nick?"

"She made them herself," Dawson explained. "Her apartment has already been searched. She had hundreds of tape recordings—audio records of her photo sessions with Nick and just about everything else she's done in the last few years. She also had a phone device that lowers the pitch of a woman's voice and makes her sound like a man."

"No wonder the caller sounded familiar." Leigh was thinking out loud now. "And I kept hearing Nick's voice when I was attacked. That must have been because she had him on tape."

"She was diabolically clever," Dawson acknowledged. "And crazy in love with him." He fell silent, studying Leigh as if trying to read her. "How about you Leigh? Are you crazy in love with him?"

It was a question Leigh knew was coming, but she'd hoped to have a little more time to prepare him. She hadn't forgotten the trial, or how he'd betrayed her, but it would bring her no pleasure to hurt him now. "Don't worry," she assured him gently. "I'm not as far gone as Paulie. But crazy? Yes, without a doubt. And in love, too, I'm afraid."

He didn't return her apologetic smile. "Are you sure, Leigh? Really sure? Because if there's a chance for us—"

"I'm sure." Her voice caught with sadness. "If Nick lives, and if he wants me, I'm his."

It was a moment before Dawson could speak. "If that bastard isn't good to you, if he ever lies or cheats or hurts you in any way, I'll come out of retirement and kill him."

The savagery in his voice surprised her, but not as much as the information he'd revealed. "Retirement?"

He massaged the bridge of his nose. Without his glasses, he looked pale and rather boyish. "I'm turning in my badge," he said. "It's time. I've done things that make me sick to my stomach, especially to you."

"But, Dawson—"

"It's worse than you think, Leigh. When I found out Paulie was the killer, it made me see exactly how far I'd gone. I would have sacrificed anything to win the Montera case. In fact, I did. I sacrificed you."

He hesitated, struggling with something. "I love you," he managed at last. His voice seemed to thicken with emotion as he fought to express himself. "I didn't know how much until now."

Leigh didn't know what to say. She wanted to stop him, but he so clearly needed to go on, to talk. "Dawson, I'm sorry—"

"No, don't be. This misery is the least I deserve for being such an ass. I fucked up everything—our relationship, the court case. I even had Paulie Cooper under surveillance at one point," he admitted, "but not because I suspected her of the murder. My real concern was the threat she posed to me because of what Jennifer might have told her. All along Paulie was the killer, and I missed it completely."

"Jennifer Taryn?" Leigh was remembering Paulie's comment about Dawson's relationship with the model.

He hesitated, clearly torn about whether or not to go on. "You might as well hear it all," he said finally. "I'd be a liar if I pretended that what happened has been weighing on my conscience for twenty years. It hasn't. I thought I was doing the right thing back then. Now I don't know. Shit, I don't know anything."

"Twenty years ago? You must mean Nick's trial?"

"Yes." He slipped his glasses back on. "I had just started with the prosecutor's office when Montera first came up on manslaughter and rape charges. I was assigned the task of interviewing Jennifer Taryn, who, as it turned out, was the black sheep of a well-connected family. The Taryns were friends of the DA, and word came down from on high while I was interviewing her that there could be gang reprisals if Jennifer told her story on the stand."

Leigh wanted to make sure she understood. "Her story being that she and Nick were caught together by the gang leader, who then attacked Nick?"

"Exactly. She was going to testify that Nick killed the leader of Los Coyotes in self-defense, but I made sure she understood what could happen if she did. I explained the gang would hold her responsible for the leader's death because she'd cheated on him and provoked the fight with Nick. She knew what the gang was capable of. She'd seen the violence firsthand, and when she took the stand, she told a completely different story."

"And everyone believed her?"

"Everyone, except Montera, of course, and nobody cared about him, one more screwed-up *vato* from the barrio. We were preventing gang reprisals against an innocent family, who, not uncoincidentally, had friends in high places. It was the right thing to do, or at least that was how I rationalized it."

A high-pitched screech warned the waiting-room occupants that the toddler had broken loose again. But Dawson didn't seem to be aware of his surroundings anymore, or even of Leigh. He was completely caught up in the recounting of what had happened.

"I kept in touch with Jennifer afterward," he went on. "I helped her out financially from time to time—in return for her silence. Everything was fine until a few months ago, when she told me she couldn't live with the lies any longer. She was going to tell Nick the truth and ask his forgiveness. She assured me that I wouldn't be involved. She only wanted to clear her conscience of what she'd done."

He exhaled heavily and rubbed his jaw, obviously weary. "I thought I'd talked her out of it, but apparently I hadn't. When she turned up dead, I really believed that Nick had done it this time, especially when I saw the body."

Leigh had to wonder if part of Dawson's motive for prosecuting Nick so vigorously had been to protect himself. He'd known Jennifer might tell Nick the whole story at any time, including Dawson's part in it, which meant that Dawson himself had had a reason for wanting them both out of the way.

"I've withdrawn my name from the ballot," he said. "And I've tendered my resignation as well. I'll be leaving at the end of this term."

"What will you do?" she asked him. She felt about him the way she had about Paulie. No matter what he'd done, she didn't want to see him suffer.

"I don't know. I'm weary of the rat race. Maybe I'll get a cabin in the mountains, fish a little. Maybe I'll sell cars."

He let out a sound that was meant to be laughter, but Leigh could hear the pain cutting through it. He was giving up everything, she realized. Perhaps he had just realized he loved her, but he'd loved his political ambitions, too. She was sad for him, but she knew he'd made the right decision. He'd been hungry for the wrong things, for power and prestige, and that hunger would have kept his judgment forever in question, his ethics at the mercy of the highest bidder.

"Do you want something to eat?" he asked her. He'd just become aware of the high drama at the candy machine, where all three kids were now clamoring for Reese's Pieces, and Mom looked as if she were about to give in to forces greater than she.

Dawson rose from the couch. "How about a candy bar? Or something from the cafeteria? They've probably got sandwiches and coffee."

Fatigue washed over Leigh, and she slumped back against rock-hard, overstuffed green plastic. "Thanks, but I wouldn't have the energy to eat it." Exhaustion overrode any need for the normal comforts, including food. Closing her eyes, she left Dawson to his own devices. Heaven is a waiting-room couch, she thought. If she could just take a nap, maybe when she woke up she would find that it was all a dream, and Nick would be all right.

Please God, she thought, let him be all right. If he doesn't live, and it's because of me, I don't think I'll be able to go on. I love him so much.

A horrified gasp brought Leigh's eyes open wide.

She sprang up from the couch in time to see Kate Rappaport enter the waiting room and freeze in shock at the sight of her daughter's dishevelment. Hysteria bubbled up, and Leigh almost laughed. She hadn't realized she looked that bad.

It took Kate a second to shake herself loose, and then she stormed forward and began plucking at Leigh's torn clothing. It was Kate's way of dealing with a crisis, Leigh knew. She couldn't manage motherly, so she opted for orderly.

In the next moments, as Leigh described the nightmare of the last few days, Kate busied herself, restoring Leigh to civility.

"You look like an earthquake victim," Kate muttered.

Leigh smiled. "You never thought your daughter would be this notorious, did you?"

"I never thought my daughter had this much courage. I see how wrong I was."

Kate stopped fussing then and met Leigh's eyes for a moment. Leigh could feel her mother's concern. She could see it. There was a stab of anguish in Kate's gaze as she reached out and caught hold of Leigh's hands. An awkward silence ensued as the two women hung on to each other. They'd touched and hugged many times, but not with this kind of feeling.

A warmth passed between them that was as much physical as it was emotional, Leigh realized. The awareness brought a rueful smile to her lips. Her fingers tingled as if they were coming back to life, as if she were coming back from some cold place.

"Ms. Rappaport?"

Leigh looked around as the doctor strode into the room and stopped dead center in the middle, his hands on his hips.

"The man you shot?" he said. "He's going to live."

Leigh dropped her mother's hands and swayed forward with the staggering force of her relief. She would have fallen to the floor if Kate hadn't been there to catch her.

"Aie yi yi!" Maria Estela Inconsolata Torres moaned dramatically. *"El destino!* I knew someday he'd be shot through the heart by a woman!"

Leigh stood back from the small crowd gathered around Nick's hospital bed, watching as Nick's housekeeper fussed over the wounded warrior. Nick hadn't been shot through the heart. Leigh's bullet had hit him in the solar plexus, missing his heart by some considerable distance. But Estela wasn't concerned with technical details today. She was much too busy wringing her hands and praising the heavens for having spared such an unworthy, unrepentant sinner as Nick.

Leigh smiled good-naturedly. It had been like this all morning. Nick had been allowed visitors today for the first time, and he'd been drawing record crowds since breakfast. If it wasn't a bevy of nurses and attendants clustered around him, each more anxious than the next to change his bedpan, it was a reporter wanting an interview. Even Alec Satterfield had put in a brief, surprise appearance, bringing Nick a fifth of Russian vodka and pouring him a shot before he rushed off to talk to the media, who were camped at the hospital entrance. Right now little Manny Ortega was next in line to pay homage.

"You're a real *bandido,* man!" Manny crowed, slapping the hand that Nick held up. "Now you got a gunshot wound *and* a knife wound."

"*Bandido!* What kind of talk is that?" Estela pointedly ignored Manny, who'd uttered the blasphemous word, to glare at Nick. "What kind of example you set for this young boy?" she chided. "You listen to me, Mr. Big Shot Nick Montera. You listen to Estela Torres. She's telling you what to do! She's telling you to turn your God-given talents to the photography of nature—to flowers and trees, eh? Be a good example for *el pequeño muchacho.*"

"I'm not a little boy!" Manny protested.

Nick issued a warning headshake to Manny. "Don't argue with her, *muchacho.* She's got the Big Guy on her side. Estela, for my next project, I'm thinking about a collection of hawks, lionesses, and shrew moles. How does that sound?"

Nick caught Leigh's eye and winked.

A smile bubbled, though Leigh managed to keep it nonchalant. Her throat was hot and tight, full of things she wanted to say. It had been since she walked into his room that morning and saw the man she'd almost lost sitting up in bed and looking very much the way she remembered him—as alive and golden warm as a fine, strong animal. His hair was tied back in a ponytail, but a shock of it kept drooping darkly into his eyes, forcing him to shake his head every once in a while to get rid of it. Who would've thought anyone could look this sexy and vulnerable in a hospital gown! Truly, it was everything Leigh could do not to make a fool of herself over him.

Estela snorted at him. "Where did that bullet hit you? In the head?"

"No," Nick assured her, continuing to gaze straight at Leigh. "In the heart. You were right the first time, Estela. I've been shot right through the heart."

Leigh lost the battle with her nonchalant smile.

Estela rolled her eyes and blushed.

Manny wrinkled his nose. "Mush," he opined.

"Listen up, everybody!" Nick hushed the assembled crowd, encompassing them all with outstretched arms. "How about it, guys? Could I have some time alone with the woman who shot me? She and I have things to talk about."

One by one they began to file out, Manny hanging back reluctantly and turning when he reached the door. "So what are you, a great lover or something?" he asked Nick. "The women, they go crazy over you?"

Nick cocked an imaginary gun and pointed it at the boy. "Listen up, muchacho," he said. "I have just one word of advice when it comes to dealing with women . . . learn to duck."

"That's three words," Manny corrected, pretending to dodge Nick's bullet.

Estela was the next to leave. "He gives you any trouble, you shoot him again," she whispered as she passed Leigh.

Leigh waited until they'd all disappeared down to the very last teenage candy striper before she shut the door. It didn't have a lock, but she improvised by propping a chair under the doorknob. That accomplished, she turned and sauntered slowly toward Nick's bed.

He watched her provocative approach with great interest.

"So . . . you're not a murderer," she said softly.

"Disappointed?"

She stroked her earring. "Well, there *was* some excitement in not knowing whether you were going to kiss me or kill me," she admitted.

"I'd like to do both." His voice went grainy with desire as he watched her finger the gold hoop. "Especially when you play with that damn thing."

She laughed, loving it that she had the advantage. She wouldn't have been nearly so quick to tease him if he hadn't been confined to a hospital bed, and even at that, the desire smoldering in his expression made him look very dangerous, indeed. She rather liked having Nick Montera confined this way, a prisoner of war at the mercy of her every whim.

"As long as you don't kill me first," she said. "I want to be around long enough to enjoy the kiss."

The hot sparkle in his eyes told her there were all kinds of murder, and if he had his way, he would prolong hers until she begged him to put her out of her misery, sweet as it might be.

He reached for her as she neared the bed. Anticipating him, she hesitated just outside his range. She had something to tell him and she didn't know how to do it.

"Did you get your book done?" he asked.

He was finding ways to fill the silence, Leigh imagined, but she appreciated his concern. "There was plenty of time to work on it with you in the hospital," she told him. "I sent it off yesterday. I also got a call from the ethics committee and they're dropping the complaint against me. In their opinion I acted both ethically and professionally by removing myself from the case when I realized I was getting emotionally involved."

"I'm glad you did," he said, wincing as he reached for her again.

"Remove myself from the case?"

"Get emotionally involved. Come here, you . . ."

He smiled and crooked a finger. Leigh felt that familiar tug at the very center of her being, but she couldn't go to him yet. "I have something of yours," she said, digging into the front pocket of her jeans. She pulled out the silver ring and watched his expression change, sobering.

"Where did you find that?" he asked.

"In your darkroom the night Paulie attacked me. Tell me about it."

Leigh listened intently as Nick explained that he'd been wearing the ring the night the police took him in for questioning. The arresting officers had shown him a picture of

Jennifer's body that looked exactly like his photograph of her and asked him if he recognized it, apparently hoping to trick him into saying something incriminating. At first he'd thought it was his photograph—or at least a snapshot of it—but then he noticed the marks on Jennifer's neck, one of them in particular. The police had mistaken the snake's head for a bruise, but with his eye for photographic detail, Nick had recognized it immediately and suspected he was being set up. Fortunately, he wasn't formally arrested until several days later, which gave him time to hide the ring.

"It was originally a gift from Paulie," he said, reaching out for the ring.

Leigh walked to his bedside and gave it to him, watching as he turned it in his fingers. There was only a trace of bitterness in his voice when he spoke.

"She told me she'd had it made up to go with my bracelet, and I remember thinking how thoughtful that was. All the time she was planning to set me up. She must have had another ring made up, identical to this one."

"She wanted you back desperately, Nick. She told me you had some kind of power over her, that you had enslaved her sexually."

He looked up in surprise. "Paulie and I didn't have that kind of relationship. A friendship, yes, but not sex. We were never together that way."

Leigh was astonished. Paulie had been so totally persuasive in her stories about Nick that Leigh had found herself aroused thinking about them. "I'm glad you weren't intimately involved with her," she admitted. On impulse she opened the drawer of the table next to Nick's bed, took the ring from him and dropped it in the drawer with a flourish.

"I should warn you," she told him. "I do have one characteristic in common with your cat, Marilyn."

"What's that?" Nick gazed at her expectantly.

"I'm possessive."

"That sounds promising. Can I count on you to bite my ankle the way Marilyn does?"

"That's the least I can do, since you've left little love bites all over my person." She lifted the sheets of his bed as if she were going to take a peek at him.

"What are you doing?" he asked.

"I want to feel your scar." She slipped her hands under the covers, and her fingers came into contact with the heat of his body, but she wasn't sure what part of him she was touching. "You left your mark on me," she informed him, a breathy lightness invading her voice. "Now I've left mine on you."

"Ouch!" He flinched as she found the adhesive bandages that covered his gunshot wound. "My marks were less painful."

"And a lot more fun," she agreed. "But my mark is permanent." She splayed her hand lightly over the injury and made a fierce face. "It means you're mine, Nick Montera. That nobody else can mess with you."

His laughter was rich and grainy. He dipped his hands beneath the blankets, catching hold of hers. Slowly, and with a gritted strength that was amazing for a wounded man, he drew her down onto the bed with him. His stormy, sexy expression told her unequivocally that, injury or not, he was taking control of this situation.

"You have marked me, Leigh," he said. "You've changed me."

She shook her head. "I don't want to change you, Nick. You're everything I want, exactly what I want, just the way you are."

"That's what I mean." He insisted that she understand. "You've seen the other side of me, the darkness, the rage, and you're still here. You didn't run away. There's only one other person in my life who stayed—though I'm sure many times she wanted to run—and she's gone because of my carelessness."

His voice harshened with sadness. "I'll never be careless with you, Leigh. I'll never make you want to run away."

He raked his hands into the soft tumble of her blond hair, cupped her face, and with the trembling restraint of a religious ascetic, he took her mouth. His fingers curved to the contours of her head. Her name whispered on his lips, light as the mists, soft as dandelion fluff.

Leigh shivered against him, reveling in the tenderness, fearing it *because* she loved it so much. He made her feel as if she were the most fragile and precious thing on earth—the sweet, frightened little girl her own parents had never acknowledged.

He touched her as if he knew that child as intimately as the grown woman she'd become . . . the grown woman who still needed to be cherished.

"I'm sorry I shot you," she whispered all of a sudden.

He almost laughed at her outburst. "I'm glad," he said. His eyes flared to a startlingly bright blue as he rocked back to look at her. "It's a sign that the worst is behind us. We won't ever hurt each other again. That's what it means to me."

The words echoed in her mind, and a vow was born.

We won't ever hurt each other again.

She caressed his amber smile.

He turned his mouth into her palm and nipped the firm flesh there, his teeth leaving tender pink marks. "Except in small, sweet ways like this," he promised her.

"Do you know what I want to do more than anything?" he said.

"I can guess."

"Besides that." A smile curved his mouth, but the truth of his emotions poured out through his eyes. As clear and naked as rainwater they were infused with pain and hope and every other emotion he'd ever fought to keep from feeling.

"I want to stay up all night," he told her. "I want to watch the sun come up . . . with you."